HIS LIPS TIPPED UP, HIS EYES GREW HEATED,
AND THEY FELL TO MY MOUTH AGAIN.

"Uh, Axl?" I repeated.

He looked to me again.

"I get you're a commando and all, but just so I know for future reference, do commandos need to pin women to their couches in order to share things they think are important?"

He out-and-out smiled before he answered, "Yeah."

"All righty then," I mumbled.

"You got a problem with that?" he asked.

He felt good. His body was warm and heavy. His skin under my hands was sleek, the muscle under that hard. And bottom line, I'd been wanting this in all versions of it that it might come since the first time I clapped eyes on him.

So, no.

I didn't have a problem with it.

"No," I answered.

He gave a brief nod before continuing, "Seeing as we're about to make out, might as well be comfortable doing it."

Might as well.

Yikes.

Moving on.

"Okay. Then, is there...I mean, um...*making up*?"

"Yeah," he confirmed.

"Don't you have to kind of be *together* to *make up*?"

"Hattie, this is the longest non-relationship relationship in history. We've been together since the first time you shot me down for a date and I think you know that better than me."

PRAISE FOR KRISTEN ASHLEY

Dream Chaser

"Stream-of-consciousness prose and propulsive, action-packed plotting will please old fans and draw in new readers."

—*Kirkus*

Dream Maker

"The excellent first romance in Ashley's Dream Team series… Those who like a dash of sweetness in their suspense will be delighted."

—*Publishers Weekly*

Dream
Spinner

Dream

Spinner

KRISTEN
ASHLEY

A Dream Team Novel

FOREVER

New York   Boston

Copyright © 2021 by Kristen Ashley
Cover design by Daniela Medina. Cover images © Shutterstock. Cover copyright © 2021 by Hachette Book Group, Inc.

Excerpt from *Dream Keeper* © 2021 by Kristen Ashley

Forever
Hachette Book Group
1290 Avenue of the Americas, New York, NY 10104
read-forever.com
twitter.com/readforeverpub

First Edition: May 2021

Forever is an imprint of Grand Central Publishing. The Forever name and logo are trademarks of Hachette Book Group, Inc.

The publisher is not responsible for websites (or their content) that are not owned by the publisher.

ISBNs: 978-1-5387-3393-6 (mass market), 978-1-5387-3394-3 (ebook)

Printed in the United States of America

CW

10 9 8 7 6 5 4 3 2 1

For my ice-blue-eyed protective,
possessive alpha, Axl.

I miss you.

PROLOGUE
Right at Him

HATTIE

It happened on the opening night of the Revue.

I knew it when I finished my dance.

And I looked for him.

They were there, all the guys (and Evie) to cheer us on.

To support us.

But when my dance was done, I didn't look to my friend Evie.

I didn't look to Lottie's man (and my friend) Mo.

I didn't look to Evie's guy (and also my friend) Mag.

I further didn't look to Ryn's fella (and yes, my friend too) Boone.

Or Auggie, who should be Pepper's, but he was not.

I looked right at him.

Right at him.

At Axl.

And he was looking at me.

Of course, I'd just been dancing.

But it was more.

Because I'd picked that song.

And it became even *more* when my eyes went right to his.

I saw how his face changed when I did this, and I didn't know him all that well, but I still read it.

I knew exactly what it meant, the way he was looking at me, and the fact, after I'd finished dancing to that song, I'd looked right at him.

And what it meant was...

I was in trouble.

CHAPTER ONE
Ivan the Terrible

HATTIE

I t went well."

"Tens of thousands of dollars on teachers, leotards, pointe shoes, payin' for gas to drive you to class, recitals, competitions, and you're sittin' here tryin' to convince me all that was worth it seein' as you got the big promotion from being a stripper to being a burlesque dancer."

"It's not burlesque exactly. They're calling it a Revue."

"It's a fuckin' titty bar."

I sat opposite my father and decided it was a good time to start keeping my mouth shut.

Dad did not make that same decision.

"You can try to dress it up however you want, Hattie, but you're a glorified whore," he went on. "Though, just sayin', a whore's more honest. Least she doesn't take a man's cash while she's givin' him nothin' but a tease."

I wish I could say Dad was in a rare mood tonight.

But he wasn't.

It was just that it was more foul than normal.

A lot more.

"I think maybe I should go now," I said quietly.

Dad shook his head. "You never could hack listening to reason. Or honesty. Or truth. I can see you're too fat to be in New York or London, Paris or Moscow, but for fuck's sake, not even the Colorado Ballet?" Again with the head shaking. "Instead, you're onstage at Smithie's strip club."

Yes, whenever he got into calling me fat, it was time to go.

I got up and started clearing his dinner dishes.

"I can do that," he snapped.

He couldn't.

He could barely walk.

Mismanaged diabetes.

The mismanaged part being, when I was fed up with his abuse, I'd quit coming to give him his insulin, take his blood sugar, make sure he ate, and doctor his booze by watering it down so his drinking didn't put his body out of whack.

None of which he did for himself.

Three trips to the hospital, and the subsequent medical bills, which meant selling his old house (something I saw to), downsizing (something I also saw to), and putting up with his complaints he had about having to move (something I listened to, though the move part, I saw to), meant I kept coming back.

Mom didn't get it.

She'd washed her hands of him years ago. Even before she did it legally with the divorce.

But I simply could not do nothing and let my father die.

And I knew this would happen if I did not manage his health and his life.

I took his dishes to the kitchen, rinsed them, put them in the dishwasher, tidied and headed back to the living room to remove the TV tray from in front of Dad.

Then I was going to get my purse and go.

"Hattie, it's just—" he started in a much less ugly tone as I was folding up the tray.

"Don't," I whispered.

All these years, he thought he could dig in and dig in and *dig in* because... whatever.

He didn't like his job?

He didn't like his marriage?

He didn't like his health?

He didn't like his life?

So he took that out on his daughter?

And then he has a think about what he'd said, or what he'd done, and realizes he'd been a jerk, so he decides he can say he's sorry and that will wipe away all that came before, like it didn't happen.

It didn't wipe it away.

It never got wiped away.

A person was born clean.

But I believed they died with the stains their parents gave them.

Even if they lived to be a hundred and two.

I mean, seriously?

He'd called me a *whore*.

"I just wanted more for you, sweetheart," he said gently.

I looked him right in the eye.

"I started with a tour jeté down the center stage. It was massive. I was the first solo to go out. Ian wanted their attention. And I got it. He wanted to make a statement right off the bat this was a change for Smithie's. And I made that for him, and for Smithie, flying through the air in a titty bar."

"I wish I'd seen it," he lied.

"Well, I don't," I retorted. "Because you would have found something wrong with it. And you would have shared that with me. And I don't need that. Because I thought I was magnificent, and I probably was not, but at least it's nice to think I was, even if only for a little while."

On that, I moved to my bag while Dad called, "Hattie."

I said not a word.

I walked right out the door.

It was torture—stupid—but after that conversation, I did what I shouldn't do.

When I got in my car, I cued up Anya Marina's "Shut Up" on my iPhone, Bluetoothed it to the car stereo and listened to it on my way home.

Repeatedly.

Doing this playing the dance I'd choreographed to it in my head.

And thinking about the look on Axl's face after I was done.

That first dance I danced for the first solo at Smithie's on opening night five nights ago when Smithie's Club became Smithie's Revue.

The dance was slow, avant-garde, my movements staccato.

So when I'd do my double fouettés, arabesque turns, and the final grand jeté that was reminiscent of Kitri, it came as a shock to the system for the viewer.

And by that time, I fancied, they didn't care I was dancing in a red turtleneck bodysuit that had the thighs cut up nearly to my underarms.

Even for the patrons of a strip club, it was about the dance.

Days before that, when Dorian had cornered me, saying he wanted to see all the girls' routines so he could set the lineup, I'd performed it for him, just him and me.

And when I was done, he sat side stage at his uncle's strip joint that he was reforming into something else, and he did this immobile.

"You didn't like it," I'd said, thinking the avant-garde part would be too weird for the gentleman's club crowd and I should go back to my first thought, pulling something together for "Dancing Queen."

"You're first," Ian had declared. "You're also last. If they see you first, they'll stay and drink until the lights go down on you."

My heart had thumped hard at these words.

"So you liked it?" I asked hesitantly.

Ian stood to his impressive height and stated, "Hattie, you took something beautiful and made it cool. Sexy...and cool." He nodded decisively. "You're first, baby, and you're last. Every night."

I loved that Dorian clearly enjoyed what I did.

But I worried that this would make Lottie, the current headliner (and my friend...well, she used to be), mad at me, but since I was avoiding all the girls, and had been doing it for so long (weeks!) I had it down to the art, I didn't know if she was.

Which was another reason why I was torturing myself with that song, that dance—a song I picked to a dance I put together to say things to Axl Pantera I wished I could in real life say because I knew he was going to be there.

And I was thinking all this, listening to that song, because if I thought about what I should be doing right then in order to get where I should be going that night, I'd break down, blubber like a child and probably get into an accident.

So yeah.

There it all was laid out, messy and unfun.

My life.

I had an abusive father that I, as a twenty-six-year-old woman, kept going back to and enduring his abuse.

I had Axl, a handsome man who'd asked me out, I'd turned him down, he started seeing someone else, but in the interim he saw me have a mini-breakdown, so then he tried to befriend me, which was worse than him just moving on to some other chick.

And I had a pack of friends I was avoiding because they all wanted me to go for that handsome man, even though now he had another woman, and he just wanted to be my friend. A pack of friends it had long since stopped being semi-kinda-rude (but understandable, considering how embarrassing the event was that started it) to constantly blow off and avoid them and now it was just ugly.

And that night was Lottie's pre-bachelorette-boards-at-Elvira's party, and Lottie, Ryn, Evie, Pepper *and* Elvira had all texted me to tell me they wanted me to come. And I didn't even know Elvira. I just knew she worked with the guys (that being Axl's guys, or more to the point, Hawk's guys (since Hawk was their boss): Mag, Boone, Auggie and Mo).

I'd heard Elvira's charcuterie boards were *everything*.

But no.

Nope.

Not me.

I wasn't there, enjoying life and being with my friends.

Instead, I did what I had to do to make certain my father lived another night. I tortured myself with a cool song that was a stark plea to take a chance with your heart. And I was going to go home, and I didn't know, binge *I Am a Killer* or something on Netflix, while all my friends were beginning celebrations to herald in one of the happiest times in life.

What was the matter with me?

I should go to the studio.

I should get some work done.

But that wasn't helping like it used to.

Because if I didn't have the guts to tell my father to take care of his own damned self…

And if I didn't have the courage to say yes to a handsome guy when he asked me out, further not having the backbone to accept him as a friend when he gave up on me…

Last, if I didn't even have it in me to lay it on my friends, or if not, just tell them to back off, I was dealing with my own issues, and instead, it felt like I was losing them, and it was me who was making that happen…

Then I wouldn't (and didn't) have the ability to boss up and do something with what I was creating in the studio.

So that was me all around.

Hattie Yates.

Failed dancer.

Failed daughter.

Failed friend.

Failed artist.

But really freaking good loner.

I parked at the back of the house where my and three other apartments were and let myself in the back door, thinking at least I had this.

My pad.

A weird, funky space, part of a big, old home broken in chunks. But the landlords wanted to make it cool, so they did, with up and down steps, insets in the walls to put knickknacks, interesting lighting, creamy white walls and beautifully refinished floors.

Mine was on the first level.

Living room and kitchen up front, a step up to the kitchen from the living room. A wall that was open, seeing as it was made up of open-backed shelves. Shelves in which there was a doorway with three steps down to delineate my bedroom area. That back area had a walk-in closet and biggish bath, which, no other word for it, was divine. And the only other room, what I was in now, a side area at the back that had a washer, dryer and some storage.

As décor, I'd gone with white and cream in furniture with dove-gray curtains. Some navy-and-cream throw rugs. Black-and-white art or photos in white frames.

I added to this only shocks of color here and there. In some pictures, one with a frame that was geranium pink.

Turquoise. Sky blue. Lime green. More pink.

And my prize possession, a loud beanbag in primary colors

that was covered in a print of flowers that I used as a beanbag as well as an ottoman.

My funky little me space. Small. Light. Bright. Interesting.

All things that were not me.

With ease born of practice in that small, dark room lit only slightly by the waning sunlight of a Denver summer night, light that was coming through the single narrow window, I went up the three steps that should lead me to my living room/kitchen.

And stopped dead when I got there.

Illuminated by the big wicker-globe-covered hanging fixtures, sitting back in my comfy, creamy armchair with his feet on my flowery beanbag, was Brett "Cisco" Rappaport.

The man who, a few months back, had kidnapped Evie, Ryn, Pepper and me—my friends, but also fellow dancers (except now Evie had quit and gone full time as an engineering student and computer tech).

Then he went on to kidnap Ryn again some weeks later.

He'd since been cleared of the crime he'd been framed for committing by two dirty cops who had killed another cop.

But still, not a good guy.

In my living room.

"I'm irate with you," he announced.

Okay...

Did I run?

I mean, he didn't have any henchmen with guns trained on me this time.

So that was good.

But he didn't even say "Hi" before he told me he was irate with me.

And he was nefarious, what with having henchmen and kidnapping women and all. I didn't know what he did to make a living, but I didn't think it was running an animal shelter.

"Um…" I started when he said no more and also didn't move. "Why are you irate with me?"

"Because I saw that first dance. And the second one. Also the last. And Axl Pantera saw that first dance. And the second one. Also the last. I also saw the man nearly come out of his skin, beating back the need to charge you on the dance floor, carry you to his Jeep, take you to his house, and tie you down until you swore you'd never leave him, and here I am." He extended an arm out to indicate my place while I fought to catch my breath after what he said. "Alone in your house with you, after you visited that waste of a space you call a dad. And where is Pantera?"

He leaned toward me.

I didn't move.

"*Not here.*"

"Uh…he has a girlfriend," I shared, deciding to get into that and not the information he knew I'd just come from my father's, which freaked me out.

"He's seein' a woman. There's a big difference."

"I'm not sure after all this time she'd define it as that."

"All this time…what? A few weeks?"

"More like a few months."

He shook his head. "You women have way too many scruples."

Yup.

Nefarious.

I took a chance and stepped another step into the room because I was less afraid of doing that than taking one the other way.

"Can I ask…I mean, no offense, truly, but it's a little weird…so can I ask why you're here talking to me about this?"

"Because you're my girl and I gotta whip you women into shape."

Erm.

What?

"I'm your girl?" I whispered.

His brows shot up. "Didn't Ryn tell you?"

"Uh—"

"Yeah, you're avoiding your friends. *What* is *up* with *that*?"

Okay.

Now, how did he know *that*?

"How much do you know about me?" I queried.

And, yup.

Still whispering.

"I look after what's mine."

"I'm not really yours."

"Well, see, this is how it goes."

He stopped talking, took his feet from my beanbag and stood.

I went completely still.

He crossed his arms on his chest.

And call me crazy (which on my next thought, I apparently was), but in my opinion, he was kind of cute.

In a bizarre, bad-guy kind of way.

And if indications were correct under that finely tailored suit, he had a great body.

Not to mention, he was tall.

"I kidnapped you," he reminded me.

"Yes, I remember," I told him.

"And I still assert that was Evie's brother's sitch. I mean, he was the one who swung you girls out there. I was just reacting to his bullshit."

I could argue that.

I didn't.

"But regardless," he shrugged, "I did what I did which *really* swung you girls out there so it's up to me to look after you."

This did not track.

Even a little bit.

"Uh . . ." was all I could get out to refute his statement.

Cisco didn't need me to speak.

He had more to say.

"And there's four of you, only one of me. Which means I need some assistance. Now Evan has that Mag guy. And my girl Ryn got her Boone. But still, the last two of you need to get the lead out. I work hard. I got some cake. But I can't be payin' guys to keep an eye on you girls forever. You need men in your beds."

It sounded strangled when I asked, "Am I in danger?"

"Is the sky blue? Is the earth round?" he asked questions I did not want to hear after I asked if I was in danger. "You're a woman. It's a crapshoot you just walkin' to your car out back. Hell, just bein' in this sweet, hip pad by yourself. If Pantera was here, some guy broke in to do you harm, he'd shoot him in the face."

Considering Axl was a commando as a profession, this was probably not far off the mark.

"For sure he'd scrape off that waste-of-space dad of yours," he continued.

My back went straight at that.

"You're talking about my father," I told him.

"Girl, Evie told me he was abusive. She said straight-out you had violence in your life when she was talkin' about your dad. And Ryn told me you checked out on all of them because he got in your head and you couldn't even dance all on your own and enjoy it without self-abusin' when you thought you'd fucked up. I mean, when that's the case, why do you go make dinner for this asshole every night?"

Boy, Evie and Ryn had talked a lot to this guy.

And that was the embarrassing thing that happened that made me retreat from my friends. I'd been dancing. I'd been loving it. I'd messed up. And I'd lost it...on myself.

This was embarrassing because Ryn had seen that, and I figured she'd told Pepper, Lottie and Evie about it.

Not to mention (and this wasn't embarrassing, it was mortifying), Axl had seen it too.

"He's my dad."

"Yeah, and Ivan the Terrible was a dad, and look how that turned out for *his* kid."

Now I was more confused.

Ivan the Terrible?

"What?" I asked.

"The dude beat the shit out of his daughter-in-law because he didn't like what she was wearin'. His son tried to intervene. Ol' pops cracked him on the head, killing him. And the woman was pregnant, so she miscarried. That's quite an afternoon for Ivan."

Okay, I had to take a sec because...

How had something that had started strange, gotten so much *more* strange?

"My dad isn't Ivan the Terrible," I pointed out.

"Only 'cause he's not a tsar. If he had carte blanche, where would you be?"

This was a chilling question.

"We'll let that go...for now," he allowed. "We'll let Pantera go for now too. You had dinner?"

"I was actually going to fast tonight," I told him, and not because it seemed he might ask me to dinner, but because I was going to fast that night.

His head ticked sharply. "Why?"

"Why?" I parroted, since he was looking right at me.

"Your fuckin' dad," he bit out, his tone suddenly alarming.

Right, this had to stop.

"Mr. uh..."

"Brett," he spat. "And tell me, you see the women at Smithie's?"

"Pardon?"

"Women go there. A lot. And not just since Ian switched shit up. Also not only lesbians gettin' their groove on. All kinds of women go there to party and to watch."

I nodded. "It's a thing. Women have embraced strip clubs."

And this was true, though I didn't get it. Maybe female camaraderie. Maybe they thought it was edgy and cool. Whatever it was, we had nearly as many bachelorette parties as we did bachelor ones.

"So what do you think it says, they see a woman with a healthy body flyin' through the air five feet off the ground, the back of her head nearly touching the heel of her foot?"

I again went still.

He answered his own question.

"It says they can stop eating that bullshit people been feeding them. They can be in shape and do magnificent things and they don't gotta be ninety pounds to do them. So, I'll repeat, you had dinner?"

"No," I answered.

He nodded. "We're goin' out."

"Brett—"

"Hattie, listen to me," he cut me off, his tone again different. This time gentle, coaxing. "You don't get this, you never had experience with this, and I'm seeing it's my place to show you the way. All men are not created equal. There are men who give a shit. Ryn tells me you're set for Pantera. I can't go there. And just sayin', that ass, those curls," he tipped his head to me, "you're cute. Normally, I'd be all over that. But Ryn says it's gotta be Pantera. So this is not that. We're lettin' that go. We're lettin' your dad go. You're lettin' the fast go. And I'm gonna take you to dinner and you're gonna be around a man who doesn't treat you like shit. Start you gettin' used to that. We'll go from there. Yeah?"

I didn't know what it was.

I didn't know why I did it.

But I didn't hesitate to say, "Yeah."

He smiled at me, and that decided it.

He was definitely cute.

I walked his way and he escorted me out of my own place like it was his.

The henchman was out there, folding out of the sleek Lincoln town car at the curb in order to open the back door for us.

We got in, and after Brett settled next to me, he declared, "I feel like a steak. Do you feel like a steak?"

"Who doesn't feel like eating a steak?" I asked.

"Atta girl," he muttered.

His driver glided from the curb.

And call me crazy (and I'd be the first person to do that), but when we did, I thought for the first time in a long time that things were looking up.

"At dinner, we'll talk about you wastin' your time in that studio. And we'll talk you *into* spendin' time that you don't waste in that studio. Got a coupla folks I know who own galleries. Your shit is good. Time to stop fuckin' around with that and let the world know you got talent."

My lungs seized.

Brett called out to the driver. "Call ahead. We're not waiting for a table."

Okay, maybe I was wrong about things looking up.

But for the life of me, even after what he'd just said about my studio and knowing people who own galleries, I felt I was right.

CHAPTER TWO

I Blew It

HATTIE

Sitting in my Nissan Rogue outside the studio the next morning, I again scrolled through my texts from last night.
Lottie:

Where are you?

Pepper:

Are you coming?

Ryn:

Girl. You are missing out!
Elvira's boards are EVERYTHING!

Evie:

OK. Now you're worrying me.
Strike that, you've been worrying

me. Now you're SERIOUSLY
worrying me.

My reply, copied and pasted to each of them:

Something came up! I'm SO
sorry! I hate to miss it!
Have SO MUCH fun!
xo♥♥♥

I knew I needed to give it a minute (or a hundred hours of professionally directed time while sitting on someone's couch) to try and figure out why I was so terrified of spending time with them again after what Axl and Ryn saw when I was dancing.

I had just, until then, refused to give it that minute.

But sitting in my burgundy Rogue, giving it that minute, I realized it wasn't just because it was embarrassing.

It was because it was weak.

See, Lottie had it together. She totally knew who she was and she made no apologies (not that there were any to be made, she was awesome, still, she was a stripper, and before that she'd been Queen of the Corvette Calendar, and by my estimation, 99.9 percent of the population was judgy, so *they'd* think she had apologies to make).

She loved stripping, made a ton of money doing it and was at one with her looks and her body. She also had a great house she'd pulled together herself, as well as the love and devotion of Mo, who might look terrifying in a could-be-one-of-Brett's-henchmen type of way, but he was a softie.

And Evie was a genius. Like, certifiable. I'd seen her do mathematics on the fly in her head that I'd probably mess up on a calculator. Her family was way more messed up than my dad. But she'd scraped them off and moved on, going back to college to get her degree, fixing computers, living with, looking for a new house to share and now engaged to Mag, who was a super-cool dude and insanely into her.

Then there was Ryn, who had it just as together as Lottie. She was gorgeous and sexy and sweet and strong with a fantastic fashion sense and she'd just sold her first flip, a house she'd worked on herself. Now she and Boone were in the midst of waiting to close on their second because that was what Ryn wanted to do full time. Flip houses. And with Ryn as she was, I knew that would happen.

Last, there was Pepper, who had a daughter, Juno. And Pepper was the best mom in the world with Juno being the best kid ever, even if Pepper had zero support from her family and her ex was a total tool. Motherhood seemed effortless to her. No one messed with her or her kid, not even her family...or her tool of an ex.

Then there was me.

And I was none of that.

But seriously, it *was* embarrassing, dancing free and breezy by myself in a room then screwing it up and losing it the way I did. Doing all this not knowing Ryn and Axl were watching.

No, not embarrassing.

Mortifying.

I mean, on the whole I was shy around good-looking guys.

Very few weren't.

But the one who saw me do that? The one Lottie had picked for me, tried to set us up, he'd asked me out, and I'd wanted to go, but I refused? *That* one saw me do it?

Forget about it.

And now...

I didn't know.

They were good people. Good friends.

We'd been kidnapped together!

But what did I say?

When they were so together and didn't let anyone shit on them, how did I explain why I continued to take care of my dad?

Especially when they knew it was him. They knew it was my dad who was the reason Ryn and Axl saw me self-harm.

And how did I share what I'd never shared? That I rented studio space, and worked on pieces, but never even attempted to show one, much less sell one?

Bottom line, how did I tell four totally together women who had been in my life for a good while, who all counted me as friend, that I had not let them into my life hardly at all?

Do unto others, right?

And I thought, if I cared about someone, gave them my time, and they didn't let me in, how would I feel?

Not good.

Of course, I could just let them in.

But the longer I left it, the harder that became.

And now . . . was now.

I'd blown off Lottie's pre-bachelorette party to go out to dinner with a (probable) felon.

And none of them had texted again after my text.

I wasn't sure I could come back from that.

The only thing I was sure of was that, right then, I was going to head into my studio. I hadn't been there in at least a week.

And maybe, what it used to be able to do—give me focus, calm, and an outlet to express things I didn't even admit to myself—it would do again.

Not to mention, Brett had told me last night over steaks that he'd had a look (breaking in to do so, and how I didn't feel disturbed and invaded by that, I had no idea) and he thought my stuff was "the shit."

"Want that piece in my living room. The girl folded in on herself," he'd said. "Think about how much you'll charge. I'll get you the cash and arrange to have it moved."

He'd actually said that.

And the girl folded in on herself, a piece I called "After," made of concrete and rusted iron with some copper wire and carefully selected bits of stone, was one of the favorite things I'd done so far.

I didn't want to sell it.

It was me.

But if someone wanted to buy it…

On this thought, I got out of my car, went to the door of my studio, unlocked and opened it, walked in, and for the second time in less than twenty-four hours, stopped dead.

Because Axl Pantera was standing right next to "After."

Right next to "After."

In my studio.

Where I expressed…

Everything.

My heart lodged in my throat.

He was tall.

Beautiful body (and I meant *beautiful*, so beautiful I wanted to form it from concrete and shiny steel so it could live forever).

A thick head of spiky silver hair atop fabulous features—strong nose, square jaw, gorgeous full lips and the most remarkable ice-blue eyes I'd ever seen.

Truth be told, he wasn't handsome in a classical sense.

He was more rough, though I'd prefer to call it roguish. With a high forehead, heavy dark brows, hooded eyes that were quite deep set and downturned at the ends which gave him a look like he was always alert, always assessing, didn't miss a trick.

I had no idea where he got that silver hair. He couldn't be much older than me.

But he worked it.

"How did you—?" I started to ask how he knew about my studio.

"Stood them up," he stated. "Again."

What?

"Pardon?" I asked.

"Lottie's big thing. Gearing up. That was last night. Shower is coming up. Bachelorette party after that. Next day, wedding. And last night you're... what? Kissin' your dad's ass?"

And for the second time in less than twenty-four hours, I found my body stunned still.

This time it was to fight the pain.

"Told myself to have patience," he continued. "This shit isn't easy. I know. My dad didn't hide the fact he wasn't all that thrilled with the way I turned out either."

Uh...

What?

He was...

Well, Axl was...

Perfect.

How could his dad not be thrilled with how he'd turned out?

"You, it was dance. Me, track and field. Dad was a track star. Sprinter. Long jump. I was the same, but better. A lot better. Didn't make the Olympics, though, and you would have thought me not doing that when the vast majority of athletes can't, I was patient zero with the coronavirus."

"I—"

"And I still see him. He's my dad. Now he thinks I'm an idiot to quit school to go into the service. I wasn't a gold medal winner with millions in endorsements, he wanted me to be what he became. An attorney. Work at his firm. He's in the thick of it. He gets off on it. He doesn't see or tries to ignore or just enjoys the fact the prosecutorial system in this country is fucked to the point it's a joke. The penal system is the same. And I don't find justice a game where you rack up wins and losses on your personal score sheet and that proves how big your dick is when sitting next to you is a person whose life is at stake. He does not appreciate my opinion on these subjects, but he's a scrapper. His description of himself. So he brings it up *all the fuckin' time*. Just to get a rise out of me. I try not to take the bait, but he won't let it go until I either walk out or double down."

"That doesn't sound—"

"Good?" he interrupted in order to finish for me. "No. It isn't. I hate it. It drives my mother crazy. But I love her and I want to see her and that comes with seeing him. And he's my dad. There's a pull. Nearly impossible to fight. So I get it. How it's hard to let go. Hard to stay away. But my father never hit me."

All right.

I was beginning to rethink my friends being much better friends than me. Because it seemed *everyone* knew what I didn't quite openly share (but I still shared) during our kidnapping. This being about my dad getting physical.

And really, what happened during a kidnapping should stay with the kidnapping.

"Axl—"

"He never drove me to harming myself."

I closed my mouth.

He looked down and touched "After," a piece that came to his hip, and then his attention returned to me.

"This breaks my fucking heart," he declared.

I held my breath.

Oh yes.

He knew that this studio was where I expressed things.

"It's you as a girl and it's you as a woman, cast in cement, formed of iron, and I get it's hard to break free. What I don't get is that it isn't hard to come out of yourself and take someone's hand. You got at least half a dozen of them extended to you. Why the fuck would you not only avoid them, but slap them away?"

Since he wasn't letting me talk, even if he asked a question, I didn't say anything.

"Lottie's hurt, Hattie," he shared.

Oh no.

I closed my eyes.

"Yeah," he said.

I reopened them.

He kept going.

"She likes you. You mean something to her. Last night was so important, everyone's gathering, Elvira's pulled out her boards, all so they can celebrate one of their own, and where the fuck are you?"

"I had something come—"

"Don't give me any of your shit." He shook his head sharply. "I don't buy it."

I shut my mouth again.

"Mac has a heart of gold." "Mac" being what the guys called Lottie, seeing as her last name was McAlister, at least for the next few weeks. "What the woman doesn't have is the patience of a saint. So you blew it last night, Hattie. Fuckin' huge."

With this statement, suddenly, breathing felt alien to me.

Axl walked my way.

He got close.

He stared down his nose at me.

And breathing was a memory.

"And you dance for me," he said quietly, but not a sweet quiet, an angry one, "begging me to kiss you like I mean it. I wait over an hour for you in the parking lot after, and you run away. You dance for a room full of people, but it's all about me, then *you run away from me*."

God.

I'd done that.

After the opening night of the Revue, I'd delayed as long as I could before I'd gone out.

Partly because the girls and guys were all meeting at an after-hours bar to celebrate, and I intended to do a flyby, but the longer

I delayed getting there, the less time I'd have to spend there before I could say I was tired and leave.

Mostly, though, it was because I worried, after I looked at Axl when the dance was done, that he'd be waiting for me.

And he was.

Right outside the door.

And I'd run from him.

I hadn't even allowed myself to think about it since.

But now that he brought it up...

Humiliating.

"The girls tell me you're shy," he said. "They tell me I gotta put in the effort. I do, and time and again, you make a goddamn fool of me."

Oh no!

I didn't want him to feel like a fool.

"Ax—"

"So yeah, Hattie, last night, hurting Lottie, you fuckin'," he got nearly nose to nose with me, so close, I could see thin threads of midnight striking through the steel of his eyes, "*blew it.*"

And with that, he moved away, walked around me to the door, and he slammed it behind him.

I didn't even turn to look at it.

I stared at "After."

He was right.

That was me.

After my failed audition for the Chicago Academy for the Arts.

Mom had been there, and of course Dad, both of them together, even though she'd moved out and got her own apartment at least a year before.

I'd been fourteen.

Two years before that, my ballet teacher had told my father, "Don, she's talented. There's no doubt about it. She just doesn't

have the body for it. Through no fault of her own. Hattie's healthy.
Fit. Limber. She has grace and power. She's just too tall and big
boned. She simply isn't built to be a prima ballerina."

And even before *that*, Mom had said, "Hattie, sweetie, dance *for
you*. If you're not dancing for you, you need to *stop dancing*."

I thought I was dancing for me.

I loved dancing.

I loved dancing and painting and calligraphy and helping Mom
decorate her cakes.

"My artsy girl, my free spirit, my rainbow," Mom used to
call me.

But I'd messed up, twice, during my solo routine at the audition
for the Chicago Academy. They'd let me start again, but not a
third time.

And after, Dad had lost it, backhanding me, catching me on
the jaw.

Right in front of everybody.

Huge drama.

Huge.

The teachers were horrified and *ticked*. They threatened to
phone the police.

Mom had lost her mind.

"If you think you're getting custody now, Don, you're *insane*.
I'll fight you 'til I die, *until I die*, you *monster*."

And I'd retreated from their hate, doing physically what for
years as they hurled it at each other I did mentally. I curled into
myself in a corner, just like "After."

A teacher and Mom had talked me out of my solitary huddle,
and all the way back to the hotel, Mom was on me, "Has that
happened before, Hattie? Has your father touched you like that
before?"

I told her no.

And he hadn't.

He'd never hit me.

But she stayed on me.

So I confessed that he'd pinch me. Grab my arm in a way it hurt. Sometimes pull my hair.

"How had I not seen this?" she'd lamented, openly torn to shreds. "How did I miss this? How didn't I know this was happening?"

I didn't have the courage to tell her it was because *I* hid it.

Though, it was out then and Mom had carried through with her vow. She dragged it all out into the open during the divorce and she won custody of me.

It came with a price though.

One I paid when I was with my father.

So my dad had hit me, my mom was a mess, and I felt guilt and shame I didn't tell her what was happening so it was me that made her feel that way, I was humiliated in front of the admissions board of one of the most prestigious performing arts high schools in the U.S., this after I failed my audition because...

Well...

I blew it.

And I stared at "After" knowing I was really, really good at one thing.

Blowing it.

My phone rang in my bag, and automatically, I reached in and found it.

I pulled it out and it was a number I didn't know.

I was so in my head, against all the laws of dealing with robocalls, I answered it.

"Hello?"

"Hattie Yates?"

"Yes."

"Hattie Yates."

"Yes."

"Nice voice."

"What?"

"Nice voice. Nice tits. Nice hair. *Great ass*. Tie you down. Tie you down *tight*. Whip that ass. Whip you until—"

I took the phone from my ear, disconnected the call and blocked the caller.

I did all of this remembering after what went down with Axl how to breathe.

And I was doing that rapidly.

Staring at my phone.

"Okay, okay, okay..." I whispered, deep in the trenches of flashback city.

Not my own flashback.

One that was about what had started all of this. Months ago. When Lottie got that creepy guy sending her even creepier letters which was why Smithie arranged a bodyguard.

That bodyguard was Mo.

Not long after, Lottie was living with Mo and fixing all her girls up with Mo's boys.

And now I had a call from a number I didn't know, someone who probably saw me dance, someone who'd found out my name, my number and was calling me telling me he was going to tie me down and whip me.

I should tell Mo, Mag, Boone...*Axl*.

I should call them and tell them what just happened.

But I'd blown it.

And it was just a creepy phone call.

Nothing to get excited about, right?

Though, they'd never shared in full, but when they found out who was sending Lottie sinister threatening letters and put him out of commission, the vibe with Smithie was super off for a while.

It wasn't just a crackpot.

It was worse.

And then there was the thing with Evie and her brother, the result of which got all of us (save Lottie) kidnapped.

Which carried on to Ryn having her thing, and a guy was shot dead on her back deck and a friend of hers was murdered.

So, I mean, it seemed like if shit could happen, it would.

And he knew my name.

My number.

Probably, if he was talking about my ass, where I worked.

And he could follow me from there to where I lived.

I shouldn't take any chances.

I reengaged my phone.

Went to Contacts.

And scrolled.

I hit the button to make the call and put the phone to my ear.

"Hey, beautiful," he answered.

"Brett, um…I think I need you," I replied.

CHAPTER THREE

Don't Give Up

AXL

He knew something was up the minute he walked into the offices the next morning after he laid into Hattie.

All his buds, Mo, Mag, Boone and Auggie, were in a huddle at Auggie's workstation two rows up in the large theater-style main space that made up Hawk's operations base.

Workstations ran across each row and were aimed at a variety of monitors on the front wall that someone watched 24/7.

And Auggie's station was the one next to Axl's.

Elvira, their operations manager, had an office on the first floor left, and there was a big conference room across the space opposite. A smaller conference room in the midsection left, with Hawk's office at the top. Walls to all of that space were windows.

To the right, the side space on the upper levels was closed from view, secured with keypads and retinal scanners and held their gear, meaning tech stuff like listening, comms and tracking devices (as well as other), protective equipment like Kevlar vests and body armor, and some weapons and munitions.

Axl looked left, saw Elvira's office empty, looked top left, saw Hawk's office dark, and this didn't make him happy because he really wanted to avoid the huddle and he had nowhere else to go.

He wanted to avoid it because first, he'd thrown down with Hattie the day before, and she was no longer tight with her girls, but he'd been such a dick, and that was something she might share.

And his brothers were not big on guys treating women like dicks generally (and the same with him, but when Hattie ran away from him after that dance, compounding it with dissing Lottie on her party—he was far from proud, but it couldn't be undone— he'd lost it).

Definitely the men were not okay with someone being a dick to a woman in their crew.

Or second, he wanted to avoid them because this could be about the dirty cop situation they were investigating that Brett "Cisco" Rappaport dragged them into when he'd kidnapped the women, a situation that couldn't be ignored, because...*dirty cops*.

Enough said.

And since there was absolutely zero movement on that, just like all the men, Axl was frustrated as fuck about how that was *not* going down.

And he wasn't in the mood to talk about either, but his workstation was next to Auggie's.

Fuck, Mag was standing right in front of it.

Axl was less in the mood when his friends caught his eye and he didn't like the change that came over their faces.

Mo and Mag, concerned and alert.

Boone, annoyed.

Auggie, prepared.

Considering whatever it was, it was better to get it over with, but regardless, they all worked in one room, and it was a big room, but they were at his station, so there was no way to avoid it, he made his way to them.

"What's up?" he asked when he got close.

The answer waited until he was there, standing among them.

"Right, brother, not sure I got a bead on where you're at with this anymore, but we've been talking and we figure you should know," Boone started it, doing that ominously. "Ryn's ride was in for servicing so I was at the club last night to bring her home, and as we were getting in my car, we saw Hattie coming out."

Terrific.

It was about Hattie.

The topic he least wanted to talk about.

Mostly because he'd been a dick, and he'd been that standing next to that statue she'd made that shared just about everything there was to Hattie Yates, and none of it was good, but none of that was on her.

And then...

Yeah.

Even standing by that piece, he'd dug right in and acted like a dick.

"And?" he prompted when Boone didn't continue.

"She got in the back of a Lincoln town car. With Cisco."

Axl felt his eyes do a slow blink.

Then, quietly, "What?"

"Don't know what that's about," Boone said. "The women are pretty pissed at Hattie for dissin' Lottie on her party so they're all about the cold shoulder. But Ryn called Cisco and demanded to know what was going on, and Cisco told her it wasn't his to share. She should ask Hattie. My woman can be stubborn so that was the end of that."

"Wasn't his to share?" Axl asked.

Boone shrugged. "No idea, man."

Axl took in a big breath.

Right.

He wanted to know what was Hattie's that wasn't Cisco's to share, but Cisco knew it and the girls did not.

No, he *needed* to know.

But bottom line, it wasn't his business.

It really wasn't.

That said, Hattie fucks with his head dancing to that song for him, afterward running away, and then, a week later, she's with fucking *Cisco*?

Denver's top crime lord and the man whose actions landed all of them in a load of shit?

What the fuck?

"Okay, I'm getting a bead on where you're at with this now," Boone muttered, watching him closely.

"Not my business," Axl forced through his teeth.

"Axe, bud—" Mo started.

"I can't kidnap the woman and make her go out with me," Axl pointed out.

The reactions to that would have been hilarious if he was in the mood to laugh.

Mo, agreement.

Mag and Auggie, intent contemplation.

Boone, open disagreement.

"Not endorsing kidnapping, but maybe the cautious, restrained approach isn't working," Auggie noted the obvious.

"I wasn't cautious or restrained when I got up in her shit yesterday morning about her missing Lottie's thing," Axl informed them, getting some widened eyes, brows raising, and Boone's head jerked. "I was an asshole. And when I stormed out, she didn't race after me in order to offer an explanation it bottom line isn't my right to have. Though, I acted like it was.

And I haven't heard from her since. I've tried the direct approach. I've tried the let's-be-friends in order to lull her into the we're-not-just-friends-anymore approach. I've tried the dickish, get-your-head-out-of-your-ass approach. I'm battin' zero across the board. I'm not sure where to go from here. But what I'm thinkin' is, after I lost it with her yesterday, she'll be even less inclined to give me a shot."

"You were a dick to her?"

That was Mo's rumble.

"You saw that dance," Axl returned.

It was weak, but it also was an excuse.

Mo's lips thinned.

He saw that dance.

He also knew what that dance was about.

So he knew it was an excuse.

"She ran away from me after that dance," Axl continued. "She's no longer replying to texts, even when she never really did, she just did it enough to blow me off without seeming to blow me off. And she wasn't replying even before I was a dick to her. I don't know what the woman wants. I think she wants me, she knows I want her, and I'm all in to put in the work, but for her sake, as well as mine, I gotta know when to stop banging my head against the wall. Because there's a line where it stops bein' about a man who thinks you're worth the effort and a man who doesn't get the hint and he becomes a creeper. And it feels like I'm edging over that line."

"We gotta get one of the girls to talk to her," Mag noted.

"That'd be Evie since Ryn is pissed as shit," Boone declared. "Missing Elvira's boards with a lame excuse was the last straw. She ranted for a whole half an hour when she got home after that."

"I shouldn't have told you Lottie got her feelings hurt," Mo remarked to Axl.

"Mac is like a sister, buddy, and I was angry Hattie hurt her.

But it isn't on you I got pissed on Mac's behalf and did something about it. That's on me," Axl replied.

"How deep does this shit go with her father?" Mag asked cautiously.

Axl shook his head. "I don't know. I didn't dig. I felt it was something, when we got together, that she'd want to find her time and her way to lay on me, not me invading her life like that."

"What?" Boone asked, but he didn't ask Axl.

He was looking at Auggie.

So Axl looked to Aug.

And when he saw the expression on Auggie's face, he demanded, "You looked into her?"

"Only to be prepared for this very conversation," Auggie replied.

Mo crossed his arms on his substantial chest.

Mag blew out an audible breath.

Boone chuckled low.

Axl just stared at his brother.

"So? What'd you find?" Boone pushed.

"I don't wanna know," Axl said quickly.

"It was ugly and then it was uglier," Auggie stated.

Fuck.

"Divorce proceedings are on record," Auggie kept on. "The custody stuff, the mom testified and Hattie was of an age, she could too. Massive control issues for the dad, and he had them with both the mom and Hattie, which was why the mom left. Mental abuse, both, until the mom left. Physical stuff was only Hattie, and it was minor, even if it wasn't, but in a way a kid might not think anything of it, except that it seriously sucked, and for Hattie, it was constant. Pinching. Shaking. Shoving. Holding her arm or hand too hard. Pulling her hair. The mom never knew about it, because Hattie didn't report it. But that escalated to what caused the mom to go balls to the wall to get sole custody of Hattie with only every-other-weekend-Saturday-afternoon visits with the dad. He caught her with a vicious backhand when she fucked up some audition for some high school in Chicago. The mom saw it and Hattie never again stayed for any length of time with her father while she was still a minor."

Axl dropped his head because he couldn't hold it up and battle the rage of fire in his chest at the same time.

Yeah.

That was ugly.

And it got uglier.

"That's tough, brother, but it gets tougher," Aug said quietly.

Axl lifted his head and stared again at his friend, that burn inching up his throat.

"Not just every competition or recital, but every *class*, which was every day, including Sunday, he was there. He'd videotape it. And from the ride home to repeated viewings of the video after, he'd dissect every second of what she'd done, highlighting the bad. Making her take notes on what she needed to work on. Report back the next day after practice on how she felt she worked on those points. Sometimes even making her do lines, like 'I will relax my arm,' and she'd have to write it five hundred times."

"You're fucking joking," Boone growled.

Aug shook his head. "She said to the judge, that when he'd pinch her or shake her, it was a relief. He'd feel bad about doing that, so for a while, he'd lay off the other stuff."

"So she was glad he'd physically abuse her so he didn't mentally destroy her," Axl stated.

He felt all the men's eyes on him.

He knew why.

His voice was not right.

The huddle became closer.

"Lock it down, Axe," Mo murmured.

Axl didn't take his eyes from Aug and went on, "But he mentally destroyed her."

"I saw that dance," Auggie said low. "And, brother, she's *way* into you. Watching that, it was like watching her say she wants you so bad, it's killing her. It fuckin' *hurt* watching her dance like that for you. So yeah, she wants you that bad and won't let herself have you, he mentally destroyed her."

Axl stepped back.

The men shifted to follow.

He stopped and stated, "I crossed that line to creeper. Could not get a lock on what was goin' on with her, so I followed her. She has a studio. Not to dance. To create shit. When she left, I let myself in. It's filled with pieces of substance. No watercolors or delicate sculptures. Big pieces. A couple that are even taller than me. They all gotta weigh hundreds of pounds. Her mediums are concrete and steel, iron and stone, marble. Even the soft stuff is hard or jagged. Like copper wire or aluminum. And you gotta have no heart in your chest if you can look at her shit and not need to fight taking a knee to battle the pain."

"Fucking hell," Mag whispered.

"I stood in that space and I got up in her face," Axl told them.

"You want to be a part of her life, a good one, one of the few," Boone pointed out. "I don't condone bein' a dick to her, but you're only human, brother. Just give her some breathing room and then go fix it."

"I'll talk to Lottie and she'll talk to her," Mo offered.

Axl shook his head. "No. No one knows about this. Her art. That space. I already violated it. I don't want to make that worse."

Mo nodded his concurrence.

"Boone's right," Mag put in. "Give her breathing room and then go and fix it."

"Not much time," Boone said. "Just don't give up."

"How much of a dick were you to her?" Auggie asked.

"I told her she hurt Lottie and I told her I knew what that

dance was about and she blew it, with Lottie and with me," Axl admitted.

"That doesn't sound like much of a dick," Auggie observed. "What you said is the truth."

"There's layin' out the honesty and bein' an asshole while you lay out the honesty, and I was the second one."

All the men knew of that distinction, so no one said anything.

"What about Cisco?" Mag asked, bringing them full circle. "Do I need to get Evan on that?"

"Let me talk to Hattie tomorrow," Axl said.

"It might not be him takin' it there, making a move on her," Boone told him. "Told you all, Cisco's got a thing about the women. He's taken them on. Feels responsible for them. Probably guilt he scared the shit out of them when he abducted them. But I gotta admit, maybe it's just that he's a nuanced guy and he's a piece of shit out there in the world, but he knows the right way to treat women."

"The man fired on Axl," Mag, jerking his head toward Axl, reminded Boone of the firefight Axl had with Cisco's associates while they were taking Ryn.

"They're either the worst shots in history, or they had orders not to hit me," Axl said and all eyes came to him. "There had to be nearly eighty rounds exchanged in that and there was a lot of damage to the vehicles parked in that parking lot, but no one was even grazed."

"So now you're on the same bent as Boone that there's more that makes this guy when he's picking up Hattie from work at two o'clock in the morning?" Mag demanded.

"I think it's clear I got more work to do with Hattie and it's not gonna help me, not even having taken her out to dinner, bein' that guy who's an even bigger ass to her, I jump to conclusions about what's going on with Cisco when, right now, strictly speaking, it's none of my business. But she knows I want it to be my business, so I ask, and she can decide if she wants to tell."

"I do not see Hattie with Cisco," Mo mumbled.

Obviously, Axl didn't either.

He saw her with him.

He saw all that curly hair of hers on his pillow in the morning and in his lap when she was blowing him.

He saw himself wading in and finding a way to guide her out of her father's life, no matter what fucked-up reason she was still in it, so he could help her find a road to healing.

And he saw himself finding ways to make her laugh and finding others to give her a life that, the next time she pulled a mold from set concrete, seeing what she wrought might bring joy, not cut you to the quick.

That's what he saw.

And if once, just once, she gave him a shot to kiss her like he meant it, she might see it too.

"Me either, I barely see her with Axl," Auggie stated, taking Axl from his thoughts. "She needs an accountant or something. Boring and no drama."

"And I'm drama?" Axl asked.

"Brother, her father's a top-of-the-heap dick, when I thought yours was. But Don Yates beats out even Sylas Pantera, something that was impossible, until Hattie. So she still deals with Yates's ass, but this goes the way you want it to, she's gotta meet your dad, and if you think Sylas won't bring the drama, you need to wake up. Because I believe in you and I saw Hattie dance that dance. So you're gonna win that battle, eventually. But with those two in the mix, that's not even close to winning the war."

"Way to be a ray of sunshine, Aug," Boone clipped.

"We're all thinking it," Auggie clipped back.

Yeah.

Axl could definitely say that Hattie meeting his dad had crossed his mind more than once.

First, she was a stripper, or had been, Sylas Pantera would look down on that, and it depended on his mood how, or more accurately, when he shared that with her.

Second, Sylas Pantera could find a mood where he felt even a stripper he looked down on was too good for his boy, and he'd find the time to share that too.

Axl sighed.

Then he suggested, "Maybe we should get some work done?"

It would seem they'd have no choice, because the men barely made their various gestures of agreement before the door opened and Hawk walked in.

None of them moved when they saw the look on his face.

He stopped at the bottom level of workstations and shared what he had to share from there.

"Got a call from Mamá."

"Mamá" would be Mamá Nana. A woman who traded in information. She did it successfully. It did not make her rich, because she was Robin Hood to her community. It did make her respected, in a variety of ways, and not just that she was Robin Hood to her community.

She was an ally of Hawk's.

And of Cisco's.

"She wants a meet. Tomorrow," Hawk went on.

"I thought Boone was Cisco's handler," Auggie noted.

"This meet won't be with Cisco, though Mamá wants him there," Hawk shared. "It's gonna be with Lynn Crowley."

All five of the men immediately went wired.

Lynn Crowley was Tony Crowley's widow.

And Tony Crowley was the cop who Cisco was framed for killing.

Then, when that frame job went south, what they now

knew was a syndicate of dirty cops moved in to clean up that business.

This being staging a murder-suicide of two of their own: Detectives Lance Mueller and Kevin Bogart. Partners as cops, partners in crime, and part of a collective of bad police who the team knew were out there, they just didn't know who they were or what they were up to.

Mueller left a bogus suicide note that explained why they killed Crowley (who was investigating them) and why he personally killed Bogart (who the note said did the kill on Crowley).

How they knew this was bigger than just Mueller and Bogart was because they had several good cops on their team. One of them was Malik, Elvira's husband. Malik got his hands on the suicide note, and they had just enough time to have it gone over by an expert to find that it was forged before Malik had to return it.

Also, before whoever was still pulling the strings got to him, the medical examiner who examined the bodies shared that Mueller was so juiced with Rohypnol, even at close range, he in no way could aim to hit Bogart dead center in the heart, because he wouldn't even have enough faculty to lift the gun to his own head. Both of which happened, shot to the heart took Bogart out, one to the brain took out Mueller.

Though, this was not in the report that was filed.

It was deemed murder-suicide and the case was closed.

Until now, even though the murder of her husband had left her with two kids and pregnant with the third, Lynn Crowley had been adamantly opposed to assisting them in any manner to find out who and what her husband was investigating before he got dead.

This told the team that she was under someone's thumb.

Now she was reaching out through Mamá Nana.

"And Heidi Mueller," Hawk finished.

"Holy fuck," Mag whispered.

Yeah.

That said it all.

Because no one had even thought to go to Heidi Mueller, Lance Mueller's widow.

Not now.

Maybe not ever.

Because she was a woman who had been through the wringer not only because her husband of nearly two decades was dead, after murdering another man and being a party to having a good cop get killed. She was also under the false impression he'd cheated on her repeatedly by coercing freebies from sex workers.

Rounding this out, the media had had a field day with this and Heidi was the current poster child for "Wronged Woman, You Decide If She Was Just a Huge Idiot or If Her Husband Was That Good at Being a Lying Douchebag." And considering the word *woman* denoted she had a vagina, the vast majority of assholes out there considered her an idiot, no matter how massive a lying douchebag her husband was.

Somehow, that was her responsibility and she took that rap.

And the last few weeks, Heidi Mueller had been living heavy with that rap.

"Boone, get on Cisco," Hawk ordered. "Mamá wants us for lunch tomorrow."

"On it," Boone said.

Hawk looked to Mo and then to Axl. "I want you two with Boone and me."

Axl nodded.

Then to Auggie, Hawk said, "I wanna know anything I don't already know about Heidi Mueller."

"You got it," Auggie replied, shifting to his workstation.

Hawk jerked up his chin then moved to the steps that would take him to his office.

"Is this a break in the case?" Mag murmured to them all.

"Fuck, I hope so," Boone answered.

Axl did too.

He really did.

Because this needed to be done seeing as they were talking dirty cops and death.

But also, he had something important to concentrate on, that being Hattie, and this bullshit was getting in the way.

CHAPTER FOUR
Whoosh

HATTIE

It was morning and I was sitting out on my side deck in my jammies with a cup of coffee and my phone, scrolling up and down.

Yes, doing this on Axl's text string.

There had been nothing new.

Not after what happened at my studio two days ago.

Instead, I was scrolling through the old from after he and Ryn saw me lose it while dancing in that studio to when I was dancing to "Shut Up" at Smithie's.

It started with:

You OK?

And then:

Hattie, just tell me if you're OK.

I'm OK.
Thanks for asking.

He gave it a couple of days and then:

You want to meet up? No pressure.
Just want to see for myself you're good.

I'm good.

Right.
You want to meet up?

To that one, I didn't answer.
Then, the next day:

Time for lunch? Going to Mustard's.
Mac says you dig it there.
Meet me in an hour?

Lottie was right. I loved Mustard's Last Stand. It was crazy, but
I was a hot dog girl.
I did not reply.
Axl didn't seem to mind, because that night, I got:

I want to reiterate there's no pressure.
This isn't about the fixup. I'm seeing someone.
You don't have to worry about that.
But even if I don't know you that well,
I give a shit about you. We're in the
same crew.
So just friends.
And as friends, I'm trying to look out for

> you. See for myself if you're all right.
> Make sure you know I'm here to listen
> if you want to talk.

I couldn't ignore that, so I didn't.

> You're very sweet. And that's very
> sweet. But I'm not lying when I said
> I'm good.

I, of course, was totally lying.
I was *so* not good.

OK, then you'd be good to hang
with me sometime.

And I was *oh-so-totally* not good to hang with him sometime.

> OK. We'll set something up.
> It's just that I'm busy right now.
> Getting ready for the Revue.

Right. Tell me when it's a good time.

> Will do! ☺

Needless to say, I didn't tell him when it was a good time.

Onward from that, he asked me a half a dozen times to meet up. Again at Mustard's. Out for a beer at Lincoln's Roadhouse. For black bean dip at Reivers.

He also asked if I was around to talk, either on the phone, or he'd come by my place with a bottle of wine and a six-pack.

I either ignored these texts or texted a day or two later, telling him I was sorry for the delay in reply, I'd been busy.

And then came opening night of Smithie's Revue.

I didn't even get home before (along with three missed calls I hadn't picked up) I got:

Babe, WE NEED TO TALK.

Obviously, I totally ignored that.

Though the "babe" part gave me a little shiver.

Which meant, not long later, I got:

Hattie, this is serious. You know it.
You made that clear. And I'm taking
it serious. But so you know, I already
was taking it serious.
We have to talk this out.

I didn't reply to that either.

Therefore, before I was even awake the next morning (not that I slept great, but I did eventually get to sleep), I had on my phone:

I don't think you understand where
I'm at. And for me to explain that to you,
it can't be over a text.
I want to see you, Hattie.
You're driving me crazy, seems you're
doing the same to you.
We have to put a stop to this.

Annnnnnd...yes.

I didn't reply to that either.

And that was the last text he sent.

I kept staring at that one, specifically the "I want to see you, Hattie" and the "You're driving me crazy" parts.

Liking the first, not liking the second (but still kinda liking it, in a very feminine, stupid, maybe even mean way that still gave me a hint of a powerful thrill), wondering how that fit in with him having a woman in his life.

I continued to do that until the phone was slipped from my fingers.

I watched Brett, wearing striped pajama bottoms, and nothing else, sit back in the turquoise Adirondack chair that was angled across from mine.

The minute he was settled, he scrolled my texts.

Important note: I was right. Brett had a great body.

Another important note: Brett took that "whip your ass" phone call more seriously than I did. Case in point, he'd slept on my couch last night *and* the night before.

Semi-important note: He was a big guy, and my couch was comfy and deep-seated, but it wasn't huge. And he didn't complain. He also refused to switch places and take my bed while I slept on the couch, seeing as he was the one doing me a favor, so I shared I thought that was only fair. He'd still declined. Which I thought was incredibly sweet.

Last important note: He made great coffee. But as we sat outside on my cute, square deck that led from a fabulous glass door in my kitchen, a deck that had high walls around it so there was privacy, but there were vertical openings with crisscross slats on them so you could see out, I kinda wished he'd put on a t-shirt. There was an intimacy to this that Brett seemed totally okay with in a big-brother way.

I'd never had a big brother, a little one, or ever been around a man with that good of a body that was that exposed outside a beach or a pool, definitely not on my deck, so I was not at one with it.

That said, after that weird phone call, I thought it was totally nice that Brett was all in to make me safe.

To the point he was hanging with me on my deck for coffee.

(Still wished he'd do it with a tee on.)

Though, it wasn't nice that he was helping himself to my texts.

"Um…" I began my effort to share this thought with him.

He stopped scrolling and looked over my phone at me.

"Can I ask why you don't go there?"

It was careful and gentle, the way this question came.

But I couldn't tell him why because I didn't know why.

I also couldn't tell him there wasn't a "there" I could go to any longer, not after the way Axl threw down with me.

I'd blown it.

It was over.

And now all that was left was to torture myself with how huge a fuckup I'd perpetrated.

I grabbed my coffee cup off the lime green ceramic stool that sat between us and served as a table, looked out the slats toward the street and took a sip.

"Message received, sweetheart, but seriously, this guy is into you," Brett stated.

I turned my gaze to him.

"He wants to be friends," I shared.

"No, he's into you."

"He has a woman."

Brett made no reply to that.

"So, again, he wants to be friends," I repeated.

"And you got a problem with that?"

"He's gorgeous. He seems really nice. I had a shot at him, I blew it. But in a perfect world, he'd be mine and now it can only be friends. Can you understand how that might be hard?"

Brett put my phone on the stool but did this with his eyes moving over me in my sleep set that was shorts and a short-sleeved pajama shirt that was pink with big, bright blue and green flowers on it. I was curled up, heels to the seat, knees to my chest.

But still, there was a lot of me to be seen.

And as he did this, he said, "I get the gist."

Oh no.

"Brett," I whispered.

His eyes came to mine. "It's okay, baby, 'cause, see, the thing is, you give a shit about someone, you take what you can get."

Oh man.

Maybe it was me who shouldn't be out on the deck in my jammies.

Maybe I should find a turtleneck and some jeans.

Bulky ones.

"You're incredibly sweet," I said softly.

"Right, the other thing is, I'm not," he stated matter-of-factly. "I'm really not, Hattie. But that's what you'll get from me. And sweet is all you'll ever get from me. But the reason I don't blow through Pantera and take what I want from you is because you don't need that in your life. So you get the sweet. And only that. But you do knowing that there's more. And the rest, well," he lifted his broad (bare!) shoulders, "I'll find a woman who can deal."

"I'm sure she's out there," I informed him.

"I need to find a Daisy. Or better, an Anya," he muttered. "I'm seein' I like the quiet ones, not the ballsy ones."

"Pardon?" I asked.

He shook his head. "Nothin'." He then pushed out of his chair. "Gonna get a refill. Check the cupboards. See what you got. Makin' you breakfast then I got shit to do."

He was making me breakfast.

Yesterday, he had one of his henchmen bring doughnuts.

I was always in for a doughnut.

I was more in for someone (not me) making breakfast.

I seriously had to scan my friend memory banks (which weren't all that hearty, sadly) and see if I knew someone who could "deal" who might make Brett happy.

I didn't share these thoughts with him.

I nodded.

He held out his hand.

I gave him my cup for a refill.

Yup.

He was sweet.

He went inside and I watched the muscles of his back (and, okay, the movement of his ass) when he did.

He was bigger than Axl, not taller, and I'd regrettably never seen Axl bare-chested.

But I'd imagined it.

Repeatedly.

And other things bared.

Those repeatedly too.

On these thoughts, I let out a heavy sigh and looked out the slats so I wouldn't grab my phone again and torture myself with the various ways I'd screwed up with Axl.

And it seemed I was really good at this, considering as I did it, I conjured up the image of Axl walking along the sidewalk in front of my house.

Though, the truth of it was, *Axl was walking along the sidewalk in front of my house*.

I sat up straight in my chair.

My movement must have caught his attention because he stopped, and his eyes caught mine through the slats.

Oh boy.

He shifted direction. No longer heading to the front walk, he was striding up the grass to the gate of my deck.

And then I lost sight of him because he was at the gate to my deck.

Oh boy!

I took my feet off the chair, put them to the rug and stood.

The deck door opened and Axl was there.

And man, he made navy cargos and a gray tee look like *everything*.

No offense to Brett, but better than Brett in practically nothing.

Crap!

I was so *in trouble*.

"Uh—" I started, panicked.

No.

Frantic.

Because he was there, and I really could not take him being mean to me again, even if I deserved it.

And...

Brett was there because I had a situation that might be nothing, but it also might be something, and I hadn't thought Axl would ever find out I had this situation.

But now he was there, and Brett was there, and to explain why Brett was there, I'd have to explain said situation.

However, as what was becoming usual with Axl, that "uh" was all I got out before he lifted a hand, palm out my way.

"No. I gotta start. Because I fucked up. I was a dick. Totally uncool."

What he said made me completely forget I had anything to say.

He dropped his hand and kept talking.

"I was pissed, and I've been frustrated for a while you won't let me get to you and that came out. No excuses. I should have locked it down, sorted through it before I came to you. But I didn't. And I apologize. Seriously, Hattie. What I did was fucked and I wished I didn't do it. But I did. And there's nothin' left but for me to say I'm sorry."

Ohmigod.

That was so nice!

"I—"

I again got no more out.

"You're beautiful."

I blinked and my belly felt funny.

Um…

I was?

I mean, I knew I wasn't hard to look at.

But…*beautiful*?

"And you danced that dance for me," he continued. "It messed with my head. It was…" He shook his head. "I'd never seen anything like that. *Felt* anything like it. No one had ever given me anything as gorgeous as that. It was too much. Too big. And the only person I could work that out with was you, and you cut off every avenue to you, and I needed to process what I was feeling. I couldn't hang on to it anymore."

"Axl—"

Yup, again, that was all he let me say.

Though, I was glad whatever I was going to say didn't stop him from saying what he said next.

And the *way* he said it.

Low and tortured and thick and *amazing*.

"Christ, baby, I can't get it out of my head. I go to sleep, thinking about you dancing. I wake up, and the first thing I see before I open my eyes is you looking at me after that dance. I—"

Okay.

Done.

I moved the five steps to him, put my hand to his chest and whispered, "Shut up."

He stared down at me, unmoving.

I stared up at him, the same.

The air around us grew heavy.

And he was so gorgeous, saying such incredible things, not to mention right there, and I was touching him, I couldn't stop my lips from saying, "Shut up, shut up."

The words that came after that lingered in the air unsaid, but they were there.

Kiss me like you mean it.

And he heard them.

I knew he did when his arm sliced around me and my hand on his chest was forced up into his spiky hair because my body was plastered to his.

And his mouth was on mine.

He kissed me.

Axl kissed me.

And he did it like he meant it.

His other arm swept around me, and I came up on my toes, his head angling, mine tipping the other way. He held tight and I pressed deep and I tasted, and I took, and I gave, and I drank, and he plundered, and he sucked, and his tongue danced with mine and yes...

Yes.

He kissed me like he meant it.

And I kissed him back the same way.

"Okay, the very last thing I wanna be doin' right now is interrupting this."

Axl tore his mouth from mine and looked over my shoulder at who I knew was Brett.

And those steely-blue eyes grew stone cold.

But his arms got so tight, I was having difficulty breathing.

Please tell me this was not happening!

I looked over my shoulder and there was Brett, bare-chested and in pajama bottoms.

And there I was, in my jammies in Axl's arms.

For the first time, in Axl Pantera's arms.

After he kissed me.

This was happening.

CRAP!

"Before you lose it, I sleep on the couch," Brett declared. "And we don't got time for you to lose it anyway, because, Hattie," Brett looked to me, "you need to see this shit."

He then waved something he was holding in his hand that I hadn't noticed, what with my freak-out that he'd interrupted Axl and my first kiss.

But it looked like pictures.

And a large manila envelope that vaguely, in my hazy mind, I remembered came in the mail yesterday. It had no return address. My address was handwritten. I didn't know what it was. I figured it was marketing material, but regardless, I didn't open my mail because I was busy getting ready to go to work.

"Why's he sleeping on your couch, Hattie?"

At Axl's question, slowly, I turned my head back to him.

His eyes were still cold.

"Well—" I began.

But now Brett was interrupting me.

"It's good you're here," he stated, and I could tell by his voice he was getting closer—even if, on that little deck, it was hard to be too far away—but still, *he was coming closer.* "And it's good you're not fucking around with working shit out, finally. But what seemed like a low-key sitch is now officially a serious fucking *sitch.*"

At that, I looked to my side and down at what Brett was holding.

Pictures.

Black and white. Eight by ten.

Porn.

Hard-core, BDSM *porn.*

And it did not look like the woman tied up in a very unsexy way (to my inclinations) was enjoying it.

My skin chilled.

"The fuck?" Axl whispered dangerously.

His skin didn't chill.

It seemed to heat.

And his arms got tighter.

"There's three pics," Brett explained. "This one's the least fucked-up. And it came with a note that said, 'This is you.'"

Suddenly, Axl let me go and took a step back.

That chill on my skin turned to ice.

"The fuck?" he repeated.

I looked up into his eyes.

But Brett answered for me.

"She got a call two days ago. Man said her name, threatened to tie her down and whip her. Odds were, he was just a crackpot fan. Now, think he isn't just fucking around."

"That's why he's picking you up from Smithie's," Axl said to me.

Okay, well, as I suspected, Boone and Ryn saw me get in Cisco's car.

And Boone told Axl.

"Axl—"

"That's why he's sleeping on your couch."

"Okay, see, the call came in when—"

"That's why he's on your deck hardly wearing anything, while *you* are on your deck, also hardly wearing anything."

"Well, I wouldn't exactly say this was hardly any—"

"And you didn't call me."

His voice was so flat in delivering that, I closed my mouth.

"You didn't call me or Mo or Boone or even Smithie. You called Cisco."

And that was an accusation.

"Okay, I see that isn't—"

"And you kissed me like you just kissed me. What's the matter with you?"

And again, I shut my mouth.

Because that?

I did not like the tone of that.

It hurt.

"You know, think I made it clear I'm in to do the work, Hattie. But there's only so much a man can take," Axl declared.

"Listen, brother—" Brett tried to get in there.

Axl's head jerked his way. "I'm not your brother."

"Just calm down and let Hattie get a word in."

"You got advice for me with this?" Axl asked, flinging a hand out my way.

Right.

First I was "work."

Now I was "this."

Seriously?

I mean, he always wore cargo pants. And I knew he was a commando. He'd been in on Evie's rescue the first time she got kidnapped (that one without all the girls) and Evie said there were smoke bombs and tackling involved. Not to mention, he'd charged after Ryn when she was taken, I was there as yet to be abducted, and I heard the gunshots he was exchanging myself.

So he left it in little doubt he took his masculinity very seriously.

But acting possessive and like the wronged man when he'd only kissed me *once* and he did it when he had a *girlfriend*?

(Okay, I participated in that, and encouraged it, and that was very wrong, until I understood what was up with him and the woman he was seeing, but I didn't *have a boyfriend*.)

Seriously, after he broke into my studio and was a jerk to me, then I got a nasty call when he stormed out, I could phone whoever I wanted.

Right?

Before I could share my thoughts on this, Axl's attention returned to me.

"So, official. My job in this," he cut a hand between him and me, "is done. You want it? You're up."

And with that, but no explanation to what that meant, he walked right through my gate and the entire deck shook when he slammed it behind him.

For long moments, both Brett and I stood there silent, staring at the door.

Then for longer moments, we did the same.

After those moments were over, I turned to him.

"You're a guy. What on earth was that?" I asked, tossing my hand toward the gate.

"Quiet, sweetheart," Brett said in a voice I'd never heard.

Instantly, I got quiet.

I also belatedly took in the look on his face as he continued to stare at the gate.

And when I did, I decided to give him as much time as he wanted.

He didn't take a lot of it before he rearranged his face (slightly) and turned to me.

"Now that I'm not in danger of getting my knife, hunting that motherfucker down and teaching him a lesson..."

Eek!

"...as a guy, I can tell you that he's in it so deep with you, he can't fuckin' see straight."

At that, I threw up both hands and reminded him (again), "He has a girlfriend!"

"I'll be expending some effort today in finding the veracity of that statement."

My body jolted.

"You don't think he has a girlfriend?"

"You're my girl to look after. I been doing that. This situation was not moving forward, so I had my ear to the ground, eyes I always got lookin' checkin' things out. He spends time with a woman. Until now, I thought she was a place keeper."

Uh-oh.

All of a sudden I was in serious danger of getting *insanely pissed* at a man who had not too long before shared he was "not sweet" and I knew the form this could take since I was in the room when he ordered one of his henchmen to point a gun at Pepper's head.

Still, I couldn't quite keep the ticked-off tremble out of my, "Place keeper?"

"Baby, guys are dicks. They don't mean to be. It comes naturally. Though, when they find the one for them, that's all done."

With all that had just gone on, I only had it in me to repeat an even more trembling, *"Place keeper?"*

"I'd apologize for the brotherhood if I didn't know for a fact that there are women out there who need validation or can't be alone or just want some guy around to take her car to have the oil changed, and she knows he has no staying power. Because she wants one who's better looking or has a healthier bank account, and even though she's got one, she's still looking for what's next. It goes both ways, Hattie."

Sadly, I couldn't argue that.

"You think Axl's like that?"

"I don't think a man who's like that has it in him to kiss a woman like he was kissing you."

My breath left me.

Whoosh.

Gone.

So when I spoke again, I had to force it out on a wheeze.

"Really?"

His face got soft, he came to me, and then he tucked me in a brotherly headlock to his side.

"Really," he said quietly. "And as such, I'll be checking the veracity of your earlier statement. Now, it sucks huge, but I gotta bring us back to why I felt the need to interrupt that kiss." He shook the photos again. "Hattie, this is next level. And I got resources, but I can't lift then run DNA on a postage stamp. Not unless I find a new resource that's reliable and add it to my arsenal. Which will take time. Too much of it. I need to give this to Hawk."

I had to admit, there was very little doubt my caller had sent those pictures.

So he knew where I lived.

And very likely where I worked.

And in the porn industry, it seemed they catered to their clientele thinking that a woman needed to look in pain even when she was having a non-BDSM orgasm.

Not that I watched porn (okay, full confession, I had one subscription, but they did really quality stuff, and I was a girl on my own with what seemed to be a somewhat limited imagination, so I didn't watch porn *a lot*, but I watched it—though, still in full confession, it was usually gay porn because (A) *hot* and (B) the women in the hetero stuff always seemed fake when they were having orgasms, and one could just say, a man couldn't fake it).

But what was in those pictures was absolutely next level.

Whoever this guy was, he meant to scare me.

And if Brett didn't have me in a headlock right then, I'd probably be more scared.

Fortunately, I had good friends.

Which reminded me...

"But to answer your question," Brett said, taking me out of my thoughts.

I focused on him.

"When he said 'You're up,' that means, after that kiss, and you dissin' him on Protecting Hattie duties, something I'm seeing clear now I should have strongly advised you against, then again,

I'd never seen him kiss you like that, but back to the point. The next move is on you."

Okay, *now* I was scared.

"Oh boy," I whispered.

Brett gave me a squeeze and encouraged, "You can do it."

I chewed on my lips a bit before I whispered, "That kiss was really amazing, Brett."

"That wasn't lost on me, baby. Sorry I had to fuck it up."

"I get it. Those pictures *are* next level. And obviously, Axl would have wanted to know about them. Just maybe not be blind-sided by them."

He studied me closely as he asked, "Are *you* okay about the pictures?"

A cold feeling stole through me.

"Are you—?"

He shook his head once in a firm way that was more like a jerk.

"You got me or one of my boys until you got other cover or until this is over."

I relaxed. "Then I'm okay."

"Evie was right," he muttered, gazing down at me.

"Pardon?" I asked.

"She told me when I found a woman, I shouldn't make her work for it."

"Work for what?"

"Me. Put up with my shit in order to have me. Seein' now it's the other way around, if it's worth it. You don't make them work for it. You do the work so they don't have to."

"Axl's been doing the work," I told him something he knew.

He gave me another squeeze with his arm, and he sounded almost apologetic when he said, "Your turn, sweetheart."

It was.

I didn't know what was happening with Axl's girlfriend (or him not actually having one), but Brett was also right.

A man did not kiss like that.

Unless he means it.

It was time to boss up.

Because whatever was happening was happening.

And Axl deserved it.

So it was my turn.

I chewed my lips some more.

I stopped doing that to pip a quiet, "Eek."

Brett grinned at me.

Then he turned me toward the door to the kitchen, saying, "Bacon and eggs."

Good idea.

Moving on.

"Uh, we have something else to discuss," I told him.

"Yeah?"

"Well, you opened my mail. And you read my texts. I hope it goes without saying I'm extremely grateful you're looking out for me, and I'll find some way to repay you, I promise," I told him as he shifted us sideways through the door so he didn't have to disengage in order to get both of us through it. "But perhaps we should go over boundaries."

He positioned me by the refrigerator, let me go, tossed the pictures on the counter and then opened the fridge.

"First, you don't have to repay me," he said into the fridge.

"I so totally do."

He closed the door, coming out with my eggs and bacon. "Not if I say you don't."

"Brett—"

"Second, baby, while I'm up to bat for you, I do what I have to do. With the writing on the flap, I'm surprised you didn't open it."

"What writing on the flap?"

His brows came together. "You didn't see it?"

I shook my head, my gaze going to the pictures that were upside down.

I couldn't see the envelope.

"It says, 'Whip you into shape,'" he told me.

I looked at Brett and made a face.

"Yep, this dude is fucked *up*," Brett agreed to what my face was saying. "Totally making a deal with Hawk, once we find him, I get my licks in before they disappear him."

Okay.

Hold on.

Um…

What?

"Disappear him?"

His reply to my question was offhand.

His words were *not*.

"Delgado doesn't turn shit over to the police. Delgado deals, either in house, or he contracts out. But how he deals, it's permanent."

Delgado was Hawk, that was his last name.

And Hawk, again, was Axl's boss.

"Permanent?" I asked.

Brett was getting out a skillet. "You don't know what your man does?"

"My man?"

"Pantera."

Another breath leaving me.

Whoosh.

When I got some oxygen, I drew out, "Ummm…he's a commando?"

Brett chuckled.

Oh man.

"He's not a commando?" I asked.

"Oh, he's a commando all right," Brett muttered.

"Brett!" I snapped.

Brett turned his attention from the skillet to me and he did it smiling.

Hugely.

Then he stated, "There are a variety of different types of badasses, you dig?"

I wasn't sure I dug, but I nodded anyway.

Brett read the wasn't-sure part and explained.

"Okay, you got your motherfuckers who you do not, under any circumstances, want to come up against in a street fight. But you get that same dude in a tactical situation, he wouldn't know his ass from a hole in the ground."

Well then.

That made sense.

I nodded.

"Or you got your boys who are badass behind the scenes. Meaning they can plan an operation within an inch of its life, every angle covered, every scenario accounted for."

I nodded again.

"Then you got sublevels of that, depending on terrain. Urban. Mountains. Rural. Water. Domestic. Foreign. You with me?"

More nodding.

"And then you got expertise in tech. In weapons. Then there's more expertise in types of operations. Assault. Defense. Extraction. Reconnaissance. Undercover. That sounds military, and it is, but there are a number of cases, the majority of them, where it's not. It's how a lot of us do business in a number of ways."

Oh crap.

At where this seemed to be heading, I stopped nodding and just stared.

"A man, or woman, cannot call themselves a commando unless they got expertise in *all* of that. And Hawk Delgado is the most expert in all of that I've ever seen. And he does not employ a single man who's any less than he is."

"Oh my God," I breathed.

"So Pantera, and his brothers, are not badass. Adjective. He's *a* bad…*ass*. *Noun*. And when you're a badass, you get a job done, start to finish. You don't hand shit over to anyone. So yeah, Hattie, Hawk is gonna take that on." He stabbed a finger at the pictures. "And whoever is behind that, for the rest of his days, and it'll be up to Hawk and the team how many of those there are, and how much ongoing pain he'll endure through them, will regret fucking with you."

"Maybe I should call the police," I said quickly.

And Not Sweet Brett came out again.

"Too late," he said softly. "'Cause if Hawk doesn't get him, I will. And I'm no commando, but I am a motherfucker. And I know for certain one thing in this life. A man does not fuck with a woman, Hattie. This guy obviously does not know that now. But he's gonna learn."

Hmm…

Time to belatedly rethink.

"Maybe I shouldn't have called you," I whispered.

Brett held my gaze and repeated, "Too late."

"Um—"

Brett was done.

And he communicated this by saying, "Grab a plate and cover it with paper towel. We'll need to drain this bacon when it's done. And warm up our joe. Think it got cold in the drama."

Okay.

Brett was moving on, so I'd talk to him a bit later about the lessons he was intent on teaching a man who was a creep, but he'd been that creep using the postal service to deliver a threat, so he'd also committed a felony. And the cops and prosecutors could teach him that lesson.

And if I managed to straighten things out with Axl, and Hawk took this on, I'd also share my views on that with them.

After, I'd turn this over to the police.

But for now, as Brett mentioned, there was a drama.

And I needed more caffeine, breakfast, and to get to the club to rehearse the new numbers I was introducing that night.

So it was time to get a move on.

Though, while Brett cooked, I went back out to the deck to grab my phone.

But before I came back in, I sent the first text I'd ever instigated to Axl.

> You're right. You've always been
> right. We really need to talk.
> I hate that went bad this morning.
> Let me know when a good time is
> for you.
> I'm on at the club tonight. But any
> other time, I'm yours.
> Just let me know.

Then Brett and I had breakfast.

After, Brett got dressed and introduced me to my bodyguard of the day, a man with no neck, a buzz cut that exposed several scars on his scalp (yikes!), with a very full beard, wearing a badly hidden shoulder holster under his well-cut suit jacket.

His name was Sylvester.

With me covered, Brett kissed my cheek, told me unless he heard from me, he'd see me when I was done at Smithie's that night to pick me up, and he took off.

I took a shower. Got ready to face the day.

And with Sylvester, I headed to Smithie's.

In all that time, Axl did not reply.
So yeah.
I guessed I was up.
And it was my turn to do the work.
Crap.

CHAPTER FIVE

Because We Love You

HATTIE

I had to admit, in the beginning, when Smithie and Dorian suggested the change to a Revue, I loved the idea.

But I was worried.

See, at Smithie's Club, strippers made a lot. And they could do that without doing lap dances.

And although, if there was a fabulous slab of marble I wanted to buy or I felt like a new outfit that was beyond the reach of my normal clothing budget, I was in to do a few lap dances to get them, mostly, I lived well off just salary and tips.

So the Revue worried me, because we still got tips, but we didn't dance all night. Depending on the schedule Ian set (and he shifted it nightly so patrons wouldn't become accustomed to what was on offer), it was anywhere from four to six dances a night.

And although Lottie had been making a mint off much this same schedule for years, first, she was famous, and second, she was a downright inspirational stripper.

The woman had serious moves.

But I'd been worried.

Sure, I had moves.

But I was no Lottie Mac, Queen of the Corvette Calendar and the most famous stripper west of the Mississippi, which was also the most famous east of it, seeing as Vegas was west, and Lottie was even more famous than any girl in Vegas.

So, not only was I worried because I thought my incoming cash would reduce, I thought it'd be boring, being there nine to two (which was actually a cut in hours, it used to be seven to three, but the last headliner—me—went on at 1:45 and then it was pure strippers for the next hour) and only working for maybe twelve to twenty minutes a night.

But Smithie had tripled the already substantial cover charge in order to hike our salaries.

He'd also increased the price of drinks.

And even if I wasn't onstage as often, preparing for my next dance was a total do-over in hair, makeup and costume, not to mention making sure our new stagehands had whatever I was going to use sorted.

Topping that, I had to have new material all the time. I had yet to dance the same dance twice and wasn't set to recycle for another two weeks. That was some serious work, having that number of routines performance ready.

In other words, that amount of prep and rehearsal took a lot of time.

With relief, I'd found quickly that I didn't have anything to worry about.

Smithie's used to be a hip hot spot.

Now it was a *super-hip* hot spot.

The Revue was a smash hit, even the papers were writing about it.

And Dorian had set up some social media that had gone

from around a hundred followers to over a hundred thousand in just a week.

As such, the velvet ropes were jammed outside to the point they had to turn some people away.

And my tips were off the charts.

Before the Revue, I never had a night less than five hundred dollars in tips.

Since the opening of the Revue, I hadn't made less than seven hundred in tips, and the opening night, it was over two thousand.

So even though it was weirdly more work, what with having to have so many routines, and those routines having to be amazing, it was more money.

And it was a lot more fun.

This was what I was thinking when Sylvester and I walked in the back door and down the dancers' hall.

I wasn't thinking about fun when I heard the voices coming from the main room of the club.

I hesitated.

"Everything cool?" Sylvester asked when I did.

I stared at the open door to the club, hearing Ryn's voice, and Lottie's, and in the midst of thinking I'd turn right around and text Ian, asking him to tell me when the club was empty so I could rehearse, another thought invaded my head.

This thought being it was time to grow the heck up.

These were my friends.

And I'd done them wrong.

I needed to fix that or face the consequences if I wasn't able to.

Because, just like Axl didn't deserve me sending him very public mixed messages about where I was at with him, my girls didn't deserve me acting like a twelve-year-old who didn't know how to handle her own emotions.

"Yes," I said to Sylvester, though it was a lie. "Everything's cool."

Then I might have tossed my hair (just a bit), and forcing a lot more confidence in my movements than I was feeling, I strode through the door.

Ryn and Lottie were there, that I knew.

Pepper was too.

She was onstage in some leggings and a workout bra.

The other two were sitting side stage.

All eyes came to us when we showed.

And looking at them, I realized I saw them often, I avoided them all the time, and I missed them like crazy.

They'd done their work in trying to reach me.

It was again my turn.

So I walked right up to them.

They were all eyeing me, but mostly eyeing Sylvester and me.

I'd get into Sylvester later.

Priorities.

I looked right at Lottie.

"I'm sorry I didn't go to Elvira's. It was wrong and I knew it and I felt bad about it. So bad, you wouldn't believe. But that night, my dad called me a whore..."

Gasps ensued, from all of them, with Lottie's eyes narrowing and Pepper's face getting red.

But Sylvester rumbled, "What the fuck?"

I ignored all this and carried on.

"No, worse than a whore because he says a stripper is a tease and at least a whore is honest about it. And I wish I could say that was the reason why I didn't go. But it isn't. At least not the only one. It was because I made myself so distant from all of you, and I didn't know how to come back. And then that happened with dad. Also stuff was weird with Axl because I danced that dance for him and he wanted to talk it out and he scares me so badly, even though I want him even worse, I couldn't go there. And then I got home to my house and Brett was there. And he got in my face about putting Axl off and fasting..."

"Fasting?" Ryn asked quietly.

I heard her.

But I kept going because I had to get it all out.

And it was now or never. Because further delays might mean I couldn't sort the damage.

Since I decided it was now, I had to get it all out *now*.

"Then Brett took me out to dinner, and we made friends and then the next day Axl shows and *he* gets in my face..."

"What?" Lottie demanded.

I also heard that, but I kept on my bent.

"And he was right in what he said, but he wasn't nice in how he said it. Then I got the phone call where the guy threatened to tie me up and whip me."

"*What?*"

That came from all three of them.

I still persevered with what I had to tell them, but that time, it was because I'd be answering them.

"So I made the fateful decision to call Brett because it wasn't that bad, just an obscene phone call. But, you know, shit happens."

"Shit does happen," Pepper muttered.

I looked to Ryn. "So that's why Brett is picking me up at night. And he's spending the night with me, sleeping on my couch, because he doesn't want to take any chances. Which is good. But also bad, seeing as he was there this morning with me, having coffee on my deck, but he'd gone inside to figure out breakfast when Axl showed to apologize for getting in my face and then we started kissing."

"Ohmigod," Ryn breathed.

"Right on," Pepper said.

"Then Brett broke it up because my caller is more of a stalker and he'd opened my mail and found the guy had sent me some hard-core BDSM stuff with some threats and...and...uh..."

I trailed off because none of them were looking at me anymore.

They were all looking beyond me.

I'd know why even before I turned because Sylvester greeted, "Yo, Ian."

And Dorian, who, after I turned, I saw was standing behind me, replied, "Yo, Sly."

But he did this scowling at me.

Another full confession: in the beginning, I had serious problems with Dorian mostly because he was utterly gorgeous. The most beautiful Black man I'd ever seen. And I know some might have an issue that I included the modifier of "Black" in that, but before I saw Axl, he was just the most beautiful man I'd ever seen.

Then I saw Axl.

So Dorian's title had to change, slightly.

And because he was so handsome, I was shy and awkward around him.

This, even if he was incredibly nice and he could be funny when he wasn't being serious (which was a lot, but he ran a strip club with his uncle, it wasn't just staff who could get out of hand, it was patrons, so serious was a good quality to have).

But he sensed I was shy, so he put in the work to make himself approachable to me, make me understand he wasn't just my boss, he was a friend and he cared about me, and now I liked him a whole lot.

It was on this thought I realized everyone around me put in a lot of work.

And me?

Well . . .

Hell.

"Hey, Ian," I greeted.

"You got a stalker?" Ian did not greet back.

"Dude," Sylvester said, and Ian and I looked to him. "Cisco showed me the pics this asshole sent. Now, I could do me a sweet piece in some handcuffs or creative use of silk scarves, but this shit was *extreme*."

Ian stared hard at Sylvester.

Then he dropped his head and looked at his shoes.

In order to give Ian some time, I turned to Sylvester and mouthed, "Sly?"

He shrugged.

I turned back to Ian who was still contemplating his shoes.

He then put his hand on the back of his neck, rubbed it up over his hair and then dropped it to his side, saying, "My mother told me, do not get involved in the club. Those girls will be the death of you." He lifted his head and speared me with his eyes. "She was right."

"*I'm* not stalking me," I pointed out.

"I know you're not," he clipped. "But you show with a body-guard and don't come direct to me when you got a problem?"

Hmm.

He had a point.

"You've kinda had your fair share of problems," I said.

It was lame, but it wasn't untrue.

"That's life, Hatz. You have problems. You deal. You move on. You don't know you got a problem, you can't deal, and that problem becomes a bigger problem."

Before I could agree to his wisdom, and apologize for messing up, Dorian looked to Sylvester.

"You on her all day?" he asked.

"Until Cisco pulls me, and he did not communicate he intended to pull me, so maybe," Sylvester answered.

"You do not go into the dancers' dressing room. Outside only. I'll brief security. If you're still here tonight, when Hattie is onstage, I want all eyes on the crowd. I'll give you, or whoever relieves you, a headset so you can communicate with the team. But before, I'll introduce the team to you so they know you're point on Hattie. You down?"

"I'm down," Sylvester replied.

Ian looked to me. "Right now it's a call and pictures?"

I nodded.

"To your cell phone and sent to your house?" he went on.

I nodded again.

Dorian's visible unhappiness got visibly unhappier.

"And Cisco knows this?" he pressed.

More nodding.

"What about Pantera?"

"Uh, he knows it too."

"I'll call them," he muttered, beginning to move away.

"Wait!" I cried.

He turned back to me.

"Axl and Hawk and all of them aren't *officially* on this, hence Sylvester," I shared, throwing a hand Sylvester's way.

Ian's eyes moved to Sylvester then back to me as behind me I heard Ryn say, "Sorry?" Lottie say, "Say what?" and Pepper say, "Oh man."

I turned to face them. "Axl found out I called Brett before him and he was kinda mad."

This time it was Pepper looking at her feet.

Ryn was smiling.

Lottie hitched a hip, put her hand to it and glared at me.

"I know!" I said to Lottie. "I blew it! I'm going to fix it. Promise."

Though I shouldn't promise.

Axl *still* had not texted me so I had no idea how to go about fixing it.

Though I knew I had to try.

"Hattie, attention to me," Ian demanded.

I whirled back to him.

"How bad did you blow it? Meaning, is this going to delay Delgado and his boys wading in by half an hour or half a day?" he asked.

There was low laughter behind me when I said, "Probably half an hour, seeing as Brett is going to rope them in. But I suspect, even if Axl probably hadn't calmed down, he was on the phone to the office while he drove away from my house."

Ian nodded curtly, said, "God forbid there's a next time…" and when I nodded that I got his message, he strolled away.

I took in a big breath, turned again, and looked right at Lottie.

"I hate it I missed the kickoff to the wedding festivities. I hate it. And I'm so sorry I hurt your feelings when I didn't show."

She hesitated not one second before she came to me and pulled me in her arms.

She kissed the side of my head and then said in my ear, "You don't have to let us in, but you *do* have to let us know. You need space, we can give that to you. You need to talk, we're there for you. You need someone to listen, you got ears who will be happy to hear. Just don't pull away. Because we love you and we want to be there for you, however you need that to be."

Oh no.

I was going to cry.

Oh no!

I was crying.

Holding on to her and not crying.

Sobbing.

I wasn't really a crier. I could get teary, but I'd learned to get a lock on it real quick, because Dad hated crying.

But all that had gone on… all that was going on was *a lot.*

So I was crying.

Then Ryn and Pepper pushed in, held on, and I started crying more.

When I semi got a handle on it, I pulled a little bit away, looked to Lottie and vowed, "I'm not going to miss your shower or your bachelorette party or your wedding."

"I hope not, seeing as you're a bridesmaid," she said.

"I have a fitting to get to," I mumbled.

"No shit?" she asked.

"I'll schedule that this week," I promised.

"Babe, listen to me," she said, not letting me or the other girls go. And standing in this huddle with my friends, I listened to her.

"You had big shit happening in your head and you dealt with it how you knew how. You didn't fuck up. Not with me. You did what you had to do to protect yourself. Now that I know what's going on, I'm not hurt. I get it. I sort of got it before. So don't be down on yourself. It is what it is and now it's something different. And if a friend is any friend at all, they'll get what it is, and be by your side when you move on to something different."

The tears started welling; I even felt my lip tremble.

"Oh shit, she's gonna blow again," Ryn muttered.

"No, I can get a lock on it," I said shakily.

"Cry, who cares?" Pepper asked.

"I care, I have to rehearse and you're already rehearsing. We have jobs to do," I told her.

"'What a Feeling' is tonight," Ryn declared.

I looked to her. "Pardon?"

"Black leotard, black leg warmers, I'm kicking out and pointing to everyone in the crowd with some twirls. It's gonna be *sick*."

"Ohmigod, your 'What a Feeling' is gonna *rock*," I breathed.

I knew this because I'd seen her rehearse it, standing back in the shadows, where I'd been for ages while I avoided my friends as we all polished our varied routines to start the Revue.

"I know. I've been waiting for her to pull out 'What a Feeling' since we started," Pepper said.

"That's my first dance tonight," Ryn said, eyes on me. "Ian's putting me on first. I hope that's okay with you."

"Of course it is! You'll knock their socks off. Tips will be primed for all of us," I replied.

"Totes," Pepper agreed.

"Okay, important shit, Axl kissed you?" Lottie asked.

I gave her big eyes.

"Was it hot?" Ryn asked.

I gave her bigger eyes.

"Right on," Pepper whispered.

"He was really, *really* mad when Brett showed in the middle of it," I shared. "Or, *at all*," I added.

"I bet," Ryn muttered.

"I don't think that's good. I've been, uh…messing with his head for a while," I admitted.

"Not to give the impression I think messing with a man's head is okay, but you have your reasons, and they're not about intentionally jacking him around," Lottie put in. "And these boys crook a finger and bitches fall at their feet. You don't appreciate something if you don't have to work for it. It's not a bad thing he has to work for it."

Well then.

That was sure something to think on.

"You fell at Mo's feet," Ryn said to Lottie.

"I didn't. I stalked him across my living room," Lottie corrected. "But Mo's different. He'd been jacked around by chicks. It was me that had to do the fixing."

"Oh, right." Ryn grinned.

"Is this what bitches do? Stand around in a huddle and talk for-fuckin'-ever?" Sylvester called impatiently from behind me.

We broke it off and I turned to him.

"We have stuff to sort, *Sly*," I said.

"You also have work to do," he reminded me.

"You just want to watch us dance," I accused.

"Well…*yeah*," he agreed.

"Right. I got another run-through to do. Then Ryn's up. Hattie, you're after. Cool?" Pepper planned.

"I need to get warmed up, so that works for me," I told her.

Pepper moved to jump back up on the stage.

"You want popcorn, big man?" Ryn teased Sylvester.

"Not right now, maybe later," Sylvester shot back.

Ryn smiled at him then started walking to the sound board, calling to Pepper, "Cue music!"

"Gotcha!" Pepper called back.

I moved to an open space to start stretching.

Half an hour later, I heard Sly mutter, "Best assignment fuckin' *ever*."

Ryn was doing "What a Feeling."

And when he said this, I thought it might have been the first time that day, or maybe even that week, it could even be a month...

That I smiled.

CHAPTER SIX

Anytime

HATTIE

The night was over.

Ryn's "What a Feeling" kicked butt.

Her routine was so dope, the audience was so primed for the rest of us, my tips had topped seven hundred.

I was in the dressing room, showered, had my face washed, was in civvies and ready to roll.

The girls had all gone after saying good-bye.

Brett was out back waiting for me in his town car.

Sylvester was outside the dressing room, waiting to escort me to the town car.

And the warmth of the good-bye from the girls meaning I had them back was receding.

Because I was looking at my texts.

It started with:

> You're right. You've always been
> right. We really need to talk.

> I hate that went bad this morning.
> Let me know when a good time is
> for you.
> I'm on at the club tonight. But any
> other time, I'm yours.
> Just let me know.

After rehearsal and before going out to a late lunch with the girls to catch up on life, it was:

> OK. I'm sensing you're really mad
> at me. And you have a right to be.
> I'm sorry. I should have called you first
> when that stalker phoned me.
> I'm about to go out to lunch with
> the girls. I apologized to Lottie and she's
> cool with me.
> I'd love a chance to apologize to you too.
> Will you let me?

He didn't reply.

So after Sly and I went with Ryn to check out her flip (which was crazy fabulous, even Sly was impressed)...

And before going home to tidy breakfast dishes, make a grocery list, go to my father's and feed him (in order not to have to explain things to my dad, I made Sly stay outside, and he did not demur, saying, "Good call. You don't want me anywhere near a man who called you a whore. Especially if that asshole is your father."— seemed Brett had a type when recruiting henchmen)...

I sent:

> Message is coming through loud
> and clear.

> **But just so you know, I'm in to**
> **do the work.**

Now it was 2:23 in the morning.

And Axl still hadn't replied.

It was a bitter pill to swallow, tasting my own medicine.

Dejected, I walked out of the dressing rooms and avoided Sly's eyes after catching him giving me a narrow look.

We weren't even at the back door when he repeated his question of earlier.

"Everything cool?"

"Everything's great," I lied, still avoiding his eyes.

He escorted me to the town car.

But before he opened the back door to let me in, he said, "You're a great dancer."

I looked up at him. "Pardon?"

"Best I've ever seen. I should have been watching the crowd, but I couldn't take my eyes off you, because you were that good."

Oh man.

I was in danger of crying again.

"Thanks, Sly," I whispered.

"Just tellin' you the truth," he said, and opened the door.

I folded in.

After I did, Sly bent down and exchanged a look with Brett I couldn't decipher before he closed the door.

"Hey, sweetheart," Brett greeted.

"Hey, Brett," I replied.

The car started gliding away.

"It go good tonight?" he asked.

"I worked things out with the girls," I told him.

"Yeah, Ryn texted me," he muttered.

Seriously, those two seemed tight.

We had so much to catch up on at lunch, and Evie had joined us, so I didn't get around to asking about that with Ryn.

The good news of the day, I could call her or text her or talk to her about it tomorrow.

I'd fixed that.

I had my friends back.

The other good news, the day was done.

That was all the good news.

"What about Pantera?" Brett asked after the bad news.

I looked out the side window. "I think he's still mad."

"Why do you think that?"

"I've texted three times, apologized, he hasn't texted back." I turned to him, but only to glance at him before I looked back out the side window. "He's entitled. I did the same to him."

"Mm," Brett hummed.

He then fell silent.

So I looked forward and asked, "How was your day?"

"Interesting."

He said no more.

"Well, that's good, I guess," I mumbled.

"You didn't freak," he stated bizarrely.

I again turned to him. "What?"

"When I told you some of the specifics about what Pantera does for a living. You didn't know it, but when you heard it, you didn't freak."

This was confusing.

"Why would I freak?"

He hesitated for a second before he said, "If you don't know, not sure I should tell you."

"No, tell me." I twisted fully to him. "Why would I freak?"

"The man doesn't ride a desk, Hattie," he replied carefully.

"I know," I told him. "I also know he barely knew Ryn, he heard her scream when your guys took her..."

Brett's face tightened with remorse in the streetlights.

I carried on.

"...and he raced after her and got in a firefight to save her."

"My men were under orders, no collateral damage," he declared.

I shook my head. "That's not the point I'm making. The point I'm making is, he's the type of man who, split second, charges in to save a woman from something he doesn't even know the fullness of what was happening. Just that she screamed. He doesn't have the job he has because he's a man who has the skills and experience for that job. He got the skills and experience to get that job because he's the man he is."

Brett said nothing, but he didn't take his eyes from me.

And for some reason, I felt compelled to keep talking.

"You know, I understand I'm messed up about my dad. Maybe a stronger person would cut him out of their life and move on. But part of that being messed up is not that I don't get what he did to me and the fact that what he did to me wasn't about me. It was about him. He wasn't a failed Baryshnikov. But whatever it was, he wasn't happy in his life, and he took that out on me, because it's all about him. He's my father, but if he heard me scream, I don't think he'd charge after me. He'd probably call the police. But he wouldn't charge after me. Even being around Axl a bit here and there, and this whole thing lasting what seems like a long time, I don't know Axl very well. But I know *that*. And right now, that's all I really need to know."

"Agreed," Brett said softly.

I ticked up a shoulder. "So, he is who he is. We've had one kiss, no dates, lots of nothing that feels like something, and I'm hoping to start making that something into really *something*. I can't go in being scared of who he is or what he does and wanting to change him. Honestly, I'm a mess and he seems like he's taking me as I come. He's not a mess, but he does something dangerous for a living, but the bottom line is, I don't deserve him if I don't do the same thing."

Brett again said nothing to me.

But he called to the driver, "Joe."

"Gotcha," the driver replied.

Brett then looked at me. "I'm glad you worked things out with the women."

"Me too," I returned, a little surprised at the swift change of subject and a lot confused with Brett saying something without saying anything to Joe.

Then I thought I understood why there was that change of subject.

And he'd been really nice to me.

Sure, he started that by breaking into my house, freaking me out by waiting for me to return home, and reading me the riot act.

But he was a great guy.

He just had some unusual methods to his greatness.

So I was learning.

If it's worth it, it's worth the work.

And I needed to give that to Brett too.

"Brett, if I wasn't where I'm at with Axl, and in life, honestly, if I met you free of that, I might be that girl that could deal. You're really special. In fact, you're just a great guy, and I don't care if you're also a motherfucker. But we didn't meet like that."

He reached out and slid a finger along my jaw before he said gently, "Baby, I know. Pantera can't see straight, he wants you so bad, and you been in that same space for probably longer than he has. I get it. Don't worry about me. Please."

"I think you're into me," I whispered hesitantly.

"If you were the love of my life, Hattie, and I was the love of yours, Pantera wouldn't matter. To either of us."

"This is true," I murmured.

He smiled. "It's not in the cards for us. But you're cute, and both my sisters live in Alaska, and they're all grown up, so it's fun havin' a girl to look after again. So like I said, don't worry."

"You do know you're special," I said quietly, but earnestly.

That made Brett's entire, big body tick.

Then he said, just as quietly, "No, I didn't. But I'm gettin' that, sweetheart."

I liked that I was giving him that so he could get it.

I smiled at him.

He reached out and squeezed my knee before he faced forward.

I did the same, wondering if Ryn put her phone on sleep or charged it overnight somewhere not close to her so a text wouldn't disturb her.

I decided, just in case, to wait until morning.

I then looked out the side window again.

And my brows drew together.

"Are we going to your place?" I asked the route that was not a route that took us in the direction of my apartment.

"No, we're going to Pantera's place."

I rotated swiftly in my seat, crying, "*What?*"

"I'm dropping you off so you can sort things out," he stated.

"It's after two thirty in the morning," I told him something he knew.

"Trust me, he won't give a shit, you show at his door to fix things."

Oh my God!

"I'm not prepared."

"How do you prepare for this? You don't. You just do it."

He was right.

Argh!

"I'm tired. And I don't want him to be in a bad mood because I've woken him up when I start explaining."

"Right, Hattie, you get I got a dick?"

"Of course!"

"And you get that, if outside factors did not skew shit, I could be into you in a way I'd stop at nothing to make you mine?"

Oh man.

"Uh…"

"Which is how Pantera is into you."

Yikes!

And tentatively…

Yay!

"So trust me, *he will not give a shit you show at his door at two thirty in the morning*," Brett finished with quite a bit of emphasis.

"All right, all right," I mumbled.

"You can do this," he encouraged.

"What if I can't? What if I blew things big time this morning?"

"This is how it's gonna go," he began. "He's gonna open the door. He's then gonna see you. And shit will be sorted. *Boom*."

Seriously?

"Do you really think it'll be that easy?"

"Have you looked in a mirror?"

"I know I'm not hard to look at, Brett, but that isn't the only important thing."

"You're cute. You're sweet. You're nice. You're talented. Outside a few important glitches that fuck you up, which, Hattie, everyone's got in one way or another, you got it together. Great pad. Sweet jammies. Studio full of money waiting to be made. And last, it wasn't me kissing him on the deck the way you two were kissing. You were doing that, and you can't tell me you don't know way more than me what that was about. So, not to be crude, you on his doorstep takes him a huge step closer to being in your pants. So absolutely. It's going to be that easy."

All he said was very nice.

But at the last part, my heart stopped beating.

"Ohmigod, I'm *so* not ready for sex with Axl. We have to turn back," I breathed.

Brett looked to the ceiling of the town car.

"What?" I asked.

He again turned to me. "He's not gonna jump you on his front doorstep. Stop making excuses."

I clamped my mouth shut.

"You can do this," he repeated.

I drew in a very, *very* big breath.

"Hattie, you *want* to do this."

I *so* did.

It also scared me to death.

I nodded.

"Good girl," he muttered.

Ugh.

"Are you this heavy-handed with your sisters?" I demanded.

He got a look on his face I didn't like before he wiped it and said, "Why do you think they live in Alaska?"

That wasn't the truth.

I thought I read his look, which was why I said, "You miss them."

"My sisters and me are tight. My brother..."

Unsaid: *not so much.*

"Where is he?" I asked.

"Here. In Denver."

"Oh," I muttered. Then in a normal voice, "I don't have siblings."

"You do now. We ain't blood, but you made up with four of them today, and the other one is sitting right beside you."

Uh-oh.

I might cry again.

To avoid that, I snapped, "It's getting to be freakish how sweet you are."

"I'd put that notion out of your head by offering you a Go to Work with Brett Day, but I like you think that. So we'll let it lie."

I smiled at him, the smile faltered, and I admitted, "I'm scared."

"I know you are," he said gently. "Why do you think we're going to Pantera right now? I can't let my girl crawl back into her head and not get what she wants."

No, we couldn't have that.

"I'd like to meet your sisters," I said.

"They come visit, I'll set that up."

"Brett?"

"Right here."

"Thanks for not letting me blow it again."

It was him who was now smiling.

"Anytime."

CHAPTER SEVEN

Worth It

HATTIE

Okay.

I didn't know what happened to me on the long, *long* walk from Brett's town car to Axl's front door (it actually wasn't that long, it was pretty short, it just felt that way).

But whatever it was, it happened.

And it did about the time I got over my surprise Axl lived in a cool, gray-painted-with-white-trim bungalow in Baker Historic District.

I thought condo (like Mag) or loft (like Boone).

Nope.

House.

Nice house, smallish, no yard, all of the limited space around it landscaped, great 'hood.

But I got over that mostly because I *had* to get over it.

This was happening at nearly 3:00 in the morning.

And first, I couldn't mess it up.

But second, it hit me to wonder *how* I'd messed it up.

Axl had been correct in what he'd said to me at my studio, but he hadn't been nice about it.

And the creepy call came right after that.

So, of course I wouldn't call him.

He'd just been mean to me!

And I was a grown-ass woman, and I might just be coming into my own with that, like, that very day.

But I was entitled to do whatever I wanted or call whoever I wanted when I found myself with a possible-which-turned-into-a-probable crisis.

Or anytime at all.

And Axl might know that if he *let me speak*.

He was always interrupting me.

So, when I hit his doorbell, all of that was on my mind.

Yes, I got the kind of man he was and what he was to me (even if he actually wasn't) would make it *seem* like he should be my first call.

But if this was going to work, he'd have to *listen to me* so he'd understand why he wasn't.

So this was on my mind when he opened the door.

Then nothing was on my mind because he opened the door in a pair of gray cotton jersey sleep pants with a wide navy elastic band that rode low on his hips.

And nothing else.

He had dark chest hair, not much, just enough, that trailed down to a dense line low on his flat stomach that led into the waistband of his pants.

His chest was magnificent.

His chest deserved sonnets.

The sight of his chest might make me pass out.

I couldn't even think of that line of hair that led into his pants or I might lapse into a coma.

I looked up into his semi-sleepy, ice-blue eyes.

Nope.

Not pass out.

Orgasm.

"Hattie? Is everything okay?" his semi-sleep-roughened voice asked.

What was I doing here again?

His gaze went beyond me to the curb.

His stubbled jaw hardened.

Oh, right.

That was what I was doing.

"We're going to talk," I declared, turned to give Brett a low wave, a signal I was heading in and a moment for me to pull it together because *I could do this*.

And I was going to do this.

Brett was being Brett, thus he told me he'd wait at the curb for me to text all was well and Axl was on duty, or for me to come back out so he could take me home.

Yes, at 3:00 at night.

Totally a nice guy.

Seeing as I could do this, and I was going to, I pushed through Axl to get into his house.

I only took a few steps in because there was a light coming from the back, through a door to a room on the right, but the space I was in was dark, the shades were closed, and I didn't want to mess up before I started by running into furniture or breaking a lamp.

I watched Axl standing at the door, looking out of it like I was still there, then he did a head gesture I couldn't decipher in my current panicked, anxious, scared, mildly turned-on state, and he closed the door.

Then he moved.

A lamp switched on.

In full light, him and his chest and eyes and those sleep pants . . .

Not to mention that line of hair.

Gah!

"Ha—" he started.

I put up a hand instantly. "No. Nope. Unh-unh. This time, I get to do the talking and you get to listen, but what you don't get to do is *interrupt*."

He did that man stance with hands on hips that I didn't understand if its purpose was to take up as much room as manly possible or just have something to do with his hands.

But it highlighted his chest.

His *awesome* chest.

Focus!

I launched in.

"First, I'm sorry to wake you up. But Brett brought me here after work so I wouldn't chicken out when you didn't text me, and as an excuse for the inexcusable rudeness of waking you up, I was probably totally going to find some reason to chicken out. So I'm sorry, truly, but it was now or maybe not ever."

"I do not care even a little bit that you woke me up," he stated firmly.

Oh my.

My.

That was nice.

And Brett was right.

Moving on.

"And that's not my way of saying I'm upset you didn't text me. I get it."

"I'm not sure you do since the only reason I didn't was that I had a busy day, and I wasn't able to get to your texts for a while. When I did, I could tell you were concerned, so it fucked with me I didn't have a minute to text you to let you know I was cool. I didn't get home until an hour ago, and didn't think, after you danced, a late-night texting was gonna help us work through our shit. I was gonna connect with you first thing tomorrow. Which, strictly speaking, we're doing, since tomorrow is now."

Oh, well then.

That was nice too.

No, actually awesome.

And was I a freak to feel kind of warm and squishy at the words "help us work through our shit"?

I mean he thought *we* had shit!

I couldn't get bogged down in that.

Onward ho!

"Okay, so, taking us back to where this all started, I can only hope you'd understand how embarrassing it was for you and Ryn to see me how I was that day in the dance studio. I think you understand I like you, and I wanted you to like me, and acting like a lunatic because I messed up a dance isn't going to make you like me."

He took his hands from his hips, looked like he was going to make a move toward me, and opened his mouth.

"No," I said quickly, shaking my head. "We're in the scary, soul-baring part so you don't get to talk. I'll open up discussion when I'm done. Now you need to listen."

When I said the bit about "the scary, soul-baring part" his face took on an expression I had to ignore for my peace of mind and my will to go on without skipping this part and jumping him and his bare chest.

Then he crossed his arms on that chest and settled in.

Not much better.

Perseverance in the face of his gorgeousness, clearly, was going to be the key.

I called on that and carried on.

"So, I got embarrassed about that, and I can imagine you get that. What you don't know is, that's the first time I've danced, not stripping, in maybe three years."

"Jesus," he whispered.

I allowed that since it was a reaction and not an interruption.

"And it felt really good, until it didn't, and then you guys saw me, but it just brought to the fore the fact that I quit dancing not because I didn't like it. I do. I love it. But because it came with messed-up memories and those were surfacing too. Around about the time I was dancing in that room I forgot to do it just because I loved doing it, and it felt amazing, then I did a minor screwup that meant nothing at all. But my dad got in my head. And I wasn't angry at myself for messing up so much as angry at myself for still letting *him* mess me up."

"Okay, baby," he said softly.

Oh hell.

I hadn't told him he couldn't interject, softly or other, much less call me baby.

All of which was *really* nice.

I cleared my throat.

"So, to wit," I started, Axl's lips quirked, that was hot, and annoying because it was hot since it was messing with my mojo to get this done, but I kept on, "that was where I was at with that and I just let it get the better of me."

"Understandable," he said.

Okay.

Good.

Phew.

Next!

"And I get that it may not be cool I danced 'Shut Up' for you when I was closing you out and you have a girlfriend—"

"I don't have a girlfriend."

Okay...

Um...

Oh my God.

My brain did mental cartwheels.

Then it hit me.

"A woman you're seeing," I amended to dude speak.

He shook his head. "No. We broke it off the day you messed up in that studio."

Oh.

My.

God.

"Uh..." I forced out.

"We're still friends and we hang, though," he said.

"Oh, okay," I mumbled.

"You think I'd kiss you like I did this morning if I had a girlfriend?" he asked.

"I didn't know. But Brett said no."

"For once, that guy is right," he muttered.

"Though, you told me yourself you were seeing someone."

"At that time, I still was, even though I intended to end it with her. That said, I told you that so you wouldn't feel pressure and might feel safe connecting with me. Then, when I got you to that place, I was gonna move us forward."

Hmm.

"Are you done talking so we can open up discussion now?" he asked, sounding amused.

The amused part didn't make me happy, seeing as this wasn't super easy on me.

Even so, we kinda already were discussing since I was letting him talk.

Nevertheless, I squinted my eyes at him and snapped, "No."

"Right," he murmured, now visibly fighting a smile.

Grr.

Onward!

"So, obviously, I had something to say with my 'Shut Up' dance that I wanted you to hear but I thought you had a girlfriend and I also was still messed up myself. So maybe I shouldn't have said it when I wasn't giving you the opportunity to react to it, but I had to do it and so I did. And I'm sorry if that wasn't the right thing to do or if that seemed like I was jacking you around. I can assure you, that was one hundred percent not my intent."

He said nothing.

But when I said nothing either, he said, "Is it discussion time now?"

"No," I answered.

This time, he dipped his ear toward his shoulder and twisted his neck to hide his outright smile.

Really?

"I'm not finding anything amusing," I informed him. "This isn't super easy."

He looked at me, still outright smiling. "I get that, honey. But you're not experiencing the adorableness of you."

Adorableness?

He thought I was adorable?

Wow.

Sweet.

No.

Concentrate!

"Can I finish?" I asked snappishly, or maybe somewhat fake snappishly, but whatever.

He threw out a hand in invitation to continue before crossing it on his chest again.

So I continued.

"However, even if you thought I was jacking you around, which I will repeat, I was not."

"I didn't think you were jacking me around, baby," he assured, again with the soft.

And man, did I like that soft.

"Good, but onward from that, I screwed up with the girls, and

I know Lottie is special to you, but that's mine and theirs and not for you to get in the middle of."

He looked like he was going to say something, thought better of it, and closed his mouth.

Through all this, I kept speaking.

"So, although everything you said in my studio was right, there were some ways it was wrong, but you still shouldn't have broken into my studio and confronted me. Which you apologized about and that's done. I'm not going over it. I'm noting it just to explain, maybe minutes after you left, that creeper called me so I obviously wasn't going to phone you because you were mad at me. And…the way…you left…was kind of…final…"

My words came funny, trailing off at the end, and I eventually stopped speaking because my body jerked seeing as he'd dropped his arms from his chest and started moving.

Toward me.

He did this declaring, "It's discussion time now."

I started retreating, saying, "No, I'm not done."

Though, I kind of was, outside the hard part (or, the hard*er* part), which was to share that I wanted to see where we went from here because I was really into him and he was a great kisser.

"No, you're not done," he agreed, still stalking me.

I was still retreating, and since I didn't know the lay of the land, I bumped into an end table.

I scooted around it.

He kept speaking.

And stalking.

"And *we're* not done," he finished.

"Okay, so maybe you get to talk freely now, but you don't get to stalk me around your living room."

"You'd stop moving, I'd stop stalking," he pointed out, still tracking me.

"Why did you have to move at all?" I asked, still withdrawing.

"Because we got a few more things to get straight," he answered.

"And we couldn't do it from where we were?" I queried, high-pitched and somewhat frantically, because he was getting closer.

I shifted to the side and then froze before bracing to make a dash, where to, I didn't know, because he lunged.

I didn't get the opportunity to find where to go because he caught me around the waist with an arm before he turned his hips and shifted his leg, catching me at my calves.

Yes, catching me at my calves.

Like, *kicking them out from under me*.

I swallowed a cry and grabbed on to his shoulders as I started to go down, but I didn't hit floor.

Axl moved quickly, controlling the fall, and I hit couch with Axl on top of me.

I stared into his eyes from up close.

And felt his weight on me.

Both were very nice.

"Um…" I mumbled.

"Okay, Hattie," he said quietly, "before we kiss and make up…"

Eep!

"…it's important you get it straight that no matter what, say we're copacetic, but something tweaks you or worries you and you're not sure it's a big deal so you don't want to bother me with it, or we're in a fight and you think I'm mad at you, or you're mad at me, it doesn't matter. I'm your first fuckin' call. You hear me?"

"Um…" I repeated.

"Baby, all you said is important, and I appreciate you givin' that to me. I don't have the words to express how happy I am you showed at my door at nearly three in the morning to work shit out between us. Finally. I also know how tough that was on you, so when I say I appreciate it, I seriously mean that. And eventually, when it's not three in the morning, we'll get into a lot of that or just decide to put it behind us. But this is important too. *Really* important. So confirm you heard me."

I nodded.

And I did because I got how important it was, absolutely, seeing as he had to have my undivided attention by being full-out on top of me to share it with me.

So, yup.

I totally got it.

"I get why you called Cisco," he went on. "And he sat down with Hawk today and we're all on it. Just don't do that again. Right?"

I nodded again.

He studied my face, must have sensed I was telling the truth, because a change came over him, and since he was on me, it came over me too.

I liked this change, it also terrified the crap out of me, then his gaze dropped to my mouth, and I experienced the supremely bizarre feeling of the terror receding and expanding *at the same time*.

"Uh, Axl," I called unsteadily.

His eyes came to mine.

"You guys are on it?" I asked.

"I'll brief you tomorrow, though we just got started and we got other shit happening, so we don't have anything. Yet. But yes, we're on it."

"Thanks," I whispered.

His lips tipped up, his eyes grew heated, and they fell to my mouth again.

"Uh, Axl?" I repeated.

He looked to me again.

"I get you're a commando and all, but just so I know for future reference, do commandos need to pin women to their couches in order to share things they think are important?"

He out-and-out smiled before he answered, "Yeah."

"All righty then," I mumbled.

"You got a problem with that?" he asked.

He felt good. His body was warm and heavy. His skin under my hands was sleek, the muscle under that hard. And bottom line, I'd been wanting this in all versions of it that it might come since the first time I clapped eyes on him.

So, no.

I didn't have a problem with it.

"No," I answered.

He gave a brief nod before continuing, "Mostly, though, after you gave me all of that, and what I knew it took for you to come and give it to me, and then getting down to talking about that asshole who's fucking with you, I needed to be close to you. Not to mention, seeing as we're about to make out, might as well be comfortable doing it."

Might as well.

Yikes.

Moving on.

"Okay. Then, is there…I mean, um…*making up*?"

"Yeah," he confirmed.

"Don't you have to kind of be *together* to *make up*?"

"Hattie, this is the longest non-relationship relationship in history. We've been together since the first time you shot me down for a date and I think you know that better than me."

Hmm.

"But you had a girlfriend," I reminded him.

"No, I saw a woman briefly when you were giving me nothing to go on. I liked her. She liked me. I couldn't get you out of my head when I was with her, which was fucked up and uncool. I knew just how fucked up and uncool that was when you lost it on yourself that day in the studio and my reaction to seeing your pain shared clear I needed to focus on what was important. So

I sat down with her to finish it. When I told her we were done in that way, she said, 'It's the girl you're pining for, isn't it?' So I wasn't hiding it from her either. Which was more fucked up and uncool. But she's nice. She's sweet. She talked to me about you. And she told me not to give up, you'd come around. We like the same kind of movies and she mountain bikes, and so do I, so we hit trails. Like I said, she's nice and sweet, she's also gorgeous, so she's already seeing another guy. But we've become good friends in a way she won't lose me, and I hope you aren't the kind of woman who can't handle the man in her life having female friends."

My reaction to seeing your pain.

Focus on what was important.

The man in her life.

"I don't think I'm that kind of woman," I said.

Or, if I was, after he said all that, I wasn't going to be any longer.

"Good," he muttered.

"What kind of movies do you like?" I asked.

"Lots, but with Peyton, it's horror."

I pulled a face.

He grinned at me.

"I don't mountain bike," I told him.

"I don't care," he told my mouth.

I had a feeling we were getting to the making-up part.

My hands, still on his shoulders, squeezed.

His gaze came back to my eyes.

"I have to text Brett. He's waiting to take me home."

"His car took off before I closed the door."

I felt my eyes get big. "He told me he was waiting."

"And I told him he was relieved of duty."

"You didn't leave your house."

"He got my message."

The head gesture.

Men's form of sign language.

Okay, again...

Moving on.

"Right then, can you take me home, uh, after we're finished?"

"No, 'cause you're staying here with me."

Um!

"*Pardon?*"

"Hattie, if you'd shut up, we'd make out to make up, but I'm not doin' you on my couch or in my bed before I've even bought you dinner. We're gonna make out to make up. You're gonna sleep in my bed. I'll sleep on the couch. I got shit on for tomorrow, some of that trying to figure out who's dicking with you, so I gotta take off early. You text when you wake up. Me or one of the guys will come get you and take you home. And we'll go out to dinner tomorrow, finish talking through shit, and start getting to know one another."

Oh boy.

I really wanted to do all that.

But we were already hitting a rough patch.

I started it with, "I have to be at work at nine."

"Plenty of time for me to take you somewhere and that be someplace nice."

"Well, yes, but I go to my dad's every night to make him dinner."

He didn't miss a beat before he said, "If your father can't cook his own meal, he's getting delivery."

"Axl—"

He put his finger to my lips.

That was a *way* better way to interrupt me.

"I know you don't like it when I cut you off, baby, but this is a big deal. One kiss and a whole lot of mindfuck and we're here. We're here because we both want this, we both know it and we both know how bad we want it. I wanna hear about your dad. I wanna know about your life. I just wanna know you. But we just unfucked this. Give me twenty-four hours, at least, of unfucked before we court fucking it up again."

"Okay," I whispered against his finger.

"Okay," he whispered back, taking that finger away, his gaze drifting again to my mouth.

And his head following it.

"I didn't mean to mindfuck you," I kept whispering.

His head didn't lift, but his eyes did, when he said, "One kiss, Hattie, and it was all worth it."

Oh my God!

So nice!

Then he slanted his head and gave me kiss two.

And he was right.

So right.

It was all worth it.

Totally.

CHAPTER EIGHT

Keep Putting in the Work

HATTIE

I woke feeling comfy and snuggly.

Also rested and refreshed.

That last was weird. I never woke feeling refreshed. I always woke feeling like I wanted to go back to sleep.

Or maybe it was just that I didn't want to get up.

Now I felt...

Great.

I opened my eyes and saw dark gray sheets.

This confused me because I had pastel pink sheets.

Suddenly, I smiled.

I was in Axl's bed.

And it was a great bed.

Best...mattress...*ever.*

And I could smell him.

So, obviously, *even better.*

Sun was coming from behind his closed blinds.

I wondered vaguely what time it was.

I wondered not-so-vaguely how life could get so good so fast when it seemed so bad for so long.

I wondered what was on my leg.

Wait.

What?

I looked down the bed and saw a cat, hind paws to the bed, front paws to my leg. Small, slender body. Dense gray fur. Big ears. Gold at the edge of her (his?) dilated eyes.

She (he?) studied me with curiosity and barely hidden feline distaste.

Then s/he turned and pranced off the bed.

Axl had a cat.

Axl had a pretty, dainty, gray cat with an attitude.

I would not peg him as a cat person.

Dogs.

Yes.

Pretty, dainty, haughty gray cats?

No.

Semi-meeting Axl's cat, and knowing he was a cat person made me feel like I felt when I first woke up.

Comfy and snuggly.

I sat up in Axl's ridiculously comfortable bed.

I'd become somewhat acquainted with his bedroom last night after he'd kissed me silly on his couch.

Just kissing, no feeling up, no liberties taken (not, after he started kissing me, that those liberties wouldn't be freely given).

But lots...

And lots...

Of delicious *kissing*.

Once he'd decided we were done with that (regrettably), he led me to his bedroom, gave me one of his tees to sleep in, then he took me to his bathroom, unearthed a toothbrush still in its wrapper and pulled out his toothpaste.

He told me to "sleep well" and "call out if you need anything," and then he bent in, kissed my neck, gave me a smile and left me.

I'd been too dreamy from his kisses, and maybe too sleepy from the late night, to take in much of his bedroom at that time.

I took it in now.

He decorated like me, without the shocks of color. White walls. Wooden blinds painted gray. Some lighter gray floor-length curtains at the sides. A bedspread of white with nuanced shades of gray checks.

The outlier to the gray and white was the furniture.

A modern, boxy black leather chair sat in the corner, with an ottoman and a chrome standing lamp that had a dome shade. The chair was covered in cargos, tees and my clothes.

There was also a black six-drawer dresser. And the bed frame was black, as were the nightstands. The lamps on the nightstands were chrome.

Though what caught my attention was that the only thing on his dresser was a shadow box, triangular black frame, holding a folded American flag.

That didn't bode well.

I went to throw the covers off in order to get out of bed when I saw a piece of notepaper on the pillow beside me.

Knowing it was from Axl, I snatched it up.

Classily, but surprisingly, it was heavy stock and had a dark monogram at the top that told me his full initials were ASP.

I wondered what his middle name was. At the same time, I thought I didn't know anyone who had monogrammed notepaper. And on top of that, I saw he had small, precise handwriting.

I thought all this, but I didn't think on it much.

I read the note.

Hattie~
   You're even adorable when you sleep.

Oh man.
I loved he thought that.
And I was glad, when he saw me sleeping, I wasn't drooling or snoring or anything else equally mortifying.

   Make yourself at home. If you don't know how to use it, the Nespresso machine should be self-explanatory. If you have trouble, call. Cisco dropped your bag this morning. It's on the kitchen counter.

Oh my God.
My purse!
I'd totally forgot, I left it in Brett's car.
Brett brought it around.
He was *so nice* too.
Everyone around me (outside my stalker, and, as usual, my dad) was just *so nice.*

   When you're ready, let me know and me or one of the guys will be there to take you home.

~Axl

He ended it in a way that wasn't nice.
It was *wonderful.*

   PS: Best wake-up call I ever had, honey.

Totally.
Wonderful.

Smiling to myself, I threw off the covers to get out of bed, keeping the note with me and searching for his cat.

I moved toward the wide hall, which I saw last night led not only to the bathroom, but another room at the other end.

I headed to the bathroom first, noting the hall walls were mirrored on one side, before I noticed they were actually mirrored doors to two closets on either side of the entry to the bathroom.

Interesting.

The bathroom was more of what was in his bedroom. Chrome fixtures. White walls and white penny-tile floors. White marble countertops with gray veins. But the cabinetry was navy. As were the thick towels.

I brushed my teeth.

And with what I hoped was as little snooping as possible (but I only did it with a purpose, and that was not to snoop, it was about dental hygiene), I found not only did he have floss (and he told me to make myself at home, so I tore off a string), but also strengthening and whitening mouthwash (I had this too!). So I used some of that as well.

Done in the bathroom, I wandered back out into the hall, and instead of going back to the bedroom, I went the other way.

At the other end was a room, not as big as the master, but not much smaller.

It was an office with a desk, a laptop on the desk, two handsome wire trays on either edge, both stacked with papers. Desk chair behind. Another armchair and ottoman in the corner, this one slouchy but handsome. Some shelves filled with books and what looked like trophies and medals.

And the *pièce de résistance*, a vintage stand-up Pac-Man video game against one wall.

Sweet.

Smiling to myself about Pac-Man, and still carrying Axl's note, I walked out.

In the bedrooms, the blinds were drawn so they were somewhat in shadow (though, not much blocked out the bright Denver sun, even dark blinds).

However, light came bright in the rest of the house through lots of big windows.

And I walked out of the office into a dining room area that was beyond a half wall from the living room. Black furniture. Round table. Four chairs, their backs curved, the style was elegant and classy but also modern. And in the middle of the table was a wide, squat, interestingly shaped glass bowl in hues of blue, black and clear.

It was a fantastic bowl.

It was also the kind of bowl a man who had monogrammed notepaper owned.

On this thought, I started to feel a little weird, not exactly in a bad way, as I drifted into the living room.

I'd spent time in that room last night, but I hadn't taken in an inch of it seeing as I had a bevy of other awesome (after the scary) things to occupy my mind and my time.

Now I saw it had a cool fireplace. Two couches perpendicular to it (gray). Two armchairs facing it (navy). Big TV over the mantel. Coffee table. End tables. Lamps. Black-and-white pictures on the walls, all of which seemed to be urban-life photography. Graffiti. Murals. The light rail of Denver at night.

And there was a handsome chest in front of the picture window. On it was a piece that was made of polished nickel that looked like a starburst but it was fashioned to erupt, not as if it was going out and toward you, but like it was detonating from the surface of the chest into the air above it.

It was magnificent.

Way better than the bowl and the bowl was rad.

I noted a throw blanket folded neatly on one of the couches, a pillow on top of it.

Axl was tidy.

I knew he was ex-military, perhaps that should be expected.

But outside the chair covered in clothes in the bedroom, the rest of the place suggested he was seriously *tidy*.

I wandered back past the dining area, into a kitchen.

And that was the same as all the rest.

White walls. Black-and-white-checked tile floor. White cupboards. White quartz countertop.

But black appliances and graphite countertop appliances.

Though the kitchen towels were navy-and-white stripes.

"Axl has it going on," I whispered.

And he did.

He was clean as well as tidy (which I was too). His style was stark and modern (as was my own), but it also had personality (as I thought mine did too).

And he flossed and rinsed with tooth-strengthening mouthwash, as did I.

I suddenly understood what that weird feeling was from before.

Part of it was that I'd spent so long wanting to know him, now being in his space, learning what he was like, getting to know him, even when he wasn't there, felt super nice. Not to mention, having an understanding that we were compatible in a few ways felt super nice too.

The rest of it was seeing his place was not a bachelor pad.

It was a grown man's house.

One where you lived and moved your girlfriend in when it got serious, and you stayed when you got married.

But only for a while, because when you decided to have kids you moved so you could have more room.

I got a little thrill at this thought as I walked to the counter where there was a coffee pod sitting next to a tall glass with a spoon in it that had a long handle.

Axl had set me up for coffee.

And he had cool coffee glasses.

I didn't even know there *were* coffee glasses.

But Axl had them and they were super cool.

Again smiling, I headed to the fridge to get some creamer.

And found Axl was a creamer guy.

In a big way.

Three top-shelf brands, five flavors.

I picked Starbucks white chocolate mocha, put Axl's note next to my purse on the counter, tinkered with the machine for a few seconds to find out how to do it before I set the Nespresso to running, and then moved to check out what was behind the three doors in the kitchen.

Side by side on the back wall: one, to a large garage, the other, to a walk-in pantry/utility room with washer and dryer.

The door on the front wall that had a half window led to a rectangular deck that jutted out at the front of the house. The deck was probably twice the size of mine, had high walls around it, like mine, but without the lattice see-throughs.

Total privacy.

On the deck were two moon chairs with a glass-top table, all this (except the glass, obviously) black. A black-and-white zigzag-patterned rug lay under them.

And last, there was a built-in, corner Jacuzzi, big enough for two.

That Jacuzzi didn't give me a little thrill.

It gave me a nice shiver.

Still feeling the shiver, I turned and headed back to the coffee when I noticed Dainty Cat had joined me.

She sat on the kitchen floor just inside the door, tail swishing, staring at me with eyes that were indeed golden.

And she was in full judgment.

"You'd look around too," I defended.

She silently disagreed, expressed her disdain for my actions, her dislike of my person, and her indignation I was still there, all of this with swift, feline efficiency, then she got up and sauntered out.

I watched her go, already half in love with her.

I went back to my bag, grabbed my phone, stirred my coffee with the kick-butt spoon and texted Axl.

> I'm up. Managed to figure out coffee.
> Your house is rad.
> And thanks for the offer, but I don't want
> to interfere with your busy day.
> I'll call a Lyft.
> See you tonight.
> And thanks for not minding that
> I woke you up last night.

I sent that and then sent:

> Oh, and your cat is gorgeous.

And after that, I sent:

> And your mattress is awesome!

I was so in the zone of happiness, in Axl's house, drinking Axl's coffee, being judged by Axl's cat, freely texting Axl, that it didn't occur to me not to tell Axl his mattress was awesome.

I mean, it was.

But I didn't have to tell him that until maybe later, if that fabulous time came when he was on it with me.

I barely got a sip of my delicious coffee (white chocolate

mocha, *my God*, who knew?) and nowhere near enough time to freak out about my mattress text before I got a reply.

> I want to take you home.
> I can be there in 30. You okay
> to hang until I get there?

Was I okay to hang on his deck in his awesome moon chairs staring at his two-person Jacuzzi, thinking of him kissing me in it while I felt up his chest, all of this because he wanted me to hang due to the fact he wanted to take me home?

Heck to the *yes*.

> Can I hang on your deck?

> You can do anything you
> want, baby.

Upon me reading this, Dainty Cat joined me again in the kitchen in order to confirm her worst fears: I was still there.

She then left.

In that time, I hadn't gotten over Axl's last text.

But thirty minutes wasn't three hours and I was still in his tee with bedhead.

I dealt with that, made his bed, found he had European pillows piled on the floor next to one of the nightstands. (A man who had European pillows? How did I get this lucky?)

And I was out on the deck with my coffee and plenty of time to text Brett.

> Thank you again for not letting
> me blow it.
> And I know your sisters aren't in Alaska

to put space between them and you.
I hope you feel you can tell me the
story one day.
What I know right now is that I've
never had a big brother, but still,
you're the best one ever.

I soaked up some vitamin D, drank my coffee out of Axl's hip coffee glass, and got back from Brett:

Pleased it worked out, sweetheart.
Speak soon. ♥♥

Now seriously.

What motherfucker put heart emojis on his texts?

I was still contemplating this, and a fair few other things (most of those other things having to do with the Jacuzzi, none of them having to do with contacting Dad to tell him it was pizza delivery for him that night—I'd tackle that later, after some of my joy died down and he had less time to make a fuss about it) when I heard a car approach then a garage door go up.

Not knowing the neighborhood sounds, and since the houses were close in Baker, I couldn't be sure, but just in case it was Axl, I got up and went into the kitchen.

I was done with my coffee anyway and needed to clean the glass.

I was right.

It was Axl.

And as I set the rinsed glass in the dishwasher, he came in the back door, wearing navy cargos and a navy tee.

We both froze in place and stared at each other.

We did this for a long time, like if one of us moved, the other would go up in a puff of smoke and under no circumstances could that happen.

Then we did this for even longer, like we were prepared to do it forever.

And I had to admit I could do this forever, because Axl was just that easy to look at.

But more, I liked what this said. How much it meant to him I was standing in his kitchen, which made it safe for me to share how much it meant to be there.

Dainty Cat broke it up by slithering to Axl and rubbing up against his leg.

I chanced speaking.

"Your cat doesn't like me."

"My cat doesn't like me," he replied. "She's only being nice because you're here and now she has someone to like less than she likes me, and she wants to make sure you know it."

I burst out laughing.

Axl moved to me while I did it, and he was grinning.

He stopped close, though he could have gotten closer.

Like, hello kiss closer.

Sadly, he didn't give me hello kiss close *or* a hello kiss.

When I got a handle on my laughter, I said, "If asked, I would have said you were a dog person."

He shook his head. "Dogs are easy. You get a dog. You train him what to do, he does it. There's no fun in that. You can't train a cat. A cat does what a cat wants to do. It likes who it wants to like. A dog lives to please you. A cat lives to be pleased. Randomly, every week or two, she curls into me while I watch television. I feel like I've won a medal."

Through all of this, I was smiling up at him, and when he stopped speaking, I didn't quit.

Then he kept talking.

"Though, if I wake up in the middle of the night, almost

always, she's with me at my feet or in the bend of my knees. Last night, she slept on the back of the couch. She senses me awake and then she's gone. So I know somewhere along the line, I won her. She just wants to make sure I keep putting in the work."

Keep putting in the work.

I was still smiling, but my heart had started beating a lot faster.

I ignored that and asked, "What's her name?"

"Cleo, after Cleopatra, because she's a queen."

Oh wow.

Okay.

I was getting that he really liked his cat.

"Did you rescue her?"

"Nope. I stole her."

I felt my head twitch in surprise. "You stole her?"

"Yep." He nodded. "My neighbors are assholes. Their kids are arguably bigger assholes. I saw the kids out there with her, I knew shit was about to get real. I was right. I didn't like what I saw, and I won't share what it was. I was deciding how to intervene when I was coming home from a run, and Cleo, still a little kitten, was in their backyard alone, freaked, mewing repeatedly, wandering the grass like it was a war zone and every step she took might mean she'd hit a mine. I jumped their fence and took her. The dad saw me, came over and got in my shit. I told him either he let me keep the cat or I take the cat to the vet and he can talk to a cop about why he's letting his kids abuse an animal. And I advised him to keep that in mind if he thinks about getting his kids another animal. Haven't talked to the man since. They still live there, and Cleo's three years old. And they never got another animal."

He hadn't shared the exact truth.

He did, indeed, rescue his cat.

Just not the normal way.

So, Axl was a man who would rush into danger to rescue Ryn and jump a fence to rescue a cat.

Yeah.

How did I get this lucky?

I didn't want to ask my next.

But I asked.

"Did you...take her to see a vet?"

He nodded, this time shortly.

"She was malnourished, dehydrated and favoring her back right paw, but no breaks or tears, so the vet figured it was bruised. It took me a bit to talk him into letting me keep her. He was concerned I'd done that to her. I managed to convince him she'd be safe with me. So Cleo got the realm where she'd reign and I learned that, even if your cat views you as her subject, it's seriously nice to share space with another living being who depends on you."

Okay.

He just said that.

He just said that.

"That's sweet," I whispered my understatement.

"Maybe. Mostly it's true."

I had no reply.

In fact, I didn't want to talk anymore.

I wanted a very belated hello kiss.

This must have communicated itself to Axl because he got even closer.

So much closer, I could feel his body, even if it wasn't touching mine.

And he had to bend his neck even more to hold my eyes.

"So, you like my mattress?" he murmured.

"It's like heaven," I said to his mouth.

"Hybrid," he replied.

"Mm?" I hummed.

"Memory foam and regular."

I was sure what he was saying was fascinating.

But I was fascinated with something else.

I'd never really noticed how magnificent lips were when they moved.

Especially lips like Axl's.

"Hattie?"

"Yes?"

"Do you wanna kiss me?"

"Yes."

"Then, baby, kiss me."

"Okay," I breathed, pushed up on my toes and kissed him.

No hesitation, his arms closed around me, he angled his head and he kissed me back.

Axl ended it with me pressed to the sink, my arms around his shoulders, his tall, hard body molded to mine.

Man, he was a great kisser.

And when he finished kissing me, and I swam out of how that made me feel, one could say I instantly became a disciple of that hot, hungry look on his face.

"The Pac-Man machine is my favorite part of your house," I whispered.

"Did you play?"

"Your deck beckoned."

His lips quirked. "Right. Another time."

I hoped so.

"I'm ordering monogrammed notepads this afternoon," I informed him.

His lips quirked again. "Birthday present from Mom a couple of years ago. I think that's the first note I wrote on one of them. Usually it's grocery lists."

"Did she buy you the bowl on your dining room table?"

"Yeah."

"She has good taste."

"Yeah."

"The piece in the picture window?"

"That's mine."

Nice.

"Your middle name starts with an 'S,'" I told him something he knew.

"Sylas, after my dad."

"Ah."

"Yours?"

"Marianne, after no one."

He smiled.

Then, unfortunately, he said, "As much as I'm all in to chat all day with you in my arms pressed to my sink, honey, I gotta get back to it."

He said this low, without hiding his disappointment.

I didn't hide mine either.

"Bummer," I muttered.

He gave me a squeeze. "You ready?"

I nodded.

He let me go.

I went to my bag.

When I saw his note next to it, I tried to surreptitiously tuck it in my purse.

And then I thought, it's not as if he doesn't know I like him, we'd just been making out.

And it wasn't weird for a girl who likes a guy to want to save the first note he ever wrote her. A note where he said she's adorable and he's glad she woke him up in the middle of the night to sort their shit.

So I bravely tucked it in and turned to him.

He didn't say a word.

He wasn't smirking at me.

He just moved to me, angled his head and kissed my neck.

He'd done that last night too.

I hoped that was an Axl Thing because it was sweet, and I liked it a whole lot.

He took my hand and led me to the door to the garage.
"Later, Cleo!" he yelled.
There was utter silence from the house.
Axl grinned at me as he pushed open the door.
I grinned back.

CHAPTER NINE
Porn Preferences

HATTIE

My joy faded on the drive home.

Though, it had started on an upswing, me finally in Axl's Jeep Wrangler (also painted graphite).

Jeeps were awesome, for one, and Axl was awesome, for another.

Mostly, it seemed like I'd wanted to be riding in that Jeep for decades, and there I was, riding with him in that Jeep.

But then he was quiet, and I was quiet, and being in his fantastic house after sleeping on his fabulous mattress started to wear off.

And, as I was wont to do, I got to feeling awkward.

I had a million questions to ask.

Like who was the artist who took the pictures in his living room, because it seemed like they were all taken through the same person's lens?

And did he decorate his house?

And did his folks live in Denver?

And did he have brothers and/or sisters?

Also, if he used his Jacuzzi a lot.

But this was us in a confined space. The time we'd be together was short. I'd lost the confidence I'd found when tucking his note in my purse. And even if he'd fascinated me for a long time, and I was dying to know everything about him, I didn't want to seem like I was interrogating him.

I also didn't want to communicate I was dying to know everything about him.

And he wasn't communicating *at all*.

After what seemed like forever, he called, "Hattie."

"I know," I blurted. "This is awkward."

"What?" he asked.

I looked at him. "This silence. It's awkward."

"It is?"

He didn't think it was?

"Well…"

"Babe, we don't have to talk every second we're not kissing."

Every second we're not kissing.

Mm.

Shiver.

He reached out and touched my thigh.

It was brief.

It was sweet.

And another shiver.

"I get you're shy," he continued gently. "I get this is new, even if it feels old. But don't get into your head about little things, honey. I'm just drivin' you home, glad we're movin' shit in the right direction, lookin' forward to taking you out tonight, and that's all that's on my mind."

"Okay," I said softly.

"That and to ask if you've had anything to eat."

"Just coffee."

"You want me to swing through someplace?"

I knew he was gorgeous.

I knew he was brave.

I knew he owned a Jeep.

I knew I wanted him.

I *sensed* he was nice, what with how cool he'd been through all of this (mostly).

But man, it felt great knowing he wasn't just nice.

He was seriously *super nice*.

And I could murder a bagel, but I could do that mostly to draw out the time I spent with him.

He was busy, however, and that'd be uncool.

"I have stuff at home," I told him, not exactly the truth, since I made a grocery list the day before, but I didn't go out and get any of it.

I still could scrounge something up.

"Right," he said, then he asked, "You tell your dad he's on his own tonight?"

Ugh.

Another joy killer.

"No," I answered and explained, "The less time I give him to hassle me about it, the better. I'll tell him later."

"Right," he muttered.

Okay.

Well, there was something to talk about.

Not that I *wanted* to talk about it.

But it was something we should discuss.

"We need to talk about him, Axl," I noted.

"We will tonight," he agreed. "Or maybe tomorrow. Maybe the day after." He paused. "What I'm saying is, it'd be good to have some time with just us before I get aggravated about your father."

Oh boy.

"Okay," I gave in, but importantly pointed out, "Though, just to say, when we talk about it, like you said, he *is* my father."

He glanced at me then reached my way, not to touch my thigh, with his palm up. Thus, I knew he wanted my hand.

I gave it to him.

Then he rested our clasped hands on my leg and said, "It won't be you I'm aggravated with. It's important you get that, Hattie. I told you when I was bein' a dick to you, I understand the pull a parent has, even when you wish they didn't have it. Yeah?"

I had not forgotten what he'd said about his dad.

But I also kinda did.

"Do your parents live close?" I asked.

"Cherry Creek."

"Oh."

Yup.

That was close.

And a ritzy neighborhood.

The monogrammed notepad was even further explained.

Axl kept going.

"Mom hasn't worked since she gave up her job when she had me. There are women who are good to do that, some born to do it, but she's a woman who shouldn't have done it. After she did it, she felt she had to become Supermom and Superwife. And that was her, the way she was. An overachiever. But Dad played no small part in validating it for her."

I already suspected I wasn't going to like his dad all that much.

I was thinking I might be liking him even less now.

Axl continued.

"Eventually, when I got in high school, outside coming to meets, she had nothing to do. They have a big house. Dad requires all the trappings of the status he's earned, so they also have a lady that cleans and runs errands and stocks the kitchen and sometimes cooks. Mom does some charity work because that's what Dad thinks she should be doing. Mom does not go back to work, because that's *not* what Dad thinks she should be doing. Bottom line, she's bored out of her mind, has been for twenty years, and it's torture, because it's like watching the slowest death in history."

Oh my God.

Yikes.

Awful.

"I hate hearing that, Axl," I said softly.

But I didn't ask if there was some more sinister reason why his mom didn't stick up for herself and do what made her happy and fulfilled regardless of what his dad wanted.

"I hate sayin' it, but it's the truth," he replied. "She's like…" He shook his head. "Vacant. A robot. She switches on when she's conditioned to do that by Dad. Say, he has some dinner party he wants her to give. But that's rote. And she switches on for me. And that's genuine. I bought that house, and I had some idea of what I wanted it to look like, but I worked with her in doing it. She handled the bathroom refurb and the painters and the guys who put in the blinds. Shit like that."

"I bet she enjoyed helping you," I remarked hopefully.

"Hattie, she was in software tech before she quit. In the '80s. When home computers were just taking off. Her field was highly competitive. Way more than now. It was emerging and there weren't many like her. You had to be sharp, one of the best, to land a job like that. She's kinda like Evie, just not on that scale, though not far off. And from what I can tell when she talks about it, she really liked doing it. Now she's forced into being nothing but the wife of a successful, prominent attorney who flirts with political ambitions. And that'd be okay, if that was what she wanted. That isn't what she wanted. The life she leads has choked any true enjoyment she could have out of her."

My heart hurt, listening to him.

It hurt for Axl.

And it hurt for his mom.

"God, Axl. That's awful," I spoke truth.

"Yeah. Not as bad, but still bad, Dad doesn't even fuckin' notice."

I said nothing.

Though I didn't because this made me angry.

Yup.

Official.

Even not meeting the man, I really was not liking his dad.

Axl spoke on.

"So, there you go. When we really dig into all that, it's going to be aggravating. But now you know that isn't all going to be on you, it's the same coming from my end."

"That doesn't thrill me to bits," I shared honestly. "Because I don't like that for you. Or your mom."

He grinned. "Yeah. Still."

Yeah.

The "still" part of that was that we weren't skewed with only me having the dysfunctional family.

He clearly had his share of that.

Maybe worse, having to watch his mom be like that.

"And just to say," he carried on, "you wanna ask anything about me, ask. Work is confidential. We offer that to our clients, and we take it seriously. So I'll never be free to talk about that." He squeezed my hand. "But other than that, don't hold back, Hattie. We both been waiting a long time to be right here. It feels good you wanna know about me and I want the same from you. We can have our times when we're quiet and not sharing, and that's okay. But if you don't want it to be one of those times, just go for it."

Man.

Seriously.

He was the *greatest*.

"Okay?" he prompted.

"Okay," I agreed.

"Now, do you want me to swing through somewhere to get you some food? I got shit to do, but nothing that can't wait another fifteen minutes."

And *man*.

He had a lock on me.

"I'd love a bagel."

Axl immediately started checking his mirrors.

And it was more than fifteen minutes seeing as he backtracked because we swung by Moe's.

Considering this was a special occasion (in my mind), I went all out and got the Spicy Buff breakfast bagel, Axl got the Shorty-P, and we headed back out.

We didn't talk much on the rest of the way to my pad, and not because we were eating. Axl said he'd hang with me at my place to eat and then he'd take off.

My joy came back because I loved that, after what Axl just gave me, I could settle into the quiet.

And I loved that he was going to essentially have lunch with me (since it was just after eleven).

What I didn't love was, when we were nearing my house, Axl muttered, "Shit."

I turned my attention to my pad.

Sly was standing outside it.

"Wait, is he bodyguarding again?" I asked.

"Forgot to mention, this morning when he dropped around, made a deal with Cisco. We've got a project we're working on together. Seein' as both it and you are important, we're splitting resources. This means sometimes, it's gonna be his guys on you, sometimes, it's gonna be me or my guys."

Axl offered this answer as he found a spot on the street and started to parallel park.

Of all that had impressed me that day about him, Axl talking and parallel parking at the same time was top on the list.

Though I was curious what project they were on with Brett.

Did it have something to do with him being framed for that policeman's murder?

Sadly, it was Axl's work and I couldn't ask.

Instead, I inquired, "So why did you say 'Shit' when you saw Sly?"

"He was supposed to come when I texted that I was going."

"And you're upset he's early?"

"I'm upset about the look on his face."

I stopped looking at Axl and started studying Sly, who was walking our way.

He didn't seem any different than normal. I'd noted he tended to appear to be in a bad mood, even when he wasn't. And that was what he looked like now.

I got out. Axl got out.

And Sly was all about Axl.

"She doesn't go in," he stated immediately.

Oh no.

"What happened?" I asked, feeling a freak-out burgeoning.

Did this guy who was harassing me go from ick to gross to breaking into my house and doing something extreme?

Sly didn't even look at me when he kept speaking.

"On the welcome mat. Outside her front door. I'll stay here with her."

"What's going on?" I asked.

Axl looked a mix of grim and pissed as he stalked the four car lengths to the walkway of the house.

When he disappeared inside, I turned my attention to Sly.

"Again, what's happening?"

He focused on me and his voice got soft.

Uh-oh.

"Chill, doll, it's a continuation, not an escalation."

"And you're saying that's good."

"I'm sayin', when you got some asshole bein' an asshole to you, that sucks. But him just continuing to be an asshole is better than the alternative."

Well, that semi-explained it.

"What is it? More pictures?" I pushed.

"Maybe your man should—"

"It's my life, my apartment, my stalker, Sly," I snapped.

Yeesh.

I mean, I didn't want to be ugly, he was looking out for me, and although Brett was paying him, it was still nice.

But seriously.

He finally told me.

"Rope. Red rope. Like the chick was tied up in, in the pics he sent. Coiled on your welcome mat with a note that says, 'Waiting for you.'"

"Fabulous," I hissed.

Axl came out, looking less grim and more ticked.

When he made it to us, before I could say anything, he declared, "You're going in the back way. You're packing a bag. And you're moving in with me."

Well.

Uh…

I really loved his house and I was all in for Cleo to dislike me from afar on the off chance one day I might earn a cuddle.

But…

Yikes!

"It's just rope, Axl."

"He knows where you live, where you work, and your cell number. The first and second are easy. The last, this fucker has time and dedication or resources. And this is three days, three hits. Right?"

I thought there might be a day added in there.

But yes, essentially.

I nodded.

"So he's not letting up," Axl concluded.

"But, if he's following me, he can follow me to your place and then he'll know I'm there. So…"

I trailed off.

Axl picked up the trail.

"So, I got an alarm. I got a gun safe with six guns in it. I live a block away from Aug, so I also got backup close if I need it at night when dicks like this act like bigger dicks."

These were all definite pluses to staying at his place.

Him being there when he wasn't working was another.

His place being as awesome as it was, was a third.

But he'd shown me his (essentially), I wanted to show him mine.

That was, my apartment.

To share all this, I said, "Um…"

"We'll go in, we'll eat. I'll take off. You'll pack a bag. Do whatever you were gonna do. I'll find you later and give you a key. You text me where you are so I can pick you up for dinner tonight. We have a reservation at six. If I'm meeting you here, I'll pick up you and your bag. If I'm meeting you at my place, be sure you bring your bag with you."

"I'm uncertain I want to get ready for our first date in front of Cleo. She's judgy."

Axl stared at me.

Then he did something *insane*.

That being *insanely good*.

He caught me by the side of the neck, jerked me to him (it was a gentle jerk, it was still a jerk), this movement including him making me list to the side.

He then kissed the other side of my neck, righted me so I was no longer listing, but laughed into my skin before he said in my ear (still laughing), "Then I'll pick you and your bag up here later and that means we don't have to reconnect for me to get you a key. I'll give you one tonight."

When he pulled away (but did not let my neck go), I caught his eyes and noted, "I'm okay with seeing the rope, Axl."

"I've called for one of the guys to come, have a look, take some pics, and do some dusting for prints. I don't want to disturb it until that's done. Zane's gonna be here in fifteen. So we go in the back way."

That made sense.

I nodded.

He slid his hand from my neck so his arm was around my shoulders.

Sly was there.

Whoops.

Forgot we had company.

"Sorry, we didn't get you a bagel," I said to Sly. "We didn't know you were here."

"Cisco told me to show. I showed," Sly explained.

"Food, fuck," Axl muttered, clearly remembering we'd left it in his car.

He let me go to head back to the Jeep as Sly warned, "You eat in front of me, you're gonna have to watch me eat later. I'm hungry."

"Probably not as exciting as what I let you watch yesterday, but it won't kill me."

Sly smiled his agreement to this, which I didn't think I'd yet seen him do, the smiling part. It turned him from looking like a lovable bruiser to a *cute*, lovable bruiser.

Axl re-joined us. We walked down the side yard to the back. I let us in.

And once we all got through the utility room, I watched Axl, trying not to let on I was watching him.

He certainly looked around, perhaps not with avid interest—ogling my shock-of-color art and my fantastic beanbag—but he definitely took things in.

So yes.

He'd wondered what home was for the girl who was his but not.

Like I'd wondered about what home was for him.

He didn't turn and give me a thumbs-up.

He did one better.

He looked at his boots and he did that grinning.

I took that as a stamp of approval.

And even with some weirdo leaving bondage rope on my welcome mat, again came the joy.

I unearthed the bagels and got both the current men in my life drinks.

Axl started in when we were sitting at my bar, eating.

"You date anyone recently?"

I was surprised it was getting-to-know-you time with Sly leaning on a kitchen counter right across from us.

"Uh…"

"Let me explain," he said. "This shit that's happening to you does not stink of stalker. This stinks of wronged asshole."

"Oh," I replied.

Axl explained further.

"First, he knows your cell number. It's not impossible to find a cell number, but it requires some work. Second, the threats are not escalating. He's telling you what he wants to do to you and sticking with that. Third, it's sexual in nature, which does not preclude a garden-variety stalker, far from it. But he seems stuck on one theme like he either thinks that's the threat, or he thinks that will fuck with your head or…" he hesitated, "that was something he wanted that maybe he didn't get and he's pissed about it."

"I didn't recognize his voice over the phone," I noted.

"If you know him, in order that you wouldn't recognize him, he could have farmed that part out."

Great.

I looked to Sly. "Can we have a second?"

Sly readily lifted his lemon-lime ICE and stepped out on the deck.

Yeah.

I understood his reaction.

I didn't want to be in on this conversation either.

I looked to Axl.

"The last guy I dated was a somewhat long time ago and he was really boring in bed."

"I'm sorry, honey," Axl replied.

Though, in saying this, he looked both sorry and like he thought something was funny.

I homed in on the last part.

"Bad sex isn't funny, Axl," I told him the god's honest truth.

"I know, baby. Christ, you poor thing," he soothed at the same time teased.

I looked away and took a bite of my bagel in an effort to share I was miffed.

"Back to the subject, Hattie," Axl called.

I looked back at him, and in an effort to get this done, got over being miffed.

"Do you think he might feel like you done him wrong?" he asked. "Did he want to end it? Was there a guy before him that might be a red flag?"

All right.

Well…

This sucked.

Maybe one day, in the distant future, when we were enjoying a glass of wine in his Jacuzzi, I could share about lovers past.

And maybe not ever, since there was not much to share.

But before we even had our first date?

Not a big fan.

But he needed what he needed so none of the men in my life felt I needed a bodyguard.

And thus, I had to give it to him.

"The last guy I dated was a couple of months before Lottie met Mo," I shared.

"Whoa," he muttered.

Yeah.

It wasn't years ago but it wasn't weeks ago either.

The curse of the shy girl.

I sallied forth.

"I think he was excited that he was dating a stripper. This could be why we had about three dates before he was all in to introduce me to his friends, and about a second after he said my name, he told them I was a stripper. Therefore, we had about three dates after that so I could give him the benefit of the doubt. Then I quit taking his calls. I slept with him twice in that time, and like I said, it was boring. But I didn't get to know him well enough to know if he had any latent or non-latent kink tendencies. He could be sweet, but in the end, I realized that hid he was mostly a jerk."

Axl didn't look amused anymore.

"The guy before that," I went on with a shrug. "Big spender at the club. He was the first and only patron I dated. I did this because he bought four lap dances from me and he acted during them like it was less about the lap dance and more about getting to know me while I was giving them to him."

Axl looked anything but amused now.

Nevertheless, I kept going.

"He was definitely sweet. Treated me really well. Had a nice house, a flashy car. Was decent in bed, but it could be good. A couple of months into it, he shared that he wasn't a one-woman guy. He wasn't sure he'd ever be a one-woman guy. He was seeing two other women as well as me. And he wanted to continue seeing me, but he didn't feel it was right to do that unless I knew what the future held. I liked him and he treated me great. But I wasn't a big fan of feeling like a number instead of feeling special. I ended things with him. He was disappointed and told me so. Said if I changed my mind, all I had to do was call. But he wasn't too broken up about it, even though I kinda was. And even if I was, that said I'd made the right decision."

"And before him?" Axl asked when I quit speaking.

"No one of note," I answered.

"You're sure?"

"I'll think on it, but yeah, pretty sure."

He nodded.

Then he launched in.

"I had a girlfriend sophomore through senior year in high school. We didn't last through basic training, and that was mostly on me. I loved her in high school, but halfway through basic, I knew my feelings were in a way high school was where they ended. I've dated a lot but not as much as other guys I know because I find the game playing annoying. If I ask a woman out, I know her and know I definitely want to know more about her. Not know how many days she makes me wait to get a return text. Being active military isn't conducive to relationships, but I saw a woman at the base who was also enlisted. We broke it off before I got out. Had one long-term relationship since, that lasted nearly a year. She wanted marriage and babies and made that plain. I wasn't ready, which made it plain to me she wasn't the one. And that's it."

I stared at him, liking that he leveled the playing field straight off the bat, making something awkward and not fun at this stage in our relationship something that was quick-hit sharing.

I gave, he got.

He gave, I got.

And he continued doing it.

"I'm not into kink but I am into being creative. That will range from the fact we will not only fuck in a bed, but anywhere we feel like it to light bondage and me willing to talk through shit you might want to explore. And I have a life philosophy. That being, you shouldn't just be aiming to do it right, or not at all, you should aim to excel at it. And that includes sex."

Oh my.

"You not into kink?" he asked boldly.

"I, uh…really…never gave it much thought from a practical standpoint."

"Either of these guys or any guy you've been with try to introduce it and you shot him down?"

I shook my head, going on to say, "Which is probably why I didn't give it much thought. It wasn't introduced and I've never been with a guy long enough to uh…as you say, *explore*."

A short nod, no commentary, more questions.

"Any guy tell you he wanted to take you to a sex club? Watch BDSM porn with you?"

I shook my head again, but shared hesitantly, "Though, I watch porn."

His ear dipped to his shoulder and his voice changed. "Yeah?"

I nodded my head.

"You watch with a guy?" he asked quietly.

I went back to shaking my head.

"You want to?"

"I'm into gay porn," I told him.

"Well, shit."

He grinned.

But I sat up straight.

And Axl didn't miss it.

"What?" he asked.

"Well, I watch BDSM gay porn. Some of it is pretty hard-core."

"And it's a watch thing only?"

"If you mean on my laptop, yeah."

"I mean you don't go to clubs?"

Back to shaking my head.

"Conventions? Shows?"

More shaking of my head.

"So you haven't met anyone in that world," he stated.

"No," I confirmed.

"You watch it with your curtains open, say someone can see in?"

God.

This was humiliating.

"No, in bed."

"Right," he whispered, lips twitching.

He knew I did it, and I touched myself while I did it.

Ugh.

Someone kill me.

He kept at it.

"So online pay-per-view?"

Yes, I needed someone to kill me.

"I have a subscription."

No more twitching, he smiled.

"Atta girl," he murmured.

"This is mortifying," I murmured back, turning my attention to my forgotten bagel.

"Baby, look at me."

I didn't want to, but I looked at him.

"It's natural. It's healthy. And just so you know where I'm at with it, I find it attractive. You know what you like, you got the courage to seek it out and get it."

"It's probably not what you like."

"No, but women dig man-on-man like men dig women-on-women. It's nothing to be embarrassed about."

"Do you dig women-on-women?"

"Absolutely."

A giggle erupted from me.

He smiled at me while it did.

After it was done, he said, "When we get to that point, and we're in a mutual mood, we'll go to our corners to get our thing and meet in the middle."

He'd said "when."

And also, I mean, having a porn deal with the guy you haven't quite started seeing yet was pretty awesome.

"Okay," I agreed.

He bent in, and this time I didn't get a neck kiss. I got a lip touch.

But that was nice too.

He moved back, took a bite of his bagel, I took one of mine.

But when he swallowed, he asked, "It's an outside shot, but your subscription, you have to give a cell number for that?"

"I don't remember."

"Sorry, Hattie, I gotta know the site just so we can rule that out as an avenue to you."

Fantastic.

I told him the site.

He just nodded and did nothing else.

"Well, one can say this quick ride home has been a, not so quick and b, eventful," I mumbled to my bagel, before taking a bite.

"Hattie?"

I looked to him, chewing.

"I've wanted this for months, being with you, and it's safe to say I wouldn't have started with your porn preferences, but I'll take anything I can get from you."

Okay.

Serious.

How lucky could I be with this guy?

I swallowed my bagel bite and smiled.

Axl smiled back.

Then he shouted, "Sly! We're done."

Sly came in, grousing at me, "Jesus, did you share your dating history since middle school?"

"Yes, and porn preferences," I shot back.

Sly's eyes got huge.

"But it's all about bagels now," I told him.

"How many of those girls of yours are taken?" he asked.

"All of them," Axl and I answered together.

I started laughing.

Axl just grinned and bit into his bagel.

CHAPTER TEN

Us. Here. Finally.

AXL

Axl walked into the offices, looked right, and saw the men in the conference room.

Hawk, Mo, Boone, Mag.

He lifted his chin that way but did a sweep of the room and found who he needed.

So he headed straight to Jorge.

Jorge Canseco had been with Hawk the longest, second runner-up in that was Mo. Guys had come and gone in the meantime, not many. This was because Hawk paid well, bennies were great, and job satisfaction was high.

Axl was tight with the rest of the team—Jorge, Zane, Marques and Billy. But not as tight as he was with Mo, Mag, Boone and Auggie.

This was because Jorge was older, had seniority, was Hawk's lieutenant when that was needed, was married with two kids, and he wasn't ex-military. Jorge's experience came from the street and a longtime mentorship with Hawk.

Marques and Zane were ex-military, but they were younger and newer to the team.

Billy was the newest member of their crew and his history was murky. Hawk didn't share, neither did Jorge. Definitely not Billy. Even Elvira, who was a big fan of all kinds of sharing, hadn't let anything slip.

That message was received so the men didn't ask.

Now, Axl needed to brief with Jorge before he briefed with the men in the conference room.

This being before he left, went home, showered and changed for his date with Hattie.

And he needed to brief with Jorge because his crew was his crew, but it was also Hattie's, and there were things about her the other guys didn't need (and wouldn't want) to know.

And Jorge would never share.

"'Sup?" Jorge asked when Axl stopped across the console from him.

"Day's done. Debriefing with the team, then outta here," Axl told him. Then he asked a useless question because he knew the answer. "Got anything?"

Jorge nodded.

Yep.

That was always the answer with Jorge.

You needed something, he got it.

Jorge gave Axl what he had.

"That porn site is run out of LA. They do all their filming in LA or around there. All their players are from there. They don't contract out anything, film production, tech, IT or customer service. The site doesn't have message boards. They don't ask for reviews. Customer email in and out, that's it. Unless someone hacked them. And I don't have the intel yet if someone did. I've asked Brody at Nightingale's shop to dig into that. But outside a hack, since no one involved is local, it'd be impossible for someone there to have had a personal sitch with Hattie. Not to mention, their players are gay. This is a shop by and for gay dudes. They have a mission statement about it, being a safe place for gays and kink, their actors and their viewers. I'm sure they get they have female and hetero male viewers, but I think chances are low there's some insider who wants to dick with a woman."

Axl had suspected there was nothing there.

That didn't mean there was nothing there.

It just wasn't an inside man.

"Do they require cell numbers for subscriptions?" he asked.

"Yeah. For possible tech support and payment issues purposes," Jorge answered.

"Right, then for that to be the angle for how he got her info, the guy would have to know she's into that," Axl pointed out. "Which means he's either hacked her laptop, or he's been in her apartment, got into her laptop, and checked her history."

"Already got Brody on a potential hack of her system. But for the other, we need to dust inside," Jorge replied.

"I'll tell Hattie. Any prints we can use on the rope or note?" Axl asked.

Jorge shook his head.

Fuck.

He'd hoped this was just some amateur asshole fucking with her, and because of that he'd screw up fast and they could get past this.

Then again, pretty much anyone knew not to leave prints.

"We'll get inside, Axl," Jorge said. "See if we can find anything. And we set up the cameras. Farmed out on that and they went in wearing a bogus uniform, just in case this guy is casing her, he wouldn't know the cameras were put in. If he makes another approach, we'll see."

Axl nodded. "Thanks, man."

"Don't mention it," Jorge replied.

They tipped chins at each other, and then Axl headed toward the conference room.

He did this looking at the multitude of monitors on the wall in front of the workstations.

And yeah.

There was Hattie's place. One monitor had a revolution of shots of the front door to her house, her apartment front door, the back door and her parking spot with her car. Another monitor had a revolution of sides of the house.

Of course, this meant, unless the dude could dematerialize and rematerialize in her apartment without getting anywhere near the outside of it, she was safe there. They'd know the instant someone tried to break in and they'd be able to roll out, not to mention call the cops.

But Axl preferred the added precautions his place could offer.

And walking in to see her in his kitchen.

"Anything new on Hattie's sitch?" Mag asked before Axl sat down.

"Nothing," Axl answered while he folded into one of the rolling chairs.

Mag gave him a *Sorry, dude* look.

Axl turned his attention to Hawk. "Thanks for the camera loan."

Hawk just nodded.

Then he said, "I know we all wanna get home, so let's get this out of the way. And as usual, there isn't much. Lynn and Heidi aren't budging. I talked with Mamá. She thinks they need time."

Hawk saying they weren't budging had to do with the fact that their first meeting with the two wives of the two men that were on two very different sides of this dirty cop situation had been postponed.

Though that wasn't accurate considering the meeting was never rescheduled and they weren't jumping on rescheduling.

So essentially, it had been canceled.

"Someone has gotten to them," Axl suggested.

"We can't know," Hawk replied.

And they couldn't. It easily could be cold feet that came with the desire to remain breathing and keep their children in that same state.

But it could be one of these fucks got to them, reminding them how they could be certain to keep breathing and keep their kids safe.

And even if their investigation was a joint effort with Cisco, Nightingale's crew, and Hawk's team, with Chaos Motorcycle Club offering support, they all had jobs, lives, other clients and couldn't have someone on the women 24/7.

They had bugs on both.

But that wasn't giving them anything, and whoever was leaning on them knew what they were doing.

The proof of that was that the best investigative team in Denver: Nightingale Investigations, the best scrapper crew: Chaos Motorcycle Club, and the best tactical team: Hawk and his men, not to mention five seriously invested cops, did not have dick.

The three men they had were dead.

Dead men couldn't talk.

But their wives could.

They just weren't.

Goddammit.

"So we're in a holding pattern," Boone stated impatiently. "But we suspect that whatever these assholes are up to, it isn't long term. It's a limited project. And they're close to sealing the deal. So the longer we wait, the longer they've got to do that."

None of the men said anything because there was no point in confirming what they all suspected.

In finding out from Cisco that they didn't attempt to frame him for the first murder (that being Tony Crowley, good cop doing his own investigation into dirty ones) in order to get

Cisco out of the way to take over his operations, the team was running with the theory that whatever was going down was one big score.

But at this point, everything was a theory, because, again, *they had dick*.

"Next moves?" Mag asked Hawk.

"We wait," Hawk answered.

None of the men were at one with that but none of them said anything because they didn't have a choice.

"If it lasts longer than tomorrow, I'll get Mamá to apply some pressure to Lynn and Heidi. Not to freak them. Just to show them the way," Hawk continued.

With nothing more to discuss, Hawk dismissed them.

Axl didn't take long in saying good-bye to his buds.

He had an early reservation and not a lot of time to enjoy it before Hattie had to be at Smithie's.

He headed home. Let himself in. Called to Cleo, who ignored him. Got his mail and ignored that. He then took a shower, with Cleo sitting outside the shower door, watching. He got out of the shower, which, as usual, sent Cleo scurrying.

He shaved, pulled a comb through his hair, picked a pair of dark gray trousers, a blue shirt and black shoes, and while he grabbed his wallet, phone and keys, Cleo showed some love, weaving through his ankles.

She did this mostly because she knew he was leaving, and it was an inconvenient time to give it.

She was like that.

So he picked her up, scratched her in one of precisely five places she liked to be scratched, under her chin (the others were behind her ears, her tailbone, her chest, and when she deigned to cuddle, she demanded tummy rubs).

She started purring, but he had to go, so he forced a kiss on her nose which got him the stink eye.

He put her down, smiling, nabbed his lint roller, dealt with the remains of his cat on his shirt, and then headed out to his Jeep.

Sitting in it, he texted Hattie that he was on his way, texted Sly that he was off duty, pulled out of his garage and drove to Hattie's.

And he did it trying hard not to slam his fist into the roof of his Jeep like a douchebag because he felt the deep need to celebrate the fact that his ass was in his car on his way to Hattie's to pick her up for a date.

Fucking *finally*.

He found a parking spot relatively close and hoofed it to her front door.

She didn't make him wait, opening it almost immediately, beaming up at him and saying, "I'm ready! I just have to shove a couple of things into my bag that I forgot."

She then whirled on one very high heel, the very short skirt of her dress flying out and up so he could almost see panties, and Axl didn't move because he had to concentrate on fighting getting hard.

When he managed this feat, doing it even knowing not only did they not have time to take it there after their date since she had to get to work, but also he didn't intend to take them there at all until he knew they were ready (mostly her on that, he was ready to fuck her about two months ago), he walked in.

He found her down in her bedroom area, doing something with a bag on her bed, babbling.

"It was hard to pack. I know you guys are good at what you do, so it won't take long for you to catch this jerk, but maybe it will. I've got rehearsals every day. And obviously I need regular clothes." She looked his way. "Can I borrow your teeth-strengthening mouthwash? I'll buy you a new bottle later. But we have the same brand so it kinda seems stupid to pack mine."

He had no clue why she had to put the "teeth-strengthening" part before the word "mouthwash."

But it was cute.

As she was on a regular basis.

He would not have pegged himself as a cute-girl guy. His leanings had always been toward tall, cool, slender blondes. And as such, when Lottie made her choices for all the boys, and he got a look at Hattie, he knew this wasn't going to happen.

He was seeing now it never worked out with those tall, cool, slender blondes, not because there was anything wrong with them.

But because he was about curvy women of just above average height who had a mass of loose, brunette curls, big brown eyes, a frustrating instinct for self-preservation, could soar through the air five feet above the ground with the grace of a gazelle and were cute.

Also, one more thing.

A woman who was able to select adorable, even girlie dresses that she wore like she was in jeans and a tee and it made her a thousand percent fuckable.

"You can borrow whatever you want," he told her.

His voice was not the usual.

It was lower, rougher, and it made her head jerk his way again. "Are you okay?"

Outside of needing—very badly—to fuck her in that dress?

Yeah.

He was okay.

Though the need was so strong, and now she was standing by a bed, he was just barely okay.

"Fine, baby, but we got a reservation and it isn't like we're flying to my place in Aspen. We can come get anything you forgot whenever we need to do that," he told her.

"Oh, right," she replied, her gaze drifting to her bag. It came back to him and she asked, "You have a place in Aspen?"

He grinned at her. "Sorry, no."

She grinned back, returned her attention to her packing, seemed to make a decision, finished shoving whatever in her bag and started to zip up.

Axl took that as his cue to move from where he was standing, at the top of the two steps, down into the space.

Her bedroom area had wood floors. White walls. White furniture.

Also, a white comforter.

Pale pink sheets on the bed. Dark pink throw pillows.

There were white vases with fluffy fake flowers in them in vibrant colors. She obviously read, because there were stacked books on the floor under her legged nightstands. And an eReader with a hot-pink cover sat on a night table.

The space was small. She'd utilized it well. And the way she decorated, as he'd found earlier that day, was feminine and kickass.

He reached beyond her to grab the strap of her big overnighter and hefted it on his shoulder.

Fuck, it felt like it weighed fifty pounds.

"Set up to stay awhile?" he teased.

"It's shoes," she replied, grinning and reaching for a canvas book bag that said FORTNUM'S USED BOOKS.

She scooted quickly to the nightstand, grabbed the eReader, pushed it in the bag, and put it on her shoulder.

Her *bare* shoulder, seeing as she was wearing a dress that was mushroom colored and it dropped down the sides of her shoulders, hugging her upper arms. It had long flowy sleeves and a wide, flirty ruffle at the short hem. It was belted with a thin belt in the same fabric.

She wore nothing else but earrings, those were big gold hoops.

And on her feet, she wore a pair of sandals that looked to be made with nothing but gold string crossing her foot and wrapping around her ankle. The heel was high and thin.

And yeah, he was fucking her in those shoes too.

She grabbed the last thing from the bed, a muted gold clutch, before she led the way up out of her bedroom space, and he waited at the door as she turned off lights and joined him.

Then he got her and her bags in his car and he did this hoping that she had to use the restroom while they were at dinner so he could watch her walk away in that dress.

She waited until he pulled out before she asked, "Where are we going?"

"Beatrice and Woodsley."

He felt her eyes on him. "You got a reservation at BW in a day?"

"Lucked out," he muttered, and he did. There'd been a cancellation right before he called in. "You been there?" he asked.

"Once, a few years ago, for Galentine's Day with my mom."

"Galentine's?"

"The day before Valentine's. It's just for girls."

"I know what it is, but I thought it was for friends."

"My mom's my friend."

He was glad to hear that, considering her dad was such shit.

"She was a good mom too, Axl," she went on.

"I'm glad, honey," he murmured.

"I think there was a time, after I graduated from high school, where she got kind of messed up. Wondering why she picked him. Worried about what he'd done to me and what that would mean later. I still think she worries. But she sorted herself out. We got into being mom and daughter friends, not just mom and daughter, which is way cool." Pause before she added, "She's also started dating in the last couple of years. She's gone on some vacations with friends. I think she's finally getting over him and what he did to our family."

Good news.

"You cool with her dating?" he asked.

"Definitely," she stated, a chirp in her voice that not only under-
lined her word, it was fucking adorable. "I want her to be happy.
I don't think she's been happy for a long time. I don't think she's
happy now, not really. But I want her to find that."

"Why don't you think she's happy now?"

"Well," she began. "Your mom was driven and should never
have stopped working. My mom wanted a husband, a home and
family. It wasn't like she wasn't down to work to provide. To work
to have her time and her space and her thing for herself. She likes
her work. But my aunt told me she'd always been boy crazy. Said
she went kinda nuts when she didn't have a boyfriend."

She stopped speaking, so Axl glanced at her to see she was
gazing out the windshield, looking reflective.

Before he could say anything, though, she spoke again.

"And Aunt Pam said Mom used to talk, not about her dream
of a big wedding, but her dream of a big house with husband
and kids and stuff. Aunt Pam and Uncle Dave call Dad the Big
Imposter. They said he was a charmer. They all fell for it. No
one had his ticket. Until after the deed was done, her signature
was on the marriage certificate and it was tougher for her to
get out."

"That why you're an only child?" he guessed.

"Yes," she confirmed. "It was Mom who told me that. Once we
became mom and daughter friends."

Her last was said with a smile in her voice, so he glanced at her
again and saw it was also on her face.

Pretty all the time.

Smiling?

Gorgeous.

He looked back at the road and she kept talking.

"She wanted more kids. She just didn't want more kids with

him. And I think she wanted to leave way before she actually did. But they got pregnant within a year of the wedding. It was a time she still had hope that he wasn't what he was seeming to be. Or she thought it was just youth and she'd train him to be a better husband. But..."

She trailed off.

Then again, she didn't have to say any more.

"Think my mom put it off, having more kids," he told her, seeing as she didn't end what she was saying sounding like she was smiling. So he took his turn in order to turn her mind. "Thought she'd get back to work. And then she didn't."

"Yeah," she said softly.

"In the end, it was more Dad didn't want another kid. If they had more kids, he'd have less of her attention, and less of it to take up with all the shit he thought she was supposed to be doing. And what Dad wants, Dad gets."

"Yeah," she repeated, just as softly.

Definitely the smile was gone from her voice.

He reached her way and she gave him what he wanted, her hand.

When he had it, he said, "This is a bummer. Let's have a bummer-free zone for the rest of our first date."

She let out a cute laugh and said, "That works for me."

And except for him telling her they'd set up cameras, and he had to let his guys into her pad to check for prints, and she'd have to give him her laptop and her two exes' names so they could run them, that was where they kept it.

Mostly it was Hattie talking about her day with Sly. How much he liked hanging at rehearsal (not a surprise). How much he didn't like helping her pick out her dress for that night (definitely not a surprise, no man would see that dress and like not being the one who was on the date with her, though it was hilarious, thinking about Sly sitting there while Hattie showed him dresses).

Last, how she thought it was weird, everyone involved with Brett seemed so cool when he was a self-described "motherfucker."

This was where they were at when Axl found a parking spot not close, but not far from Beatrice & Woodsley. Though, it was closer than walking there from his house, which was what he'd normally do since the restaurant was in his 'hood and they didn't only serve great food, but they had excellent cocktails. He wasn't a regular, though he was no stranger.

But after he shut the Jeep down, instead of getting out, he turned to her

"First, honey, do not get caught in this fairy godfather gig Cisco has going on. He is absolutely a motherfucker."

Her face fell and he hated that.

But he was not lying, and men like Cisco had three paths: they got caught and went to prison, they got dead, and for the rare, they retired.

Axl wanted to protect her from the first two, and he wasn't fired up about Cisco—doing what he did—being in her life whatever time it took him if he was destined to make it to the last one.

"He seems nice," she said.

"He likes you. If he didn't like you, you would one hundred percent not say that."

She rubbed her lips together.

He continued talking.

"But that's a bummer. So we're moving on. The second thing you gotta know before we get out of my car is that dress, Hattie…" He allowed his eyes to wander down then up again, and looking in her pretty brown eyes done up for him, her big mass of long, dark curly hair framing her face and falling all over her bare shoulders, he finished, his voice gruffer, "You look beautiful in that dress, baby."

"Thank you."

There was something deep in those two words, deeper than normal when receiving a compliment.

Heavy.

But he had a feeling, if he tried to tease it out, knowing it probably had to do with the fact her father treated her like garbage, it'd be a bummer for the both of them, so he asked, "I open doors for women. You got a problem with that?"

She smiled. "One hundred percent *no*."

He returned her smile, added leaning her way to touch his lips to her neck, getting the scent of her perfume, which was girlie and flowery, but subtle, and as with everything that was Hattie, he liked it.

He got out, moved around the hood of the car, helped her out and walked with her toward the restaurant.

Baker District was hip. Nighttime, it could get busy.

Once he tucked Hattie's hand through his arm, spreading her fingers over his biceps, keeping his over hers, she took his cue and walked close to him. Her shoulder to his. Her hip brushing his. Her perfume doing a number on him.

That was when he noticed it.

People looking at them as they passed.

He knew what they saw.

He liked what they saw.

He got off on what they saw.

Like his dad, Axl had gone prematurely silver in his late twenties.

His father called it the Pantera Curse.

Axl thought it was the shit, being twenty-seven and people treating him like he was forty-five.

Then again, except in the army, and after, he hadn't been shown a lot of respect by people who were meaningful in his life.

When he'd shared with his father it didn't bother him, Sylas Pantera said, "Kid, you never want to lose the advantage. Not with anyone. You want them underestimating you. Not the other way around."

First, Axl hated his dad calling him "kid."

It wasn't a nickname, familiar and loving. It was said to put him in his place, even if, when they'd had this conversation, if he recalled, Axl had been twenty-nine, and he still called him that, and Axl was thirty-four.

So yeah, he hated that.

And second, Axl did not view life as one competition after another.

He wanted people to be honest with him. He wanted them to respect him. He expected to give that first back at all times, earn the last, and return it if it was deserved.

So now, he knew the feeling he felt with the people glancing their way as they passed them, Axl walking with a beautiful woman in a sexy-as-fuck dress and arguably sexier shoes to a nice restaurant, knowing that woman on his arm was adorable, talented, loyal and a fighter.

That feeling was, he'd earned this.

He'd earned her.

And it felt fucking *great*.

His life philosophy in action.

Aim high.

And excel.

They went into the restaurant, were seated and given menus.

Hattie ordered BW's rum-based Butter Beer cocktail (and he totally could have called that, for fuck's sake, Butter Beer?—fucking adorable). He got the rye-based Edward Henry Masterman.

And the second the server wandered away after they'd ordered, she pressed into him where they sat thigh to thigh at the back of a curved booth, and she whispered in the direction of his ear, "It's so romantic here."

He pulled back a couple inches, caught her eyes but said nothing.

Still, she heard him, and he knew it when her lashes dipped, he sensed she was about to pull away, and then she seemed to make a conscious decision not to.

She lifted her gaze to him.

And knowing she'd just beat back the shyness, the instinct to retreat, Axl felt deserved a reward.

So he bent in and fitted his lips tight to hers.

He only touched them with the tip of his tongue before he pulled away.

When he again caught her eyes, her gaze had grown soft and she was now pressing even closer.

"You told me I looked beautiful, I didn't get to tell you how handsome you look," she said.

"Thanks, honey," he replied.

"And just in case I get lost in the fabulous drinks, food, atmosphere and company, and forget to say it later, thank you for bringing me here. Thank you for making this special. Thank you for knowing this is important."

He thought he knew where that was coming from, after hearing her talk about being a number with that idiot she'd dated, so he shared, "You need to know, when I'm with someone, I'm *with* them. Boiling that down, I'm a one-woman guy."

She appeared confused for a beat before she pressed even closer and said, "Thank you for that, but no...I mean, this. Us. Here. Finally. And just, well...*us*. Which is special. And important. And thank you for knowing that, showing that and giving it to me."

All right.

He was done.

The dress, the shoes, the hair, the made-up eyes, the perfume, and her being so fucking sweet?

He couldn't take more.

So he slid a hand up her jaw, into her hair, turned to her at the same time pulling her up to him, and he kissed her.

And it was not fitting his lips to hers and then tasting them briefly with his tongue.

He didn't make out with her, but he didn't leave her in any doubt about how he felt about what she just said.

He kept his hand in her hair and Hattie close when he ended it.

"Never been so proud to have a woman on my arm as I was walking that two and a half blocks with you."

Her eyes grew large.

"Same, sitting right here…with you," he continued. "So, in case I forget later, bein' here beside you, the food, booze and atmosphere, thank you for giving me that."

"You're awesome," she breathed.

He smiled. "Love you think that."

"It's true."

"Love you think *that*."

Her eyelids went half-mast and did a fluttery thing, not flirty, more semi-annoyed, semi-perplexed.

"Axl, *you are*," she stressed.

"Okay, baby," he replied, still smiling, but unfortunately having to slide his fingers out of her soft hair seeing as he could probably keep them there for a fuckuva long time, but it'd be hard to eat if he did.

"Do you not think you're awesome?" she asked hesitantly.

"Do you want a guy who thinks he's awesome?" he asked in return.

She tipped her head a little, her curls sliding over her bare shoulders when she did in a way he felt in his dick almost more than the dress, then she turned more fully to him, which meant her breast was now pressed full into his arm.

Jesus.

Dinner was going to be agony and ecstasy, he already knew that.

But he didn't know just how deep that would go.

"I see your point," she relented.

"So I'm awesome and you're the most beautiful woman in this room," he remarked,

She lifted up and gave him a smile that was absolutely flirty, as well as cock-hardeningly playful, and said, "I totally am."

He burst out laughing.

And then their cocktails came.

CHAPTER ELEVEN

B

AXL

"So, how'd it go?"

It was late the next morning and Axl and Auggie were in one of the company Hummers.

It was rare any member of the team went out in one because— shiny, black, and kitted way the fuck out—they were known by a certain element of Denver and the crew tended to operate in most cases in stealth mode.

But where they were going, they were making a statement.

Axl was driving, Auggie in the passenger seat, and they'd reached their destination, so Axl was scanning for a parking spot.

He also answered Auggie's question about his date with Hattie.

"Torture."

"It didn't go well?" Auggie sounded flipped out.

This was understandable, partly because Aug knew how hard Axl had worked to get last night, and partly because Auggie was next up with Pepper.

If he ever pulled his finger out.

Axl found a spot on the street and started maneuvering into it, saying, "When she's not shy, she babbles. It's not annoying or nervous and incomprehensible. It's her and it's cute. She reads. She's got interesting takes on movies that are deeper than the norm. She's curious about me and doesn't hide it. She's into me and doesn't hide that either."

"That doesn't sound like torture," Aug noted when Axl quit speaking.

He shut down the Hummer and turned to his friend. "And she was wearing an off-the-shoulder dress that was very short, her heels were very high, her hair was down, and at the end of the date, I took her to my place where she changed to go to work. Then after work, I picked her up and took her back to my place, where she slept in my bed and I slept on the couch. And right now, seeing as she left work after two in the morning, I suspect she's *still* in my bed."

Aug grinned. "Gotcha."

"Yeah," Axl agreed, not grinning.

They turned to their respective doors and got out.

They then moved in unison across the street toward their destination: an apartment complex.

Aug did it talking.

"So essentially, it was a great date."

Axl stopped dead on the sidewalk and leveled his eyes at his bud.

"I think you can now take it as proven Lottie knew what she was doing. Her picks for us weren't random, brother."

Aug looked toward the door of the apartment complex.

In other words: *We're not talking about this.*

"We got shit to do," Axl continued. "We don't got time to stand and chat on a sidewalk. Just…you hear what I'm sayin'?"

Auggie looked back at him. "It's not me, it's her."

"Yeah, and it wasn't me, it was Hattie."

"You've had one date," Auggie pointed out.

"Right, then wait it out. Lottie's picks turn to three matches, three wins, you need to get the lead out."

"It's not just Pepper, Axe. If it was just her, we'd be there already. She's got a kid."

Axl's brows shot up in surprise. "You got a problem with her kid?"

Aug started to look pissed. "You know it's not that. Again, *it isn't me, it's her*. She's being protective."

"Why?"

"I don't know."

"Well, find out."

Auggie's head ticked, which Axl knew stated plain he was just ticked.

And he didn't hesitate to share that verbally as well.

"All right, I see you ridin' the high of one great date, but it was *one* great date. That's it. You aren't the poster child for relationship bliss. Get off my ass."

As they all did in their crew when shit was important, Axl did not get off his ass.

"And Mag and Evie are engaged. Boone and Ryn are moving in and going into business together. Aren't those poster children?"

"We gonna get this done?" Aug asked tersely, jerking his head to the complex, bringing them back to business.

Yeah.

They needed to get this done.

Axl answered his question by moving.

They walked into the apartment building and immediately were assaulted with a variety of smells. The sweet scent of pot was the high note, mingled with the unpleasant scent of cigarettes with underlying nuances of filth and possibly vomit.

They both ignored it and jogged up two flights of stairs, walked down the hall and stopped at the door they needed.

"I'd give you the honors due to your frustration, but you just pissed me off, so I get to do it," Auggie announced.

Axl jutted his chin in assent and Aug immediately lifted his boot, landed it with no small amount of pressure right by the handle, and the door flew open.

Instantly, there was a flood of the dregs of humanity brushing past them.

A door bursts open, they assume police.

Oh yeah.

Brandi was home.

With the mass exodus, it was clear her minions had let her down with loyalty. Walking through the fetid apartment, it was also clear they let her down with cleaning.

What was unclear was why she had them in the first place.

They hit the living room at the back.

Oh, right.

That was why.

She sat her throne of an armchair Goodwill would turn down, long red dreads, raccoon eyeliner, pasty white skin that was not helped with copious contouring, massive gold bespoke hoops that said Brandi across the circle at her ears, a variety of thick chains hanging around her neck, Gucci tee and track pants, Balenciaga color-block sneakers.

None of that was fake or black-market rip-offs.

Even the gold at her ears.

So, yeah.

A girl had to find the green to get her logo, keeping minions addled in narcotics was Brandi's way.

How he grew up, Axl could do designer. And that was one thing he was down to take from his father's teachings.

He'd been in Boss last night, with Mezlan shoes.

But he wasn't sure about Brandi's switch-up between Gucci and Balenciaga. He felt it flew in the face of appropriate sporting of logo wear.

What he was sure about was his distaste for Brandi appropriating Black statements.

That woman's people had never been in chains.

Thank fuck he wasn't partnered up with Marques today. As was his right, Marques had a serious issue with appropriation, not to mention the ability to share how he felt about that in a variety of ways.

"Fuck, how'd you find me?" she demanded while the last of the queen's court scuttled down a side wall and made his escape.

"You're on Hawk's payroll, B," Auggie told her. "And as such, Hawk expects, if you need to change scenes, you send in an updated address form."

Brandi gave them nothing but a glare.

"Been a minute," Axl noted.

"Sixty times twenty-four times about ninety-five days, maybe a few of them," Aug added.

"Things got hot for me at my last locale," Brandi spat.

"Hot how?" Axl asked.

"My business is your business only if I make it your business," she stated. "That's the deal."

"Wrong," Axl returned. "Your business isn't our business unless you *make* it our business, in however we feel that might happen. And right now, ghosting us a couple of days after taking your last fee, you became our business."

She said nothing.

"Brandi, what gives?" Axl pushed.

"Right, I'll make it official. I'm getting out of the dicking-around-with-you-guys trade," she declared.

"Okay, resignation accepted," Auggie agreed readily. "So you're good to return the retainer you didn't earn, let's say, *now*?"

She made a face.

That would be a no.

"B—" Axl started.

"You boys gotta stop dickin' around with shit," she told them.

Both Axl and Aug grew silent.

This was because Axl and Auggie were there to get an informant back online.

But neither of them were ever far off the trail they'd been sniffing now for-what-felt-like-ever.

And B disappeared maybe not exactly the time a variety of crews in town got interested in Cisco, which led them to death, dirty cops and a murder-suicide.

But the timing jibed.

Jesus, did she know something?

"That's all I'm sayin', and I'm tellin' you, believe this, that warning is worth every penny of my last fee." She lifted both hands and snapped twice. "Even."

Axl broke his silence. "What do you know?"

"Okay, see, I like to," she leaned forward, "*breathe*. So fuck off. You got what you got. Be happy. And keep breathing, or not, I don't give a shit."

"Is this about the Cisco sitch?" Auggie asked what was on both their minds.

"Fuck off," she answered.

Okay, two "fuck offs"?

Axl was getting pissed.

He felt the same from Auggie.

But Axl got there first.

Crossing his arms on his chest, he educated, "See, you got a vagina or not, this is how we deal with wannabe G on our payroll who come up way short during performance evaluations. Hawk's got a place you do not want to go. We take you there and keep you there until *we* think we're even. And after, we decide how severance is gonna go down. Whether you gotta expend the effort to rebuild somewhere that is very much not here but we give you one last thing, a ride to that new location. Or we dismantle you in Denver in a way you'll never fuckin' rebuild, and you gotta make your own way to a new location. Now, we got shit to do so, you got ten seconds to make your decision. You feel like taking a ride today?"

She sat her throne with an expression that was half glare, half pout.

In that ten seconds, Axl considered the fact he knew she was thirty-nine, but she looked fifty-nine.

Thank fuck, after years of his father fucking with his head, when there was a decision to make about his future, he took the route to healthy living.

"Time's up," Auggie said.

They both started to move her way.

"Motherfuckers!" she snapped, shifting in her seat. "Right, fuck you and just to say, you and Nightingale and Chaos and fucking Sebring are all on radar. Do not think you're not."

Both men stilled.

They'd heard this.

From Kevin Bogart, dead dirty cop.

He'd made this same threat against certain players in town, including Knight Sebring, who ran a clean nightclub, but it was debatable, according to your personal philosophies, if his side business was the same.

"They are *goddamn* itching for you to fuck up, one of you, all of you, they don't give a fuck," she went on.

Both men remained silent.

"You think you own Denver," she continued, warming to her theme something that was Brandi's MO.

She pictured herself a gangster, but she was on Hawk's payroll as an informant for a reason.

That reason was why she was in this shitty apartment with a strung-out cult following.

Small-time dealer, also, when she decided not to be lazy, small-time hustler, but she was shit at both. So it was highly likely Hawk, Lee Nightingale, or some cop who had her on his CI list paid for her Balenciaga sneaks.

That reason was also because she liked to know shit you did not and then make you pay for that shit, but when she stared singing, she got off on it, so she was hella useful.

"Nightingale especially," she carried on. "That Rock Chick bullshit in those books that everyone thinks is cool?" She shook her head and dreads dragged her Gucci. "Not so much."

"We really don't give a fuck what people think of our operations," Axl remarked.

"No?" she asked snidely. "Well, when Joint Taskforce Badass Motherfuckers of Denver, and that would include Chaos, if you'll recall, got those shipments impounded some serious people got seriously deep in some serious fucking shit."

Axl and Auggie didn't even look at each other.

"Which shipments?" Aug demanded.

But he knew.

So did Axl.

"Worst thing that happened in Denver, when Chaos got out of transportation protection," she muttered. "Second worst thing, when Bounty fucked everything up and then saw the error of their ways and rebranded to Resurrection."

Axl, nor Aug, were interested in her opinions on the histories of local motorcycle clubs.

"Which fucking shipments, Brandi?" Auggie shared this by biting out.

She looked him dead in the eye. "You know which ones, Augustus." Her gaze then darted between them. "Now, we even?"

"No," Axl and Aug said together.

"All right then, you feel like starrin' at your own funeral and givin' up fuckin' that pretty pussy you been taggin'," she began, and a finger of ice trailed down Axl's spine at her mention of their women, "those shipments were meant to assure some pretty hefty retirements. And the men dreamin' of fishin' boats or drinkin' beer in oceanside bars, checkin' out chicks in bikinis they could actually afford to impress enough with their bank to suck their dicks, have not given up on that dream."

Neither man prompted her, because when she was on a roll, she didn't need it.

And she was on a roll and gave it to them.

"And when the good cops get the drop, where do those shipments go, boys?"

They were in the police impound.

Evidence that just sat there.

For.

Fucking.

Ever.

"And what does this have to do with their problem with Nightingale?" Auggie asked.

"*All* of you," she corrected.

"Whatever, B. Talk," Auggie clipped.

"This is not a new project," she told them. "You assholes running interference over the years, you been shaking things up for them for a while. They had long-term goals. You kept fuckin' with them. Those Rock Chick books come out, suddenly Lee Nightingale and Luke Stark and Vance Crowe and *Eddie Chavez* and *Hank Nightingale*," she stressed the two cops on that crew, "are famous? Untouchable."

She paused.

They waited.

"So they decided to stop fucking around, get the job done, and go for a couple big scores. And you all fucked those too."

She paused again.

They waited again.

"It's been awhile since those books came out," she said low.

"So Nightingale is a target?" Axl asked.

She shrugged. "Nightingale. Delgado. One of the Chavezes. Sebring. Rush Allen of Chaos. Who knows? Who cares? They did you a solid. Delivered those cops to you. Let Cisco off the hook. You didn't take the hint. You keep stirrin' up this hornet's nest, the gloves gonna come off."

"Why'd you mention the women?" Axl demanded.

"You boys droppin' like flies," she noted on a shrug he couldn't tell if it was fake casual or real.

"Explain," Axl ground out.

She did that. "As in, gettin' your asses claimed."

"And?" he pushed.

"Chill, asshole," she bit off. "Just that hot dick going off the market makes the rounds. Jesus."

"That's all?" Auggie kept at her.

She looked offended. "Okay, you gotta know, a sister's ass is swinging in the wind, that sister doin' her best to keep it together by strippin', I'm gonna share they got problems. They don't. If they did, like I said, *I'd share*."

They did not know that. She'd never been outspoken for the sisterhood nor had she ever shared anything without getting paid.

But she looked like she genuinely meant it.

"Now, are we done?" she asked.

"You got more?" Auggie returned.

"Dude," she snapped.

She had no more.

"Then we're done," Axl said.

"And even?" she pushed.

"We'll see," Axl muttered, giving Auggie a look and starting to turn to the door.

"Motherfuckers!" she called.

They turned back.

"I am not on your leash to yank whenever you want. You leave, we're square," she declared.

"B, you don't get to make the rules," Axl informed her.

"And you do?" she asked.

"Well, yeah," he answered.

"Fuck you," she spat.

After having hit his limit of "fuck offs," that officially hit his quota for the day of "fuck yous."

With another glance at Auggie, they moved out.

They waited until they were in the Hummer to break it down.

"Whoever this is, they've been active awhile. And right now, they're setting up to steal a huge-ass appropriation of coke and arms from evidence, move it, and then buy fishing boats," Axl stated.

"And if we get in their way, they're gonna fuck with us. And since they're faceless cops we don't know, which means they have resources, they can make that hurt," Auggie finished.

Axl pulled out of the parking spot and said, "Call it in."

Auggie called it in.

While Axl listened to him agreeing to be back at the office for a meet about it, Axl's phone binged.

He pulled it out of the side pocket of his cargos and waited for a stop at a light before he glanced at the text.

Hattie.

Telling him she was up, which was what he'd asked her to do in a note he left on the pillow beside her.

"When's the meet?" Axl asked after Aug got off the phone.

"Two."

"Right." He waited for another light before he said, "Gotta make a call."

"Go for it," Auggie muttered.

He hit buttons and put the phone to his ear.

"Hey!" Hattie greeted.

Fuck, but he liked when she was chirpy.

"Sleep good?" he asked.

"Yeah," she replied.

He did not.

He would have, if he'd been able to jack off to thoughts of her in that dress, and what he wanted to do to her in it. But he didn't want her wandering out for a glass of water and catching him jacking to her.

At least, not at this juncture.

Then again, when they got to that juncture, he wouldn't be on the couch.

"Sly there?" he asked.

"Yeah," she told him.

"Good. Tonight, I'm cooking and we're hanging before you go to work," he declared.

Nothing from Hattie.

"Baby?" he called.

"Dad," she said.

Shit.

Right.

To keep their date bummer-free, he hadn't asked how it had gone down with her dad when she told him, for that night, she wasn't going to take care of his grown ass.

And it wasn't his place to intervene with her father.

Not yet. Not ever.

That was hers and he could share his opinion and advice.

But he couldn't get in the middle of it unless it was harming her.

And after she broke it down for him the night before last about what was messing with her head in that studio weeks ago, he had yet to ascertain if it was still harming her, or what harmed her was in the past and the man had lost his power, outside what he'd done to her back then and how it still messed with her head.

"Okay, how do we juggle that?" he queried.

"Pardon?"

"I wanna make you dinner. I want time with you. You need to see to him. My guess, you're not ready for me to go hang with your father while you sort out his dinner. So how do we juggle that?"

She didn't readily answer.

So Axl got in there.

"What time does he eat?"

"I usually go over early because I don't eat with him and I have to fuel before I dance."

"What's early?"

"Five."

"Okay. Sly can take you over to deal with him and I'll have dinner ready for us six, six thirty. Cool with you?"

There was a hesitation before, "Yeah."

"Anything you don't eat?"

"What are you making?"

The first meal he was cooking her?

Totally pulling out all the stops.

"Tuscan chicken."

Auggie made a noise.

Axl ignored it.

"What's that?" Hattie asked.

"You like chicken?"

"Yes."

"Prosciutto?"

"Definitely."

He grinned. "Spinach? Goat's cheese? Sun-dried tomato?"

"Yes. Absolutely. Yes," she answered in line.

His grin got bigger. "Then you'll like this."

"I'll be home by six."

"Okay, honey, see you then. You got the key I left?"

"Yes, and Axl?"

"Yep?"

"I really like our bummer-free zone. We'll talk about Dad when that time comes. But it means a lot that you know how, uh…he was and you're not being…"

She didn't finish that.

"You don't have to say that. Get yourself coffee. Enjoy the deck. Play Pac-Man. I'll see you later."

"Later, Axl."

"'Bye, babe."

He disconnected.

Instantly, Auggie asked, "Can I come to dinner tonight?"

"Fuck off."

Aug chuckled.

Axl drove.

It took some time before Auggie said quietly, "I'm glad it's going good, Axe."

"Yeah," Axl replied.

And he let it be.

Meaning, he didn't get into Pepper again.

Auggie was right. He'd had only one date with Hattie.

But Aug didn't know about her art, and as such, hadn't seen it.

He also hadn't been there to see her dancing that day Axl and Ryn saw her dance. Falling in an elegant heap on the floor. Soaring through the air in a way Michael Jordan would say, "*Damn*."

And Aug had not been woken up in the middle of the night to witness a tough woman who had no idea she was tough, she was amazing, she created beauty in a variety of ways from her art to her dancing to decorating her apartment to the dress she put on for him, pull it together to finally sort their shit.

So he'd let Auggie off the hook.

For now.

CHAPTER TWELVE
Safe Place

HATTIE

S hit, you two are killing me."

This was what Sly said after he entered Axl's house in front of me. This being once I was done dealing with my dad and he drove me there.

I understood him.

The place smelled like heaven.

And I got to eat whatever that was, and Sly didn't.

Axl appeared in the dining area.

Yup.

Heaven.

Axl kept moving, doing it smiling at me at the same time looking like he wanted to pounce on me.

I watched him moving, not smiling, but knowing I definitely looked like I wanted to pounce.

Gone was his usual work gear of cargos and tee.

In their place: supremely faded jeans, a different tee, this one dark heathered gray with yellow letters that said BLACK

Rifle Coffee Company around a knife, and his feet were bare.

Oh yes.

I wanted to pounce.

Axl made it to me, hooked me around the neck with his arm, I hit his body and his mouth hit mine.

We didn't go at it.

But I got a reminder he sure tasted good.

"I do still exist," Sly griped.

We broke it off, but Axl didn't let us break apart. He kept his arm around my neck but positioned me to his side.

"And you guys suck," Sly finished.

"Apologies, man," Axl said, miraculously sounding both apologetic and not.

Sly hulked to the door.

"Thanks for keeping me safe today," I called.

He stopped at the door and pinned me with a look.

"Your shit is great. Stop fucking around," he ordered.

And with that, he left.

"What was that?" Axl asked.

I looked up at him to see him looking down at me.

And did it make me a freak I could stand there, claimed by him, gazing up into those steely blues *for the rest of my life*?

"He came to the studio with me today."

Axl's dark brows shot up. "You worked in the studio?"

I shook my head. "First, I rehearsed. One of my routines tonight has some tricky lighting, so I had to go through it with the lighting guys."

Axl shifted us around and started walking us, attached, to the kitchen, saying, "And?"

"Then, well...I'm feeling the bug. Got something in my head. I had to go to the studio to check materials. And I found what I knew I'd find. I needed to make an order. So no, I didn't work. But I'm going to get back to it once my order comes in."

"Mm," he hummed, detaching from me in the kitchen and pulling a stool from the wall that had a chrome base and footrest and black leather seat with back.

The only stool of its kind in the kitchen, but it was kickass.

He adjusted it to a place by a counter where it looked like he was making a salad and then shifted me so I knew he wanted me to climb up, which I did.

Once I was there, he moved to a cupboard, opened it, and I saw upside-down hanging wineglasses.

He commandeered one—awesome, wide-bowled and tall. He came back to the counter where the salad prep was happening, and I saw there was another wineglass there, filled with red. Not to mention the bottle.

He nabbed the bottle, poured and handed the glass to me.

"So what else did you do today?" he asked, picking up a knife and going back to cutting cucumber.

Okay.

Um.

Okay.

Was all that just…*awesome*?

"Hattie?" he called.

"Remind me, if I get a chance, and I'm home before you're home, to be equally awesome with you."

His expression changed, and apparently he liked what I said so much, he felt it needed to be communicated beyond that change.

So he put the knife down, came right to me in a way I had to open my knees so he could get between them. Once there, he took my jaw in both hands, and yeah.

That time we went at it.

When we broke off the makeout session, I was minimally

panting, Axl was all I could see, and I was in no doubt he liked what I'd said.

"So, good day?" he asked.

A giggle erupted from me and I answered, "Yeah. And it keeps getting better."

His eyes glittered with icy-blue goodness before he slid his hands away and went back to cucumbers.

I took a sip of my (excellent) wine and inquired, "How was your day? Or can I ask that?"

"You can ask that, if you don't mind non-detailed answers," he shared. "And we had some movement on a case. That movement is promising only because there's been no movement for weeks. So, bottom line, it's good."

"Great," I said, before I asked, "Where's Cleo?"

"Hiding and preparing her complaint there's someone in the house that divides attention from her, which she'll add to her on-going, active, but contradictory complaint about not having the house to herself where I only visit to feed her and appear when she's feeling like getting some love."

That didn't get a giggle.

It just made me laugh.

He shoved the cucumber aside, grabbed a carrot and asked nonchalantly, "How's your dad?"

Dang.

He looked at me out of the sides of his eyes, "Honey, we're gonna have to go there."

I sighed.

Then I said, "He was a jerk."

And he was.

Not calling-me-a-whore jerk, but, say, in the mid-to-lower range of Dad's multiple levels of jerkiness.

Axl looked down at the carrot in a manner I knew he intended to look down at the carrot so he didn't do something else, like press me for details, demand I never see my father again, or get one of his six guns and go shoot him in the kneecap.

"I like to think that it's because he's lonely and he misses me," I said.

"But?" Axl prompted me for what I obviously didn't say.

"He wasn't pleased he had to order pizza. Not that he doesn't like pizza. Just that he's into control. And when I show at his house, he knows he's controlling me. And I don't know if you know, but he has diabetes. The kind you have to closely manage. So when he doesn't check his blood sugar or take his insulin, it's a way to control me. It's all an exercise in control, even though I'm not ten anymore and even then, the way he did it wasn't okay. Mostly because controlling anyone isn't okay at all, ever."

Axl spoke no words.

But the carrot was getting decimated.

"I know, I know," I guessed his reaction. "He can take care of himself. Or he could get someone to come in and do a few things to look after him without leaning so heavily on me. He has money, not a lot of it, but he has a pretty good income from a work-from-home job. He's got a nest egg. It was bigger before he had a couple of hospital visits that bit into it. But we sold his house and downsized him—"

He turned just his head my way. "You mean *you* sold his house and downsized him."

I rubbed my lips together.

"That means yes," he said, watching my mouth.

I nodded.

Then I said, "We don't have to talk about this."

Axl put the knife down, grabbed his glass, took a sip of wine, and I watched his throat work while he did that.

So it took a second for me to shake myself out of the fascination when his focus came back to me and he spoke.

"You lay this stuff on your mom?"

I shook my head.

"It pisses her off," he deduced.

I nodded my head.

"You give it to your girls?"

"Well, until recently, I wasn't really speaking to them."

"Before that?"

I shook my head again.

"Intend to do that?"

"I can, but I haven't and...I don't know. I don't think they'll be judgy, but they care about me. They've never met him. Pretty much anyone I talk to about this, Aunt Pam, Uncle Dave, Mom, my high school friend Tammy who lives in Wisconsin now who I FaceTime with a lot, and she knows all about Dad, they think I should tell him to jump in a lake."

"So I'm your safe place."

The whoosh of warm, sweet, pure goodness that came from that nearly knocked me off the stool.

"Yeah, Hattie?" he pressed. "I'm your safe place. I cannot guarantee that won't come with reactions. It goes against the grain, knowin' a woman I care about, the woman I'm seein', the woman who's sleeping in my bed, walks into her dad's house with a target on her back for abuse. But even telling you that, it's only so you know I give a shit about you. It is not judgment. It isn't pressure. It's not up to me to stop it. It's up to me to support what you feel you have to do, and support it if you feel you have to keep doing it, and then praise God if the time comes you're done and you stop."

"Okay," I whispered, having heard all he said, but mostly the part about him caring about me was rattling around happily in my head.

That and all that stuff about supporting me.

"And eventually, my ass will be with you when you go and then you gotta let me do what I gotta do."

Oh God.

The happy stuff stopped rattling.

"Axl—"

"And that would be, I am not witnessing that shit, Hattie. You can tough it out with him when you're alone. But I'll make it plain he does not do that shit in front of me."

I wanted to see Axl tell Dad that he had to treat me right.

I really, really, *reallyreallyreally* wanted to see that.

"Well, uh...that time will be a ways off," I noted.

"Fine," he replied.

"And, you know, if your dad ever acts up, I'm your safe place too."

"Well, batten down the hatches, baby, because that shit's happening on Monday."

My hand tightened on my wineglass so much I had to force it to relax before the glass shattered, and my voice was kind of squeaky when I asked, "What?"

"Part of my day." He set his glass aside and went back to the carrot. "Mom called. She wants me over for dinner. I told her I'm seeing someone and it's serious. So she wants you over for dinner too. You don't dance Monday nights. We're going over for dinner."

Full-on squeaky with, "We're *what*?"

He bent down, got a bowl from the cupboard (shiny black, big, nice lines, perfect for him and his home décor, because he was perfect, except when he was jumping the gun and setting up a Meet the Parents before we'd even been together a week, gah!), put it on the counter and reached for a bag of cleaned spinach.

"Dinner. Mom and Dad's house. Monday night."

"Axl, this is *waaaaaaaaaaay* early," I pointed out, feeling I had not elongated the "way" nearly enough.

"Early for what?" he asked after dumping the spinach in the bowl.

"We've had one date," I reminded him.

He turned again to me, put a hip to the counter, and said, "Theoretically, if not practically, you've been mine for what? Three months? Six? Ten years?"

I had to smile at the "ten years."

But I said, "Okay, but—"

"And that means I've been yours that same time."

Hmm.

Nice.

"Even when I was with Peyton."

Hmm!

"So I think the time is right, don't you?" he asked.

"Well, I think *you* think the time is right since you made a date with your parents without consulting me," I replied.

"What would you have said if I consulted you?"

"Please, God, no."

He burst out laughing and came to me so I again had to open my knees to let him in.

With him laughing like that, I didn't mind.

He then bent to me, one hand on my thigh, one hand he wound up in my hair and held it to my neck.

In position to successfully scramble any thought process I might have, he said, "I knew you'd say that so I circumvented you saying that and I did it for two reasons. You down with hearing them?"

"Maybe."

He grinned and kept talking.

"One, it's gonna happen, and trust me, it's better not to procrastinate. We get it out of the way and move on."

Okay, well, his surety in the solidity of our togetherness didn't suck.

However....

"And two, for future reference, we need to understand how

huge a dick my dad is gonna be so we can plan how to handle that later. Or if I tell him to fuck off and arrange it so I see only my mother until Dad apologizes for whatever Dad is gonna do."

"Wh-what," I swallowed, "what's your dad going to do?"

"That's got a few parts too."

Fantastic.

"Hit me," I invited without a great deal of enthusiasm.

"First, you're a dancer. Which he will look down on. But before, you were a stripper, which he'll absolutely look down on."

Really not feeling the love for his dad.

"And that would be about him being a snob," he continued. "But you could be a lawyer, a doctor, have your art in the Guggenheim or work for fucking NASA, and he'd still find something about you that was not good enough for his son. And that would just be him being Sylas Pantera."

Okay. Then, Sylas Pantera was an equal opportunity meanie.

Not better.

But at least I was forewarned.

"Second," Axl carried on. "He'll lay into me. It could be subtle, it could be overt. But it will happen."

"Oh boy," I mumbled.

"Yeah," he agreed.

"Just to say, my dad will charm you. He'll be funny and interesting, and he'll talk sports or current events and you'll think, 'This guy is not so bad.' Then, when he gets comfortable around you, he'll let things slip. He's so good at it, the first half a dozen things will happen, and you won't even notice them."

"Wanna bet?"

I took in his expression.

Nope.

I did not want to bet.

What I knew from his expression, his actions, not just that night, but for a long time, was that he was serious about this.

About us.

And I was serious about us.

Absolutely.

And thus, he was right.

Get over the crappy stuff in order to move forward armed with the knowledge of how it would be so you could prepare for that.

I needed to focus on the good parts: we were together, that appeared to be solid, and the fact Axl was intent to move us forward.

We'd fought hard to get here. It'd be nice to have some time to glory in the spoils. And not just one fantastic date where Axl liked my dress, listened to everything I said, fed me amazing food and acted like he truly thought I was not only the most beautiful woman in the room, but the most interesting one in the city.

And, obviously, whatever he had on tap for that night, which at the very least smelled *divine*.

But it wouldn't feel very glorious, having stuff hanging over our head that would spoil our spoils.

Anyway, it was Thursday. Monday was forever away.

And Monday came after Sunday, when the Revue was not operating. It was straight-up strippers at Smithie's Sunday and Monday nights so the girls could have a rest.

Hopefully, Axl had Sunday off.

Also hopefully, he'd spend it with me.

Suddenly, he bent and kissed the side of my neck where he wasn't holding my hair.

"All right," he said there after the kiss, then pulled away and looked at me. "I see this really flips you, and you're right. It's too soon. I'll put Mom off."

"Axl," I said quickly when it looked like he was going to move away.

He stopped.

"I get it," I continued. "And that 'it' has two parts too."

"Sorry?"

"The first, I'm a procrastinator. You learned that the hard way. If something scares me, I avoid it."

"Hattie, baby, this isn't me saying—"

I shook my head and put my hand to his chest.

He shut up.

"I conditioned you to that because that's me. Seriously. I have to own up to it. And honestly?"

"Yeah?"

"Meeting your folks terrifies me. So, if I had my choice, I'd meet them on our wedding day, *after* the actual wedding."

He got a look on his face that made me keep going.

Fast.

"Not that I think we're getting married or anything."

That look interpreted itself when he started laughing, something he had been holding back.

"Are we doin' that shit outdoor or indoor?" he asked through his laughter.

Well.

Phew.

He wasn't freaking about me bringing up our wedding when we'd been seeing each other (officially) for two days.

"Shut up," I muttered through a grin.

"White cake, baby, with lemon filling, and that whipped cream frosting. None of that heavy buttercream crap," he ordered.

"So noted," I said, still grinning.

He sobered and said, "I hear you about avoidance."

"Good call, cutting that off at the pass," I told him.

He just studied me with a warm light in his icy eyes.

"Part two is, you're right again. We're doing this. So why wait?" I concluded.

"That mean I'm gonna meet your dad soon?"

"Uh…"

He smiled, touched his mouth to mine quickly, then let me go and turned back to the salad, saying, "I called the meet with my folks. You get to do the same with your dad."

"Appreciated," I replied.

Dad could definitely wait.

But I had a feeling Mom was going to love Axl.

Hmm.

I sipped wine while he tossed veggies into the salad, put it in the fridge then checked a rice cooker on the counter.

"Chicken's almost done, rice not quite," he announced. "I'll make the sauce in a sec."

"It smells awesome."

He shot me a smile while he nabbed his glass then something caught his eye.

He drank some wine, set the glass aside, and I watched him move to a pile of mail.

He then did exactly what I did.

Walked right to the recycle bin because that was where most of it was going to end up.

He hit the pedal and yup.

There it went.

Flyer.

Flyer.

Something in an envelope.

Postcard flyer.

All I could see was vast space filled with tree stumps that used to be a forest with confused deer wandering around and fumes from the postal workers' Jeeps.

Conversely, I again thought I was all kinds of weird that it felt super nice, sitting, sipping wine, food cooking, and watching Axl doing something everyday, like going through his mail.

"What the fuck?"

My mind went from my apocalyptic thoughts about the environment, and my happy thoughts about Axl, and my eyes went from the bin to Axl when he said this.

He dumped the rest of his mail on the counter (what appeared to be coupon papers, which in my opinion, you should be able to opt out of if you didn't clip coupons).

Then he came to me, envelope out.

Big manila envelope.

Like the one the pictures came in from my stalker.

"Oh my God," I whispered.

When he got close, I saw, handwritten on the front it said, To HATTIE'S FUCK.

"Oh my God," I repeated.

Axl ripped it open.

"He knows I'm here," I said.

"Yep," Axl replied tersely.

And I didn't know if a facial expression could be described as terse, but if it could, his was.

"Jesus," he muttered.

"What?" I asked.

"Note says, 'I'll do you too,'" he shared, then flipped a picture around.

A naked, tall, muscular man, bent over a table, tied to it, taking it from behind from a man in a black leather, full-head mask.

Same theme, the man getting it did not look like he was enjoying it.

In fact, like the pictures he sent me, everything about it seemed violent, even having no small amount of experience watching scenes like that in action and knowing getting it good could look like it was bad.

The pictures he selected seemed designed to denote pain, not pleasure.

And this was mega creepy beyond the fact that all of this was just super creepy.

"He put this in my mailbox," Axl said.

I didn't know what that meant so I looked from the photo to him. "Pardon?"

"He *put* it in my mailbox, Hattie." He showed me the envelope again.

No address.

Just the words.

"He didn't post this to me, he opened my mailbox and put pornographic materials in it," he stated.

"Is that, uh...actionable?"

"Mailboxes are the remit of the United States Postal Service. They have protections. And those protections are federal. Think a cop wouldn't be all fired up if you got pissed some landscaper or housekeeping company put some marketing material in your mailbox. This?" He shook the envelope. "Yeah. A cop would get interested. So would the Feds."

I found this hopeful on one front.

I put that hope into words.

"Maybe we should hand this to the police."

"We will. I'm telling Eddie and Hank tomorrow. About this and about the threat he mailed to you, which is also actionable, not to mention the rope. It was harassment before. That's official now. His shit is racking up."

I felt relief, mostly because I didn't know who this loser was, or how much *more* of a headache he'd be to Axl as well as Brett if they caught this creep and that did not go well.

Apparently, you could prosecute someone for using your mailbox inappropriately.

You could also prosecute them for things such as, say, illegal seizure and assault.

I didn't share this with Axl.

I asked, "Did your guys go in and dust for prints?"

He nodded. "They're running things, but all they've found so far is yours and Cisco's."

Hmm.

"And my laptop?"

He shook his head. "It wasn't hacked and that porn site you subscribe to wasn't hacked either. We're running your two exes, but so far what we got is they're clean."

Boy, he wasn't messing around with this.

And although they weren't getting much, that felt nice in a number of ways. Including, importantly, that even with this creepiness happening, I felt safe.

"What does that picture say to you?" I went on. "Is that an escalation?"

"Yes, in terms of the fact he's obviously following you, you clearly have a man in your life, as well as constant protection, and he's not letting shit go. So I'll be having words with Sly tomorrow too."

When he caught the look on my face, he continued.

"Chill, baby. Not angry words. I've been so caught up in you, I haven't been vigilant in looking for a tail. It could easily have been me that led him here."

It was cool he held up his hand like that.

One lesson my father taught me that was worthwhile: you didn't pass the buck. It was a supreme weakness to blame someone else. It took courage to admit you screwed up and take responsibility.

Of course, he often thought I'd screwed up when I didn't. But that was beside the point.

"Are there other terms?" I pressed.

He shook his head. "No. He hasn't gone off message. He just wants to keep tweaking you. Though, there's a possibility he's bi. But that's irrelevant, unless we can get a lock on some kind of description and can start looking for him in earnest. And if he's bi, that means he might be trolling for action in a number of lanes. And that opens the field of search, which always sucks because it's a drag on time and resources."

Well then, bad news, the creeper hadn't lost interest.

Good news, he was still just a creeper and not a total, whackjob, "it puts the lotion on its skin" creeper.

Mixed bag.

Axl was clearly finished with this topic.

I knew this when he went back to the mail, put the picture and envelope on the counter, dumped the newspaper coupons in his recycle bin, and announced, "Time to make the sauce."

"Can I help?" I offered.

"Yeah, top up my wine and take us into bummer-free zone. Tell me what we're doin' after dinner. You in the middle of bingeing something? Or you wanna stream a movie?"

Hanging with Axl in front of his TV sounded awesome.

Even so, I said, "Pac-Man."

He turned his head my way. "Tourney?"

"Absolutely."

He smiled and got out a saucepan.

I topped up his wine.

He made a roux, then he made the sauce. When the rice was done, he served up, we ate at his dining room table, and cleaned the kitchen together.

And he kicked my ass at Pac-Man.

Mental note: practice Pac-Man tomorrow.

Second way more important mental note: stop delaying in tackling things that terrify you.

Because you never know.

The spoils might be sweet.

CHAPTER THIRTEEN
Fireman's Hold

HATTIE

I threw back the curtains, and on shiny, bronze, sky-high stiletto heels, I walked out to "oo's" and "ah's" and some clapping hands.

"Thank God, it fits you like a glove," Lottie breathed in relief.

It was Saturday. We were at the bridal shop for my bridesmaid dress fitting.

And Lottie was right.

Thank God my dress fit like a glove because, when I called for a fitting, it took days to get an appointment, and they'd told me then that the wedding was so close, "if alterations are significant, you might have to find an outside seamstress."

Since I'd delayed this way too long, I was down with that and paying extra if needed.

But fortunately, it didn't seem to be needed.

"The hem is even perfect," Lottie's mom, Nancy, said, coming toward me.

"Jump up on the pedestal, babe, turn to the mirror, let's have a look," Lottie ordered.

I did as told and looked into the mirror.

My hair was piled up on my head in a curly-haired girl's messy bun, wavy tendrils floating down.

The bronze heels were what I was wearing to the wedding.

Along with, obviously, the dress, which was the sexiest brides-maid dress I'd ever seen.

A shiny, soft, light brown satin with spaghetti straps, cleavage cut down to the midriff, and a slightly overlapping side slit that went all the way up to the waist that made underwear nearly impossible.

Though, I was going to try to find something. I could do commando, but it unnerved me, especially with that slit and the need to be walking down an aisle. If the material shifted in a bad way, which it could because it had a small train that added weight, shit could get real... *in a church.*

That said, I was not surprised about Lottie's choice.

She was openly sexual, she didn't care what anyone thought about it, and before I started to avoid the girls, I'd been with her on her three Say Yes to the Dress appointments. Thus, I'd seen the wedding gown she selected, which might be the sexiest of all time.

Lottie was twitching the skirt of my gown, Nancy was standing a couple of feet away, tipping her head this way and that, looking me up and down, and my attention moved from my image in the mirror to the girls behind me who were sitting on couches, studying me.

Evie, Ryn, Pepper, and Lottie's sister, Jet.

Since Axl was doing something for work, and doing it with Boone, and Mo wasn't allowed to know anything wedding, my bodyguard for the day was Evie's man, Mag.

We were having lunch after this.

And one could say, I needed girl time.

Bad.

But this wasn't about me.

It was about Lottie.

And I was being a baby.

It had only been a few days.

A few days in Axl's house, some of the time with Axl, and some of that time with his mouth on mine.

And that was it.

We made out, and he didn't take it any further.

At all.

Him being him, sweet, handsome and supportive, tall, strong, funny and a *great* kisser, it was driving me crazy.

I needed more.

Like, lying in his bed Thursday night (and it was worse last night) restless, needy, fighting the desire to go out and jump him on the couch kind of crazy.

He was taking it slow. He knew I was shy. And that was sensitive and thoughtful. I shouldn't only be cool with that. I should be happy he was like that.

But not even feeling me up?

"Is it too tight?" Nancy asked. "Do they need to let it out?"

Since a bra was also impossible with this dress, if they let it out, with my bazungas, I'd be flopping all over the place.

"I need the support, Nancy," I told her.

"Yeah." Lottie was now standing by her mom, also tipping her head this way and that. "But is it comfortable?"

Actually, it was.

"Yeah." I shifted my focus back to the mirror. "And it's gorgeous."

So gorgeous, it fit me so well, showed so much cleavage and leg, I wondered what Axl would think of me in this dress.

I also wondered, since it looked like I'd be able to do so, if I took that dress home with me that day, put it on, and modeled it for him, if Axl might pounce on me in that dress.

Of course, if he did that it might require cleaning and/or pressing.

But at least he'd *pounce on me*.

I mean, again, we hadn't been together for years, but we also hadn't been together for hours.

And again, he was sweet, touchy, funny, affectionate, teasing, a great kisser...*hot*.

I loved all that.

But he needed to *fuck me*.

"You don't look happy," Lottie noted.

"I'm happy," I told her. "It's fantastic. I blew it with a late fitting, but it doesn't need alterations, so you don't have to worry about that anymore, and I don't have to worry about worrying you. So it's all good."

"Then why don't you look like it's good?" Lottie returned. "And don't blow sunshine, Hatz. If you need something changed, we'll get it sorted. It's not like the wedding is tomorrow. We have a couple of weeks."

"Honestly, it's great."

Nancy leaned to her daughter and murmured, "She doesn't look like it's great."

"It really is," I asserted.

They stared at me.

Heck.

I was worrying them, and I'd done enough of that.

And this was Lottie's time, prep for Lottie's big event, so worry should not be part of the equation.

"Axl hasn't had sex with me yet," I blurted.

Nancy's brows shot up and her eyes closed and stayed closed for a second before she opened them.

Lottie's head jerked and her tumble of blonde hair jerked with it.

And every single female ass on the couches behind me got up and walked to stand in front of me.

"What?" Ryn.

"Really?" Pepper.

"Whoa." Evie.

Jet said nothing, just studied me.

I looked at Lottie. "This isn't about me. It's about you."

"It's about you now." She lifted a hand my way, shook her head and said, "And don't. I don't mind. Honest to God." She dropped her hand and asked, "You've been living with that man now three days, and he hasn't done you?"

"We make out. A lot," I told her, or more aptly, all of them. "He touches me. A lot. He's very affectionate. All the time. It's sweet. He kisses me before he drops me off at work. We make out in the doorway of his room before I go to bed in his bed. He sleeps on the couch. And last night, after dinner, before work, while watching TV, we cuddled on the same couch and eventually started necking. But he hasn't even tried for second base."

"*What?*" Ryn.

"*Really?*" Pepper.

"*Whoa.*" Evie.

"*I know.*" Me.

"I'm outta here." Mag, from where he stood behind the couches.

Mag then took off.

"Have *you* tried for second base?" Lottie asked.

"Second base?" I parroted, confused.

"Gone for his package. A man gets the message real quick when you grab his dick," Lottie explained.

That was the girl take on second base?

That seemed a third-base maneuver, totally.

"I'm just going to...tell them we're good and we're leaving with the dress," Nancy murmured, lips tipped up, as she walked away.

"Uh..." was my answer to Lottie's question.

"She hasn't," Ryn said under her breath to Pepper.

"I'm kind of . . . not assertive like that," I shared.

Lottie put a hand to her hip, hitched out that hip, and returned, "Well, sister, you wanna get laid, you better get assertive. You led that boy on a long, drawn-out chase. No shade. Just sayin'. But translation for a dude with a brain and a keenly honed capacity for sensitivity who's into the chick who led him on that chase, he's not gonna jump you, push you or pressure you. He's gonna *read* you and wait for you to give him the next signal. You gotta give him the signal, Hatz."

"You do." Ryn.

"Totes." Pepper.

"Absolutely." Evie.

Jet again said nothing to me.

Though she did to Lottie.

"It isn't that easy for everybody, Lottie."

It *so* wasn't.

I mean, I loved kissing him. A lot.

But I wanted more.

A lot more.

Especially after all that kissing.

I just didn't know how to communicate that mostly because I thought I already was.

I was participating in our makeout sessions—avidly—and if memory served, I didn't think it was me—not once—that ended them.

If you were too shy to speak the words, how else did you tell a guy you were ready for more, outside grabbing his dick?

Jet turned to me. "Take your time. If he's worth it, he'll wait."

Ryn made a noise that sounded like she was being strangled.

I homed in on that. "What?"

"Well, just saying, he's been waiting awhile."

He totally had.

Way longer than three days.

Bah!

"So, have a conversation about it," Jet said to Ryn. "She doesn't have to go for the gusto."

A conversation might be doable.

It might not.

Axl and I now seemed to have no problem communicating.

But how did you bring up the conversation that essentially said, "Dude, I want you to fuck me."

I absolutely wanted him to fuck me. If he could kiss that well, I was really looking forward to what else he could do.

Again...

Like...*a lot*.

I just didn't know how to get him to *do it*.

I mean, he hadn't even gone for *my breast*.

It was excruciatingly frustrating.

"I think it's sweet he's taking things slow," Evie remarked.

"God, if Boone slept on the couch while I was in a bed a room away, for *three nights*, I'd have to figure out how to muffle my vibrator, I'd be she-bopping so much," Ryn declared. "We actually had a conversation about taking it slow. Our slow lasted a day."

Oh God.

Seriously, I felt that.

After all our snogging?

Then Axl just kisses my neck, tells me to sleep well and closes his bedroom door on me?

Man.

It had been crazy hard not to crawl between his sheets and have a little me time that I wished was *we* time.

"Talk to him, grab his dick, whatever. The conversation, verbal or physical, will last less than a minute before he does something—" Lottie cut herself off as she looked to the door.

The way she did that, I looked that way too.

And, to my surprise, incoming were Axl and Boone, with Axl looking...

Looking...

I braced because I'd never seen him look like that.

But it was not hard to read that look.

He was *enraged*.

Oh no.

What now?

My stalker had taken a day off. There'd been nothing from him on Friday.

Was he back with a vengeance?

"Oh shit." Ryn.

"Holy hell." Pepper.

"Oh boy." Evie.

"What are you doing here?" Lottie.

Axl stopped by the pedestal I was standing on, his eyes raking me, they came to mine, and he demanded, "Jesus, fuck, what are you wearing?"

"Uh..."

"A bridesmaid dress, Axe," Lottie answered for me. "Seeing as we're at a dress fitting, and you know that. But I'll repeat, what are you doing—?"

"Your father called you a whore?" Axl bit out, ignoring Lottie.

I looked to Boone who was looking apologetically at Ryn, which made me turn my attention to Ryn who was in full-on *Eek!* face.

Ryn told Boone, Boone told Axl.

Now Axl was here.

Enraged.

Damn.

"Eyes to me, Hattie," Axl growled.

I turned instantly back to him.

"Uh..."

"And you've been *fasting*?" he clipped.

My gaze took the journey from Boone to Ryn again, which bought me another growled, "*Eyes*," from Axl.

I started to move off the pedestal to him, seeing Mag now standing behind him with Boone, and I did this saying, "Honey, I—"

He shook his head, I stopped moving, and he stated, "Oh no, baby. Fuck no. Shit just changed with how we deal with your dad."

Uh-oh.

"Listen, maybe we can talk—" I tried again.

"You're not a whore," he declared.

"I know that, but—"

"Does it even penetrate how entirely *fucked up* it is for a father to call his daughter a whore?" he asked.

I shut up, and not simply because, in truth, it actually hadn't. It hurt he said that. I knew he was wrong about it. But it didn't occur to me to take that one step further and think that was, indeed, entirely fucked up.

What it was, for me, was Dad just being Dad.

I also shut up because I'd learned this. That "this" being, when Axl got pissed and had something to say, I didn't interject, even when he asked me questions.

"And you have a beautiful body," he announced.

Oh.

Wow.

"What the fuck? Fasting?" he went on.

When he didn't say anything for a while, I opened my mouth to share, but before I could, he threw up his arm, indicating me, and said, "For Christ's sake, look at you. You're fucking perfect. And you don't need that dress to be that, but, baby, you in that dress. *Fuck*."

I stood still.

I felt the girls go still.

The air went still.

Maybe even the earth stood still.

Because...

Perfect?

Oh man.

Okay.

Official.

I *really* needed my guy to *fuck me*.

"And you're fasting," Axl continued. "Because that asshole gets in your head. I told you, baby, he harms you, I intervene. I'm intervening."

"It's intermittent fasting," I said softly. "It's a program to—"

"Lose weight?" he asked curtly.

"Yes. I could stand to shed a few pounds."

Like, maybe, twenty-five (okay, thirty) of them.

"Why? You out of shape?" he queried.

"Well, no."

"So?" he pushed.

"What I'm trying to share is, it isn't him. It's something I want to do for me."

"Think real hard, Hattie, honey. Isn't it? Is. It. Not. Him?" Axl challenged.

Okay.

Um...

Heck.

It was.

It was him.

Whenever I felt crap about myself, it was always Dad.

"Yeah," Axl said quietly, reading that realization on my face.

"Axl," I whispered.

"We'll talk about this more tonight," he said, much more calmly. "But I am no longer okay with you walkin' into his house with that target on your back, Hattie, knowing the extremes of his abuse."

"Okay, we'll talk about it," I quickly agreed.

He nodded, turned his eyes to Lottie and said, "Apologies for interrupting, Mac."

"Not necessary. In fact, I wish I could do an instant replay," Lottie replied.

Even if that was kind of funny, Axl was in no mood, so he didn't even smile.

He looked back to me. "I'll be home around four. Will you be back?"

I nodded.

"Good," he muttered. "We'll finish this then."

Great.

I started to move to him because it seemed like he was leaving, and I wanted to give him a kiss good-bye, but with a sharp movement, he lifted his hand my way, and I stopped again.

"Don't get near me in that dress," he warned.

I felt a flutter, two tingles, and a spasm, all of these in different places in my body, all of them *awesome*, all of them familiar, and all of them *frustrating*.

His face grew a little soft (but only a little, he was still ticked), and he said, "See you later, beautiful."

Beautiful.

Oh God, the waterworks were coming.

I trusted myself only to nod while I tried to get a lock on the tears, both of which I accomplished.

There were general farewells all around with Boone going to Ryn and laying a hard, closed-mouth kiss on her before he and Axl departed.

The door barely closed on them before Lottie said, "You absolutely need to pounce on that man."

"Oh my God, *yes*." Ryn.

"Put him out of his misery." Pepper.

"I mean, seriously." Evie.

"I'm outta here again." Mag.

"I was like you, before Eddie," Jet said, referring to her husband, Eddie Chavez, and I focused on her. "I put him through the wringer. He had to do all the work. That meaning *all the work.*"

I *so* caught her drift.

"But, honey," she kept on, "as much as I get you, that man really, *really* needs to fuck you."

Oh boy.

Yikes!

"Do you think . . . him losing it like that about Dad . . . is because he's frustrated?" I asked.

"No," all of them, every single one, answered at the same time.

Okay, so that sitch wouldn't have an easy fix.

My eyes wandered to the door.

"Are you in any doubt he wants you . . . and *bad*?" Pepper asked, and I turned to her. "I mean, Hatz, he couldn't even let you get near him wearing that dress for fear of what he'd do if you did."

"Fireman's hold then sex noises from behind the curtain in the dressing room," Ryn guessed.

"I think, since it would be their first time, he'd have it together enough to take her to his car, drive her home and do her in his bed," Evie shared her version. "Though, he'd take her to his car in a fireman's hold." Pause, then, "And the same when he took her to his bed."

"Nope. He might get her to his car, but he'd do her there," Pepper put in.

"Okay, we all need to stop talking about Axl doing me now," I warned, visions of me in a fireman's hold on Axl's shoulder dancing in my head and the flutters, tingles and spasms were back with a vengeance.

The girls grinned at each other.

And that included Lottie, but she did it noting, "What they're saying is, you can share with him what you need. He needs it too.

As bad or worse than you. You guys have been waiting a long time for this. And you can trust him with it, Hattie. You can also trust him to take care of the both of you."

She was right.

There was one thing I was getting, and that was coming in strong.

I could trust Axl Pantera to take care of me.

It still wasn't going to be easy.

But I was avoiding avoidance.

I was tackling things that scared me.

Right?

Right.

Damn.

*   *   *

At around four that afternoon, I was on Axl's deck with Evie and Mag when Mag suddenly said, "We are *so* gone."

That was right before we all heard the garage door going up.

Oh God.

Axl was home.

Evie was in a moon chair beside me, Mag's (very, the man was six foot four) long body was sprawled in a lounge on the steps up to the Jacuzzi, I was in the other moon chair.

But, as one, we all rose from our positions.

I knew, however, I was the only one who did it nervously.

Good-bye hugs were swift and out on the deck.

By the time we all piled into the kitchen, Axl was also coming into the kitchen.

I might have stared at him like a deer caught in headlights (actually, I was pretty sure I stared at him like a deer caught in headlights).

Axl was staring at me like he really wanted to say something, but whatever it was, he couldn't do it in company.

"We gotta bounce," Mag said into our staring contest, going to Axl and doing the bro hug of hands clasped before them, chest bump, back thump, release.

Evie went in for a regular hug.

When they cleared away, Axl looked to me, and like we had a mind meld, we both moved to each other, then moved together behind Evie and Mag to follow them to the front door.

And Axl took my hand as we did.

We stood at the front door, calling good-byes, Mag saying we'd get together, and he'd do his grilled pizza (*grilled* pizza?).

Then they were gone, the front door was closed, and Axl and I were standing at it, still holding hands, and staring at each other again.

As usual, he got there before me.

"I need to apologize for busting in on your time with Mac and the girls," he said. "That was uncool. And I'm sorry. Though, honey, I gotta say, I'm not gonna apologize for being insanely pissed about that shit regarding your dad. We need to talk this through, but now, I gotta reiterate something I didn't leave any real doubt about earlier. I got a serious problem with you going to see your father without me. At least until he gets, from me, that you now have a man in your life that won't tolerate him being a dick to you."

"I need you to fuck me."

Yup.

It came right out just like that.

And I knew it wasn't a figment of my imagination, me thinking it and not saying it (like should have happened) when his head cocked sharply to the side.

Damn!

"What?" he asked.

"Uh…" I answered.

His hand in mine got tighter and he started moving, and since

I was connected to him, I started moving too, him going forward, me going back.

"Say that again," he ordered.

"It's just that, um...I really like kissing you," I said.

He shifted us so we'd round the armchairs.

And our destination was clear.

Oh man.

"That wasn't what you said," he noted.

"Well, uh...you, and, um...me, that is—"

I didn't finish that, not that I really started it. He gave my arm a jerk, I slammed into his body, his other hand tangled in my hair and his face was in mine.

"You need me to fuck you, baby?" he whispered.

"Yes," I whispered back.

Okay, there it was.

Out there.

I thought he'd kiss me.

He didn't kiss me.

He let me go and disappeared because he bent to put a shoulder in my belly and then I was up.

In a fireman's hold.

There were no flutters or tingles with that.

It was all spasms, and these were concentrated in one place.

"Axl," I said to his superior ass.

Okay, it was more like I *panted* his name.

He was tall, his strides wide, so I wasn't on his shoulder for long before I was on my back on his bed.

And he was on me.

But he again didn't kiss me.

He framed my face with his hands and stared down at me.

"Axl."

That time, it was a plea.

Only *then* did he kiss me.

Me on his bed, *with him*, this going somewhere, *finally*, I might not have reached for second base right off the bat.

But while his tongue plundered my mouth, my body responded (wildly), and I tugged hard at his tee.

He shoved up to his knees, straddling me, and *whoosh*, the tee was gone and there was his chest.

God, I'd missed his chest.

I started to push up to touch it, but he came down, rolled us, then we were up again, both of us, with me straddling him, and *whoosh* again, *my* tee was gone.

He was staring at me straddling him in my bra and a noise like a low purr hummed from his chest.

Good freaking *God*.

Hot.

Hearing that sound, instantly, feelings neither of us let loose while we were just necking exploded all over the place.

I wanted to taste him, so I did.

His neck.

His ear.

He wanted to taste me, so he did.

He sank his teeth into the curve of my breast above my bra.

Oh yeah.

"Yes," I breathed.

I'd barely hissed out the "s" when my bra was gone.

"*Yes,*" I gasped.

His hands were at my breasts.

Both of them.

God, it felt nice, their weight held in his strong, long-fingered hands.

Then my nipple was in his mouth.

He drew hard.

No spasm at that.

My sex clutched like he was already inside me.

Need.

Oh, *man.*

I moaned.

My other nipple was in his mouth.

I ground into his promising bulge between my legs.

And when I did, I flew through the air as he whipped me on my back, and he was off the bed.

I had no time to protest the loss of him.

One sandal...gone.

Okay, I was with his program.

I undid the button on my jeans.

The other sandal...gone.

I unzipped my jeans.

With Axl tugging on the hems, my jeans scored down my legs, taking me partially with them.

Which was good, since my panties were now in easy reach for him to curl the fingers of both his hands in the sides and yank them down to my calves.

This he did.

I felt a rush of wet between my legs.

Or, another one.

I wheeled the panties off and then Axl had his arm around my waist and I was again going through the air.

Colliding with him.

I wrapped my legs around his hips as he entered the bed on his knees.

And we were kissing.

Kissing hard.

I had one hand wrapped around the back of his neck, the other one was tugging at his belt.

He broke the kiss and muttered, "Hold tight," against my lips.

I stopped tugging at his belt and curled my arm around his shoulder.

We went back to kissing, and I was so into it, his taste, his tongue, the smell of him, the feel of my skin against his, my bare breasts crushed against his hard chest, when I felt more skin. The skin of his hips against my legs after he tugged down his cargos.

Then his hand was between us and I felt him rubbing the tip of his cock against my clit.

My pussy spasmed and electric currents rushed over my thighs.

Finally.

Oh yes.

So good.

So, so, so, so *good*.

I tore my mouth from his and panted, "*God, honey.*"

"Yeah?" he asked.

"Yeah, yeah, yeah," I answered.

He shifted his cock to my entrance.

Finally!

I focused on his blue eyes.

"Yes," I demanded.

He fell forward, pulling me down on him, filling me, and then I was on my back, and Axl was on me and in me.

In me.

Part of me.

Then he was gliding gently, in and out.

I used my legs around his ass to lift my hips to meet his strokes, our gazes locked.

"Beautiful," I whispered.

"That's my line," he whispered back, angled his head, and kissed me again.

Then he started fucking me, the strokes turning to thrusts, his hips shifting, finding the right spot to make me gasp, moan, his hands on me, mine all over him.

It built.

It surged.

It carried me away.

The thrusts became drives.

I dug my nails into skin, sucked hard on his tongue.

The drives turned into pounds.

Yeahyeahyeahyeahyeah.

I broke our kiss, shoved my face in his neck and wrapped everything I had around him.

Everything.

Tight.

"Christ, yeah," he grunted.

And that was when I came.

Explosion.

Fireworks.

Then obliteration.

Nothing but sensation.

Elation.

Completion.

God, this was perfect.

God, *he* was perfect.

God, he was everything.

Everything.

My orgasm began drifting, he was still driving deep, I could hear his labored breathing, and I was cradling him, squeezing him, rising to meet him.

"Hattie," he whispered in my ear before he groaned deeply, pressing his face hard in my neck, burying himself to the root.

Yeah.

Yeahyeahyeahyeahyeah.

As he coasted with his climax, I petted him, out of the zone of need, aware of everything now. The feel of his skin, the heat of it, the muscle under it. The heft of his cock, filling me full. The scent of him, man and soap and hints of shaving cream. The aroma of sex.

Of us.

He shifted his head, trailed his tongue around the groove behind my ear, down my neck to my throat, dipping it into the hollow at my clavicle, and then his head came up.

I saw his face just a moment before my eyes floated closed because he was kissing me, soft and sweet and sated and unhurried.

That kiss said we had now, and tomorrow, and the next day, and week, and years and years besides.

It was a kiss that said this was our beginning, and there might never be an end.

That kiss wasn't a promise or a vow.

It was just reality.

The here and now.

And forever.

I wasn't just moved by that gorgeous kiss.

I was shattered by it at the same time it held me together.

He was the only man who'd ever kissed me like that.

And I had a strong feeling deep in my heart that he was going to be the last man who would not only kiss me like that.

But kiss me at all.

He broke our kiss, slid his nose down the side of mine, over, down the other side, and God.

God.

He was perfect.

Everything.

"No more sleeping on the couch," I said quietly.

He lifted a hint away and grinned at me. "Right."

"Do you have tomorrow off?"

He nodded.

"Will you spend it with me?"

"Absolutely."

I trailed my hands up his back, over his ribs, up his chest, his neck and cupped both his cheeks.

"You're beautiful too," I told him.

A glitter hit the ice of his eyes.

"Thanks, baby," he replied.

"That was awesome," I said.

"Yeah it was," he agreed.

"I would say it's a case for delayed gratification, but I don't want you to wait three days before we do it again."

"Three months," he corrected.

"Three months," I relented.

"Maybe six."

I laughed softly.

"Felt like ten years," he muttered.

"Totally," I concurred.

"Need to deal with this condom, honey," he said.

That surprised me.

"You put on a condom?"

"Yeah. You missed it. You were in the zone of showing me how to tongue fuck your mouth."

Like he needed me to show him.

He did *not*.

I just encouraged it.

"I sense you probably already knew."

"Always good to have a refresher."

I grinned at him.

He kissed the grin on my face, slid off me, but rolled me to my side, closing my legs and catching me behind my knees with his arm to curl them up for maximum comfort.

Yeah, I should have known that was something Axl would do.

Not leave the bed with me spread eagle and make me move my own limbs.

Looking after me.

Taking care of me.

Thinking of everything.

I watched him hitch up his cargos that he hadn't fully taken off and disappear in the hall on his way to the bathroom.

I then saw movement, shifted my gaze, and Cleo jumped on the arm of the chair.

Her tail twitched and she shared her hearty disapproval of the recent activities.

When Axl returned, still in cargos, but *sans* his boots and socks, Cleo turned her attention to her daddy and communicated her revulsion of our carnality with an irate flick of her tail that Axl didn't miss.

"Sorry, my queen, you're gonna have to get used to it," he warned his cat.

Mm.

Another irate tail flick.

Axl put one knee in the bed, and suddenly I was all tangled up in him, mostly on my back, partly on my side, all of him on me.

Snuggly.

Nice.

"Bummed you have to go to work," he said to my lips.

"I don't have to leave for hours," my lips told him.

His gaze lifted to my eyes. "But I have to fuel you before you go."

"Will you stay?"

"Sorry?"

"For the show? Will you watch me dance? I'll sit with you when I don't have to prep for my next one."

A change came over his handsome face.

A gorgeous change.

This before he said softly, "I'd love that."

I loved that he'd love that.

I'd love it too.

I didn't have any deep, abiding messages to send to him through any of the numbers I had planned for that night, but

I wanted to know his eyes were on me as I was doing what I loved to do.

He slid the hair off the side of my face, my neck, then wound his fingers in it, his eyes watching.

I pressed closer and Axl adjusted his long legs in mine, the scrape of the material of his pants against my skin wildly erotic.

This meant I fitted my hips more closely to his.

His attention went from my hair to my face.

"That was big, wasn't it?" I asked.

"It was big," he confirmed.

At his confirmation, feelings overwhelmed me. Feelings so huge, it was good I was lying down, or they would have brought me to my knees.

I dipped my head, pressed my face in his throat and his fingers sifted into my hair.

"You okay?" he asked, his lips in the top of my hair.

"I don't know what this feeling is, but I do know it's a whole lot more than okay."

His arm around me squeezed tight.

"It's always been big, what's between us, you know?" he whispered into my hair.

Oh, I knew.

Kiss me like you mean it.

Not once, not a single kiss, not even a lip touch, did he ever kiss me like he didn't mean it.

I nodded.

"The first time I saw you dance," he said.

I closed my eyes.

That was when it happened for him.

The first time he saw me dance.

For me?

When he walked into that studio, trying to pretend everything was cool, and I knew he'd seen me lose it, and the expression on his face said he wanted to sweep me away.

Take me someplace safe.

Slay dragons for me.

No one had ever looked at me like that in my life.

So yeah.

That was when it happened for me too.

"Yeah," I said against his skin.

"You're remarkable, Hattie."

I flattened my hand against his back, pressing in.

My voice was husky when I said, "You too."

"No, listen to me, hear me, baby, *you're remarkable, Hattie*."

I pulled my face out of his throat, tipped my head back, slid my hand up into his hair and drew his mouth down to mine.

I kissed him.

And I meant it.

He then kissed me at the same time he rolled me.

We went slower that time, and he lost the cargos completely.

But in the end, it was just as big.

CHAPTER FOURTEEN

Scratched the Surface

HATTIE

Hands woke me.
        And lips.

I stretched, languorous.

Axl, his heat spooning me in his bed, slid his mouth from my shoulder to my ear.

"Mornin', baby," he murmured there.

I stretched again, more languorously.

He was here.

With me.

He'd slept here.

With me.

"Morning," I whispered.

His hand hit my hip.

"Wanna go down on you," he said.

Oh yes.

We hadn't done that yet.

I twisted my neck and caught his eyes.

So beautiful.

"'Kay," I agreed.

Those icy-blues shone with humor and something even better before he took my mouth in a slow, Sunday morning kiss.

Then, with that hand at my hip, he pressed me to my back, and he wasn't kidding.

He wanted to go down on me.

I was sleepily surprised that, without preamble, he slid my panties off, opened me to him, and dipped right in.

I didn't need any preamble when he got down to business.

Holy heck.

Axl purred when he ate a woman out.

It was *sublime*.

* * *

Croissants, butter, jam, coffee, me in my nightie, Axl in his sleep pants (these black with a black elastic band), post-orgasm (me, two, Axl, one) and his bed.

I'd never had one, but I recognized it immediately.

My perfect morning.

"What do you wanna do today?" he asked, twisting to put his coffee mug to a nightstand after taking a sip.

Go down on you, fuck, you go down on me again, fuck more, move on to making love and sometime in there eat and snooze before we pass out for the night, I did not say.

"I don't know, what do you wanna do?" I asked instead.

"Finish breakfast, fuck, nap, fuck, eat lunch, maybe a quick tourney of Pac-Man, fuck again, eat dinner, watch a movie, fuck then sleep," he said mostly what I thought, with some welcome alterations.

I bit off a hunk of croissant and jam and smiled at him with my mouth closed.

He watched my mouth as he queried, "Is that indication you're down with my plan?"

I nodded exuberantly while chewing.

He chuckled and grabbed the knife that was in the jam jar. A jar that sat on a dinner plate which was acting as a tray on his bed.

He thus commenced in loading up his croissant.

He liked a lot of jam.

So did I.

Mm.

"You were beautiful last night, baby," he murmured before he took his own bite.

Yes.

He'd told me that last night.

Not that a repeat sucked.

"Thanks," I said shyly.

"Particularly liked 'Do You Wanna Touch Me.'"

He would.

"I got that when you touched me *there* a lot after we got back from Smithie's," I joked.

"Punk in pointe shoes," he muttered, going for some butter to prepare his next bite. "Fuckin' genius."

I felt something skate over my skin.

And the sensation was like someone was trailing a soft cashmere blanket over my body.

That said . . .

I didn't often pull out the pointe shoes at Smithie's. If it didn't work for the routines—which were meant to be provocative, titillating, not a showcase of dancing talent, so they didn't often work—I didn't try to fit them in.

But there was something gloriously suggestive in adding the grace of being *en pointe* with the hard chords and blatant invitation of that song.

I couldn't run away *en pointe*.

So if you wanted to touch, all you had to do was reach out, and I couldn't get away.

You had me.

But genius?

"Thanks," I repeated, my voice funny.

His gaze came to me.

"What?" he asked.

"What what?" I asked back.

"What's with the voice?"

It wasn't like he was deaf, though it was coming clear he wasn't one to let things slide.

"Just…" I tipped my head to the side, "genius?"

"You think I'm full of shit?" he asked bluntly.

Nope, definitely not one to let things slide.

"No," I answered. "I think you want me to feel good about myself."

"And you think I'd do that by feeding you a line?"

I studied him closely.

He didn't seem mad.

He seemed inquisitive.

"I…don't know," I told him honestly.

"Okay…" he began.

He then tossed the last bite of his croissant on the plate and focused on me.

Or focused *entirely* on me.

"I wouldn't do that," he stated.

"All right," I replied.

"Also," he went on, "I'm aware I'm not gonna fix all your father broke down in you by blowing sunshine up your ass."

Oh boy.

"Okay," I said.

"Which brings us to talking about your dad."

Ugh.

"Can we just . . . not?" I requested.

"Why not?"

"Because we're having a perfect Sunday morning."

His expression warmed with that.

But sadly, that warmth did not mean I was off the hook.

"Okay, honey, then when? In the mornings, I'm out of the house before you. I come home to have some dinner with you, and there's not time to do much more. And regardless, it wouldn't be great to get into the heavy with you right before you have to work."

This was a valid point.

"You didn't go to your dad last night," he noted.

No, I didn't.

"I texted him at lunch," I told him. "After the, uh . . . sitch at the bridal shop, and, well, the state I was in, I thought it was best to concentrate on you."

He grinned.

It was a nice grin.

It was a hot grin.

Then he asked, "And how'd he handle that?"

"He didn't reply."

Which meant he was ticked.

Further, that meant I'd catch it the next time I saw him.

I didn't share that last part with Axl.

Then again, I might not catch it, since apparently Axl was coming with me to Dad's when I went.

"And tonight?" Axl pressed.

Bluh.

I totally didn't want Dad encroaching on my Sunday with Axl, not this conversation, not having to leave the house to make him dinner.

In fact, until Axl just mentioned it, I hadn't given a thought to Dad.

Which, really, was a first.

I gave a thought to Dad a lot.

Hmm.

"I hope you know, if your dad was a loving father, and genuinely needed your day-to-day assistance, I would not have an issue with that," he remarked.

"I know," I replied quickly. "Of course I know."

"This is something else."

I knew that too.

I delved into the butter and made a study of carefully spreading it on my croissant.

"Hattie," Axl called.

I looked up at him. "I can't stop. He won't take care of himself. And he's my dad."

"Okay, then as I told you, tonight, I'm going with you."

Oh boy.

"Has he met any of your other boyfriends?" he inquired.

Whoa.

Just…*whoa.*

Axl was my boyfriend?

My boyfriend?

Major flutter.

"Hattie," he called again, a little less patiently this time.

"You're my boyfriend?" I asked.

"Were you there post-first-fuck convo yesterday?" he returned teasingly.

I so was.

Thank God.

Okay, he was my boyfriend.

There was that cashmere blanket again.

And okay times two, we were talking about this.

Last, I was procrastinating again.

We could either have this conversation now, or have it when I had to leave to go to Dad's, something I actually *couldn't* do without Axl because I hadn't been behind the wheel of my car in a week, not to mention, my vehicle wasn't even there.

"We need to go get my car," I noted.

"Baby," he murmured.

Procrastinating!

"Right, no," I belatedly answered. "About the boyfriends. And that's not a hard no, because I actually have, but it was a high school boyfriend and we went to Dad's so he could take pictures of us before prom, so it kinda counts, but also doesn't. Because...high school."

"And how'd that go?"

"Dad was charming and funny, and at my next visitation with him, he told me Tyler was a loser."

"Was he a loser?"

I shook my head. "No, he was nice. Then he went off to school at Cornell. He broke up with me his second week there. It bummed me out."

"Sorry, honey," Axl said through a grin.

The grin was cocky and amused.

Then again, if Tyler hadn't moved on from his high school girl-friend, I might not be in bed with Axl eating croissants and being annoyed by my father who wasn't even there.

"But he was the only one," I continued. "Tyler, I mean. Dad might actually like you," I added. "He's a man's man. You being all commando-y, he might understand I scored a winner."

Axl's lips quirked. "Commando-y?"

"Even in sleep pants, you look like you could topple a dictator."

Axl burst out laughing.

"It's the chest," I pinpointed it.

Axl laughed harder.

I smiled and watched while he did.

Then I realized, with him being my boyfriend, I was his girl-friend, and this afforded me certain rights and privileges.

So I took advantage of one, pushed up to my knees and kissed his morning-stubble jaw as he did it.

While I was moving away, he caught me by the back of my neck, pressed his lips hard to mine, and only after he did that did he let me go.

I sat back on my ass as Axl said, "You know, a real man's man does not depend on his daughter to check his blood sugar and cook his meals."

"Mm," I hummed noncommittally.

"Right, let's boil this down," he suggested.

I shoved my last bite of croissant in my mouth and gave him my full attention.

"Obviously, I think any adult should be responsible for their own life and health."

"Hmm," I agreed, but only tonally.

"And obviously, I'm not a fan of your dad abusing you, not only verbally, but by controlling your time and thus your life by landing a heavy responsibility on you that you have to consider every fucking day, so essentially, he's got you on a lead he yanks every fucking day."

I said nothing to that, not even making a noise, because...

Holy shit.

He did.

Onward from my earlier realization that I gave a lot of thought to Dad, I also had to fit him in every day.

Which meant I not only had to think of him, but actually *fit him in*. What I'd make him for dinner, then make it. If he had groceries, his prescriptions, and if he didn't, buy them.

All of this countless times *every single day*.

It was just my day, and I did it.

I didn't think about it, except to think it was inconvenient, or to worry about what other people thought that I did it.

I knew it was control, but I hadn't really grasped how far that went.

"We don't need to go over my opinion about his verbal abuse. I think that's clear," Axl went on.

It sure was.

"And I sense you have no real idea how much through his past, and likely his current abuse he's inserted himself in your life, your thought processes, the image you have of yourself. I think he controls a good deal of your thoughts without you even realizing he controls them."

Okay, I had to admit, this had come clear with the whole fasting thing and it was something I needed to take some time to ponder.

Though not over croissants on a perfect (or it was) Sunday morning with my brand-new, super-fit, had-the-chest-of-a-god boyfriend.

"So," Axl sounded like he was about to sum up, "if it were up to me, you'd tell him to kiss your ass and be in touch only if he wanted to take you to dinner or a Rockies game."

Wow.

Wouldn't that be a dream.

"Hmm," I repeated to share that thought.

"It isn't up to me," he kept going. "That's your choice. And I'd like to tell you I won't go over there tonight and tell him that I know he called you a whore, and then explain somewhat thoroughly how I feel about that, and how I'd like him to refrain from allowing it, or anything like it, ever to happen again. But I can't tell you that. Because when I go over there with you tonight, that's precisely what I'm gonna do. With my job, I can't be there every time you go over to see him. I can only hope you won't hide that shit from me if it happens, so if I have to have another conversation with your father, I can get on that without delay or without him breaking down what I built up."

All that was awesome, and scary, in equal measure (maybe a wee bit more scary).

But...

Hang on.

"What you built up?" I queried.

"Babe, you gotta learn how to take off the blinders he put on and see you."

"Okay, I like that, honey. But you don't have to make a job of that."

In fact, I really didn't want him to make a job of that.

I wanted to be his girlfriend.

No, I *was* his girlfriend.

What I wasn't was so deep in the la-la land of Axl Pantera (and his bare chest) post-orgasm, croissants-and-coffee-in-bed goodness that I didn't think that we'd hit rough patches and it would take work to keep our relationship strong. And frankly, at this point, build that relationship. Because we were in our infancy and anything that was shiny and new was exciting and seemed like it'd never lose its luster, but it always did.

But I didn't want to be a job to him.

I didn't want to be work.

His head ticked. "Sorry?"

"You don't have to make a job of that," I repeated.

"What do you mean?"

"Telling me all the time I'm beautiful and perfect and you like how I dance and stuff like that. Make it your job to do that."

He fell silent.

So silent, his silence was the definition of silence.

And after it went on awhile, it started freaking me out.

"Axl," I said.

"I thought we went through this," he replied, his voice strange. Low. Careful.

"We did."

"I'm not blowing sunshine."

"Okay."

The silence came back and now he was examining my face in a way I felt he might be able to count my pores.

"Axl." That one came out as snappish.

Because, what was the deal?

Again with the careful tone. "You're not hearing me, Hattie."

"I am."

He shook his head. "No. You're listening. But you aren't hearing."

"I don't get what you mean."

"I'm not feeding you a line."

"You've said that, now repeatedly," I reminded him.

So suddenly I jumped, he reached out and caught my face in both hands and brought his so close to mine, all I could see were his eyes.

"Fuck," he muttered.

"What?" I breathed, now not starting to freak out.

I was in a freak-out, full bore.

"You were beautiful in that dress yesterday, Hattie."

"Okay."

"Listen to me."

That was not careful.

It was deep. Resonant. Luke-I-Am-Your-Father *intense*.

"When you were doing those twirls up on the tips of your toes to Joan Jett—"

"Pirouettes," I corrected.

"Yeah, those," he said. "The table next to me gasped. Punk is pounding through Smithie's sound system and I could hear them gasp."

Wow.

That was huge.

I stared into his eyes.

"You doin' ballet to Joan Jett with dark eyes and safety pins in your shirt was *genius*."

My heart started beating hard.

Axl continued.

"You say 'Okay,' you say 'Thanks,' you brush it off when I'm telling you the god's honest truth. I told you that you were remarkable—"

"I know and that's sweet and—"

His hands pressed in and he got so close, the tip of his nose was brushing mine. "I told you that, Hattie, because *you're remarkable*."

Okay.

Wow.

I began panting.

"You have no idea because you heard him tell you over and over again that you're not. But he's wrong. You are. And it's not because you have a fantastic body, and I swear to fuck, it took a lot out of me not to drag you to the dressing room and bang you against the mirror when I saw you in that dress yesterday. It isn't because you trained for years and know the moves so you can execute them. You make people feel when you dance. You make them *gasp*. Your dad's been a dick to you all your life, he messed with your head, hurt you, and your loyalty to blood doesn't break. Your art, babe, we haven't even gotten to that. Fuck, we haven't even scratched the surface of you."

Scratched the surface of me?

Yup.

Definitely panting.

"I'm not tellin' you shit because I like you or I wanna get in your pants. I'm telling you the truth. I misspoke when I said I was building you up. I didn't mean propping you up. I meant putting back together the pieces he tears from you. Pieces that are already a part of you. They're who you are. The compliments I share with you aren't a means to any end except to remind you of who you are."

Okay.

Enough.

Putting my hands to his shoulders, I kissed him while shoving him to his back.

He rolled me, and I was pretty sure jam and butter got on his sheets, and even if his hands had a firm clasp on my ass, he lifted his head and said, "Hattie, not sure we're done talkin' about this."

I had a firm hold on his head and was trying to pull it down to me. "We're done."

He pushed back on my pull. "I need to know you heard me."

"I'll assure you of that after I suck you off."

There we go.

A steely flash of blue in his eyes and then he quit talking and let me pull him down so I could kiss him.

This I did.

Hard.

And so, he could do no preamble before giving head?

I could too.

I planted a foot in bed and rolled him.

I slid down his body.

No, wait.

Maybe I couldn't dispense with any preliminaries.

Because there was his chest.

I sucked in a nipple.

And shift...

I raked my teeth over the other one.

The noises he was making?

The way his long, strong body was shifting under mine?

I sucked that nipple too.

He wasn't playing fair, and I knew this when he cocked a knee, separating my legs, which meant his thigh was pressed to the heart of me.

Well, since it was there…

I rubbed against it.

"Jesus, Hattie," he growled.

As I started to head to that line of hair that pointed to buried treasure, I lifted my eyes to his.

Man.

Those eyes all turned on…

I shivered.

He helpfully straightened his leg that I was straddling so I could reach my goal.

"Shift, beautiful, wanna play with your pussy while you go down on me," he invited.

"No, just you."

"Baby, get your cunt up here beside me," he ordered roughly.

Okeydoke.

Shivering again, I modified positions as he wanted.

He yanked my panties down to the bend in my knees.

That caused a quake.

I yanked his waistband down his hips.

His pretty, heavy, rock-hard cock jumped free.

My mouth watered.

And now was no time for preamble.

I swallowed it whole.

"Christ," Axl groaned, driving his hips up and sliding two fingers inside me.

Yeahyeahyeahyeahyeah.

I got in position to bob, to suck, to use my hand when needed.

Then I did all that.

And yup.

His cock was hefty.

Way more than a mouthful.

Delicious.

Eventually, after I spent some time licking, sucking and pumping, while Axl stroked and rubbed, Axl tore my panties over my calves, off my feet, caught me at my hips, lifted me bodily up, and planted me on his face.

Then he sucked hard on my clit.

My head jerked back, and I rocked against his mouth.

He pulled me down deeper.

"No fair," I gasped.

He tongue fucked me.

Totally no fair!

But God.

So good.

"*God, honey.*"

I lost even the visual of Axl's cock (not that I was in the state to do anything with it anymore) as he slid up between my legs.

"Stay still," he rumbled.

I stayed as I was on knees and elbows.

I heard the crinkle of plastic.

Seconds later, he was inside me.

Oh yeah.

Yeahyeahyeah.

"Sit up, lose the nightie." His voice was gruff.

I pushed up on his cock and pulled off my nightie.

One of his hands trailed up my belly, my ribs and cupped my breast.

The other one just moved up, up, and around the back of my neck, into my hair, pressing my head down.

I watched my body bounce as he drove his cock up inside me.

Man, that was hot.

"Axl," I whispered.

"Fuck," he ground out, grinding something else too (*nice*), and twisting his fingers in my hair. "This mane."

He shoved me down into the bed again, coming with me, covering me, mounting me, and fucking me.

His hand at my breast went to my clit.

I bucked under him when he hit and rolled.

"That's my girl, Hattie," he grunted in my ear. "Reach for it."

"Honey," I breathed.

He went faster, deeper.

I didn't have to reach for it, my orgasm was speeding toward the finish line.

"Come, baby," he whispered in my ear.

I exploded, pounding back into him, whimpering into the sheets.

"Yeah," he groaned, pushing up to his knees, holding my hips and thrusting into me through my orgasm until he found his.

He barely finished, and I was still shaking through mine, when he pulled out, rolled me to my back, and settled his weight on me and a forearm beside me.

And he was still breathing heavily when he invited, "Feel free to use that as your way out of any and all conversations you're done having."

Not having quite caught my breath either, I still burst out laughing.

When I came out of it, he was smiling at me.

I smiled back at first.

Then I stopped and said, "I heard you."

"All right, Hattie," he said softly.

All right.

"Is there jam and butter all over the sheets?" I asked.

"I don't care," he said as answer.

"Do you have extra sheets so, since a nap is next on our agenda, we can take it, get up, shower off jam and butter and change the sheets so we can fuck again after we eat?"

His body was shaking on mine with his humor when he

answered, "Yeah. I have an extra set. Though, maybe we should shower and switch 'em out before we nap."

I smoothed my fingers along his cheekbone into his silvery hair and suggested, "Works for me. Now, let's go back to our perfect Sunday."

He moved in, touched his mouth to mine.

And agreed, "You got it."

CHAPTER FIFTEEN

Back on Track

AXL

Hattie sat beside him in his Jeep, fiddling with her phone as they drove to her father's.

"What do you think it means, two days, no stalker?" she asked the side window.

She wasn't thinking about her stalker.

She was thinking about where they were going and asking about her stalker in order to stop thinking about it.

"Babe, I'm not a stalker," he said quietly. "Got no clue what it means."

Though he did.

There were three scenarios.

One: he lost interest.

Two: he finally processed she had a man in her life, and constant protection, and he decided it wasn't worth the hassle.

Or three: he was gearing up for something big.

Obviously, Axl was pulling for one or two.

And more with the obvious, on her way to see her father with her new boyfriend was not the time to chat about it in case number three freaked her out.

"It's our perfect Sunday, yeah?" he reminded her, even though they were taking a detour from that right now.

He'd get her back to it when they got home.

"My dad tonight, your dad tomorrow night," she said softly.

"Hattie."

He sensed her turn her eyes to him.

He glanced and saw he was correct.

"Done and then done," he stated. "And just to say, I'm not gonna be a dick to your dad. I'm just gonna be honest and firm in letting him know you got a man in your life and where that man stands on how he expects the people in it to treat you."

"Okay."

She didn't sound convinced.

"You got something on your mind, now's the time to talk about it, before we walk in there," he told her.

"You know I heard all you said to me this morning," she noted.

"Yeah," he replied.

"And you know, we've been having sex, eating, snoozing, and you kicked my ass in Pac-Man again."

He grinned. "Yeah, I was there through all that."

"I'm totally practicing Pac-Man while you're at work tomorrow."

"Honey, I've had years to become a master."

"Well, your turns are very long at the video machine because of it, and as utterly fascinated as I am at witnessing your Pac-Man superiority, I have to admit that, at times, my mind may have wandered."

Ah.

"Yeah?" he prompted on a smile.

"You've said things that have made me think."

He wasn't sure if that was good or bad.

What he knew was, they didn't have two hours to go through

it. They had maybe fifteen minutes before they got to her father's.

Even so, he said, "Sock it to me," because if she needed it, he'd stop and talk to her for two hours and that was not about avoiding her dad.

It was to give her what she needed.

"One day, just, you know, on a roll, watching documentaries on Netflix, I watched the Amy Winehouse doc. Did you see that?"

"No."

"Well, we can just say it didn't depict her dad in the greatest light."

There it was.

"Okay," he said.

"Then, I don't know, it was a bummer, obviously, since she's lost to us now, and she was so amazingly talented. And Lady Gaga is so badass. So, in order to cleanse my palette, I watched Gaga's documentary. And her dad is in it. And he's awesome. Very supportive."

No.

There it was.

"Yeah," he said quietly.

"Did you see that one?" she asked.

"No, but I get you," he told her.

"I never really . . ." She paused. "It's just my life. I never really stopped to think about it."

"And now you are."

"Yes. And what you said about loyalty. I don't know if that's true."

"Baby, you go there every—"

She cut him off.

"I go there to win his approval. I'm realizing now that I'm still trying to win his approval, Axl."

Well.

Shit.

He hadn't thought of that.

"I can't say I don't love him," she carried on. "He's my dad. And like I told you, he can be charming. Funny. Not just to others, also to me. It isn't just ugliness and yuck."

Yuck.

So damned adorable.

He fought smiling.

"So, it's not all bad times," she continued. "But it isn't even that. It's just…" Another pause. "I want what I can't have because he's not going to give it to me because if he did, he'd lose his ability to control me."

Shit.

She was onto something deeper and more sinister than what he was seeing as an outsider who hadn't even met the villain yet.

"Yeah, it's why he tells you you're less when you're more," he concurred.

She didn't reply.

He reached out and touched her thigh then kept his hand there, the back of it on her jeans.

She slid her fingers around his.

He brought their hands to his leg.

"The sky is not green, it's blue," he said. "You just need to find the place where you see the color of the sky through your own eyes. You with me?"

"I'm with you."

"And it fucks me to say this, but if you got that, if you're firm in that, in understanding who you are, you can take care of him and it won't be a threat every time you go over there because he can say what he wants and it won't affect you because you'll know it's bullshit."

"*If* I go over there," she mumbled.

He felt a weird thump in his chest.

"Sorry?" he asked.

"I have a lot to think about, honey," she said. "And you're right. He messes with my head. I don't know if I can...if I..." It took her a second, but she got there, "If I can get myself straight while he's messing with my head."

Fuck, in that Jeep with her, he could not shout in triumph.

Instead, he kept a lock on it and said, "Told you, I'm here to support you. We've had to adjust that considering how shit is. But that doesn't change the support part."

She squeezed his hand. "Thanks, babe."

"And something else to think on," he continued. "It is without a doubt that our upbringing is a huge factor in the people we turn out to be. But Amy Winehouse's dad didn't pour booze down her throat to make her drink herself to death and Lady Gaga is a straight-up boss. You gotta find that line you draw where it's *you* who decides your future."

"Yeah," she said quietly.

He let it go at that, fucking elated that some of what he said was sinking in and she was reconsidering where she was at with her dad.

Her phone binged with a text and she slid her fingers from his hold to pull it out of her bag and check it.

She'd texted her father earlier to let him know she was bringing someone over while she got his dinner together.

These texts had been Axl's first experience with holding his tongue when it came to this sitch, because her father texted right back, saying he didn't want company. Thus ensued a back-and-forth of her standing her ground that Axl was coming. A back-and-forth Axl felt badly about, but he couldn't back down, because it was his opinion she shouldn't back down.

He worried, her dad knowing that the time was nigh for her being over there, that text was him giving her shit.

"Your dad?" he asked when she was moving her thumbs over the screen in reply.

"Pepper," she answered. "During your marathon turns to kick my ass in Pac-Man, I told the girls we were officially boyfriend and girlfriend in all that conveys. They're pretty excited."

At least there was something good coming over her phone.

They hit her father's house, which was small, but in a good 'hood, and there was a fairly new model, relatively stylin' Buick in the driveway.

On sight of the Buick, the question begged to be asked, why couldn't the man use that to get his own ass to the grocery store?

Even if it begged to be asked, Axl didn't ask it.

He parked.

They got out, and as Hattie made it around to his side, she rubbed her hands down the front of her jeans with nerves.

Watching her do that, the bad feelings Axl had during the text exchange came back.

And he reconsidered.

Was this knee-jerk?

He'd lost his mind when Boone told him her father had called her that name. Shy, sweet, adorable Hattie was not a whore. And no father should be flinging words at his child like that, but with Hattie in his life, he couldn't let stand hers did.

But it was more.

He saw her weeks ago in that dance studio, slamming her fists into her thighs repeatedly, harming herself.

Because she'd been harmed.

Knowing what he knew about her history with her father, when he heard the abuse was still occurring to that extreme, his first instinct was to come between it and her.

But now, with her nerves, he was concerned he was the one doing her harm.

He focused on her pretty, flowery, ruffly, girlie-as-fuck top and her tight faded jeans, as well as her high wedges, and more importantly, how she could be cute and sexy at the same time, and tried not to focus on her anxiety.

He failed.

He took her hand when she made it to him.

"Hey," he called.

Her eyes came to him.

And yep.

Now it was him that was causing her harm.

"I got caught up in my anger when I heard what your dad said to you," he told her something she knew. "And because I did, I didn't ask how you felt about me having a chat with him. But we're here and we need to have that discussion. Now, I'm prepared to go in there and have that chat with him. Or this can be a meet-the-boyfriend thing and nothing else. But it's up to you how I play it."

Surprise flashed in her eyes before she leaned his way a little and said, "I kinda made it clear at the time I wasn't a fan of what he said."

He nodded. "Then I'll make the meet-the-boyfriend play."

"No one has ever stood up for me, except Mom. Aunt Pam and Uncle Dave, even my grandparents, I knew it concerned them, and when I got older, they spoke to me about it. But when I was younger, they never did anything. Not because they were weak, or they don't love me. I think they felt their hands were tied. I think that because I could feel their frustration. Also, their relief when Mom left him, and I went with her when they divorced. My family showed me a lot of love and that was their way to make up for what he was doing. But they never stood up for me."

He wasn't sure what to do with that.

So he asked, "What are you saying?"

"I'm saying, we're official boyfriend and girlfriend now. And we should have a deal. If you let me be me, I'll let you be you.

Free to be who we are, do what we think is right, even if it's doing something for the other. In other words, if I had an issue with it, honey, I would have told you. And even as angry as you were, I sense you would have listened to me."

At first, hell no.

Later.

He hoped so.

"But more," she carried on, "I can't say it sucked you were so angry on my behalf. It didn't. Not even a little bit. And when you first told me you might come with me to share what you had to share, I wanted to see how that would go, when someone stuck up for me to Dad." Her curls slid as she tipped her head to the side. "Does that seem childish?"

"No," he said firmly.

She gave a small nod and went on.

"Even so, I think in a way we're always little kids with our parents. And because of that, they always have the ability to do good things, make us feel better when life is crap, or we want them around when we're sick because they give us comfort. But they also always have the ability to do bad, like what Dad does. On the other side of it, they always see us as their kids, and they're the authority, so they might not listen. I think he knew he hurt my feelings when he called me that. I also think he felt badly about it afterward. But from experience, that won't make it stop. Now I'm wondering, if someone else says, 'Listen, that isn't okay,' if he'll hear that and maybe realize it isn't okay and stop doing it. Or at least try."

"You have hope you can salvage shit with him," Axl murmured.

"Well…he's my dad."

Yeah.

He was her dad.

"How about we see how it plays out?" he suggested.

She smiled at him, her unease not entirely gone, but it wasn't as bad as before.

"That sounds like a plan," she agreed.

He bent to touch his mouth to hers before they walked to the front door.

She let them in.

Once in, she called, "Hey, Dad!"

There was no response.

The place was nice, not anything like Axl imagined: run-down and unkempt.

Decent furniture. Clean. Ordered.

They moved out of a small foyer into a living room and there he was in a recliner, a Rockies game on.

He turned a surly face their way and Axl was surprised again.

He was good-looking and appeared fit. He'd be tall when he stood, which was a surprise since Hattie wasn't short, but she wasn't particularly tall. Further, her dad had to be in his fifties and he was holding on to a good amount of dark in his thick hair. And his brown eyes were clear.

He wasn't sunken, sallow, over- or underweight.

And the instant his gaze hit Axl, his expression shifted.

Surprise, first.

And then ingratiating as he pushed himself up from his seat.

Hattie popped forward, still attached at the hand to him, which meant she pulled him forward.

And when she did, Don Yates's eyes fell to their hands and locked there.

"Dad, I want you to meet Axl, my boyfriend. Axl, my dad. Don Yates."

And…

Shit.

Axl thought he could call this.

But the mild tick to the man's head, the shock that registered in his expression, followed by a rush of warmth and…

Fuck.

Gratitude.

He loved his daughter.

Fuck.

Don Yates loved Hattie.

Axl didn't ask what she had texted him, but obviously she didn't share who was coming.

And now the man was meeting his girl's boyfriend. And the fact he hadn't met one since the one she had in high school had to scream this was important.

And Don Yates knew that.

It meant something to him.

It meant something his girl would bring her man to meet her dad.

Don knew he treated his daughter like garbage. He knew it was duty that brought her to his house.

And now Axl knew he played her because he'd fucked up so huge with her, he was continuing to play her to make excuses to see his girl.

Don moved forward, it was cumbersome, like his feet hurt, and he did it with his hand extended.

"Axl?" he asked as Axl let Hattie go to offer his own hand.

"Yeah, Don, nice to meet you," Axl said as they shook.

"You too, uh...yeah." He cleared his throat. "You too. Um," he looked to his daughter, "honey, why didn't you share you were bringing your boyfriend over?"

"I told you it was someone special I wanted you to meet," she replied.

"Well, yeah, darlin', but...right...okay." He returned his attention to Axl, swinging an arm to the couch that sat at corners to his recliner. "Please, have a seat."

Axl nodded but looked down at Hattie. "You gonna hang with us, baby, or get down to dinner?"

"I thought dinner," she said and turned to her father. "Sorry, Dad, but we have plans."

They did.

To eat their own dinner at his house, watch a movie, fuck and sleep.

Nothing major.

Or at least not *that* major they had to cut something as important as a Meet the Dad short.

She wanted this done.

Then she wanted out.

"You need my help?" Axl asked her.

She tipped her eyes up to him. "No, honey. You and Dad, uh...talk."

"Right," he murmured.

She again looked to her father. "I thought a pork chop with rice and some peas and corn."

"We got hot dogs in there, darlin'. And crescent rolls. How about pigs in a blanket and mac and cheese?"

Axl knew zero about diabetes, but he knew good fuel and that wasn't it.

"Dad—" she began.

"It'll be quicker and then you and your man can get on with your evening," Don said, now the thoughtful father.

She hesitated, muttered, "Okay," then asked, "You guys want a beer or something?"

"I'll have one," Don said and, magnanimous, "Axl?"

"Sure, I'll go with Hattie and bring them in," he offered.

But Don shook his head.

"No, no, sit. I'll go with my girl. Take a load off." He was pulling it together. Smiling. "Make yourself at home. I'll be right back."

With a glance to Axl, Hattie headed to an inner doorway, her father following, his hand hovering on her back like a doting dad.

Axl took his seat and it was good he had a second because he had to rethink this situation.

Because it was not a situation where he could get up, even mildly, in a dickhead father's shit for treating his daughter like crap.

This situation was something bigger and he didn't know how to proceed.

Goddamn it.

Don came back in, not at one with his body, though Axl could see, in the past, he probably was built.

On closer inspection, the guy looked older than he probably was, and he moved even older than that.

Axl partially got out of his seat to take the beer offered when Don made it to him.

He resumed his seat, Don sat, and Don started it.

"Hope you like Fat Tire."

"Don't think you're allowed to live in Colorado and not like Fat Tire," Axl replied.

A pleased smile before Don sucked back some beer.

Axl followed suit.

"So you're why my girl's not been coming around to see her old man," Don noted when he was done swallowing.

"Yeah," Axl confirmed.

"How did you two meet?" Don asked.

Now they were in Dad Interrogation Zone.

"A friend set us up."

Don nodded. "Yeah, well, yeah, that's the way it goes." His gaze moved from Axl's head to his running shoes and the interrogation continued. "What do you do for a living?"

"Contract tactical security," Axl semi-told the truth, semi-lied, using terminology the whole crew used that said some of it, not nearly all of it, was confusing and easily blown off if secondary questions came like, "What's that?" they could say, "It's complicated."

Don's eyes did the up-and-down-again thing before he murmured, "Right." Then, without asking Axl to expand on his earlier answer, "You been doin' that long?"

"Few years." Axl took a sip, swallowed and said, "I was in the army before that."

"Well, son, thank you for your service."

Never quite knowing what to say when people said that, Axl rarely said anything.

Like now.

He just jerked out his chin.

Don pressed on. "You see any action over there?"

Axl felt his neck muscles tighten. "Had a few tours."

Don looked him direct in the eyes and said quietly, "Right, son. Right."

Don then nodded, not losing eye contact, and...

Fucking hell.

"You serve?" Axl asked.

Don nodded again. "Right outta high school. Didn't know what to do with myself, enlisted. I was army too. Just did my four years and got out. Knew myself better by then."

"Yeah, tend to learn a lot about yourself when you're in."

"Yeah," Don confirmed.

"You guys doing all right?" Hattie yelled from the kitchen.

"We're good, honey!" Don yelled back, took a sip of beer and looked to his knees.

"Listen, Don—" Axl began, and Don's head shot up.

"She dances. You seen my girl dance?"

"Yes," Axl replied.

"You, uh...know *where* she dances?"

"Sat through her show last night."

Don blinked.

"She was magnificent. Danced ballet to a punk rock song," Axl told him.

Don's chin shifted to the side. "She what?"

"Joan Jett. She danced to Joan Jett and the Blackhearts. She had four other numbers last night, she's always great. But that one blew the audience away."

"I…" Don looked toward the doorway to the kitchen and back to Axl. "You're, well…good with her working there?"

"It's her life, she can do what she wants," Axl said on a shrug. "But I think she likes it better now that they've switched to a Revue. She can be creative. And she's really good at that. Shines. Headliner used to be a friend of ours, the one who set us up, Charlotte McAlister. But Hattie's the main headliner now."

"She is?"

This news visibly rocked him.

Good.

Axl nodded and drew back more beer.

Then he told him, "You should follow the club on social media. Sometimes, they post videos. Can't say I have time to check very often, but from what I've seen, management uses a lot of Hattie. She's drawing a big crowd for them. Always had a velvet rope, now they have to turn people away. Even if the cover charge has tripled."

"Well, I'll be damned," he said under his breath. He took a second to think on that, then back to a normal voice, he asked, "How long you two been seeing each other?"

"We've known each other awhile now," he hedged.

"You meet Sharon yet?"

Sharon was Hattie's mom.

He shook his head. "Not yet."

It was the first time since he met the man that he saw something overt he didn't like.

A smug smile.

He got to meet the boyfriend first, and that meant something to him, like it was a competition.

Axl had a lot of experience with that and he didn't like any of it.

"She doesn't have to go make dinner for her mom," Axl pointed out.

The smile died.

"And she asked me to spend the day with her, I promised I would, so here I am," he went on. "But thanks for letting me crash your party."

He said that last, but after what he'd said before it, it was clear that it was Don who was crashing the party.

"She takes care of her old man," Don told him.

"Unh-hunh," Axl replied. "She's a good woman."

Don looked a touch ashamed.

Hattie came in, right to Axl, sitting on the arm of the couch next to him, and sharing, "Waiting for the water to boil and the oven to heat up. We should have you sorted in about twenty minutes, Dad."

"Well, that'll be good, honey. Though, you get those pigs in the oven and the pasta on to boil, I'll finish up," Don said.

Hattie's back went straight.

"But what about cleanup?" Hattie asked.

"I'll clean up after myself tonight. You and your man go off and have fun. Okay?"

"But your fee—" she tried.

"I got it, darlin'. Okay?"

"Okay," she replied and looked down at Axl.

He shook his head slightly, indicating he hadn't gotten into it.

She then asked him, "You okay?"

He nodded, murmuring, "I'm good, baby."

Her gaze moved to the television. "How are the Rockies doing?"

"There's ups, there's downs," Don didn't exactly answer.

They all sat in uncomfortable silence before Hattie got up, saying, "Going to go check the water."

Axl watched her walk out, threw back more beer, then he made a decision.

This man loved his daughter. It was fucked up how he did, but he did.

And Hattie wanted a healthy relationship with her father.

Axl couldn't tell the future to know if that was a possibility.

Though it was more.

A good deal more.

Because, since he didn't know if that was a possibility, he also didn't know if she should continue to hope, and onward from that, if he should champion it for her, or try to find a way to cushion her by leading her to the understanding it wasn't going to happen.

And if she continued to hope, Axl wasn't certain what part he should play in helping her try to find that way.

But in the now, she had hope.

So something had to be said.

He pushed forward to sit on the edge of the couch.

He then rested his elbows to his knees and called Don's attention from the TV, saying, "Listen, Don, I gotta admit something to you."

Don looked to him, eyes wary, head tipped to the side in query.

"See, it's come to my attention you're not a big fan of where Hattie works, and you weren't real nice to her recently in how you shared that, callin' her a name."

There was surprise.

Then Don's face closed down.

Axl ignored both and kept going.

"Now, I get I'm very new on your scene, but I'm not on Hattie's." Another semi-lie. "And I hope you get where I'm comin' from, and even feel relief she's got a man in her life who would step up for her in this way. But it upset her and I'm not big on her bein' upset. Now, this isn't about comin' between a father and his daughter. This is about me looking after my woman. So I really gotta ask you to adjust the way you communicate with her so you don't do her any harm."

"I'm not sure I know what you're—"

"You called her a whore, Don."

His face got red.

"She's not a whore, Don," Axl kept at him.

He shifted in his chair, and Axl knew the bluster would come before it came.

And it came.

"She's a classically trained—"

"I know what she is. And what she's not. And I feel I gotta repeat what she's not is a whore."

"Do you have children?" Don asked.

"No," Axl answered.

"So, you don't have kids. When you do, you'll understand. You put effort into something. They put effort in it. And then—"

"This isn't about her dancing. This isn't about your hopes and dreams for her. This isn't about *her* hopes and dreams for her. You called her a whore, Don. And not only is she not that, you calling her that upset her. And I can't have that."

"I was having a bad night," Don said tightly. "I know my Hattie is no whore."

"You'll probably have more bad nights, though I hope you don't. But if you do, gotta ask you to refrain from taking it out on Hattie that way. We clear?"

Don stared hard at him.

Axl didn't know if it was about control or the new guy coming in and laying down the law or embarrassment or what it was. He was not a man like Don Yates. He'd never know.

But they went into staredown and it was a good thing.

Because Don had no choice but to take Axl in. Not only that he wasn't backing down, but everything about him.

He knew he didn't look like a guy you wanted to fuck with.

So if it ever came down to having to pick, would she choose a father who called her a whore, or a boyfriend like Axl who had her back?

Don knew the answer to that question and shared it with Axl when he said, "We're clear."

Axl quickly finished it.

"That was uncomfortable for the both of us. I just hope, when you have time to think on it, you're pleased your girl has a guy who's looking out for her."

Don nodded stiltedly, turned away and sucked down a massive slug of beer.

Axl shifted again into the couch and threw back some of his own, just not that much.

It took a few beats, and the man didn't look at him when he did it.

But he did it.

"I love her, you know."

That was currently the fuck of it.

"I know."

"I want the best for her."

"I can imagine."

Don tossed back more beer.

Axl sensed movement in the doorway to the kitchen so he looked that way and saw Hattie joining them again.

He could tell by the expression on her face that she read the room.

He shot her a smile.

It didn't work, her worry remained.

"Pasta's in, Dad," she said. "Colander in the sink. Everything's measured for you to make the cheese part. Oven timer is for the pigs. Microwave timer is for the pasta. By the time you've got the pasta together, the hot dogs should be done."

"Thanks, honey," Don muttered. "Now give your old man a buss, and you two go on with your night."

She did that, bending to kiss his cheek.

Their good-bye was awkward, Don getting up to walk them to the door, make a show all was well, Hattie anxious because she knew it wasn't.

Unfortunately, at the door she had to make it worse.

"I can't come tomorrow night again, Dad. Axl and I have, uh...plans that we can't—"

"That's okay, darlin'. I'll order some Chinese," Don assured. "Don't you worry about me. Just, uh, well...real glad you got other places to spend your nights."

Right.

Like she was coming to him because she was lonely and wanted company.

Hattie didn't call him on that.

She nodded, studying her dad closely, before she got up on her toes to kiss his cheek again, saying under her breath, "You check your sugars today?"

"I'm good, honey," Don replied.

She studied him closely again, apparently saw what she needed to see, and moved to the door.

Don didn't offer Axl his hand this time.

But Axl did.

Her father had no choice but to take it, and Axl held firm as he said, "Good to meet you, Don. Thanks for the beer."

"My pleasure." It was not. "Have a good night."

"Will do," he replied.

They were then out, and they didn't talk on the way to the Jeep.

But he was sure to hold her hand again.

He'd barely switched on the ignition when she said, "Right, from the arctic air I'm guessing it didn't go too great."

"It went. And it's done. And we're all moving on."

"Are you okay?" she asked.

"I'm fine."

"Was he okay?"

"Don't think it's a surprise that he wasn't happy the guy he just met was telling him what to do in his own house. But considering what we were talking about, he gets me, and he didn't push back."

She had nothing to say to that.

"You think you'll catch it next time," he surmised.

"I don't know. Like I said earlier, I've never had anyone stand up to him for me before, except Mom, which just started a fight."

"I'm not gonna start fighting with your dad, beautiful," he assured her.

"Yeah, it's a different thing, and I just . . . well, honey, I just have a lot to think about."

They both did.

Because he did what he had to do.

But there was something more there.

Axl just didn't know what to do with it.

One thing he did know was that, right then, he wasn't going to be able to do anything about it.

Though, there was something he could do something about.

"Ever had Coca-Cola cake?" he asked.

Her reflective air shifted to excited air.

"Are we going to a bakery?"

He grinned at her. "Yeah, the bakery that's my kitchen."

Both words were pure shock when she asked back, "You bake?"

"Sure," he said, then repeated, "Have you ever had Coca-Cola cake?"

"No."

"Well, that's too bad and we'll make that next time. This time, we're making it with Dr Pepper."

There was a smile in her voice when she said, "Sunday night baking at Axl's."

"Yep."

"Perfect," she said softly.

Yep.

And they were back on track.

CHAPTER SIXTEEN
That Path Is Always Open to You

AXL

Mid-morning the next day, Axl was in the office, Hawk was in the office, and Elvira had just walked out.

With the coast clear from Elvira sticking her nose in it (he loved the woman, and she was wise, but this was another deal and it was the kind of deal she'd sniff out in a flash and stick her nose in), Axl left his workstation and took the steps up to Hawk's space.

He knocked on the doorframe even if Hawk was already looking at him.

The man was standing because he rarely ever sat. Axl didn't know what he was doing, but whatever it was, it was on his phone because he had his cell in his hand and that hand was up.

"Yo, Axe," Hawk greeted.

"You got a minute?"

In answer, Hawk tipped his head to the chair opposite his desk and tossed his phone on the top of it.

Since Hawk rarely sat, the men who visited him didn't either.

But for this, Axl closed the door behind him after he entered, moved to a chair, and put his ass in it.

Hawk watched this, and he hesitated, but then he joined him, sitting behind his desk.

"Is everything cool?" Hawk asked.

"I got a sitch. Personal. And I was hoping you might talk it through with me. Maybe have some insight."

"Hit me," Hawk invited.

And there was one of the bennies of working for Cabe "Hawk" Delgado.

He was a good boss, generous with his knowledge, gave credit where it was due, didn't get in your face if you fucked up and held up your hand that you did...

And he had time for you even when he didn't.

"I met Hattie's dad last night."

Hawk's lips thinned.

Right.

His boss might not be in on their chats, but not much happened with his crew that Hawk didn't know about.

So he knew about Don Yates.

"I got blindsided," Axl told him.

"How?" Hawk asked.

"He loves her, Hawk."

Hawk held his gaze a beat before he sat back in his chair.

Yeah.

This was going to be a conversation.

Hawk's voice was lower when he inquired, "He loves her, and he hits her?"

Axl shook his head. "I got no excuse for that. Or the verbal abuse he keeps doling out. What I know is, recently, he called her a whore."

"Jesus," Hawk clipped.

"She didn't tell me that. She told Ryn, Ryn told Boone. And

I got it from Boone. But before..." He paused, then got to it, "I can't step in with her dad. She knows their relationship is dysfunctional. She feels beholden. I could only have her back. Until I heard that. Then I shared I was going to have to have words with her father."

"Good," Hawk murmured.

"Then I got there, and the man was practically beaming, he was so fuckin' happy Hattie brought her boyfriend over to meet him."

"Fuck," Hawk grunted.

"So we sat down. He gave me the 'What do you do for a living' and 'How'd you meet my daughter' gig. I answered. All was good. Then I told him I couldn't have him upsetting Hattie like he did by calling her a whore. He tried to explain it by saying he was in a bad mood. I told him, in future, if he was in a bad mood, he needed not to take that out on Hattie."

"On your first meeting," Hawk noted.

"On our first meeting," Axl confirmed.

"Which happened...what? How long have you been seeing her? A few days?"

"Yep."

"You laid down the law with your woman's father the first time you met him after you've been with her a few days," Hawk laid it out.

"Yep."

"Christ, Axe, you don't fuck around," Hawk muttered.

"This isn't really something you fuck around about."

"No, it isn't," Hawk agreed.

It was time to give Hawk the fullness of it.

"She goes every night to make him dinner and clean up after. She runs errands for him. He's a part of her day-to-day life. And the man I saw last night wasn't the picture of health, but he could see to himself, even with the errands. What I told her was that I was there to support whatever she felt she needed to do. But full transparency, my hope was that she'd find her way to helping him move on without him infiltrating her life on a regular basis the way he does. Now, I'm not certain."

"Men do this," Hawk stated.

"Sorry?" Axl asked.

"We see another man and the shit he's in and we don't realize we put ourselves in his shoes. Without knowing where your thoughts have turned, you're thinking, if I had a daughter and I loved her and I fucked up with her in immense and arguably unforgivable ways, I would not want the door closed to redemption."

"That makes sense," Axl said.

"Is Hattie an only child?" Hawk queried.

"Yeah."

"And her father is ill?"

"Diabetes that he doesn't manage very well."

"So she'll manage it for him," Hawk deduced.

"Correct. But he has a nice house. A newish car in the drive. She says he has a job where he works from home and makes good money. She started dinner, he was down to finish it and clean up after so we could get on with our plans. She's had to skip a few nights with him last week, but neither he nor his home looked neglected in any way. He doesn't walk freely, but he can have groceries delivered. He can also drive through a pharmacy."

"It's bullshit."

Axl nodded once. "It's control. She knows it. We've had some talks. She's thinking on things and part of what she's thinking is she wants to pull back from him so she can get her head straight about what he's done to her and how it continues to affect her."

"And now that you know he has genuine healthy feeling for her, you're not sure that's the right path."

"That's why I'm talking to you. I honestly don't know where to go from here. Again, Hattie and I are new. We've talked about the mental abuse, but not him hitting her. But needless to say, because there was both, it seemed cut and dried."

"And now it's complicated."

"Now it's complicated," Axl affirmed.

"Have you spoken to her about where the dad might be at?"

Axl shook his head. "No, I didn't want to give her hope because even with all that, she wants what everyone wants. Her dad to be a good dad."

Hawk gave it only a beat.

Then he broke it down.

"First, as an only child with a father who has a chronic illness, one as significant as diabetes, it is inevitable there will come a time where he will need her. And if she feels she must do what she's currently doing, which she does, because she's doing it, she'll feel duty bound to meet those needs when they become more considerable. But it is my strong opinion that now is absolutely not that time. She needs to wean him off her. And that isn't about abuse. It's not about control. It's about dysfunction in a family unit that needs to be rectified. She will be in her twenties and falling in love once in her life. She doesn't need a family member sucking her time and energy when she should be enjoying being young and falling in love."

Falling in love.

"And straight up," Hawk continued before Axl could recover from the velvet hit of those three words. "The man isn't ninety, but he is ill. He's got a life to live that is likely going to be abbreviated by his condition. So he needs to be encouraged to live it."

"Yeah," Axl grunted, still stuck on the thought of Hattie falling in love.

With him.

Which he was doing with her.

He'd just not consciously acknowledged it.

"The second is harder, which is why you're here," Hawk

carried on. "But if you had no problem getting down to important business on your first meeting with this guy, I'd find your times to continue to go over when she's with him. Regardless of the rocky start, try to establish a relationship with him. And then point out, if he loves his daughter, he should get his head out of his fuckin' ass and put the work in to build a relationship with her that isn't based on shit."

"Yeah," Axl repeated.

"That's harder, Axe, 'cause you can't go in there doing that without her knowledge. Which means you gotta point out to Hattie in the middle of sorting her head out about past and current issues that there's healthy emotion mixed in that. And since there is, you think it's worthwhile you both work on him in coaxing it out."

Hawk leaned forward.

Because he wasn't done.

"But you gotta be certain you're at one with thinking it's worthwhile to coax it out," he warned. "If you're not, then you should keep doin' what you're doing. Support what she feels she has to do, and step in when he crosses a line."

"Right," Axl said.

Hawk's gaze remained steady on Axl.

"It's been a rough road for you with her, what she experienced growing up, even when you got together, it wasn't going to be easy," Hawk remarked. "Still, sucks to hear that it's not only not easy, but also confusing."

"Definitely sucks," Axl agreed. "Though, appreciate you talkin' it out with me."

Hawk sat back again and replied, "Anytime."

Axl stood.

Surprisingly, Hawk didn't.

"Again, gratitude," Axl said. "I was at a loss. Now I'm not. It's important so it's good to have a path."

Hawk nodded.

Axl moved to the door.

"Axe?" Hawk called.

He turned to his boss.

And it felt like someone punched him in the sternum when he saw the look on Hawk's face.

A look he couldn't quite read.

But he could feel it.

"You know what fucks me?" Hawk asked quietly.

"No," Axl forced out.

"That you came to me with this."

And a sock to the gut.

"Sorry, I—"

"No," Hawk bit off. "That you came to me because you can't go to your dad. That fucks me, Axl. Because I'm honored you felt safe sitting across from me and talking this through. But you should feel safe with your dad. You do not. And that pisses me right the fuck off."

Axl said nothing.

He felt a number of things.

But he said nothing.

Hawk did.

"I got two boys," Hawk told him something he knew. "If I knew Asher or Bruno went to another man for advice on anything, something important like this, or which protein powder worked best, I fuck you not, I'd die a little inside."

It wasn't easy, but Axl swallowed.

"What I'm sayin' is, I get you're flyin' blind with this," Hawk continued. "You don't have a father who acts as a foundation for you, Hattie doesn't either, so you gotta search for the path forward rather than knowing it or having your personal path lead to your father's door for guidance. So I'm glad you took the time to come up here, man. I just caution you to realize you are lacking the same thing Hattie is and don't get lost in that. You made the right choice today, coming up here. And as shit progresses with Hattie's dad, remember, that path is always open to you. I don't have all the answers. What I will always have is the time to listen and work shit through."

His throat feeling tight, Axl nodded.

Hawk was older, but not old enough to be his father.

But fuck, he was glad he'd found a man like Hawk to be his mentor.

"Right. Later, Axl," Hawk finished it for both of them.

"Later, Hawk."

And with them exchanging chin lifts, Axl walked out of Hawk's office.

CHAPTER SEVENTEEN

Two Drawers

AXL

That evening, twenty minutes later than he wanted to do it, Axl walked in from his garage, calling, "Hattie, baby, I'm home."

And within seconds, Hattie came flying into the kitchen, barefoot, wearing a long, yellow dress with little white flowers on it. It was fitted to her torso, had ruffles for the short sleeves, a flowy skirt and a slit up to the knee on her left leg.

Her hair was piled on top of her head and her face was panicked.

"Okay, I thought I had it together, but I didn't," she announced. "So I made Sly go shopping with me today and I bought seven dresses. I've switched out which one so many times, I think Sly might beg Brett to be taken off Hattie Detail. But I think this is the one. What do you think?"

He didn't tell her what he thought.

He told her what he knew.

"You look beautiful."

"No, seriously, what do you think?"

Axl was confused seeing as he'd just answered that question.

"Honey, you look beautiful."

Looking down at herself, she shifted her hips side to side, which meant the skirt drifted around her legs.

Axl was watching that as she asked, "Is it too casual?" Then she decided for him. "It's too casual. It doesn't say Cherry Creek."

He tore his eyes from her hips and stated firmly, "Hattie, look at me."

She looked at him.

"You. Look. Beautiful," he declared.

She kept gazing at him for a few beats before she said, "Okay. *Phew*. Now, hair up or down?"

He didn't hesitate. "Down."

"Right!" she for some reason cried loudly, then rushed out of the room, her skirt flying out behind her.

He found her in the bathroom, leaning over the sink, yanking something out of her hair.

It came tumbling down.

Well, hell.

That went straight to his dick.

He had to shower, and they had to get on the road. They didn't have time for a quick fuck.

"Babe, I need to shower."

She turned to him. "If my hair is down, I need product. And fiddle time. Are you okay to shower with me in the bathroom?"

"Of course."

She grinned at him. "Then shower."

And back she went to her hair.

He moved to his room, pulled off his clothes, tossed them on the chair, boots and socks remained on the floor, then walked naked back into the bathroom.

She turned to him again, her eyes doing a full body scan, but sticking on his cock.

This meant he got behind her, fit himself to her body, bent

in and kissed her neck, getting a whiff of her perfume, feeling his cock stir (again), and he said in her ear, "You can have it later."

"Mm," she hummed.

He kissed her neck again then went to the shower.

When he got out, Hattie was still at the sink fucking around with her hair, but now she was doing it with Cleo sitting on the bathroom counter, tail swishing, staring at her in fascination.

Axl didn't question that.

He understood a fascination with Hattie's curls.

But when he reached for a towel, Cleo remembered nothing fascinated her. And doing so, she tossed him a look, jumped down, and Axl stopped and stared as she ran her body along the backs of Hattie's legs as she strutted out.

"Jesus, what'd you do to my cat?" he asked.

"Well, as she's a girl," Hattie told the mirror, "and I'm a girl, I realized the best way to win any girl over was to offer her girl time." She stopped fucking with her hair and turned fully to him. "In other words, I took some time with Cleo, and she and I had a chat which was mostly me chatting, and Cleo snarfing down a bowl of tuna."

"In short, you bribed her with food."

"Totally."

Axl chuckled.

Hattie leaned a hip against the basin and watched him towel off.

"Babe, it'll take me five minutes to dress and we need to be out the door in five minutes. I don't have time to fuck you which means we don't have any for you to change your mind seven more times about your dress, or your shoes, or—"

"I got it, I got it," she said, whirled, her skirt flew, and she was out the door.

He seriously wished he had that twenty minutes he'd wanted to have before they needed to leave when he walked from the hall, dressed in jeans and a white button-down, his shoes in his hand, to see Hattie rise from the bed wearing a pair of high-heeled yellow sandals with a thin ankle strap, a little gold at her throat and wrist, and a sheen of gloss on her lips.

He'd woken her up to fuck her that morning before he had to get up and shower, then leave.

With Sly at the door to take duty, he'd left her in his bed.

That fuck, officially, wore off the minute he saw her in those shoes with that lip gloss.

Now he was wishing even more than he did before—and he wanted this visit out of the way, but he'd never been looking forward to it—that he hadn't caved when his mother pushed for this dinner.

He beat back the need to at the very least kiss her, and hard, which he knew would lead to them both wanting other things, which in turn would mean his resolve would buckle, and he got on with putting on his shoes.

She grabbed her purse. He grabbed her hand.

And at the door to the garage, he called, "Later, Cleo."

Nothing.

"Later, shmoochmagooch," Hattie called.

A distant meow.

"Shmoochmagooch?" he asked.

"During our chat I learned she likes baby talk," she told him.

Fucking hell.

This made him grin and he kept doing it even when he was backing them out of the garage.

Bad news, they were on their way and it was always a crapshoot with his dad how things would go.

Good news, Hattie seemed a lot calmer than when he walked into the house.

"You good?" he asked to confirm.

"Absolutely not. I'm totally freaking out," she answered.

He glanced at her and saw none of that.

"You seem good," he noted.

"I'm faking it."

Back came his grin.

"Honey, it's gonna be okay."

"Mm-hmm."

"It is. Most importantly, it's going to happen, and that means eventually it'll be over, we'll be home, and it'll be behind us."

"Smart advice. I will now commence visualizing the ride home." She then put her hands up at her sides, tip of her thumb to tip of her middle finger, and she began chanting, "*Om*."

Now he wasn't grinning.

He was laughing.

Fuck, she was something.

Yeah.

Cute girls totally did it for him.

She stopped chanting, dropped her hands and asked, "How was your day?"

"I had duty at the monitors," he shared. "We take turns having to sit there and stare at them. I got three days of that and then I'm back out from behind my workstation. Which I already know will be the best day of the week."

"Man of action," she noted.

"Definitely not a man of sitting on my ass all day," he replied.

She didn't say anything, and at a glance, he saw her lips tipped up, looking amused, staring out the windshield.

It was a good segue, so he took it.

"Sometimes, depending on what jobs we're on, I got night duty doing that," he told her.

"All right," she said.

"That's not a problem?" he asked.

"Honey, I work nine to two in the morning. Is that a problem?" she asked back.

"No."

"I can hardly be ticked at you that you have to work nights when I work nights."

Right.

"Yeah," he said through his chuckles. When he stopped chuckling, he asked, "Did you get to your studio today?"

"I was in the middle of a tourney of Pac-Man with Sly, and, by the way, he's nowhere near as good as you, so I kicked his ass, when I decided the dress I picked to meet your folks in didn't work. We went to four stores. Sly carries a gun. That's the only reason it wasn't five. I felt the need to make up for it, so I took him to Cherry Cricket for lunch. He was feeling the burn of me kicking his ass so he forced a short first to win two takes it all at the video machine, which I won. Commence freak-out about the dress, because I decided on a red one, but obviously, since I'm not wearing it, it wouldn't do. So that would be a no on the studio."

"Maybe tomorrow," he replied.

They fell into a comfortable silence, and during that silence, Axl contemplated two things.

One, it was nice coming home to her.

Two, they were falling in love with each other.

With this in mind, he told her, "I've never lived with a woman."

"Pardon?"

"I've never lived with a woman," he repeated.

"Um…okay."

"That said, my last long-term relationship, she was over a lot. We both preferred my place when one of us slept over. So I gave her a drawer."

"A drawer," she said, partly contemplative, partly teasing. "That's big stuff."

"I thought it was. She was ticked it was just a drawer."

"If I had a diary, and therefore wrote in a diary, and you gave me a drawer, I'd have to go out and buy heart stickers and glitter washi tape so I could fully commit my 'Dear diary, today, Axl gave me a drawer,' memory as it deserved."

He started laughing again.

"I haven't lived with a guy either," she told him.

"Seems so far we're both naturals," he remarked.

A wave of warmth hit him from the passenger side of the vehicle.

He then saw her out of the corner of his eye move in so she could kiss his jaw.

She sat back and it took a minute before she queried, "Can I ask why you mentioned that?"

"Never in my life came home to a woman."

Hattie didn't respond.

"Been comin' home to you now for days, didn't think on it, all that was going on. Had a second to think on it, and I like it. So I thought you should know."

At that, she pushed the limits of her seatbelt again to give him another kiss on the jaw, this time wrapping her hand around the other side of his neck to give him a squeeze.

He felt her touch and smelled her perfume.

Yeah.

He liked her in his Jeep too.

Axl enjoyed her kisses, but he decided not to share that in case she did it again, and her touch prompted more action, the kind where he'd turn around and dis his mother on dinner.

They drove the rest of the way, back in their comfortable silence.

Until he pulled into his parents' side drive.

"Holy crap," she whispered.

As they passed by, he studied the sprawling house with its red brick, black shutters, white woodwork, and curved portico.

The green lawn was perfectly manicured. The front hedges flawlessly clipped. The dual elms on either side of the front of the house mature and towering.

An opinion on something Axl had never considered hit him with a surety that surprised him.

He hated his parents' home.

It was classic, pompous, had zero uniqueness, no personality, and the best things you could say about it were that it was big, it was sturdy, and at a push, it was stately.

But it was boring.

If you had to guess who lived in that house, you'd probably say conservative, elderly and uptight.

Except the elderly, all true.

He drove around back to the huge area that included four garage doors, an archway covered in some flowering plant that didn't quite hide the pool and tennis court beyond and the small detached mother-in-law house where his mom and dad's assistant/housekeeper lived.

And he hadn't felt the feeling he was feeling as he parked since his dad reamed his ass in front of his teammates and coaches for coming in second in the hundred-yard dash in regionals his sophomore year.

But he knew what the feeling was.

He was embarrassed.

"Okay, so your dad isn't like, a successful attorney. He's, like, a super-duper, mega successful attorney," Hattie noted.

"We'll just say his firm does the very least pro bono work they can do and not look like complete assholes rather than total assholes. Every hour is a billable hour. And he works a lot."

"Axl," she called, her voice searching, soft.

He turned to her to see her gaze the same as her voice.

"Are you okay, honey?" she asked.

Shit.

He wasn't.

"We do it, it's done," he said.

She let her seatbelt go that time, came in and touched her glossed lips to his.

She pulled back, still staring into his eyes.

"There's one thing I already know I'll always love about your parents. They made you."

Fucking fuck.

Another punch right to the sternum.

She read his intent before he did what he intended.

He knew it when she ordered, "Don't mess up my lip gloss."

"I'm gonna mess up your lip gloss, beautiful," he warned.

And then he did.

When he was done, he wiped his mouth on the back of his hand as she reapplied.

They got out of the Jeep, walked to the house and went in the back door, which led them into the massive kitchen.

And to his mother hovering while Lisa, their woman who did everything, was cooking.

This was something else that hit him as a surprise, like a shot.

His mom was just his mom. He'd always thought she was beautiful in a detached way any kid would think their mom was beautiful.

But as he took her in right then, he saw she really was something.

Tall, blonde, features that were classically attractive, she'd always been slender. Though the last year or so he'd noticed abstractedly that she'd been putting on weight, it looked good on her. It made her look healthier. Even more animated.

And in the moment of coming to this realization, Axl noted something else.

Her clothes were more casual than usual.

Hattie and he were dressed more formally than she was, something Axl hadn't noticed his mother ever do "in company." And they would consider the first visit with Hattie to be having company.

She was wearing pressed chinos, a crisp white Oxford shirt with the collar popped and a pair of neutral flats.

He knew the shoes were Louboutin, but unless someone recognized the style, or saw the lipstick-red sole, they wouldn't.

What they weren't were Chanel, his father's preferred footwear (and accessories) for his mother.

And that was so much so, even Axl knew it. He couldn't count how many times he'd heard his father say, "Rachel...no. You need to go back and put on the Chanel."

There was something almost rebellious about those Louboutins.

And definitely the chinos.

"Sweetheart," she greeted, moving direct to him while smiling at him, at the same time darting curious glances to Hattie.

"Ma," he greeted back.

She arrived at him and did the mother thing with her hands on his shoulders. He put one to her waist and bent down for her to kiss his cheek.

He straightened and put a little pressure in his hand as he turned them to Hattie.

"Mom, this is Hattie Yates. Hattie, baby, this is my mom, Rachel Pantera."

Hattie had a hand up and a smile on her face that did not look fake, but he could tell by the stiff line of her neck and shoulders that she was nervous.

"Mrs. Pantera, really lovely to meet you."

"Hattie, please call me Rachel," his mom invited, taking her hand then covering it with her other and holding it. "Nice to meet you too, and what an amazing dress. So effortless but so chic."

"Wow, thank you, Mrs.... sorry, Rachel."

Before Axl could introduce Hattie to Lisa, his father made his entrance.

"Did I hear...?"

Axl tensed when he heard his dad's booming courtroom voice.

"...Axl's Jeep?" The man appeared in the kitchen. "Yes! There's m'boy."

And then there was his father.

To make certain you didn't miss how important he was, he hadn't changed from work. His look gave the implication he'd just arrived home, shrugged off his suit jacket and pulled off his tie. But never fear, he'd arrived in the nick of time.

Axl had inherited a good deal from his father. Not just the dark hair turned silver early, but also his height, his build and his blue eyes.

His mom moved away from Hattie and immediately Hattie edged closer to Axl.

So close, her shoulder brushed his.

He slid his arm around her waist.

"My God, look at you," Sylas Pantera said to Hattie. "Aren't you a pretty little thing?"

Every fiber of muscle in Axl's body strung tight.

She wasn't a fucking pretty fucking *little* fucking *thing*.

Fuck.

Right off the bat, reductive language to put Hattie in her place.

So yeah.

It was going to be one of those nights.

Fuck.

"Mr. Pantera," Hattie forged in, not leaving Axl's side but lifting her hand Sylas's way.

His dad waved in front of himself, booming, "No, no, no. Sylas. Call me Sylas."

Then he took her by the shoulders, pulled her from Axl's hold and bent down to kiss her cheek.

He let her go and Axl instantly claimed her again.

"Kid," Sylas greeted him.

"Dad," Axl replied.

"You look fit," Sylas stated.

"You do too," Axl returned.

"Work good?"

"The usual."

His father's mouth tightened.

Work was a thorny subject, mostly because his dad didn't exactly know what Axl did, and even if he did, he wouldn't know exactly what that entailed because Axl couldn't tell him.

And Sylas didn't like not knowing things.

So much so, there was a likelihood that his father had Hawk's operations investigated. He had an in-house investigator, and as named partner, his father wouldn't hesitate to use firm resources as he saw fit.

But even if he did, there was only so much to be discovered.

And Sylas would know just how much was not.

"I guess that's good," Sylas said tightly. "Now, are we going to stand in the kitchen all night, or am I making cocktails?"

"I could use a cocktail, darling," his mom put in.

"Always," Sylas returned, with an ogle to Hattie and then a dismissive, "It's martini time."

Rachel swayed back an inch at the not-so-veiled insult couched in an inference his mother had a problem with alcohol.

Something, to Axl's knowledge, she did not have.

Axl fought punching his father in the throat.

Hattie forged into the breach.

"I love martinis too, Rachel. Are you vodka or gin?"

"She's both if it has an alcohol content," Sylas answered for his wife.

And there it was again.

What the fuck?

Dots of pink hit Rachel's cheeks, she didn't quite hide the side eye she shot at her husband, and Hattie's fingers curled over Axl's at her waist.

That was when he realized how hard they were digging in.

He released the pressure and dropped his head to look at her.

"Sorry," he muttered.

"Don't be," she whispered back, keeping her fingers around his.

"What's this?" Sylas asked.

"Nothing," Axl said shortly. "I could use a martini too."

Sylas looked to Hattie and jerked a thumb at Axl. "Gotta get this kid to start drinking scotch. Now, that's a man's drink."

Hattie, doing her best to defuse the tension, shot him a bright, playful smile. "Well, Sylas, James Bond drinks martinis and I'm relatively sure everyone thinks he's pretty danged manly."

"Yes, but he's fictional," Sylas parried.

And then Hattie did something brilliant.

She capitulated immediately, stating "Touché," in a way she made it clear she couldn't give fewer fucks about what Sylas thought was a manly drink, so she certainly wasn't going to argue about it.

Which brought Sylas up short, physically.

His body jerked with it.

Done with him, Hattie looked to his mom.

"Rachel, this *kitchen*. It's *amazing*. I hope we have time tonight for a tour of your home."

"How about we do that now while Sylas is making our martinis?" Rachel invited. His mom looked to his dad. "And mine will be *vodka*, Sylas. Like it always is."

Hattie, looking up at Axl, began, "Oh, I don't—"

She didn't want to leave him with his father.

"Go, honey," he encouraged. "Vodka or gin?"

"Vodka."

"Olive or a twist?"

"Either," she replied, squeezing his hand and then smiling gamely at his mom as she let him go and moved out of the curve of his arm.

Axl stuck close in order to say hello while Rachel introduced Hattie to Lisa.

Then the women took off and Axl followed his dad into the library, which was where he kept their drinks cabinet, so it was where they did a lot of their entertaining.

This so he could thrill people with his massive book collection that covered the floor-to-ceiling shelves on all the walls, impress with his baseball signed by Johnny Bench or bask in the gasps when people noticed his Chihuly Persian set.

"You really want a martini?" Sylas asked, picking up the shaker.

"I really want a martini. Vodka. Olive. Dirty. Same for Hattie."

His dad prepped to mix, but after he had the ice in, the olive juice, he reached to the vodka and looked to Axl. "You didn't know which she preferred."

"I don't know if she likes celery or how she feels about the polar ice caps melting either. We haven't been married for five years. But I'll find out."

"How long have you been seeing her?"

Long enough she's living with me, about four days.

That would make his father's head explode, and as such, he wanted to say it, but since he wasn't five, he didn't.

"Not long," he said instead.

"Not long," Sylas repeated under his breath. "It's like pulling teeth."

"We're new, Dad. Mom called to ask me over to dinner. I let it slip that I'd met someone special who I think is important and Mom wanted to meet her. So Hattie's here. And I'd appreciate it if you'd be cool while she is."

"I'm always cool," Sylas replied.

"Calling her a pretty little thing isn't cool."

Sylas stopped pouring Cîroc and lifted his brows at Axl. "She's pretty, and my guess, she's eight inches shorter than you, if she wasn't wearing those heels, so that's little."

Axl drew in a deep breath, turned his head to look out the window, then he went to a couch and folded his body in it.

"You've always been so fucking sensitive," Sylas said in a voice that it was like he didn't want Axl to hear what he said, but he absolutely wanted Axl to hear what he said.

He should let it go.

He did not let it go.

"Could it be, with a woman who is right now touring my parents' home with *my mother*, which means she's important to me, that I'm sensitive to the fact that I want her to like my parents?"

"I can't imagine why she wouldn't like us."

"You've never been called a pretty little thing. If you were, you might reconsider that opinion."

Sylas stopped fixing the top on the shaker, set it down and turned fully to Axl.

And the games were about to begin.

He was not proved wrong.

"Well, fuck, my boy's one of those enlightened men who maybe shouldn't call themselves men."

"Only you could take the word *enlightened* and make it seem like a bad thing."

"It is when it really means you're a pussy."

"We're done."

Axl didn't say that.

Hattie did.

His head jerked toward the sound of her voice and he saw her standing in the doorway with his mother, both their faces flushed with anger.

Surprisingly, since she'd shown so little emotion around his father for as long as he could remember, his mother looked ready to detonate.

But Hattie...

Jesus.

Hattie.

She turned to Rachel and said, "I'm so, so sorry." And then to Axl, she stated, "Axl, I'd like to go home now."

He rose from the couch, having no clue how to play this, considering he was falling in love with her and she was going to eventually have to have a relationship with his parents.

Though he was leaning toward getting the fuck out of there and trying it again once his father got his shit together.

But Sylas moved to the center of the room, and in a cajoling voice said, "I know what that must have sounded like. You don't understand. My son and I have a certain kind of banter."

"Well, regardless that it didn't sound at all like banter, I know you used the word *pussy* in a derogatory way, and since I have one, and it's rather precious to me, I find that offensive," Hattie returned.

Axl had to look to his feet to concentrate on not shouting with laughter or walking across the room to give her a high five.

He lifted his head when Hattie continued.

"But that's beside the point. Your son means a great deal to me. He's a really good man. He's funny and he's sweet and he's insightful and he treats me with kindness and respect. He's protective and he's supportive. And he's a fantastic cook. And if you think all of that is 'pussy,' well, I agree. Because it's pretty damned fantastic, if you ask me."

"Brava, Hattie," Rachel crowed.

Hattie's body jolted like she had no idea anyone else was in the room.

"Sylas, apologize to Hattie," Rachel demanded.

His dad knew many things, as he'd be the first to tell you, and one of them was: when you face a surprising adversary, you use any means available to find a way to best them.

This time, he picked contrition and charm.

"You're absolutely right, Hattie. For too long that word has been used egregiously, and it was equally crass, my usage of it."

He went for the gusto, putting his hand on his chest. "Sincerely, I apologize."

"It wasn't me you were baiting," Hattie returned.

Well, shit.

Axl couldn't stop smiling.

His father turned to him and the skin around his eyes was tight.

Yep.

Axl was probably going to smile all night.

"Sorry, kid, I took that too far."

"You did," Axl agreed.

"Okay then," Rachel said loudly, taking hold of Hattie and moving her into the room. "That's done. How about we move on? Hattie," she looked to his woman, "I understand if you're uncomfortable, but really, we'd like you to stay. And I promise, Sylas *can* behave himself."

She ended that on a look at his father that Axl had never seen.

It was so pointed and sharp, it was a miracle Sylas didn't start bleeding.

Hattie looked at Axl and she did it hard.

"I'm good, baby," he said.

She instantly turned to his mother. "We'll stay."

Okay, yeah.

He knew it before.

He knew it a fuckuva better right then.

He was totally fucking falling in love with this unbelievably kickass woman.

Hattie moved from his mom to him.

"Finish the martinis, Sylas," Rachel hissed, walking toward her husband.

"At your service," he muttered, an edge to his tone, and he was heading back to the drinks cabinet.

Axl sensed that wasn't about what just happened.

But what just happened didn't help.

He was watching his parents when he felt Hattie's fingers close around his.

So he tipped his head down to catch her gaze.

He then bent and kissed her neck so he'd be in position to whisper in her ear, "Proof, beautiful. You're goddamned remarkable."

She pulled her head back to look into his eyes.

And then she said out loud, "You are too."

After that, she yanked him down on the couch so forcefully, another ounce of pressure, she'd dislocate his shoulder. And once they were down, she practically fused herself to his side, which made Axl's stomach hurt from trying to fight laughter.

She then pinned her eyes on his mom.

"So, Rachel, Axl tells me you were a software wizard before he came into the world. Axl and I have a mutual friend, she's studying to be an engineer. She knows everything about computers. I bet she'd love to chat with you about all things tech."

His mother appeared startled, as she would be, seeing as nothing in this house was ever about her, before her face warmed. "I'd...well, I'd love that."

Hattie smiled gorgeously at her.

"I'll bet, when she finds a job, they won't make her wear skirts and hose to work," Rachel commented.

Hattie leaned slightly forward, and openly horror-struck, said, "*No*. They made you wear hose? Really? That's almost barbaric."

Both women burst out laughing.

Axl shifted back because his father's arm was in his face, extending a martini toward Hattie.

She took it and spared him only a glance, saying, "Thanks, Sylas. You're a doll."

At once, she returned her attention to Rachel and started gabbing.

Axl watched her, settling into the couch, sliding an arm around her to settle her with him, feeling his lips twitch.

Yeah.

Hattie Yates was something.

And that something was fucking amazing.

*   *   *

She moved on top of him, her arms wrapped around his shoulders, stroking his cock with her pussy, his mouth drawing at her nipple.

She was moving slow, like she wanted him to feel every centimeter of her as she took him.

And, oh yeah.

He felt it.

She was making love to him.

And after the things she said about him to his father, Axl was not down with that.

So he gripped her behind a knee, lifted it, released her sweet, tight nipple from his mouth and rolled them so she was on her back and he was the one on top doing the stroking.

Slow.

Making love to her.

His sweet Hattie who showed zero hesitation in taking on a hellcat.

For him.

She pressed her legs to his sides, her hands roamed his back, over his neck, his hair, but they stopped with her fingers on his cheeks.

"So handsome," she whispered.

He showed her how he felt about that by kissing her.

The warm, wet generosity of her mouth paralleled what he felt between her legs.

It was the first time he'd had her ungloved.

Her suggestion, after she shared she kept up to date on a birth control shot and he shared he hadn't gone in ungloved since his last long-term girlfriend, but Hawk required biannual physicals, his last was six weeks ago, and he'd come up clean.

He knew she'd decided the time to dispense with the condoms was now because she experienced what she experienced with him that night.

She wanted them close.

She wanted to give him that.

Nothing in between.

And for a variety of reasons, that felt *great*.

He broke their kiss when her hands went to his ass, no roaming, it was a demand.

He nipped her earlobe and moved faster.

She responded by hooking a leg around the back of his thigh, putting her other foot to the bed, and pulsing up into each thrust.

Fuck yeah.

"So sweet, baby," he murmured against her lips.

She kissed him.

He went faster, she encouraged it every way she could, pushing him to the edge.

He sensed she wasn't there, and he needed her there.

So he slid a hand between them, pressed and twitched her clit with his thumb, as he went faster, harder, and she gasped against his tongue when she came.

He slid his lips to her throat, but his head jerked back when it hit him, suddenly, unexpected.

Hard.

So hard, he only vaguely felt her proprietary grip on the back of his neck and her satisfied, "Oh yes," seemed far away.

His orgasm receded as fast as the shock of it coming, which meant he collapsed on her, but at least he had the presence of mind to roll them so she didn't have to bear his weight for very long.

Their breath evened out while she was touching him, tasting him.

He did the same.

Sometimes you said a lot with no words at all.

This was one of those times.

Even though she'd never done it before, Axl knew what it meant when she trailed a thumb along his throat to his chin, along his jaw and kissed his ear when her thumb arrived there.

He let his hands fall away.

She slid off him and out of bed.

Since it was her first time, he didn't know where she was at with cleanup, if she wanted privacy or not. So he lay in bed, waiting for her to finish in the bathroom, instead of joining her.

When he saw her enter the room, he got out of bed. They met halfway, touched lips, and he hit the bathroom, cleaned her from his cock, quickly brushed his teeth, and headed out.

She was in bed in a nightie, and he knew, panties. She didn't sleep bare in any way.

He didn't either, so he pulled on some sleep pants.

He joined her and tangled them up.

She cuddled closer, tucking her face in his throat.

"You felt really good tonight, baby," he said quietly into her hair.

"You always feel really good, baby," she replied.

He grinned. "I meant, it was nice to have you like that."

He meant more than dispensing with the prophylactics.

"Yeah," she whispered.

She knew what he meant.

He gave her a squeeze with his arms.

"Thanks for having my back with Dad."

"Mm," she hummed.

She did not like his dad. She didn't warm up to him once all night. No matter how obsequious Sylas was being, she put up with him and that was it.

It was his father's loss.

Then again, his dad had been losing out on a lot for as long as Axl could remember.

Through this, his mother was entirely unoffended.

In fact, Hattie and his mom bonded.

Extreme.

He liked it.

But there was something he didn't like.

"I think something's up with him and Mom."

"Mm," she repeated, but it was different.

"What?" he asked.

"I don't know," she answered.

"You kind of know," he returned.

She tipped her head back. "Tonight was rough for you."

"Tonight was worse than sometimes, not the worst it's been. It's annoying but I'm used to it and it's annoying *because* I'm used to it."

She nodded against the pillow. "I feel that."

Yeah, she did.

"You mention that because . . .?" he prompted.

She was hesitant when she said, "I don't know how raw you are."

"She's done with him," he stated.

She pressed her lips together tight and lifted her brows.

Yeah.

His mother was done with his dad.

Hattie could even read it and she barely knew them.

"Thank fuck I don't have a guest room," he muttered.

She grinned up at him. "Your mom gives me the impression she can take care of herself."

He didn't know about that.

"You haven't mentioned anything about this being a possibility. Is this out of the blue for you?" she asked.

"I would have wanted her to leave him twenty years ago. She just seemed like she was so stuck in it, she was never getting out."

"Maybe something happened," she suggested.

"He tends not to dig in with her. Tonight, he dug in. She seemed surprised he did it in front of you. But I'm not sure she was surprised he was doing it. They weren't at each other's throats, but it was clear it took effort for them to even be civil."

Hattie had nothing to say to that.

So they had his mom gearing up to do whatever she might be doing, Hattie's dad maybe being someone worthwhile, and Axl and his teammates were on a stalled mission to root out a pack of dirty cops.

"At least your stalker seems to have lost interest," he remarked.

"You think?" she asked.

"It's been a minute," he said. "I told Hank and Eddie about it, gave them the pictures. I'll call a meet. Sit down with them and Hawk. Ask their take."

"'Kay."

She sounded like she was getting sleepy.

He shifted so she had some of his weight and they were closer.

"You take a stalker in stride," he murmured.

"I have people looking out for me," she replied.

Definitely sleepy.

"Yeah, you do, baby. Go to sleep."

"'Kay," she repeated.

"Hattie?" he called.

"Yes?"

"We feel you're clear from this guy fuckin' with you, and you wanna go home, I'm givin' you two drawers here, and I want one at your place."

Her body tensed, then relaxed.

Completely.

"Two drawers. I need a diary," she mumbled.

He chuckled.

She pressed her face in his neck.

Not long after, they were both asleep.

CHAPTER EIGHTEEN

Off

HATTIE

I was in my bed in a post-sex haze when suddenly I was no longer in bed.

Well, half of me wasn't.

My upper half was in Axl's arms and his face was buried deep in my neck.

It felt like he was giving me a hickey, I liked that feeling, then he sank his teeth in, and I liked that feeling *so much* better.

After he did that, he growled in my ear, "Creamer."

I smiled.

Pulling my head back, he got my message and lifted his to catch my gaze.

"Take care of my guy," I whispered.

He watched my lips speak before he kissed me hard and closed mouthed when I was done.

He let me go, touched his lips to my temple and then he was off the bed again and heading to the steps to my living area.

I settled back down and watched him go.

It was Friday morning, and after dinner with his folks on Monday, it had been an eventfully uneventful week.

Quick catch-up:

Nothing happened Tuesday, except when I went over to take care of Dad, he seemed reserved. Not unfriendly. Just quiet and in his head.

Which I guessed I should have expected.

Wednesday, when there was still no more from my stalker, and since I wanted to get in my studio—and honestly, I really liked Sly, he was funny and sweet, even if it was likely he might engage in criminal activities—but I didn't know if I could create with him there.

But I wasn't feeling like trying.

And anyway, I hadn't had hardly any alone time in over a week.

I hadn't even been in my car in that time.

I didn't know it about myself until then, but I was learning I was an alone-time type of gal.

In fact, I was jonesing for it.

So, after morning sex on Wednesday, I begged Axl to talk to Hawk and his cop buddies to see if they thought it wise I was released from constant detail.

I had a feeling it was partly because I timed the ask right, partly because he read me, but he didn't mess around.

In other words, he met Sly and me for lunch at Mustard's.

There he told us they'd had a sit-down and they had no idea if this hiatus meant whoever was screwing with me was moving on, but...

"Since we got cameras outside your house, if you're good for us to put a tracker on your car, a tracking app on your phone, you carry a panic button, and Ian sees to things at the club, you're also good to go it alone. Unless he hits again. Then we reconvene."

I was very much down with that plan and told Axl so.

However, even though I shared this might happen, Sly looked kind of bummed when he found he was going to be off duty.

So yes.

The guy was sweet.

And I felt a little bad.

But seriously, a girl needed some time to herself.

As what seemed like kind of our last hurrah (as such, though I hoped I'd see him again), Sly had lunch with us before he took off.

Axl drove me home, gave me the panic button, downloaded the app on my phone and set it up, put the tracker on my car, and then said, "You got my key. You can go get your stuff. Or you can leave it. I'll clear your drawers tonight."

Which (*obviously*) led to a makeout session he had to end because he had to get back to work.

I went to his place and got some of my stuff (though I left some of it too).

But I didn't do that until I cleared a drawer for Axl at my pad.

I found not long after I got home from Axl's that Brett was not at one with me being unprotected.

I found this when he called and shared it with me.

"Brett, the guy hasn't been in touch in ages and I have to have some alone time," I told him.

"I can get that, Hattie, but in an uncertain situation, you proceed with caution," he'd returned.

"They've given me a panic button and put a tracker on my car and there are cameras—"

"Don't give a fuck. But the decision has been made. And you need alone time, okay. My boys'll still be doin' drive-bys and they won't go stealthy. This guy is watching you, he'll know you got protection. They'll also be keeping an eye on the club. Smithie still make sure all the girls got escorts to their cars at night?"

"Yeah."

"Pantera keeping you company at night?"

"Yeah."

"Fine," he grunted. "But Hattie, next time a decision is made like this, I sit at that table."

He'd then hung up.

I had a feeling that was partly about his feelings being hurt and I got that. He'd stepped up. And obviously Axl hadn't called him in on the powwow.

I texted Axl to inform him of this misstep, and he'd texted back it was noted.

Hopefully, the stalker was done with me.

But if he wasn't, I'd make sure Brett was in on future decisions about my safety.

And I took this as indication that no matter what Axl said, or Brett said, he was no motherfucker.

Dad had been in the same reflective mood that evening. And even though Axl had told me he'd have to work late so I was on my own for dinner, thus I told Dad I could hang with him for a while, he'd said something he'd never said before.

"No, sweetheart. I'm sure you got a lot of other things you'd rather be doing than spending time with your old man."

He was right.

Still, it felt weird to be let off the hook like that.

Though, it seemed meeting Axl had had an interesting effect on my father.

I just wondered if that would continue to develop, how it would, and if whatever that was, was good, and finally, if that would last.

On the way home from Dad's, I got a call from Axl whereupon, immediately after exchanging greetings, he asked, "After you work, yours or mine, baby?"

First, I loved, even though I was no longer staying with him, that didn't mean I didn't get to sleep beside him.

Second, I wanted him to fuck me in my bed.

"Mine."

"Right. Text me when you're on your way home from Smithie's. I'll meet there."

"I'll give you a key tomorrow."

"Cool, beautiful."

A week and a day together, we each had the other's keys.

I thought that was seriously, freaking *rad*.

After I got home from work, Axl meeting me at my place then fucking me quick and hard (and the usual *fantastic*) before we both passed out was even more seriously, *freaking rad*.

Axl was gone before I even got out of bed in the morning on Thursday (also stuck in a post-fuck haze, that said, his day started super early, he was always out the door before seven, sometimes earlier than that, and I wasn't usually out of bed until nine, earliest, more often closing on ten).

But when I finally pulled myself out of bed and got down to loading up the Smeg, I opened up the fridge and saw my lonely, woeful salted caramel creamer and kicked myself for not hitting the grocery store on the way from Dad's after my phone conversation with Axl.

I rectified that yesterday (we now had white chocolate mocha, cinnamon, vanilla, toffeenut and the aforementioned salted caramel).

And he'd noticed.

Rounding that out, Thursday included Dad calling me and saying he was good on his own.

Which prompted a short conversation that he did not get impatient with (first shocker), that included me asking if everything was all right with him (he assured me it was). If he was taking care of his health (he assured me of that too, second shocker, because he sounded like he wasn't lying). And if *we* were all right.

"It's just that meeting your man made me realize I lean on you too much," he'd said to that last (third shocker). "I love to see you, Hattie, but you're a young woman. The last thing you need is to be spending every night with your father."

He was right about that.

It was still a shock.

Thus Thursday also included me calling Mom to share not only this turn of events, but belatedly share that I was seeing someone, I really liked him, and it'd be good if we all found a time to sit down together.

She'd been wary of Dad, "He's pulling his usual stuff, Hattie, don't fall for it," and ecstatic about Axl, "I can't wait to meet him! We'll fix a time!"

Though, the second seemed weird and forced. However, not forced in the fact she was excited I was seeing someone I really liked, but the fix-the-time part.

Which was something to think on, though not at that time push her about.

Because Mom had had a few years of being in what, at times, I worried was a concerning funk, but the last couple of years, she seemed to be moving on from it.

But she never didn't want to see me.

I didn't like that and put it on my mental agenda to give her time and deal with it later.

Thursday also included me talking all this through with Axl after he took me out for our second date, Mexican at Blue Bonnet.

Axl concurred with Mom about being wary of Dad, and since he'd never met her, "Got no take, baby, but I'm lookin' forward to meeting her."

He also drove me to work, because he intended to stay for the show, and hang with me during my free times, because, "It'd suck, date two ended at eight o'clock."

I mean, for heaven's sake.

Was this guy awesome or what?

Which brought us to now.

Back at my place.

And Axl had discovered the creamer.

He hadn't filled his drawer (though I'd shown it to him, and the slow smile was *so* worth the struggle of trying to make space for him—what could I say, I liked clothes and I had a walk-in, but it wasn't Kardashian level).

I hadn't filled the drawers he'd cleared for me.

But this was real.

It was happening.

And all those things I'd discovered about him that first day in his house were panning out.

We were compatible.

Like, *crazy* compatible.

He hung up his towel.

I did too.

He rinsed his whiskers from the sink (he'd brought over a razor, and shave cream).

I had no whiskers, but if I did, I'd rinse them.

He put his coffee mug in the dishwasher, I did as well.

We both liked Mexican.

We both liked going down on each other.

We both liked lots and lots (and lots) of sex.

I liked to dance when he was at the club.

He liked to watch me.

I mean, were we not perfect?

On this thought, he came down the steps into my bedroom carrying two mugs of coffee.

I pushed up on an elbow. "Which one did you go for?"

"I got a toffeenut and a cinnamon. Which one you want?"

Hmm.

Tough choice.

He sat on the bed facing me and I asked, "Which one do *you* want?"

"I don't care. You got all the best flavors. I'm good either way."

I was too!

See!

We were *perfect*!

Since he didn't seem prepared to head straight out the door, in order to get caffeine and more time with Axl, and not spend that time talking about who wanted what, I decided, "Cinnamon."

He handed me a mug.

I adjusted the pillows and scooched up to rest a shoulder against them so I could take a sip.

"You down with me putting a litter box in your utility so Cleo can come over?" he asked after he took his own. Then he shot me a handsome grin. "Like the other girl in my life, she likes alone time, but I got the cold shoulder yesterday when I went over to give her breakfast. She didn't even come into the kitchen. Just sat in the doorway giving me the evil eye."

I was surprised this wasn't Cleo's normal morning ritual.

Still, I replied, "Oh no. Totally, it's okay to set her up here. Since you're working, I'll go out and get the stuff. Is she particular?"

He grinned again. "What do you think?"

She was particular.

Man, I liked that cat.

"I'll text you a pic of her sitch at my place and the brand of litter," he said.

"Cool."

"You got Mac's shower tomorrow," he noted mysteriously.

"Yup," I confirmed.

"Sunday, wanna take you and your dad to a Rockies game. They're in town and got a day game."

Mystery immediately solved.

But all I could do was stare at him.

He didn't miss me staring at him, and not only because he couldn't, considering he was practically sitting in my lap.

"You don't think that's a good idea?" he asked.

"I…don't…" I pulled it together. "I don't think I've done anything fun with Dad in, uh…I don't know. Maybe ten years."

"Then it's time," he stated.

Maybe he was right.

"I'll call and ask him."

He nodded.

"Is there a reason why you want to take Dad to a baseball game?" I queried.

"Only that, if he's been thinkin' on shit, and sees that your relationship hasn't been healthy, and sees at this time in your life, you shouldn't be weighed down with the health and welfare of a parent, maybe you should show him it's time to be father and daughter friends. Like you're friends with your mom."

Friends with my dad.

Doing something fun with my dad.

"He really likes baseball," I said quietly. "When I was young, he'd take me to games a lot."

On this thought, one I hadn't had in a long time, I felt something happen in my belly.

Something weird.

Warm, but not.

Because that "not" part was scared.

"I think that's why I like hot dogs," I shared. "Because that was the only time he'd buy me something crappy to eat and not give me shit about it. All the pressure that seemed to be there between us wasn't at the ball field. We'd have fun. He taught me how to keep score. He explained strategy. I wasn't really interested in it. But I was interested in being like that with my dad."

"Then I hit on the right thing," Axl said softly, his eyes the same on me.

"I'll call him," I decided to take the risk. Give in to a little hope. Think positively when I thought about my dad for the first time since I was fourteen. "See if he's up for it."

Axl replied, "Good," before he took a sip from his mug.

I did too.

And when I swallowed, I suggested, "For Cleo's sake, maybe we should be at yours tonight."

"I was gonna say that."

Totally . . .

Compatible.

I smiled at him and asked, "Can I make you dinner?"

"You can do what you want, honey."

My mind started whirring through ideas.

"Anything you don't eat?" I inquired.

"Not a big fan of tomatoes and hate squash."

When he said no more, I asked. "That's it?"

"There a lot of food you don't like?"

"I don't care for tomatoes much either."

"Celery?"

Something about the way he pinpointed that singular food item caught my attention.

"Celery?" I parroted.

"Yeah."

"Well, fill it with peanut butter or cream cheese, it's a relatively inconspicuous vehicle to eat peanut butter and cream cheese. That's about all I can say about it."

He started chuckling.

Then he asked bizarrely, "How do you feel about the polar ice caps melting?"

"I'm wholeheartedly against it."

At that, he busted out laughing.

I liked to make him laugh, but I was confused.

"What was that about?" I asked when his laughter died down.

"Dad tried to find out where we were at by making mention I didn't know what kind of martinis you liked. Instead of just asking about you. About us. About how I feel about you. Where I met you. What it meant that you were at his house, meeting him and Mom and having dinner with them. Sometimes, being his son is like being on a witness stand. He tries different tactics to get the answers he wants. Even though I'm not a hostile witness. I'm his son. And he can just ask."

His dad was really a trip.

A bad one.

"Yeah," I whispered.

"I told him I didn't know if you liked celery or how you felt about the ice caps because we hadn't been married for five years. But I intended to find out." He took a sip and then finished, "Now, I know."

"Now you know." I gave it a second and then queried, "You heard from your mom?"

"She's dodging calls and her return texts are vague. We got your dad and the Rockies Sunday. We'll figure her out next week."

I wasn't sure he should wait.

But I nodded anyway.

He bent to me and touched his mouth to mine.

When he pulled away, he said, "I gotta get to Cleo before I go to work."

"You want me to go take care of her?" I offered.

"Babe, she already likes you more than me because I'll baby-talk . . . maybe . . . when I have a baby, not before. Don't take my role as breakfast slave away."

That had me chuckling.

It also had me thinking about giving Axl ice-blue-eyed babies.

He lifted his mug. "Can I nab a travel mug?"

"Help yourself. Top shelf over the—"

"I saw 'em."

Another lip touch before he got up and I got to watch his ass in his black cargos as he walked to the living area.

I pulled myself out of bed so I could give him a proper good-bye kiss at the door.

I gave it and good before Axl was off.

Then, since I was up in a way I was *up*, I went about my usual morning business (during which I saw I had a faint mark on my neck from Axl, which made my toes curl).

I decided I'd do an early rehearsal so I could get to the studio. My order wasn't in for the materials I'd purchased, but I could start constructing the mold.

After my shower, in order to give my hair some time to dry naturally before I hit it with the diffuser, in my robe, I sat down on a stool at my kitchen counter with my laptop to check the tracking for the stuff I ordered, and pulled up email as a matter of course.

That was when the texts started coming in about Lottie's shower, which Jet was throwing for her sister, but we were all coordinating presents so we didn't double up on teddies or the like.

I copied and pasted a photo of the racy red number I got her (that was a stop at the mall Sly didn't mind), along with a couple's spa collection (I wasn't sure Mo could fit with her in a bath, I was sure he'd be down to try), and a nice bottle of champagne.

And that was when I noticed my email was hanging.

I hit the send/receive status, and it was churning, but...

A message downloaded with the subject SOMETHING TO LOOK FORWARD TO.

I clicked on it and it had two .mov files.

So that was why it was hanging.

Movie files.

Big ones.

Huge.

Two of them.

One was titled "For You" and the other "For Him."

There was nothing in the body of the email.

A chill raced down my spine and I instantly called Axl.

"You good?" he asked as greeting.

"I think I got an email from my stalker," I told him.

His voice was different—crisp but cautious—when he asked, "Why do you think that?"

"Because there are two rather large movie files on it, one is titled 'For You' and one 'For Him,' the email address is obviously a bogus gmail, because it starts with whowantsyou, there's no message and the subject says 'Something To Look Forward To.'"

"When did it come in?"

I hadn't checked emails in a while, so I scanned the date.

Dang.

"Saturday," I told him.

"You go through your postal mail since being home?"

"Yes."

"Nothing?"

I shook my head regardless he couldn't see me and told him what he had to know since I would have shared if there was.

"Nothing."

"You open those movie files?"

"Not yet."

"Everything you got on your computer that's important backed up in the cloud?"

"Everything."

"You good to open them and tell me what you see, or you want to wait for me to come get your laptop?"

"I can open them."

"Okay, I'm on my way, but open the 'For Him.'"

Of course he was on his way.

And…

Of course he'd pick that one.

Because he didn't want me to see what this lunatic thought he had in store for me.

I double clicked on "For Him."

It started right in on some porn well after any preliminaries.

This guy was going for a quick response, because on my screen was a man, again muscular, on his back on a table, long legs spread wide and tied high, arms tied down over his head. He was being finger fucked, not delicately, and jacked, also not delicately, by a tall, hooded, bare-chested man in black leather pants.

The man being worked looked in agony.

"Gay porn, male, BDSM," I told Axl.

The finger fucking stopped, and Black Leather Pants man grabbed a short, multi-tailed whip and started swatting at his subject's cock.

Ouch.

Seriously.

I could totally feel that, and I wasn't a guy.

And yeah, even more agony.

"Now whipping," I reported.

"Close it and don't open the other," Axl ordered.

"Axl—"

"I'll call Cisco, see if Sly is free. If not—"

Argh!

There went my alone time.

"Axl—"

"Babe, no," he bit off.

I shut up.

"I'll be there in ten," he grunted.

Someone was not happy.

I wasn't happy either.

Because not only had alone time vanished, so much for going to the studio.

"Okay, honey," I murmured.

He disconnected without saying good-bye.

I watched until it was over, which was only maybe another minute.

But during that minute, there was a further splice, a jump in the action, so I was clear on the outcome.

Well, one thing could be said about this dickhead, he intended things to come to fruition.

I was about to close it when something struck me.

Instead, I started it again and watched the whole thing.

Then I opened the other one and I didn't sit through the whole thing, I skipped to the end.

She climaxed too (or faked it).

I went back to the first, watched very closely, specifically the man at work, not the one being worked.

Then I went to my porn site.

It took a lot of scrolling through their library, but I found it.

I clicked on it.

And the movie started.

I hit mute and fast-forwarded to where the worker was barechested (the workee had long since lost his clothes).

And yes.

There it was.

I'd never seen this one, but I'd gone through the short highlight reel they offered so you could make your selections. None of the action my stalker picked was on the highlight reel, but I remember the guy on the table (before he was tied to the table). I thought he was good-looking, had a great body, but another film had caught my eye, so I'd passed it up.

But I remembered the tattoo that slithered up his hip from his leather pants.

I was watching it when Axl walked in.

As he strode purposefully my way, his eyes did a quick scan of me before they dropped to the laptop.

"Is that it?"

His voice was abrasive with anger.

"No, it's from my subscription site. But it's the movie he used."

Axl stopped beside where I sat on one of my kitchen stools. "You've seen it before?"

I shook my head. "Just scanned the highlights."

"So, what are you—?"

"I'm going to tell you something and you have to promise and swear that you won't say anything. To *anybody*."

I could make a case that the steel-blue of his eyes was actual steel with the way he was looking at me.

"Promise?" I pushed.

"Promise," he grunted.

"Ryn told me about this site because—"

"Boone and Ryn are Dom and sub, which means BDSM is their thing, and she likes watching man-on-man too."

Whoa.

That was even more than I knew.

I blinked up at him.

"He doesn't get into the nitty-gritty, but we share," he said like he was forcing it out. "Though I'm just guessing about Ryn digging watching man-on-man."

He guessed correctly.

I didn't get into that.

"Okay," I replied quickly, wishing to move us along not only for me, but also for him, Boone and Ryn. "So, you took my laptop to see if it was hacked, I wonder—"

I didn't finish that.

Axl had his phone out so fast, I didn't think he moved to get it. It was just that one second, he was standing there, scowling down at me, the next it was at his ear.

"Yeah, Boone, can you bring Ryn's laptop in? We need to check if it's hacked," he said into the phone. "This asshole who's fuckin' with Hattie sent her an email. And there might be more. I'll explain when I get to the office." Pause then, "I don't know. But Ryn recommended a website this guy is using and obviously she has Hattie's email." Another pause, then, "Yeah, thanks, brother."

He disconnected and I said, "Maybe it's more than just how he got my email."

"Did she send you a link to that site, or did she tell you about it?"

"At first we talked about it. But she sent the link with her subscription info so I could give it a go before I committed to subscribe."

He nodded. "When was this?"

I shook my head. "I...really don't remember. But it's at least a year."

He nodded again. "Cisco says Sly's busy. He'll be free in a couple of hours and he doesn't have anyone else available. Neither do we. Though I suspect Boone just freed himself up. But that means, in the meantime, honey, get dressed. You're goin' to the office with me."

Oh boy.

I was curious about where he worked.

But this wasn't how I wanted to get my first tour.

"Axl—"

"Babe, I know you're probably freaked. But I need you to get a move on. If he's in Ryn's laptop, I'm thinking less good thoughts than I was before. But a hack can be traced. If he left that trace, we can find him. I want on that right away."

"Okay, I'll be fast but, he finished."

"What?"

"They both did."

He took a quick breath, but it was big, expanding his chest, all this in an effort at patience, before he demanded, "Explain fully."

"I know you told me not to, but I watched the end of the one for me. And I finished the one for you. And they both climax."

"I see you think this is important, so I need you to explain that."

"I think, I don't know . . . but if he wanted to hurt me, or you, or freak us out, would he show them finishing?"

Axl didn't reply.

"It's like, again, I don't know, but it feels like . . . *flirting*. Or a come-on. Or an invitation or something."

"You think this whackjob genuinely has a thing for you outside being a whackjob who clearly has a thing for you?"

"For us."

"Hattie, I can see wanting to think that in order to make it less disturbing, but I'm not sure it says that."

"Okay," I muttered, starting to get off the stool so I could go and get dressed.

"Babe," he called, wrapping a hand around the side of my neck, so I stopped moving and looked up at him again. "You want someone, you approach them at a bar and hand them a line. You do not send them pictures and movies without even introducing yourself. Again, Boone doesn't get into the nitty-gritty, but they find partners in the normal way. A lot of the time, they can just sense who is who and who likes what. They also have signals, like shit people wear, bracelets and necklaces and stuff. And they got their own thing going on where they can be around like-minded people and meet potential partners at bars, clubs, parties. They don't find someone they like who they have no idea if they're in the life or not, follow them, leave unsettling presents on their doorstep, and invade their lives."

I nodded.

That made sense.

"Yeah?" he asked, even though I nodded.

"Yeah," I answered.

"You okay?" he pushed.

I couldn't shake something.

I nodded again.

"Tell me the truth, Hattie," he said gently. "I wanna deal with this," he indicated my laptop with his head, "but you're more important so I need to know you're good."

"I'm good. I just think…" I shrugged and finished, "Something is off."

"Something is definitely off," he agreed.

"Not just this guy being whacked. Something else."

"We'll get down to it." He gave my neck a squeeze. "Get dressed, honey. We gotta go."

I nodded again, he gave me another squeeze and then he let me go.

I ran and got dressed.

*   *   *

We were all standing around Axl's workstation (and, by the by, Axl's workplace was serious *cool*, precisely what you'd think of as commando central!).

All of us (though, I wasn't standing, Axl told me to take a seat in his chair, which I thought was sweet).

That all of us included Axl, Boone, Ryn, Axl's boss, Hawk, and the office manager, Elvira.

They'd connected remotely with some IT guru to Ryn's computer and he had some diagnostics running.

But they were watching the montages sent to me on mine.

As was not in question, I liked porn.

Watching porn montages sitting at Axl's workstation with our friends, his coworker and his boss?

Awkward.

"Well, not much you can say about this dude, 'cept he's got good taste in porn," Elvira remarked.

Ryn made a choking noise and I knew why because I was swallowing my own laughter.

"Vira," Hawk's deep voice tumbled from one side of me, where he was standing, to the other, where Elvira was, and I fought holding on to the arms of Axl's chair so the force of his unhappiness wouldn't knock me over.

FYI: pre-Axl, I would probably be apoplectic around Hawk Delgado (much like the semi-functioning apoplectic I was around Axl).

Yes, he was that handsome.

Then again, none of the guys were slouches, far from it.

But they'd been picked for my girls.

Hawk, though (even if he was *very* married).

Dayum.

I looked up at him.

Dayum to infinity.

His face was carved in stone.

One could say he did not like his boys dicked with, especially not through their women.

Or just not at all.

But one of his men having an issue was one thing.

Another one dragged in?

Man, whoever was doing this was up shit's creek.

"I watched this one," Ryn declared. "Start of it was a three out of ten, but I was bored so I let it roll. Totally ended on a bang." Pause. "Literally."

Elvira laughed.

Ryn laughed with her.

I chewed my lips in order not to laugh with them and wondered how they could sally forth in such a manner with the suffocating, pissed-off, alpha-male vibe weighing down the air.

"Hattie, could you place any of the pictures this guy sent?" Hawk asked me, muffling the fury in his tone, but just barely.

"Did he take stills from porn movies you may have seen and that's what he sent to you?"

I shook my head at him.

Hawk shifted his gaze.

"Ryn seen the pictures?" Hawk asked Boone.

"Not yet."

"Show her, see if she can place them," Hawk directed.

"I'll get 'em," Axl said, then he was off.

"Play it again," Elvira said.

I looked to her then down to my laptop to see the short, three-minute clip had ended.

I reached out to hit play when Hawk repeated, "Vira."

"What?" she asked.

Nothing from him for a second, then an audible sigh.

Before I could hit go, Axl came back and handed a folder to Ryn.

She opened it, studied what was in it, turned one of the photos over, and went completely white.

Oh no.

"*What?*" Boone barked.

Barked!

Yikes.

Her eyes drifted up to him.

"Can we talk?" she asked in a strangled voice.

Oh no!

Quick as a flash, he had her hand and was dragging her down the row.

It was safe to say this was not good.

Everyone watched as they had an intense discussion with Boone's neck bent deep so he could get his ear close to Ryn's lips.

And this discussion did not go well, and I knew that starting with the muscle that played in his cheek, but also because eventually Boone's face . . .

No . . .

Every inch of his body nearly screamed he needed to hurt someone.

"Oh no," I whispered.

They came back, and Ryn looked sheepish, Boone still looked murderous and he was walking like his shoulders were a wall of cinder blocks swinging to and fro.

Eep!

Still, he did it again holding her hand.

Sweet.

"Well, some of you know, some of you don't, and it's never fun to be outed when you don't call that ball, but here we go," Ryn started. "I'm in the life. I had a Dom and he tied me up just like this chick." She lifted the folder and shook it. "*Exactly* like this chick. He was not a good Dom and I don't mean that in the conventional, I-didn't-enjoy-him way. He didn't play by the rules in a way that could have been dangerous for me."

Right.

Before, I realized that I was breathing relatively easy.

Now the pissed-off alpha vibe was suffocating.

But my heart hurt that Ryn experienced that.

"She told me about it," Boone growled. "I found him, had a few words, shared a few other things nonverbally. Had a few words with some important players in town too so his shit would be shut down. His shit, disregarding safe words, is serious, so the players I talked to assured me that he'd find some difficulties feeding his need. That said, way I left him, I felt sure I taught him a lesson in etiquette. I'm seein' now I left him with a few questions on that."

"This isn't about Hattie, it's about Ryn," Axl said.

"Yeah," Boone grunted.

"He's fucking with Hattie and me to get to you and Ryn," Axl went on.

"Yeah," Boone bit off.

"Ding, ding, ding," Elvira suddenly, and weirdly, said.

And more weird, not a second later Axl's phone sounded.

He took the call.

But I looked to where Elvira was looking.

Ryn's laptop.

The diagnostics were no longer running.

"Yeah," Axl said. "Yeah." Pause. "You got a location?" Listening. "Leave it to us. Thanks, Brody." He disconnected and announced to all, "She's been hacked."

"Fuck," Boone clipped.

"I'm so sorry, Hattie," Ryn said.

"Why?" I asked. "You didn't stalk me."

"Brody doesn't have a location yet," Axl kept going. "We need to get on that."

"Dude's name is Laszlo Kovack and I know where he works and where he lives," Boone supplied.

Both Boone and Axl looked to Hawk.

"Go," he bit out.

Boone turned to Ryn and Axl looked down at me.

"You stay here until Sly gets here or you hear from me, okay?" I nodded.

He bent in and kissed me quickly.

Then he and Boone took off, both of them with their phones to their ears.

I thought about Laszlo Kovack.

And what I thought was, I'd like to have a conversation with him about why he played this the way he did.

Not that I wanted him to play with Boone and Ryn.

Just that...I didn't get it.

"Did he like you?" I asked Ryn.

"Well, we connected, so he was attracted to me," Ryn replied. "But for me, he was definitely a one and done."

"I think he didn't want to be a one and done," I surmised.

"Just, you know," Elivra began, "takin' up the slack while Hawk here tamps down his inclination to chase up Axe and Boone so he can work out his current murderous tendencies, this Kovack guy thought you'd share with her." She tipped her head to Ryn. "My guess, this started before you and Axe got together?"

I nodded.

"So...yeah," Elvira said in conclusion.

"But then he knew I was with Axl," I pointed out.

Elvira shrugged. "That, I don't get. Unless he got into it and found he was getting off on it and didn't feel like quitting."

It was more than that.

I felt it.

But I focused on Ryn. "You okay?"

"Yeah."

She didn't sound convincing.

"I'm sorry that happened to you."

"No big deal, it's over. I'm sorry it leaked to you."

"That isn't on you."

She nodded.

"He bi?" Elvira broke into our back-and-forth to ask Ryn.

"No clue," Ryn answered.

"He's bi," Elvira said.

"And?" I asked.

"And, have you seen Axl?" she asked back. "Or Boone?"

Well then.

There you go.

"He wanted him," I surmised.

"He wanted him. He wanted you. He wanted Ryn. Maybe even wanted Boone. Who knows? That video," she tipped her head to my laptop, "says 'Come and play.' It does not say, 'Come and play, and after, I'm gonna wear your skin.'"

Yeah, just like I thought.

Totally no *Silence of the Lambs* vibes.

Totally an invitation.

But…who does that?

And it wasn't just rule-breaking BDSM guy stuff.

I just couldn't shake that it was…off.

"Boone did not share the details of his 'conversation' with Laszlo, but I'm thinking he left it without question that he was not down to play," Ryn noted.

"This guy doesn't play by the rules, right?"

"Right," Ryn said miserably.

"Ryn, honey, it isn't your fault," I reiterated.

"It still sucks. I mean, what a dick," she replied.

"It does suck, but whatever. They'll get him so it's almost all over." It was a lame attempt to reassure her, but it was all I had.

"They'll get him," Hawk rumbled.

I jumped, not believing I kinda forgot he was standing there.

Hawk then turned and prowled down the row, and at the end, he jogged up to his office like he had energy he needed to expend.

Hostile energy.

Eek!

"So, you know, you gotta hook a girl up with the shops you go to," Elvira said to Ryn. "I mean, marriage is *da bomb*, but you gotta keep things in the marital bed hopping, you feel me?"

Ryn lost some of her gloom and semi-smiled. "I can totally hook you up."

"Porn too. Malik won't do all boys, but a girl can take her laptop to a bubble bath and get herself in the mood before she pounces on her man," Elvira declared.

Ryn's smile strengthened. "Totally."

Elvira's voice changed abruptly, and it did this in totality.

"You are never responsible for a violation. You will almost always feel like you are, but it is not yours to take on. It is *never* yours to take on. Do you get me?"

"I get you," Ryn said softly.

Elvira looked down at me. "Do you get me?"

"I get you," I repeated Ryn's words.

"Right, this pretty much shouts time for a cosmo. Who wants one?"

A cosmo?

As in, the drink?

"Vira, it's not even ten in the morning," Ryn noted.

Yes, the drink.

"And?" Elvira demanded.

Neither Ryn nor I had the answer to that.

Though I had another note.

"Bars aren't open yet."

"You think, I work with these boys, I don't have a setup in my office?" she asked.

Considering this was a place of business, a kickass one, but still a place of business, I wouldn't have thought that, no.

Though, thinking on it then, if I had to work with an office full of hot guys, I'd have a drawer of goodies to help me get through.

"Ten or not, it's girl time," Ryn said, grabbing my arm and pulling me up.

I hadn't even had breakfast.

Still.

"I'm in," I said.

We moved down the row with Elvira declaring (to me), "Girl, you miss my boards again, I'm banning you for life."

I knew one thing in that moment.

I really liked this woman.

So that could not happen.

"Cross my heart, never again," I promised.

"Best stick to that," she warned.

We hit her office.

She opened a cabinet, and this was not clandestine.

There was a fancy shaker, stylish martini glasses and everything.

Even a mini ice maker!
I'd heard a lot of talk about Elvira.
I was now seeing why.
Because straight up.
She was the shit.

CHAPTER NINETEEN

Setup

HATTIE

After work that night, I opened the door to the dancers' dressing room and saw Axl out in the hallway.

He was shoulders to the wall, ankles crossed, arms crossed, and his head was bent in contemplation of his shoes before I walked out, and it came up when I did.

It was not a pose of patient waiting.

It was a pose of annoyed reflection.

I knew two things about seeing him there in that stance.

One, Sly was off duty.

Two, they hadn't found Laszlo Kovack.

"Hey," I greeted cautiously.

"Hey, baby," he replied, pushing from the wall, uncrossing his arms but staying put as I made it to him and laid my hand on his chest.

He dipped his head to get my touch on the lips then took my hand and started us to the door as he said, "Caught your last dance. Usual awesome."

"Thanks," I murmured.

He pushed through the door and we nearly ran into Ian, who was coming in from escorting Pepper out.

He gave us both a look, a nod, and I said, "'Night, Ian."

"'Night, Hatz. Pantera."

"Walker."

They added chin lifts to their macho, last-name farewells, and I wondered why men used last names instead of first.

I didn't wonder long because in the end, it was just masculine, and in the case of Axl and Ian, hot.

Axl put me in his Jeep, rounded the hood and angled in beside me.

We belted up and were on our way.

As this happened, I thought that it sucked, this guy was screwing with him and me, Boone and Ryn.

It sucked my alone time and studio time was gone again.

And it sucked that, because of this, I wasn't able to cook for Axl that night.

I hadn't cooked for him yet, and truth be told, my cooking wasn't all that much to write home about, but it wasn't the worst.

And I wanted to do it for him.

I forged into the glum silence.

"Let me guess, you didn't find him."

"Nope."

"You will. It's just been a day," I reassured.

"This guy is a shit Dom for fun, and he's an insurance adjuster for work. He's not a master criminal. We should have had him in an hour. He's nowhere to be found."

Oh boy.

"Well, maybe he knows who he's dealing with and taking precautions," I suggested.

"Yeah," he muttered, making it clear he was unconvinced.

Back to the reassurance. "Tomorrow is another day."

"Yeah, and we were gonna kick back and grill some burgers with Mo while you women did your thing with the shower. That's off because we gotta find this guy."

Another reason to be angry with Laszlo Kovack.

And since he'd racked up quite a list, I fell out of Reassurance Zone and slid into Annoyed Zone.

"This guy is such a jerk," I snapped.

"Agreed."

"And I don't get him," I kept bitching. "I mean, none of this makes sense, the latest of which is you guys can't find him. But I've been thinking on it all day, and I cannot buy the leap from him being pissed at Boone for sharing justifiably how he felt about what this guy did to Ryn, to him bothering you and me. If he's mad at Boone and Ryn, not that I want him to take that out on Boone and Ryn, still, why wouldn't he take it out on Boone and Ryn? How do I factor into all of this? And you?"

Axl said nothing, but the air in the car had shifted.

It felt tingly.

"Axl?" I called.

"Shit," he whispered.

"What?" I asked.

"So caught up in what he was doin' to you, didn't see it," he said.

"What?" I repeated.

"It's a setup."

"Pardon?"

"You were right, my dad was baiting me."

I was perplexed.

How did we get from talking about Kovack to something about a setup to him mentioning his dad?

"Okay," I said slowly.

"He doesn't give a shit what anyone thinks about him. He has no problem being an asshole. But he knows I do. It's a game. He wants me on my back foot. He wants to manipulate me into being an asshole. And if I take the bait, he wins. And I end up not only feeling like an asshole but feeling like a chump because I got played."

"Yes," I agreed, still confused.

Axl didn't enlighten me.

He was digging in his side-leg cargo pocket for his phone.

He handed it to me and said, "Code seven, three, three, nine, two, eight. Call Boone."

I couldn't be ecstatic that not only did I have the key to his house, he had mine, we had drawers (as yet to be filled, still), but he also just gave me the code to his phone.

The vibe of his voice made me engage his cell and do as he said.

It was connected to his Jeep, thus rang in the car, but it only did this once before Boone answered, "All cool, brother?"

"It's a setup," Axl repeated.

"Sorry?" Boone asked.

"They got eyes on us. They know about this guy. And I'm not sure it's this guy doing it. They're leading us to this guy. Makes no fucking sense he's stalking Hattie, tagging me in on that, maybe trying to tweak me, thinkin' I'd have an issue with the bent of his threats to me, instead of targeting Ryn 'cause he's got a history with her, or you, because you got up in his shit. Hattie should have nothing to do with this. Me either."

"Fuck," Boone said.

In other words, whatever Axl was talking about, Boone agreed.

But Axl wasn't done laying it out.

"This guy can see her at work, follow her home. But getting her cell number and email takes resources. Hacking a computer takes resources. Becoming a ghost takes resources. Resources this guy does not have."

"*Fuck*," Boone clipped.

Yup.

He agreed.

"They went after Hattie to drag me in, pull you in through that and Ryn's history with him, and through you and me, get up in Hawk's face, all to manipulate us into doing what we were going to do if we found him today. We rolled Eddie and Hank into it, something they could guess we'd do. So it's a stretch, but not too much of one to tag them in. They knew we were investigating it. Even though Eddie and Hank now are also investigating it, they didn't put a stop to us doing the same. You laid him out, statute of limitations is not expired on that first assault. Add another one, we're vulnerable. If they're pissed enough at us, and they're pissed at us, if they got hooks in the DA, and they seem to have hooks in everybody, we're fucked. Assault charges for you and me, and Hawk, Eddie, Hank, even other members of the crew who knew about this could get done for conspiracy or aiding and abetting."

I wasn't sure what he was talking about.

Though I knew none of it was good.

"Christ, makes sense," Boone said.

"B lied to Aug and me, brother. She mentioned the women. She said it was just about us being off the market. It wasn't. They're on the offense. They intended to use the women to get to us, and this is how they're doing it. They're trying to force our play to take us out."

I didn't know who "they" were, but I knew I didn't like them.

Axl kept going.

"If they did a direct assault, we'd keep our shit and plan accordingly. Hit one of our women, straight thinking goes out the window. Even Hawk was off his game today, he was so pissed."

"Motherfucker," Boone bit.

"Hunt is off for Kovack tonight, and maybe permanently," Axl said. "I'll call this in to Hawk in the morning and we'll meet."

"Yeah," Boone agreed. "Good grab, Axe."

"Yeah," Axl said curtly. "Later."

"Later, bud."

The call disconnected and I handed Axl his phone.

"Was I supposed to hear any of that?" I asked.

"Some of it, no, but since it pertains to you and you're not gonna say anything to anybody, it doesn't matter."

Point taken to keep my mouth shut.

Next up.

"Assault?" I asked quietly.

"With their gig, in BDSM, trust is paramount. This guy put Ryn in a position where he could do absolutely anything he wanted to do to her and she was helpless to stop him. In that world and any other, that amounts to rape. Ryn's tough, but it understandably fucked with her. But even if she shrugged it off, that's enough to send Boone over the edge. The fact this guy could be doing it to others, he had a statement to make. He made it."

"Were you two going to find him in order to—?"

"Definitely."

I said nothing to that.

"Tease that out, honey," he said in a gentler tone. "Ryn takes that to the cops, how do you think that'd go? She decided to have sex with that guy, in their scene, and from the cops' perspective, they could think it's just that she didn't like the way he did it. Even if they found some charge to lay on him, she put that in front of a jury, a defense lawyer would chew her up. She consented but didn't like the way it went. The fact he rendered her defenseless in a way she did *not* consent to, and doing it, probably scared the shit out of her, wouldn't matter. A case could be made that was what she wanted. And maybe it was on the bones of it, but the way he did it, it absolutely wasn't. And he's free to keep doing this to women? No."

He was right.

No.

"Okay," I said.

"Okay," he replied.

I took in a deep breath.

And got to something else that was now very heavily weighing on my mind.

"It isn't lost on me there's an element of danger to your job," I began, and stopped.

"Mm-hmm," Axl hummed in an encouraging way for me to go on.

"And it's very much you. We haven't talked about it, but I think it feeds something in you."

"It does," he confirmed.

"Okay, that may be for a deeper discussion later. But for now, with whatever you were just talking about, are you in more danger than normal?"

He reached his hand out to me.

Like always when he did that, I took it.

When he had it, he said, "It's going to be okay. I'm going to be okay. The guys are going to be okay. We got our teeth into something that's tough and we aren't finding it easy to tear it free. But we'll get there, and we'll be good when it's done. Promise."

"Can you make that promise?" I asked.

He didn't hesitate.

"Yes."

It was because this was Axl.

And the zero hesitation helped.

But I believed him.

"Okay," I repeated.

"Okay," he replied.

We were quiet the rest of the way home.

Only Axl was quiet on the way into the house. I baby-talked Cleo when I saw her and Axl learned I not only called her shmoochma-gooch, but also Supreme Queen Grayfur and Sleekmeister General.

So he wasn't entirely quiet.

He chuckled.

We did the couple's bathroom dance when we brushed our teeth and I moisturized.

We both changed into sleepwear in the bedroom, and we both tossed our clothes on the chair as we undressed.

But when we got in bed, on his back, Axl tucked me to his side and that was it.

I had my head resting on his shoulder, my hand on his ridged stomach, and I didn't know what to do about this situation.

Because I wanted to have sex.

And if he wanted it, he went for it.

I always wanted it from him, so I gave it.

Now, I wanted it and I thought maybe he needed it.

He'd had a frustrating day. He needed sleep.

And maybe connection with me.

But I didn't know how to initiate intimacy because I'd never done it.

And if he wasn't doing anything, did that mean he didn't want it?

I licked my lips, rubbed them together, then decided to go for it.

If he said he wasn't in the mood, he just wasn't.

Things were heavy.

It didn't mean anything more and I knew one thing for certain.

I loved that he was into me and showed it in a lot of ways, and one of those ways was copious, and that was sexually.

So we had an off night, we'd have more.

On the other hand, guys were guys, but they probably needed that sometimes too. The "that" being your partner sharing they found you attractive by sharing they wanted to have sex with you.

Right.

I pulled it together, slid my hand to the top of the waistband of his sleep pants and trailed my nails lightly along it, tipping my head back and whispering, "I wanna go down on you. Is that okay?"

As he dipped his head to put his face in mine, he took my hand in his, pushed it under the waistband and wrapped it around his hardening cock.

And thrillingly unnecessarily, he growled, "It is absolutely okay."

I smiled, slid up a little to touch my mouth to his then I touched it to his throat.

He used my hand to stroke his dick.

Okay.

Nice.

As I made my way down his chest, though, he pulled our hands out and adjusted himself in bed at the same time tugging down his pajamas.

He tossed them to the side, positioned on his ass with his back against the headboard, and he spread his legs.

Knees cocked.

Axl Pantera laid out for the taking.

Okay.

Um…

Niiiiiiice.

I moved, curled up, took hold and went in.

Seriously, my mouth full of his cock?

Delicious.

That purr I loved came from his chest, his legs tensed, and then he relaxed, his hand going in my hair.

And as I blew him, he played a lot with my hair, arranging it across his lap in a way that made me clench and fight squirming.

Because it was like I got to touch him without, in a certain sense, me being the one who touched him. Also, I loved that he dug my hair so much. And last but *so* not least, it was just plain hot to be draped around him in that way while I was sucking his dick.

Eventually, however, after a good deal of sucking, licking,

rolling the tip, pumping with a twist (I'd discovered he liked that a whole lot), his hand fisted in my hair and he started pulsing up into my mouth.

Oh yes.

Taking his gentle face fucking, and getting into it, I couldn't fight the squirm, and even though Axl was purring consistently now, he didn't miss it.

"Shorts off, get up here," he ordered roughly.

Without delay, I released him with a hard draw and a final stroke, sat up, pulled down my sleep shorts and panties, fell to a hip, kicked them off and climbed right on.

Axl helped, holding his cock ready for me.

I glided down, taking it.

"Yes," I breathed.

"Fuck yes," he corrected, his hands going up my cami at the back and around.

He palmed both my breasts.

I started riding.

He tweaked my nipples and warned thickly, "Need you to get there fast, Hattie."

I started riding faster.

He squeezed my nipples.

I bucked.

"No, baby, finger to clit," he corrected.

Could I do that riding him? Touch myself right in front of him?

I put my finger to my clit and trembled head to toe.

I could do that.

"Yeah," he whispered, rolling both nipples.

Oh my God, *yeah*.

I bounced on him, up quick, slamming down hard.

His hands slid up, my arms were forced up, and the cami was gone.

He then grabbed both cheeks of my ass, gripping them in a

touch that was over the edge of gentle, and I jolted and started to ride wild.

"That's it, fuck me, baby," he grunted.

Yes.

I understood it.

That hold on my ass was possessive.

That wasn't my ass.

It was his.

I was his.

And I loved being his.

I rode harder.

"Christ," his fingers dug in, "Fuck yeah. Ride me, Hattie."

I rode. I soared. I came and did it hard, crying out, catching him at his neck, grinding down.

I didn't stay down.

I lost him when he pulled me off, planted me on my knees, positioned behind me, shoved a hand in my back so I arched for him and both my hands were forced to brace against the wall, and he pistoned back in.

Oh my God.

Amazing.

"Axl," I gasped.

He wrapped an arm across my chest, fingers at the side of the base of my neck, holding me steady as he drilled me.

Oh *my...*

God.

"Axl," I whimpered, and like a shot, came again.

He squeezed my breast as I swayed my hips to meet his thrusts, reeling from my orgasm.

His hand went down over my belly and in between my legs to cup us as he fucked me.

"Best goddamn tits, juiciest fucking pussy," he growled into my neck.

Oh God.

Could I come again?

Even if I wasn't quite done with the last one?

I was almost there.

"Baby," I moaned.

He pinched my clit.

I whinnied as I exploded.

He purred, then grunted, then shoved his face in my neck before his head jerked back.

He drove up and groaned, deep and rumbly.

Best sound ever.

Ever.

Honestly, I liked his orgasms even better than mine.

No joke.

He sat back on his calves, taking me with him, so I sat on his dick.

And his hands went back to my breasts.

It was not lost on me he was a tit man.

And since I was ultra-sensitive there, it also wasn't lost on me this was (high) on the long-and-getting-longer list of how we were compatible.

"Seriously," he murmured into my neck, giving gentle, kneading squeezes that were way better than a post-fuck cuddle. "Best tits ever, baby. Beautiful."

"Thanks," I wheezed.

I was pretty sure I felt him smile.

"And sweet, juicy pussy," he continued. "So goddamn wet, you're all over my thighs."

I shivered.

"Even when I'm fuckin' you, my mouth is watering with the need to eat you."

Another shiver.

"I can't touch you, honey," I voiced my complaint.

"No," he agreed, and didn't move.

Oh my.

Yes, I was his.

I loved that.

One hand left a breast, moved over my belly, which normally, I didn't like. It wasn't concave or even flat, and I'd always been conscious of it.

But he palmed it with the same reverence he gave my breast and any notion of embarrassment or discomfort that might have formed vanished in an instant.

He then slid his hand back up, the other one moved, and they changed tits as he crossed them over me, but he still held the weight cupped in his hands.

"Before I had you, would jack myself, thinking of you sucking me off with all this gorgeous hair all over my lap," he shared.

"Honey," I whispered.

"I think with that ride, Hattie, you broke us both in. We'll find time where we got a good amount of it to get creative."

Oh yeah.

"Okay," I agreed.

His hands went to my waist, he pulled me up and got out of bed.

Then he hooked me with an arm and my knees skidded across his sheets before he swung me up in both of his arms and carried me, not in a fireman's hold, but groom and bride, to the bathroom.

He set me on the counter.

I had not recovered from the Groom and Bride Maneuver when, for the first time, he got out a washcloth, wet it with warm water, pressed it between my legs and cleaned me.

Rinse, and I watched as he cleaned me from him.

Another rinse, and he draped it neatly over the sink (exactly what I would do).

And in another surprise move, he caught me under the arm with a swing and I was on his back.

On.

His.

Back.

Playful and sweet.

Oh my God.

This man.

I tucked my thighs to his hips, wrapped my arms around his neck, and he flipped the light switch as he carried me out and dropped me down beside the bed.

He handed me my shorts, panties and cami, reached to grab his pajama pants, we dressed and Axl pulled me into bed.

He yanked the covers up and this time he wound himself up in me, front to front.

"I don't think, ever in my life, I've initiated sex," I admitted.

"Time for me to buy a diary. Though, no heart stickers, but definitely a thick black Sharpie to record how fuckin' thrilled I am I was your first."

I started giggling.

He touched his mouth to mine while I did it, again when I was done, then tucked my face in his throat.

"Go to sleep, Hattie."

"Okay, Axl."

"Thanks for the fantastic head and the ride of a lifetime."

I was giggling again.

Through it I said, "I can't go to sleep if you're being sweet and funny."

"I'll shut up."

I didn't want him to, but I did want him to sleep. He'd had a trying day.

So I didn't say anything.

Not much time passed before a certain feline made her way up our bodies.

Cleo stopped with a pair of paws on me at my upper arm, and the way I felt them, the other pair was on Axl.

I felt her censure through the dark as she stared down at us.

She then jumped clear and I suspected she was done with us and had gone to sulk somewhere free of the humans until Axl said super quietly, "She's at my feet."

"She still loves her daddy."

He gave me a squeeze.

And with the gang all there, settled in and safe, finally, I fell asleep.

CHAPTER TWENTY

Tripped

AXL

It wasn't the time.

He wasn't ready for it.

He wasn't sure Hattie was ready for it.

But it happened.

The next morning.

After a quick fuck, a quick shower, and Hattie launching into getting ready for Lottie's brunch bridal shower at Jet Chavez's, Axl made some calls.

First, they had to hit Hattie's place to get her present, then he was going to drop her at the party, and with all the women there, the men were going to meet.

It was time to go, but when he went to the bathroom to hustle her ass up, she wasn't there.

She wasn't in the bedroom either.

He used that door to the living room to see if somehow she got past him and went to the deck, when he saw her in the living room, the handle of a cat toy with a feather on the end of it in her hand.

Cleo was nowhere to be seen, and he was about to tease Hattie about her ongoing efforts to steal his cat's affections when he noticed why Cleo wasn't playing (if there was one thing his cat loved, she loved to play).

Hattie had lost focus on the toy and was staring with not a small amount of interest at the piece on the chest in his front window.

He felt a clutch in his chest, and it wasn't the first time.

He shouldn't have bought it.

He should sell it.

He just couldn't.

"Babe, we gotta go," he called, and he hadn't managed to hide that clutch sounding in his voice.

She started, and her head turned his way.

"You okay?" she asked.

Yep.

She heard it.

"Yeah, but we gotta get on the road."

Her study of him became acute. "You sure you're okay?"

"Yeah," he repeated his lie. "Ready to go?"

She nodded.

And she was.

That day, it was the red dress day, he saw, and unfortunately, no matter how gorgeous she looked in it, he had to agree it was a good call she didn't wear it to his parents'.

Because it had a short, flirty skirt, a halter-like top with a straight edge under her collarbone and slender straps, and those straps crossed over her bare back. She wore her big gold hoops with it and a less-dressy pair of gold high-heeled sandals.

And unlike the yellow dress she'd worn to meet his folks—which his mom was right, was effortless and chic—the red dress said she was an adorable, but hot fuck.

And she was.

But his father would have torn that apart like a vulture.

Due to the way that night went, the discussion of what Hattie did for a living didn't come up.

That red dress would have pushed it in that direction, and it would have been Hattie in the firing line and Axl blowing his stack.

So yeah.

It was good they avoided that.

They got in his Jeep and she picked Supreme Queen Grayfur to call out good-bye to Cleo so he was smiling when he got behind the wheel.

But that smile didn't last long.

Hattie didn't miss it.

"You're not okay," she said.

"I'm fine," he lied.

"I'm sorry this stuff is hanging over all you guys' heads."

That wasn't what he was thinking about.

"Yeah," he agreed.

"Like you said, it'll all be okay," she assured him.

Shit.

"I know. That's all good. I'm not worried about that, Hattie."

"Okay," she said hesitantly.

Shit.

She did not need to think he was worried about that, because she was being super chill about all that was going down. She hadn't freaked once.

But if she thought he was worried about it, she might start worrying about it.

"That piece is titled 'Tripped.'"

"Pardon?"

"The one in the window. It's titled 'Tripped.'"

She said nothing, but he felt her gaze keen on him.

"I had a buddy in the service. We were tight. He stepped on a land mine."

She gasped.

Yeah.

That was not even close to it.

"Axl," she said gently, her fingers curling on his thigh.

"He was in front of me. I saw it."

"Oh my God, *Axl*." Her fingers squeezed tight and didn't let up.

"So," he cleared his throat, "yeah."

"So that piece…called 'Tripped'…is a representation of a land mine exploding?"

Yep.

She got it.

"Yeah."

"Why…I…it's…" She pulled it together. "It's an amazing piece, but why do you have it?"

"A vet who's a friend of another buddy of mine, also from the army, got into art when he got out. That's his thing. Making stuff like that into what you see in my living room."

"Making an instrument of death beautiful?"

She sounded horrified.

"Fucking with your head that an instrument of death could be beautiful. It's not. It's hideous and destructive. It's a political statement that the men who sit at desks, never in danger, never even under imminent threat, should be very clear in making decisions about when and why they send men and women into that. The cause should be just. It should be to protect our loved ones and our way of life. Not protect their financial interests."

"Although I hope it goes without saying that I agree with all of that, I hate to say this, but I didn't get that from that piece," she said carefully.

"That's the point. You'll never get it, Hattie, not really. And I thank fuck for that. They won't either."

She fell silent.

He spoke into it.

"I went to a show of his. I was in a mood. In a mood to support a fellow vet, because that piece cost a fuckin' fortune. And in the mood to be confronted with that reality in my living room."

"Axl—"

Christ, he'd started.

Now it didn't seem like he could stop.

"The flag on my dresser came from his casket. He was a foster kid. He had no one else for them to give it to. No one but me. He fought hard not to get caught up in bad shit growing up. And part of that fight was to enlist and have a job that was good and right and far from all that in a way, even when he was out, he could go to school and stay away from it forever. He didn't get that shot."

She was rhythmically squeezing his thigh now.

But when he was done, she said, "Maybe we should talk about this when we have time and you're not driving."

"I don't talk about it."

"What?" she whispered, and there was a thread to it, worry, maybe even fear.

"To the guys...yeah." That was a grunt. "To you, this is all there's gonna be."

"Honey—"

"That's what it looked like, except in the middle of it, flying apart, there was a big Black man that had a huge smile, a sense of humor so wicked good, he could have been a standup comedian, and he was such a solid guy to his core, he never had anyone give it to him his entire life, but his sense of loyalty was second to none. That piece is what a land mine looks like when it's triggered. Exactly."

She didn't say anything.

And he knew why.

"So that, Hattie, is why we won't talk about it. Because now you have some small sense of how hideous and destructive it is, and outside this, I'm not gonna lay that on you."

She slid her hand from his thigh.

He glanced at her.

Maybe for the first time since he met her, he couldn't read her face, and it wasn't because it was in profile.

And he did not like that at all.

"Babe, it's too much. If I need to, I talk to the guys. If they need to, they talk to me. That doesn't touch you."

"What was his name?"

"Jordan."

"First or last?"

"First. Full name Jordan Bridges."

Then . . . nothing.

"I shouldn't have said anything," he muttered. "You got a shower to have fun at and—"

"I'm shy, and there are things about me that are messed up, but I'm not weak," she declared.

"I know you're not," he said fast. "I know that, honey. You're tougher than you think."

"No," she stated, and he knew she was looking at him. "I'm tougher than *you* think."

Shit.

Now he was getting pissed.

"It's not about that, and not to be a dick, babe, but it's also not about you."

She grew quiet again.

He drove.

They didn't speak all the way to her house, and because they didn't, because she didn't set shit straight, he got more pissed.

So they also didn't speak as they went in the back door and she grabbed her present.

And they didn't speak all the way to Jet and Eddie's.

He stopped, idling at the front, and looked to her.

"Text when you're done," he said shortly.

"All right," she replied.

She turned to the door.

Then she turned back.

And laid him out.

"You're right. It isn't about me. It's yours to give if you want, to withhold if you don't. But something to think on, Axl, my situation with my father is mine. It isn't yours. In a certain sense, it's none of your business at all. But in what we're building, it's totally your business. If you let me struggle with that on my own, you'd be the shittiest boyfriend in history. You lost someone you obviously cared about deeply, and I cannot even imagine how it felt watching him die. I hate that for you. I *hate it*. But I need to know Jordan Bridges, not just because, with every passing minute I spend with you, you mean more to me, so I need to know you. But more importantly, I get the strong sense Jordan deserves to be known. I love how protective you are of me. But this isn't going to work if you protect me from you."

And with that highly successful speech, she turned from him and threw open her door.

Then, with a ballerina's grace, she jumped down from his Jeep in her high heels, slammed the door, and holding Mac's present to her chest, the gift bag with a bottle of champagne in it dangling from her other hand, she skip-ran up Jet's front walk.

He watched the whole show.

And then he muttered, "Fuck."

* * *

Mo was waiting for the elevator on the parking level and Axl would learn he was continuing to do a piss-poor job of hiding what he was feeling when Mo turned as Axl walked up to him and his big, bald head twitched.

Fantastic.

"Everything good?" Mo asked.

They had a deal.

They did not keep shit from each other.

Not ever.

And when this kind of thing came up, stuff that surfaced about when they served, absolutely, one hundred percent not ever.

"Hattie knows about Jordan," he said as the elevator doors opened.

They walked in, Mo tagged the button, and turned to Axl.

"And?"

"I gave her the brief, and it was brief, and told her that was all she'd ever get. We won't talk about it again."

"Axe," Mo said low.

"Yeah," he muttered. "Not a good call."

"You gotta be ready to talk about this shit," Mo stated. "I don't know how this started, but you obviously weren't ready to talk about it. Just tell her that. She'll get it."

"She reminded me that the fallout of her having a dad like she has isn't mine unless she makes it mine, but I made it mine before she gave that to me."

"It's not the same thing."

"Isn't it?"

Mo didn't reply.

"And she said if I let her deal with that on her own, I'm the shittiest boyfriend in history. And she's right. She also said we won't work if I protect her from me."

"She's right about that too," Mo said carefully.

"How do you deal with it with Lottie?" he asked as the elevator doors opened.

They stepped out.

But they didn't go to the office.

They stood in the hall and Mo answered, "I don't, she does."

"What?"

"She does," he repeated. "To use the correlation Hattie's making, you told me you laid it out for her dad. *She* didn't have that conversation with him, you did. She wasn't dealing with that, you were. Shit gets real for me, you guys aren't close, Lottie rolls in. I feel it, she absorbs it. We all know there's a never-ending well of it. She just wrings herself out so, when it comes again, she can suck it up."

He hated that for Mo.

And he hated that for Mac.

And he didn't want that for Hattie.

"And that doesn't gut you?" he asked.

"I fuckin' hate it. But she doesn't. She loves me and that's a part of me and she has all the patience in the world for it, all the time I need, because she has both of those for me in everything, and this is part of that everything."

Shit.

With Hattie's last speech she was telling him she was that kind of woman.

More.

She needed to be that woman for him.

"I fucked this up," Axl stated the obvious.

"Listen to this, brother. If she is who she needs to be for you, she would hate with everything she's got that you feel that way. Text her. Tell her you'll talk later. And I'll bet you a thousand dollars standing here right now, you'll get a text back in less than a minute."

He pulled out his phone, saying, "I won't take that bet."

Mo grinned at him, it was slight, imperceptible to the untrained eye, but he did it.

He then slapped a hand on Axl's shoulder that nearly sent him two inches into the floor.

Mo went to the office.

Axl stayed in the hall to text Hattie.

That didn't go well. I was unprepared.
So fucking sorry I acted like an ass.
We'll talk about it later, baby.
Enjoy the shower.

And he was barely inside the door to the office when his phone chimed.

You didn't act like an ass.
We were both unprepared. I didn't
handle it great either.
We'll talk, but only when you're
ready.
Now you badasses are only
allowed to plan an end to
whatever is going on.
Not take over the world.
xxx♥♥♥xxx♥♥♥

He grinned at her quip, but more, her indication they were okay.

So when he lifted his head and saw Mo's eyes sharp on him, he jutted his chin.

Mo jutted his back.

He entered the conference room and noted immediately this business was getting crowded.

Their crew: Hawk, Mo, Boone, Aug, Mag, Jorge and Axl.

Nightingale's team: Lee, his right-hand man Luke Stark, and his stealth guy, Vance Crowe.

Chaos: Rush Allen, their president, Tack Allen, their past president, also Shy Cage, Joker Steele and Dutch Black.

Sebring: Knight, and his first lieutenant, Rhashan.

Cisco: Brett and his driver, bodyguard and general Man Friday, Joe.

The cops: Eddie, Hank, Malik and Hawk's two other best buds outside Tack, Mitch and Brock.

And last, a free agent, Ally Zano, sister to Hank and Lee, resident badass with a pussy.

Chairs had been brought in, but Mag, Vance, Joker, Dutch, Joe, Rhashan and Eddie had all opted to hold up various walls.

As Mo took his seat, Axl moved to stand by Mag.

"Right, let's get this shit out of the way so we can all have a Saturday," Hawk started it and then looked to him. "Axe, break down what you told me this morning."

Axl gave it to them about the setup.

When he was done, Hawk shifted his attention to Lee, "You're up."

Lee nodded and launched in.

"Part one, I had Brody on something else yesterday, so it sucks you lost a day when he could have saved you that time, but he had to put your search aside until this morning. But he got on it and Laszlo Kovack took a company transfer about a week after Boone handed him his ass. He's currently up to his neck in packing to move to Portland, Oregon, something that's scheduled to occur next Monday. And as a farewell to Colorado, he's up in Vail right now, and this morning he had a Denver omelet for breakfast prior to gassing up and heading back down. However, what there is absolutely no evidence of him doing is dicking with Axl and Boone. So it'd come as a big surprise to him if you boys showed and handed him his ass again."

And there it was.

They were being played.

And Axl bet there were eyes on Laszlo Kovack's house so they could get caught in the middle of handing a man his ass.

But now, they couldn't look for those eyes because, in how they needed to look, it was very illegal, so they couldn't get caught trying to find the means set up to catch them out.

"Onward from that," Lee continued, "Brody confirmed Kovack's computer was also hacked. He sometimes takes pictures of his partners. And those are the shots that were sent to Hattie. So as Axl figured out, it was a setup." Lee looked to Boone. "He's bi, he sometimes does multiple partners, but there aren't any shots of your woman."

Some of the tension shifted from Boone's shoulders.

"Part two," Lee carried on. "We finally got something interesting on the ME that reported the Mueller/Bogart double murder was a murder-suicide, before he changed his findings in the official report. He's been laying low, keeping his nose clean. Though, it seems the high stress of his job had to be addressed. And he did that by sorting a vacation on a houseboat on Lake Powell, something he and his wife like to do once a year. Thing is, this time, he bought the whole fucking houseboat. And two jet skis. And to round that out, a powerboat. All with cash."

And there that was.

He'd been bought.

"At least he didn't sell his soul on the cheap," Shy noted with open disgust.

"Yeah," Lee replied.

"That needs a follow-up, he needs someone leaning on him about that," Tack noted. "And since Eddie already got up in his shit about it, it can't be a cop."

"When's he going to Lake Powell?" Knight asked.

"Next week," Lee answered.

Knight nodded. "I'll talk to Sylvie and Tucker. They can plan a family vacation. Head up from Phoenix, track his ass down and finesse a conversation."

There were nods of assent all around that was the way to go.

"Now for another break," Hawk said then he focused on Jorge. "Jorge?"

"With Brody hung up, but the diagnostics run, we picked shit up on Ryn's laptop. She had three hacks. One to download her web search history. One to download her email. And one to download all her documents and pictures."

Boone already knew this, since it was one of the things they were following up yesterday, but Axl still looked at Boone to see his face hard, his jaw clenched.

He wasn't over that violation of Ryn.

Not surprising.

Jorge kept going.

"These originated from three different Internet cafés. We followed up at the cafés. They got records that show three different bogus IDs were given when he bought time. We ran them. One was from a dead guy. One from an incarcerated guy. And one from a guy who doesn't exist."

"Another dead end?" Ally asked.

Jorge shook his head. "Nope. Checked in with some boys I know who deal fakes. One of them remembered the name that the guy asked for him to use for an ID, since it's apparently some famous porn star's name, Phil Charismo."

"For fuck's sake," Knight muttered.

"Yeah, pure class," Jorge agreed through sarcasm. "He remembered the name, remembered the guy and remembered the guy visited him with another guy. He thought it was a sting. Patted them down. Asked if they were cops."

"He sold them an ID when he thought they were cops?" Rush asked.

Jorge shook his head. "Not Phil Charismo. But the guy with him, my dealer says he'd lay money on that guy at one point having been a cop. This guy does good fakes. He's also greedy.

What I wouldn't call him is smart. He thinks if he asks a cop if he's a cop, the cop has to say."

The mood in the room lightened a fraction as they silently shared humor about a criminal committing a crime and being this stupid.

"He give a description?" Brock asked.

"Not exactly. Though, he says he wouldn't forget him. But he won't play unless he's paid."

"We'll handle that," Hawk said and looked between Axl and Aug. "B needs another visit. She knows more than she said, and I don't pay to get jacked around."

"She's moved again," Rhashan informed them.

"You got a location?" Hawk asked.

Rhashan shook his head.

"I'm on that and I'm on Brandi," Ally declared.

"It's not you she fucked over, Ally," Hawk pointed out. "Wearing my money and knowing my boys walked out of her place with an operation already underway to take them out, and that operation was using their women, when she specifically said the women were not involved, I'm not okay with that."

"Let's just say I got a way with girl talk," Ally replied.

Hawk didn't argue that.

He nodded.

"Brandi and I need a conversation as well, I work with you," Cisco put in smoothly.

"When I work, I'm a loner type of girl," Ally told him.

"Trust me," Cisco said on a smile. "We'll have fun."

Ally studied him, saw whatever women saw in him, and smiled back.

Jesus.

That was when Hawk went back to Jorge's news.

"We're lookin' into the other two fake IDs to see if either of them have ties to cops. Obviously, the incarcerated one does, but he's from Maryland and doing his time there. Doesn't mean this doesn't have that reach, cops know cops. But that's going to take awhile."

"I can get Brody to help with that," Lee offered.

Hawk nodded again then looked around the room. "Everyone's computer needs a hefty firewall. You don't have a source who can do that for you, get them here. We'll handle it for you."

Axl made a mental note to get his and Hattie's laptops into the office.

He then said, "We need to fuck up without fucking up."

Hawk looked to him. "That was my take."

"I'm not comfortable with that," Mitch put in.

"Nothing that will stick," Hawk returned.

"They can make shit stick, Hawk," Mitch shot back.

"It'll out some players and we need some threads to pull to unravel this, brother," Hawk replied. "We'll be careful that the fucking-up part has a stronger *not* fucking-up part."

"And while some member of your team deals with legal issues because he put himself out there to be arrested, we've lost resources that could be put to better use," Mitch retorted.

"Let me talk to Resurrection," Rush suggested.

"Room's already pretty fuckin' packed, man," Luke noted.

"Resurrection won't mind a couple of brothers going down for something they didn't really do," Rush replied. "As long as we make sure their asses are pulled out of that sling. And anyway, back in the day when they were Bounty, if B can be believed, they were in bed with these assholes without knowing they were in bed with them. They were the ones who were running security for those transports that were taken down. If that was me and my club had that in its history, I'd wanna know. Having it in their history without knowing it makes them vulnerable. It also makes them motivated to find out who was really behind that shit. So them getting involved in this won't come as a surprise. They had men who did time back then, ties like that bind. We're allies. If I don't share that with them, they find out we knew, we'd lose that, and we need shit copacetic with MCs all the time, but now especially."

Axl didn't miss the proud look Tack Allen had on his face when his son was talking.

And he thought it'd be interesting to know how that felt, having a dad that was proud of you and did not hesitate showing it.

Though he suspected he'd never know.

"Mitch, you good with that?" Hawk asked.

"Plan carefully, Hawk," Mitch said quietly. "We do not need innocent men behind bars and dirty cops free."

No one said anything because no one disagreed.

Hank broke the silence.

"By the book."

Yeah.

Fuck.

From here on out, they had to keep their noses clean.

Or be even more careful when they didn't.

"Hawk, you definitely. Lee, you too. And Knight, you watch your back," Hank went on.

Knight's lips thinned.

"Brandi mentioned you and Eddie specifically, Hank," Aug reminded him of something they'd already reported.

"We're clean," Eddie grunted.

He and Hank were partners.

Hank knew the rules, and for the most part, played by them.

It was lore that Eddie Chavez had always shot from the hip.

If it wasn't this situation, this would almost be funny.

But it was this situation.

So it was not funny.

"We're up," Malik put in. "Me and Mitch and Brock. We can't swing our asses out there, but you got inside shit you need done in a cop shop, you come to one of us."

There were general murmurings of agreement all around.

"Right, we have movement," Hawk said in a way they all knew he was ending it. "Not much, but there's something there now when before, we had nothing. Cisco and I are still on Mamá to get to Lynn and Heidi. For now, we just had a huge fuckin' wake-up call to stay smart and vigilant. Let's not drop that ball."

There was more murmuring of concurrence.

And the meeting was adjourned.

* * *

After the meet, they'd had time to grill burgers at Lottie and Mo's while the women continued to do whatever women did at a bridal shower.

Hawk joined them, and not only because his wife, Gwen, was at the shower.

Boone was pissed.

And Axl had walked into the meeting raw from a conversation with Hattie.

Boone wasn't hiding his and Hawk was the kind of man, part because he was their boss, part because he was a good guy, and part because he was a vet himself, who would not miss the kind of raw Axl was feeling.

Not to mention, one of his own was imminently getting married to a fine woman who loved him more than her own life.

So he stuck with his men.

They all started getting texts, though, and none of them fucked around with moving out to go to their women.

As Axl passed the house, he saw Hattie come out of it and he knew she'd been watching for him.

Looking out for him.

Feelings invaded, some of them bad—Jordan coming up, how he hadn't handled that well with Hattie.

A lot of them good, culminating in him having to park three houses down from Jet and Eddie's, but by the time he got out of the Jeep, Hattie was skip-running his way.

He was on the grassy verge up from the curb, hadn't even made the sidewalk, when she hit him, and he immediately curved his arms around her.

She arched in, one arm around his shoulders, one hand wrapped around the back of his neck.

She'd gripped his neck like that before.

That night they made love.

He knew right then it was her brand, hot on his skin in a way that radiated out and released the tension from his neck and shoulders better than any steam or massage.

"Hi," she said softly.

Christ, his girl was something.

"Hey," he replied. "Have fun?"

"It was a blast."

He grinned at her, but it was small, and it died fast.

"Babe—" he started.

"You don't have to—"

"I do."

She went quiet.

"I wasn't ready to talk about that piece, or Jordan. But you're right. It's a part of me and with what we're building, I need to give it to you. And I should have just said I wasn't ready instead of being a dick to you."

"And *you* were right," she instantly returned. "That wasn't about me. I should have let it go and then brought it up later, letting you know it was important to me to have it, but you could give it to me when the time was right for you."

"Okay, but I could have been cooler in how I communicated to you."

"Axl, honey, I want *you* just as you are. Not diluted. Not

careful with every step you take or word you say. You were feeling something, and you let it out. My point is, I can take it."

"Yes, I know, you've been taking a lot from your father for a really fuckin' long time."

Her entire head jerked, her curls bouncing.

"That's not like my dad."

"It's—"

Her hand on his neck squeezed hard.

"Axl, it is not one thing like my dad. We're going to fight. There are going to be times when you're not cool, or I'm not cool. We just experienced one. That isn't like what my dad does. It's being in a relationship."

His voice dipped. "I never wanna hurt you, Hattie."

Emotions moved over her features, at first surprised, then gorgeous and shining.

Oh yeah.

She was falling in love with him.

Maybe already there.

After today, he knew he was.

And wasn't that the fuck of it.

Jordan would have been all over his ass for being a dick to Hattie.

But he would have loved it, knowing a fight that was partly about him, led Axl to truly realize the kind of woman Hattie was and that she was the woman for him.

"Please stop being so hard on yourself," she urged. "That upsets me. Having honest reactions and being real with me does not."

Yeah.

She was the woman for him.

On that thought, he decided it was time to kiss her hello.

So that was what he did.

And he did such a complete job of it, Elvira clicked by them, ordering, "Good Lord, take it to a room."

That was also a good idea.

So Axl broke the kiss, took her hand, moved her to his Jeep and helped her in.

Then he got in and took them to a room.

CHAPTER TWENTY-ONE
Stolen Base

AXL

It was Sunday morning, they were out on the deck with fresh coffee, warm biscuits from a tube that Axl had thrown into the oven, a plate of butter and a jar of apple butter.

And Hattie had just declared, "Tonight, Jacuzzi time," when his phone rang.

He looked down at it on the table, saw it was his dad, and he really wanted to ignore it.

Especially since he'd rather talk about planning Jacuzzi time with Hattie.

It'd be the perfect thing to look forward to if shit went south with her dad at the game that day.

Don had said yes.

Axl was a little surprised.

A little encouraged.

And a lot concerned.

But considering how cagey Axl's mom was being, he figured he should talk to his dad just in case, by some minor miracle, Axl could ferret something out of him about what was going on with those two.

"Definitely," he said to her as he reached for his phone. "Gotta take this, babe."

She nodded, staring at his phone like it was a snake that could bite him.

He put it to his ear. "Hey, Dad."

"The girl you're dating is a *stripper*?"

"Be back," he said to Hattie, rising from his seat.

She watched him closely but said nothing.

"Is she there with you right now?" his father demanded incredulously.

"Yeah," he answered, moving into the house and making certain the door was shut behind him.

"How serious is this?"

"She's been to dinner at my parents' house. How serious do you think it is?" Axl returned, stopping at the kitchen sink and aiming his eyes out the window.

"I cannot believe you brought a stripper into your mother's and my home," Sylas bit out.

"I cannot believe you investigated my girlfriend."

"We have an in-house investigator, as you know, and you come from money. I wouldn't be a good father if I didn't do it."

Axl couldn't believe his ears.

"Right, and what else did you find, Dad? That she's an artist as well as a dancer? That she pays her bills, has never been arrested, has no problems with drugs or alcohol, has a lot of good friends who love her and are loyal to her because she's lovable and inspires loyalty? Did you find all that out and then call me to bitch about her having been a stripper? Is that what a good dad does?"

"I can't understand you," Sylas spat. "You're a good-looking man. You have a nice home. A job that pays well. You could have any woman you wanted. What on earth are you doing with a stripper?"

Axl had a ready reply, but he didn't get to say it because his father spoke again, not to Axl.

"Yes, I'm confronting him about it. Of course, I'm confronting him about it." A pause and then, "Are you *insane*?"

"Dad," he clipped.

His phone buzzed in his hand.

He looked down at it and saw he had an incoming call from his mother.

Jesus Christ.

He put it back to his ear only to hear his father demand, "Do not answer that. We're not done."

"'Bye, Dad," he said, selected the button to disconnect and pick up, put the phone back to his ear and said, "Ma, I'm good."

"Don't listen to your father, Hattie's a lovely girl."

"I know that, Mom."

"Hang up with him right now," he could hear his father ordering.

"I'm not hanging up with my son," she snapped. "And I'm not letting him listen to your rubbish."

"This is unbelievable. He's a smart guy. How he can be this stupid is beyond me. She's after his money," his father declared.

"You mean you think she's after *your* money," his mom said.

"*Family* money," his dad shot back.

"*Your* money, Sylas. And I regret to inform you of this, but it is *not* always *all about you*."

"Rachel!" It was a distant shout.

She was moving away.

"Axl, sweetheart, forget this even happened," she urged into the phone.

"That's impossible because this is serious, Mom, what I have with Hattie. And he has a choice to accept her and be kind and respectful to her or he doesn't see either of us. Is this understood?"

"Perfectly," she stated with no hesitation. "Now, on another note, I need some of your time soon. Later in the week. Could you have lunch with me?"

Shit.

He put it right out there.

"You're leaving him."

There was a hesitation then.

"I...well, darling, how did you know?"

She sounded freaked.

The door opened and Axl spoke his next while looking in Hattie's eyes as she came inside.

"You always put up with his shit. You're not putting up with his shit anymore."

"Rachel!"

"I can't talk about this now, Axl," Rachel said quickly. "And I hope I can trust you not to mention anything to your father. I don't quite have all my ducks in a row."

"This secret is seriously safe with me," he assured.

"Thank you, sweetheart."

"Give me your phone," he heard his father demand.

"I'll be in touch. Tell Hattie I said hello and a bit later...well, I'll contact her, and we can plan some girl time."

"I cannot even *believe* you're championing this!" Sylas shouted.

"I'm certain she'd love that," Axl said.

"Good, and have a nice day, darling. Speak soon. Love you."

"Love you too. And I know you can't talk about it right now, but before we hang up, you have to know. I'm glad for you. I want you to be happy and I've wanted that a long time. I'm pleased as hell you're going for it and I'll support you any way I can." He let that sink in and finished, "Later, Ma."

Another hesitation before he got a husky, "Good-bye, Axl."

She disconnected.

He dropped his cell on the counter and shared with Hattie, "She's leaving him."

She came right to him, put both hands on his chest and asked, "Wait, was that your mom or your dad?"

"First, Dad."

"Your dad phoned to say your mom was leaving him?"

"My dad phoned to share he'd investigated you, knows you stripped, and is pissed as fuck I brought a stripper into his house and I'm so stupid I don't know you're after his money."

She began to take a step back, but he hooked her with an arm and waylaid her.

"You know I don't believe that shit," he growled.

"I know," she whispered, hands pressing in.

"He's a goddamned dick."

"Honey."

"They got in a fight while Dad was spewing his shit, and then Mom called. She walked away from him and said she wanted some time this week. I put it out there, she confirmed."

"Well, that's good," she said hesitantly.

"It's fuckin' awesome."

He was still growling.

She pushed in with more than her hands.

"I'm okay," he lied.

"You so totally are not."

At that, his head dropped.

Just dropped, like he wasn't in control of it.

It hit her shoulder.

That was when she slid her arms around him, held close and pressed against him tight.

She said nothing, just held on.

When he got it together and lifted his head, she caught his eyes.

"You're not stupid," she said softly.

"I know, baby." He let his gaze move over her face and then asked, "How hard is it for you to keep your shit right now?"

Her voice was vibrating when she answered, "Very."

"I'm okay." It wasn't a lie that time.

"All right, honey," she said, then moved totally in, turning her head and resting her cheek to his chest.

And yeah.

It wasn't a lie.

Now he was okay.

* * *

"Gonna get us some hot dogs, nachos and beers. Babe, you wanna go with me to help carry?"

It was the fourth inning.

And something bizarre was happening.

Don looked to Hattie.

Hattie looked to Don.

Don jerked his head.

Hattie looked to Axl and smiled big and bright. "Of course."

For fucking certain.

Something weird was happening.

"Anything else you want, Dad?" she asked as she got up.

"Beer, hot dogs and nachos sound like just the ticket." Don's gaze came to Axl. "Thank you, son."

So fucking weird.

"Yeah," he grunted, grabbed Hattie's hand and all but dragged her up the steps from their seats he paid a fucking fortune for to get on the first-base line.

Things did not start out weird.

They met Don at a handicapped parking spot and Don was as Axl would have expected. Guarded and reticent.

The vibe was awkward and stilted as they hit Will Call, went in, got their programs and found their seats.

Through warm-ups, the same.

Before the game started, Axl headed up to get them their first round of beers, and when he got back, that was when it happened.

No longer stiff and uncomfortable, it was a father out with his daughter and her boyfriend, kicking back, watching a ball game and having a great time.

Don thanked him for the tickets and said next time, it was on him.

Don asked him how his job was going.

Don asked him how he felt about the Rockies' stand against the Mets from which they just got home.

Don asked him if he'd ever been down to Arizona to catch spring training.

Don told him he'd followed Smithie's Instagram and saw Hattie dancing, "And maybe you and me can take in a show sometime, if that isn't too weird."

And no, that wasn't weird.

The rest of it was.

He stopped his woman in a concession stand line, let her go, got in front of her and looked down at her.

"What the fuck?"

She was very bad at trying to look innocent. "What the fuck what?"

"What'd you say to him?"

"Um…"

That gave him nothing and she didn't expand.

"Hattie," he prompted.

"Okay, so maybe I told him that your dad called you stupid and a pussy and that you found out today your mom was leaving him. And he was really flipped out about your dad calling you stupid and a pussy. He said, 'Jesus, barely know the guy, and still know he's far from stupid and for sure, he's no pussy.' Then he got kinda...*angry* on your behalf."

For the second time that day, Axl couldn't believe his ears.

"Let me get this straight, your whole life, he is not cool with you. He hears about my dad not being cool with me, and he's angry on my behalf?"

She shrugged.

"Jesus," he muttered.

"Hattie?" they heard.

They both looked in that direction.

And fuck him.

Automatically, his jaw tilted sharply, and his back went straight.

A dude was looking Hattie up and down, smiling, and getting in their space.

"Jesus, Hattie, hey," the guy said, the smile going broad.

And then he went right in.

Right...*fucking*...in.

With an arm snaking around her waist, he bent and kissed her cheek.

"Uh, no," Axl ground out.

The man's head turned his way, and way too fucking slowly, he let her go and stepped back.

"Shit, sorry, are you—?" he began.

"Yeah," Axl bit off.

He looked to Hattie. "Sorry, honey. I just saw you and..." Another step back. "You're looking good."

"You too, Flynn. Um...this is my boyfriend, Axl. Axl, this is Flynn," she introduced.

"Axl," the guy said.

"Flynn," Axl returned.

Flynn looked right back to Hattie. "Boyfriend?"

This was an ex.

And two things Axl knew about him.

One, he wasn't the dickhead who was up his own ass about dating a stripper.

Two, he was the one who let her go because he wasn't enough of a man to stop being a boy who wanted all of his toys and he was either far more broken up about it than Hattie realized, or he understood what he lost after she was gone.

"Hey, I called," Flynn said to Hattie.

Yep.

He understood what he lost after she was gone.

And he was scratching into that right in front of Axl.

Motherfucker.

"I know, I just thought...a clean break," Hattie stated uncomfortably.

"I wish you would have picked up, honey."

"You do get I'm standing right here," Axl noted.

The guy turned his attention to Axl.

He was good-looking. Tall. Built. Could probably hold his own with ninety-five percent of the population and best a lot of that.

Axl could totally fuck him up.

And fucking *Flynn* didn't miss it.

"Sorry, I—" he started.

"No, you're not," Axl cut him off.

"Axl," Hattie said softly, edging close to him and taking his hand.

His fingers wound around hers tight.

Flynn didn't miss this either, and goddamn it, he really liked her.

When he saw her holding hands with her man, that was when he backed off.

"It's real good to see you, Hattie," he said.

"Yeah, Flynn. You too."

He took her in...

No, *drank* her in, and the flash of pain he couldn't hide disappeared behind a mask of fake friendship.

"See you around, yeah?" he said.

"Yeah," she replied.

He looked to Axl. "Axl, nice to meet you."

Axl just jerked up his chin.

After another look at Hattie, Flynn turned and walked away.

Axl moved them forward in the line.

"Okay, that was unfun," she mumbled. And louder, "Just in case you didn't get it, that was one of the guys I used to see. The one who wasn't into exclusive."

"He didn't want it to end," he told her.

"I know. He told me that when I broke it off with him. I just didn't want to be one of many."

"How many times did he call you after?"

She considered this a second and...

Christ.

Hattie.

"I don't remember. Five, six."

Axl looked to the ceiling, then twisting his neck along the way, he looked to his shoes.

"What?" she asked.

His gaze went to her. "You really have no fucking clue, do you?"

"No fucking clue about what?"

He noticed the line moved again, and he moved them with it, saying, "No fucking clue how hot you are."

"You like me," she said.

"Yeah, babe, and I started to like you because you're hot."

"And because Lottie set us up."

"No, because you're hot."

She stared at him, befuddled.

Christ.

Hattie.

"You took one of those calls, honey, and he would have told

you he's scraping off his other women to go exclusive for you," he informed her.

She shook her head. "No, he seemed pretty clear—"

"Hattie."

"What?"

"That man who just walked away is kicking his own ass right now, what he's pretty much been doing for months, because he let you slip through his fingers. And now, you are *very* with another guy, and he's blown his chance, and he knows it."

"You can hardly get that in a two-minute interaction with him."

"Wanna bet?"

She stared at him again, this time hard.

"You're gonna get another call from him before this day ends," he told her. "This one he's gonna make to ascertain he actually did blow his chance because he's gonna ask you where you're at with me."

"I really don't think that's going to happen, Axl."

"Naked Jacuzzi sex says it does."

"You can't wager something the other person wants."

He grinned at her.

Then he used her hand to pull her to him so he could bend and press his mouth to hers.

He pulled back an inch and said, "He's gonna call."

She rolled her eyes and said, "Whatever."

He grinned again and moved them forward in line.

They got the beer, dogs and nachos. Hattie loaded up her hot dog along with her dad's, Axl took care of his, and they took them back down to their seats.

And after they passed the food out, Don kept laying it on thick.

"The best. Beer. Ball field hot dogs. Nachos. My girl and her man."

And Axl was done.

He leaned forward to look beyond Hattie and said to her father,

"I know Hattie told you I had a family situation this morning, Don. But I can assure you, I'm fine."

Don leaned forward too.

"My girl is not what I called her, and to my dying day, I'll regret I called her that."

Axl stilled.

Hattie went solid next to him.

"That's my penance," Don went on. "And I hope your father understands that's his too."

"He doesn't understand that, Don."

"Then I'm sorry for you, son. But I'm sorrier for him," Don returned. He looked to his daughter, patted her leg, and said quieter. "I'm sorry, honey."

"It's okay, Dad."

"It's not. But thanks for that anyway," he replied, sat back, aimed his eyes at the field and took a big bite of the hot dog Hattie had covered in ketchup, mustard and onions for him.

Axl turned his eyes to Hattie.

She was staring at him with hers swimming in tears.

"You okay?" he mouthed.

She nodded, sniffed, pulled her shit together, looked to the field and took her own huge bite of hot dog.

Jesus Christ.

Axl sat back and stared at the field.

"The runner should stick closer to the bag, right, Dad?" Hattie asked.

"No, honey, he's a fast one. Got twenty-five stolen bases this year already. Pitcher doesn't keep an eye, he's gone," Don answered.

Five minutes later, Don was proved right.

Stolen base.

* * *

Axl put his phone down at the side of the Jacuzzi and looked to his girl, who was straddling his lap wearing a red-and-white polka-dot bikini.

Yeah.

A fucking polka-dot bikini.

"She says she's okay," he told her about the text he just read from his mom after he'd texted her to ascertain that very thing.

"I really hope after all this drama that we have some smooth sailing for, oh, I don't know, a year or five," she replied.

He smiled at her.

"At least until Lottie and Mo get married," she said.

"Yeah, at least until that," he agreed.

She reached, grabbed her glass, and sucked back some margarita.

He didn't go for his beer.

He went for her ass.

She put her glass back and looked down at him. "I knew I'd love your Jacuzzi the minute I saw it."

"Always liked it. Can't say I ever loved it, until now."

She smiled at him.

"You good with that thing with your dad?" he asked.

"He's never..." She brought her shoulders forward, released them. "He could be apologetic, but that was different."

"Okay."

"I don't know what it means, but I think he had a really good time with us today. I don't think he's been to a game in a long time. He doesn't leave his house much. I think maybe, I don't know..."

She didn't finish that.

He still said, "Yeah."

"It kinda feels stupid to hope," she said softly.

"It's never stupid to hope, baby," he replied.

"Would you take him to a show?" she requested.

"Absolutely," he answered.

"He follows Smithie's on Insta. That's totally not Dad."

"I told him about it."

She looked surprised. "You did?"

"Said they use you a lot to draw an audience."

"Whoa."

"You're special, Hattie. And he knows it. He's always known it. And I can't speak for how he tried to draw it out, push you beyond what you were capable of giving to make you more when you were already great. My sense is, now he's realizing how great you are and always were. And that doesn't have to do with your dancing. It has to do with you being a daughter who would stick by her dad even when he didn't deserve it."

She made a study of watching her finger track his cheekbone, down past the corner of his lips, to his jaw.

"Babe," he called.

Her gaze came to him.

"It's never stupid to hope," he repeated.

"Yeah," she whispered, dipped her head and kissed him.

It got serious.

And then her phone rang.

They broke it off and she reached out and looked at the screen.

It said, FLYNN CALLING.

"Take it." His voice was shaking with laughter.

"Axl, I don't—"

"Take it, baby, naked Jacuzzi sex is on the line."

She shot him a look then took the call.

"Hey, Flynn." Pause then, "No. Um…" Pause then, "Well, actually, honestly, no. We haven't been seeing each other very long."

Axl beat back the audible laughter, but now his entire body was shaking with it.

She shot him a harder look.

And kept talking.

"Sorry, just to say, even so, we've known each other for a while, and I have the code to his phone."

Axl made a noise like he was strangling.

She smacked his shoulder and got water in both their faces.

He didn't mind in the slightest.

"Yes, well, I don't know what to say," she kept going. "I'm sorry about that. I just liked you a lot and it hurt to break it off, so I didn't take your calls because, well, it hurt."

Axl quit laughing.

"Yes, I would have known that if I took your calls, but...I'm so sorry to say this, Flynn, I didn't, and I moved on and now I'm with Axl and this thing I have with him is really going somewhere. So you were honest with me. And even if it hurt, it was a nice way for you to be. So now I have to be honest with you and say there isn't really any chance of that." Pause then, "Yes. It would have been good to know then." Pause and finally, "Yes, you too. It was...it was good between us. And I'll always remember that."

Ouch.

"Yes, 'bye." She beeped to disconnect and put her phone down.

"I don't wanna hear it," she said.

He didn't care.

"Did he break up with them?" he asked.

She grabbed her margarita in an effort to look anywhere but at him.

But she answered, "No. Though he said he was prepared to."

"I bet he was," Axl murmured.

After taking a sip, she put her drink down and narrowed her eyes on him. "I'm glad you're into me, but I'm not all that."

"You so fucking are."

"Well, as it's good not having a boyfriend who thinks he's awesome, it's good you've got a girlfriend who isn't up herself and thinks she's all that."

"Oh no," he said, hooking his thumbs in her bikini pants and shifting her to float just beyond him so he could get them down her thighs. "That's not good. I want you to know exactly how hot you are."

"Axl—"

"Naked Jacuzzi sex, baby. Lose the top," he ordered.

She kept her eyes narrowed on him.

Axl freed the bottoms from her feet and tossed them over the side where they made a wet slap.

He then pulled her back to straddle him, yanked down his trunks, and over the side they went.

And he waited.

Not long after, Hattie lost the top.

CHAPTER TWENTY-TWO

In Her Corner

HATTIE

Thursday late morning, I walked into Smithie's and the gang was almost all there.

I headed to where Lottie and Pepper were sitting on the front edge of the catwalk and Lottie greeted, "Yo," while Pepper greeted, "Hey, Hatz."

"Hey," I returned. "Do you know what this is about?"

We'd been called in by Smithie for a full staff meeting.

The last full staff meeting had been to share with everyone we were moving to a Revue, though the dancers, including me, had known about it beforehand seeing as Smithie and Ian had talked to us about it to make sure we were onboard.

Having no idea what it was about, I didn't think this meeting boded well and I was prepared to be seriously bummed about it if it wasn't good news.

Because, so far, the week had been awesome.

Like, *really* awesome.

Starting with Monday night, when Axl came over to my place

with Cleo after work and I got to give him the equal goodness he'd shown me when he cooked Tuscan chicken for me.

I didn't cook him anything as fabulous as that as I didn't have anything like that in my repertoire. But after he got in and got Cleo sorted, I sat him on a stool, gave him a glass of red, and then served up stuffed shells and garlic knots with a salad and tiramisu for dessert.

And he really liked it (especially the tiramisu, and I made mental note that Axl was an all-around coffee guy).

That night, he also brought over a bag full of stuff, and now he had sleep pants, boxer briefs, tees and socks in his drawer and there were some jeans, shirts and cargos hanging in my closet, as well as some running shoes on a shelf.

Now . . . See?

The week even *started* awesome.

We both fretted (well, Axl didn't fret, but I could tell it was a concern) that Cleo wouldn't take to her new circumstances. But the second she was let out of her carrier, she looked around, went right to my colorful beanbag, jumped on it, collapsed to a hip and started licking her foot.

So, the queen accepted her new dominion by immediately finding her throne.

All good.

It was back to life after that, and that was normal life with some (tentatively) fantastic twists.

It had been deemed safe for the women to do their thing without being protected, so I was able to get back into my studio and start working on the new piece I'd been wanting to dive into.

And when I did, I realized it was a mild form of torture to have to tamp down the need to create.

It was heaven being in the studio. Almost as good as choreographing a new song.

Okay.

No.

Maybe better.

And that was a point to ponder, though I wasn't prepared to ponder it just then.

Onward with the awesomeness, Dad had surprised me when I went over on Tuesday because he'd discovered online grocery shopping with delivery.

And when I inspected what he got, I saw he didn't buy a bunch of crap. Most of it was actually healthy.

He also told me I didn't have to come over Wednesday, because he'd reconnected with his bud, Jim, and they were going out to some sports bar to have dinner and watch the game.

I remembered Jim. He was a nice guy. He and his wife had gotten divorced around the time Mom and Dad did.

And I was glad Dad was finding ways to get out of the house and be with people that weren't me.

Dad also let me off the hook for that night, saying he was going to try some new recipe, which meant Axl and I could eat and hang before I had to go to work without me having to be anywhere it wasn't really my choice to be.

And tomorrow night, Dad was going out to dinner with me and Axl and then he and Axl were going to take in the show.

I was a little nervous about that.

But I was also a little excited for Dad to see that I was dancing because I loved it, and although the memories were jaded, the bottom line was, he played a part in giving me that.

The only thing hanging over our heads was that Axl had double parent duty tomorrow, seeing as he was having lunch with his mother.

He'd heard not one word from his father, which I thought was awesome.

And from his take on his mom's texts, he said, "She sounds like she has it together."

So that was tentatively awesome too.

And last, Axl and I had brunch plans with my mom on Sunday.

I wanted to see Mom, I missed her. It'd been way longer than a minute (too much longer).

But I had to admit, I really loved my first Sunday with Axl when it was just him and me most of the day. Being lazy and making love and eating when we were hungry and playing Pac-Man.

With our schedules, and just how life had been when we started, it'd all been go, go, go and drama. We didn't have a lot of downtime.

And that Sunday, I'd discovered that rejuvenating with Axl was *the best*.

So after this brunch with Mom, I was going to suggest to Axl that, if we could, we made Sundays our days.

I had a feeling he'd go for that.

But now, we'd all been called in for a meeting at the club and I had no idea why.

I just hoped they hadn't assessed how the Revue was doing, weren't pleased with it, and we were going back to just stripping.

I didn't want to go back to stripping.

I didn't have a problem with it. I was good at it, made great money, the club was safe, classy, for the most part the clientele was all right, my fellow dancers were the best, so was management, and I could move my body and get in the zone.

But being able to build my routines and roll them out, that had been another creative outlet I'd come to seriously enjoy.

So on the way to that meeting, I'd realized, with Axl in it, and my relationship with the girls back on track and as strong as ever, not to mention Dad being cool, and work having turned into something that I dug doing, I was in a zone where I actually liked my life.

No.

I loved it.

For the first time, I thought...ever.

And that was mammoth.

So I didn't want anything messing with it.

Although I worried (because that was me), it would surprise me that the Revue wasn't working. The place had been packed every night, regardless of the higher cover charge and drinks prices.

But I was a dancer, I wasn't a businessperson.

What did I know?

"No clue," Pepper answered my question about the meeting, but although she was answering me, she was smiling across the room.

I looked that way to see Ryn approaching.

"Could be anything, knowing Dorian," Lottie said.

She was right.

Dorian was a rare breed. Idea man as well as action man.

And he didn't let grass grow.

We greeted Ryn and she asked the same thing as me.

"Anyone know what this is about?"

We all shared our negatives, then Pepper went on to share she had the same worries as me.

"God, I hope we don't go back to just stripping. I haven't shown my tits since I did 'Cold Hearted' that second week. And I gotta say, it's kinda refreshing being able to keep my kit on."

The last couple of waitresses straggled in as Smithie and Ian came down the stairway that led to Smithie's office.

But Smithie didn't approach the gang gathered around the edge of the catwalk.

He took a seat at the bar as Ian came to us carrying something that looked like rolled-up plans.

Weird.

I mean, we all knew Ian was Smithie's right-hand man.

But Smithie had never taken a backseat.

Dorian did a scan as he approached, probably to see if everyone was there.

He then stopped in front of us, crossed his arms on his chest, which made his pecs bulge under his midnight-blue dress shirt (and I took that opportunity to appreciate it), the roll of paper in his hand peeking over his left shoulder.

"Right, you all got shit to do so we'll make this fast," he began. "The Revue has been very successful, much better than we'd forecast, and it doesn't look like that's gonna slow down," he announced.

Well, then...

Shoo.

Also...

Yippee!

"So in two weeks, we're gonna close," he went on.

There were murmurings of surprise and discontent, swaying of bodies, shuffling of feet.

"For three weeks," he continued.

Everyone shut up and stopped shifting.

"We've been covered in calls from people wanting VIP seating," he shared. "And they're willing to pay for it. So we're constructing booths down each side of the catwalk and elevating the floor so the people behind these new booths can see the stage. The far wall will also be a closed-off VIP area that will serve as a place for larger parties, and when we have celebrity clientele, entourages. Further, we'll be adding lighting embedded in the edges of the stage that can be programmed to a variety of colors, flashes, streams, etcetera."

"*Rad,*" I breathed.

Ian wasn't done.

"And installing apparatus so dancers can make an entrance from above the stage on hoops, in cages, on ropes and poles and most anything else they can dream up."

How cool!

"*Rad*," Pepper, Ryn and I whispered at the same time.

Dorian kept going.

"It's going to be a tight turnaround, but we don't want to lose momentum, so we're hoping our contractors can hit the deadline. During that, the back rooms where the private dances took place will be repurposed into a kitchen. A questionnaire we sent to patrons strongly suggested that they like to stay for a while and they don't only want to drink, they want to eat. To fill that need, we've hired Joy Anderson to take over the kitchen."

"Joy Anderson, the woman who does the Joy of Food food trucks?" one of the waitresses asked.

"Her," Ian confirmed. "It will be an extensive, gourmet appetizer menu."

"This is so fucking *cool*," Ryn said under her breath.

It totally was.

They were taking it from a classy strip joint to a straight-up class club.

And we were in on that. We got to watch it unfold. Help them.

On these thoughts, I studied Ian even more closely.

He seemed his usual.

Confident.

Sure.

But it couldn't be denied.

He was reaching for something.

Working for it.

Risking it.

Going for his dream.

And we got to be a part of that for him.

Yes, this week was *totally awesome*.

"New furniture will replace the old," Ian carried on. "More comfortable and styled to match the booths, which will be red velvet."

"I am loving this so much," Pepper whispered.

"We've also begun booking talent," Ian stated.

"Uh-oh," Lottie muttered.

Yeah.

Uh-oh.

More dancers?

Like...

Better ones?

"We currently have three up-and-coming comedians who will be doing routines intermingled with guest MCing the program," he shared. "We're looking at more and we're in search of a talent who can be the resident MC and provide filler so there will only be burlesque routines with the headline performances. No outright exotic dancing until two in the morning after the last headliner leaves the stage. But when we reopen, there'll be no nudity. We'll provide costumes, which will be attractive, sexy, and brief, but they will also provide coverage."

"Wow," I whispered.

Ian looked to us girls. "I need all the headliners here next Tuesday at eleven. I'll tell you which of your dances I want you prepared to do. We're having videographers come in to film your routines. We're updating our website and we need content for that, as well as teasers and marketing promos to keep our clientele's interest and get them to return when we reopen."

I didn't even know Smithie's had a website.

"Down," Lottie called.

"So down," Ryn said.

I just smiled hugely at Ian.

He took in my smile and his lips quirked.

He then uncrossed his arms and showed us the roll of paper.

"These are the plans. I'll lay them out and you can have a look if you're interested. Any questions?"

"Are we gonna get paid for that three weeks?" a bartender I

didn't know all that well, though he'd been around awhile (and he was kinda annoying, which was the reason I steered clear) named Craig asked.

"Yes," Dorian answered. "Any other questions?"

There were more questions, a lot of them (hate to be judgy, but seriously, ugh) were kind of unnecessary (these mostly coming from Craig), seeming like folks just wanted to suck time or make people listen to them talk (again, mostly Craig).

Ian seemed to have all the patience in the world for them (though going on like that was keeping me from the studio), something Smithie would not have. On question two, Smithie would get ticked, ask if he'd ever left anyone hanging, wonder aloud why he got no respect (which, honestly, was a good question), and tell us he had better things to do before he took off and did those things.

Eventually, it seemed we were going over old ground and Ian ended it.

He then told us if there was anything anyone wanted to discuss in private, they could find him or Smithie.

He unrolled the plans on a table, thanked us for our time and strolled away.

He met Smithie where the big boss still stood at the bar and I felt a little thrill run down my spine.

Not only at the way Smithie was looking at Dorian, with pride and respect.

But there was something different about Smithie.

He looked...

Chill.

"The handover is complete," Ryn remarked, and I looked to her and saw her watching Smithie and Ian go up the steps.

"Yeah, it isn't official, but it's still totally official," Pepper agreed.

"Good for Smithie," Lottie said. "He deserves to take a breather from all the time-suck and drama. Craig asking if we were gonna get paid, then asking if PTO would still accrue, then asking if we'd have an employee discount for food, then that shit about a health and safety course to best navigate the elevated floor. I don't know how Ian does it. The dude is a tool."

I admired Lottie's ability to be judgy, but sound like she was just saying it like it was.

Then again, she was.

Craig was a tool.

We all hung back and waited until everyone drifted away from the plans before we went to go look at them.

"Killer," Pepper said, gazing down at them.

And, man...

She was right.

"I thought the club was hot before, but this isn't next level. This is five levels above that," Ryn noted.

She wasn't wrong.

I continued to study the design, thinking that I wanted to tell Axl to cancel plans with Dad for tomorrow and make them after the renovation had been done.

Which reminded me.

"Axl and Dad are coming to the show tomorrow night," I announced.

"No shit?" Lottie asked.

"Whoa," Ryn said.

Pepper just stared at me.

"No, it's good," I said to Pepper. "Axl's going to take him home after my last dance so he won't have to sit next to him during any out-and-out stripping. Because, you know...gross."

"If you think it's good, then I think it's good. But just sayin', all this stuff that's going on with your dad, it's like a whiplash turnaround," Pepper replied.

She could say that again.

"I know," I agreed.

"Keep your guard up, babe," she warned. "It's my experience a leopard doesn't change its spots."

I nodded to her, and when I thought she'd looked away, I gave eyes to Ryn and Lottie.

"What's with the eyes?" Pepper asked.

Okay, maybe I should have made sure that she'd looked away.

But she saw them, and I'd learned of late that avoidance was something to avoid.

Not to mention, my girls were my girls. They could take and give the honesty, and I'd discovered it wasn't ever ugly.

So I went for it.

"Just, you know, maybe Dad had reason to have a reality check when Axl had words with him."

"Maybe he did, all I'm saying, Hatz, is be careful with your heart," Pepper replied.

"No, what I mean is, Axl is an outsider to the unit, but one who cares about me. So it was objective, but wasn't, if you know what I mean. And sometimes, an objective opinion can make people think. Though, I don't know if that's all there was to it. I think another part was me telling Dad that Axl's father said such nasty things to him. I think that was his, 'Hey, wait,' moment. You know, something like, 'I did that too and it was really uncool.' You know?"

"Okay, but still...look after yourself," Pepper reiterated.

"Right, I'm butting in here to say what Hatz isn't outright saying, Pez," Lottie did, indeed, butt in. "You need to stop dicking around and go out with Auggie."

"Exactly," I concurred.

"Totes," Ryn added.

"How is what she said—?" Pepper began.

"Axl was hands on," Lottie stated. "That might not be where it's at for you. But bottom line, you need a buffer from those jackals you call parents, that maggot of an ex of yours, and what she didn't say, but I will, is, girl, it's been a dry spell from hell. You need to get laid," Lottie expounded.

"Word," Ryn agreed.

"Listen—" Pepper tried.

"Nope." Lottie held up a hand and shook her blonde locks. "It was touch-and-go there for both Rinz and Hatz when Boone and Axl started seeing other bitches. You don't need Aug to give up and start looking. Serious, with Axl, it was a close call, since Mo said the chick he was seeing was solid."

"I know, *phew*," I put in. "He really liked her. They still text a lot."

Pepper did a slow blink at me.

She then asked, aghast, "You let him text another woman?"

"Well, sure. They're friends," I answered.

"She's someone he dated," Pepper pointed out.

"I know," I told her.

Her face twisted in a weird way. "Hatz, babe, he's probably been inside her."

Um…

"I try not to think about that part."

"I wouldn't be able to stop thinking about it," she said.

Hmm.

"He's with Hattie," Lottie noted firmly.

"He isn't Corbin," Ryn put in.

Oh yeah.

Right.

God.

How could I forget?

Corbin, Pepper's ex, cheated on her to the full extent of the definition of cheating (and then some).

In other words, he'd moved in with her, committed to her, had a baby with her, and kept fucking his ex-girlfriend through all of that, and obviously, she didn't know.

The ex-girlfriend didn't know.

But getting away with it for years, he eventually got lazy, left a trail Pepper followed, there were a variety of nasty confrontations, and *boom*.

Suddenly she's a very young single mom, her ex is pissed that she rained on his parade, he takes it out on her, uses their daughter as a weapon, and insult to injury, Pepper's parents made members of the moral majority look like hippies. They'd washed their hands of her when she moved in with Corbin out of wedlock, without washing their hands of her, since they intermittently got in her space to share she was going to hell.

"I know he isn't," Pepper said to Ryn.

"And Auggie isn't Corbin," Lottie added.

"I know he isn't," Pepper repeated to Lottie, a wee bit more impatient this time.

"So, what gives?" Lottie asked. "I mean, she shoots, she scores, three times, babe," Lottie reminded her of the wins she'd had with Evie and Mag, Boone and Ryn and me and Axl, doing it pointing to herself then Ryn and me.

"It's more complicated when you have a kid," Pepper said.

"It is not," Ryn returned. "You're being chicken."

"I'm not being chicken," Pepper snapped.

"I'd make chicken noises, but I'm above that," Ryn said to Lottie.

Lottie laughed.

Although that was funny, I was seeing they weren't getting this wasn't a funny moment for Pepper.

I kept my gaze on Pepper and suggested quietly, "Maybe we should lay off."

"Yeah, that'd be good," Pepper said curtly.

"As far as I know, you're not Benjamin Button," Ryn told her. "You dig what I'm saying to you?"

Pepper stepped back from us.

Yup.

This wasn't a funny moment.

I braced.

And it was a good thing I did.

"You know, I would never want to have a psychopath obsessed with me, like you," Pepper said to Lottie. "Or have a friend murdered and some guy whacked at my back door, like you," she said to Ryn. "Or have someone send me dirty pictures and emails like you," she said to me. "Or gambling addict fathers." Back to Lottie. "Alcoholic brothers." To Ryn. "Or abusive fathers." To me. "But I have never, *never* been loved by my parents. I have always, *always* been an outsider in that family. I meet a guy who I think loves me, loves...*me*. He wants to make a family with me and build a future with me and every year it's going to be putting up the Christmas tree and taking out the ornaments with the years on or remembering when we got them on vacation or when we had another baby or that year we made decorations as a family. And he was *fucking around on me from the start*."

Oh man.

We totally should have laid off.

She was far from done.

"And since I found out and we were over, he's just been *fucking with me*. And I have you guys, and *that's it*. My sister is programmed to their bullshit. My brother took off to escape it before I even graduated from high school and no one has heard from him since. So day-to-day, hour-to-hour, minute-to-minute, except for Juno, *who is my kid*, and I have to protect her from all this, I'm very, *very* alone."

She took a huge breath as we all stood there, silent and still, listening.

And I knew for me, but I figured the same for Lots and Rinz, hurting for Pepper.

Then she launched in again.

"And with what I endured growing up. And what Corbin did to us, and he did it *to us*, me and my baby girl, and keeps doing, I know one thing. I need to protect my daughter. So yeah. Auggie is hot. He seems nice. Lottie wouldn't fix me up with a loser. But I come with baggage." She focused on me. "The kind that *no way in hell*, when he's with me, I'd let him text some woman he's fucked." She glanced around. "And these guys are who they are. They do what they do. And so he gets with me and finds my baggage too much to bear, my hang-ups tying him too tight, and he scrapes me off, it isn't about just me losing him. Which is bad enough. My daughter loses him too. She's already been through that and I'm not gonna put her through it again. So maybe you can put yourself in my shoes for a hot fucking second and then *back off*."

"Maybe he won't—" Ryn began.

"*Back off!*" Pepper screamed.

Dang.

"Pepper," Lottie said softly.

"Are you backing off?" Pepper snapped.

"Sure, girl, if that's what you need," Lottie gently replied.

"I gotta go," Pepper suddenly announced.

"Hey," I called as she started to take off, not liking her leaving in that state.

"I can't, Hatz, okay?" she asked. She looked to Ryn. "I'm sorry I lost it."

"I'm sorry I pushed," Ryn replied.

"Right. Cool. Now I gotta go. Later," she finished.

And then she went.

We all watched.

When she disappeared out the front door into the sun, Ryn murmured, "Okay, well, shit on a stick. That didn't go too good."

I said nothing.

Lottie said nothing.

Since it was weird Lottie said nothing, I looked to Lottie.

She was gazing across the room.

So I turned my attention there.

And Dorian was standing a couple steps into the club from the stairs to the office.

He had his hands on his hips and his eyes on the front door.

Seemed Ian witnessed that, and although he couldn't hear our conversation, he couldn't miss Pepper screaming at us.

His face was inscrutable as he continued to look at the door before he dropped his hands, turned and moved back up the stairs.

"Okay, well, one, she wants Auggie bad, she won't let herself have him, and all her closest babes are loved up and it's tearing her apart," Lottie declared.

I started staring at her because I didn't get that from Pepper at all.

What I got was, she was protecting her daughter, and her heart, and Auggie was not a possibility because I got her.

These guys were these guys and you had to be in the position to let them be who they were.

They did the same, of course.

But I could totally see Pepper needing more from Auggie than he might be comfortable giving, this so she could trust him, when it wasn't Auggie that broke her trust, but he'd be the one who'd have to build it again (if that was even possible).

And just how much it would hurt to find out he wasn't comfortable giving that, and as such, not going there at all.

For her.

And for Juno.

"Totes," Ryn replied to Lottie.

Hunh?

Lottie again said nothing.

So I asked, "What's two?"

She turned her attention to me. "There is no two. There's just that one. You can lead a horse to water and all that. Now, we back off. I gotta talk to Ian real quick. See you tonight."

And then she was off, walking with a purpose toward the stairs.

Ryn came to stand at my side so we could both watch her go.

When we couldn't see her anymore, Ryn said, "She totally has a plan."

She totally did and that concerned me.

Because not only was she Lottie, and one of her plans meant I was sleeping beside Axl every night, but also because she was headed to Dorian.

And as I'd previously noted, Dorian was an action man.

"Totally," I agreed.

"I'm glad I'm not the last one standing, that would suck," she went on.

It seriously would.

"Totally," I repeated.

I mean, it was bad enough seeing how happy Lottie, Evie and Ryn were when my guy was within reach and I wasn't reaching.

It'd be so much worse if it wasn't just being scared to take the risk but feeling like I *couldn't* reach.

"Maybe we should tone down the domestic bliss," I suggested.

"Maybe, I don't know."

I looked to her. "Why don't you know?"

She turned fully to me. "I was in the offices when Gwen brought all her and Hawk's kids in. And all three of them, like a shot, the two boys and his little girl, went right to Aug."

"Oh man," I said.

"Yeah, he loves kids. Like, a lot. And they love him back."

And thus, one reason Lottie picked him for Pepper.

"My mom said something to me, when shit got real with my brother," Ryn continued. "About how happy she was that I finally had someone in my corner. Pepper's got it going on, but she also takes a lot of shit from a lot of directions. It'd be good to see her have someone in her corner. And not just us."

Pepper did take a lot of shit.

So it *so* would.

And this got me to thinking, maybe I was wrong.

Mag stepped in, and the stuff with Evie's family had been extreme. They put her in some serious shit. Mag got shot in the middle of it.

And now they were getting married.

Ryn's sitch hadn't been that dramatic, but she definitely had some baggage, including, I'd recently discovered, a past partner breaking trust with her in a fundamental and fundamentally terrifying way, and she and Boone were completely solid.

Shit had been real from the beginning with Axl and me, and except for us not very successfully navigating the situation with his sadly departed friend, that had been brief, and other than that, between him and me, it was all smooth sailing.

Lottie hadn't just wanted to see her girls and her guys happy.

She'd been very deliberate about all this.

And she was not unaware of Pepper's past, and the important aspect of Juno being in that mix.

I'd been so deep in all the things I was dealing with, it hadn't occurred to me to look more closely at what Pepper's day-to-day life would be like.

And my friend really needed someone in her corner.

And not just her girls.

So, to communicate I agreed, I repeated myself again.

This time with feeling.

"Totally."

CHAPTER TWENTY-THREE

She Was Mine Before

HATTIE

Having left the club, on the way to my studio, I called Axl.

I was kinda bummed because, after that scene with Pepper, I wasn't thinking about the piece I was working on.

I was thinking about my friend and that maybe I needed to spend more time in her corner.

Like, say, after we inadvertently upset her (a lot) and she'd gone off on her own, instead of going to my studio to work on my art, find her and share I was in her corner. Also admit I might not have been real good at doing that in the past. But now I was all in.

So, yeah.

I was bummed I wasn't in a work-at-the-studio mood.

But more bummed that my friend was in a bad place.

And I decided, once I got to the studio, I'd text her. See if she wanted to meet for a coffee.

Or something.

On this thought, Axl picked up.

"Hey, babe."

"Hey, uh, heading to the studio," I told him.

"Cool," he replied.

Okay, now...

Um...

Where to begin?

"You good?" he asked.

"Well..."

In truth, I knew where to begin.

I just didn't know if I should begin there.

That being, feel him out about what to do about Pepper and Auggie.

And by feel him out, I meant enlist his services to get Auggie to get the lead out in going for Pepper.

"Hattie," Axl prompted.

"Okay, well, the meeting was about Smithie's closing for three weeks," I told him. "They're doing some renovations. VIP seating and putting in a kitchen because they're going to start serving food. It's all good, including for us. We'll keep getting paid. And Smithie covers tips. Truth, I can have better nights than he covers, but I won't be hurting."

"Right, then yeah. All good," he said. "And that gives you free time to be in the studio."

I hadn't said anything outright, but he sensed I was jonesing to get back to it.

My guy.

Such a *good* guy and so tuned to me.

"Yeah," I agreed.

I said no more.

Axl waited.

Until he was done waiting.

"Babe," he pushed, knowing there was more to say.

"Okay, we had a blowup with Pepper when we pushed her about getting together with Auggie."

"Shit," he muttered.

And the way he did, I knew now he had more to say.

"What?" I asked.

"I take it she was resistant to going there with Aug?" he asked back.

"Very," I answered.

"Right, well, not too long ago, I got up in Auggie's shit about this same thing. And, babe, prepare. Because she's not giving him anything and he gets why she isn't. He digs her and wants to go there, but you don't push a woman with a kid. So my guess, he's going to be moving on if he isn't in that zone already."

That wasn't good news.

But I was stuck on something else.

"You don't push a woman with a kid?" I asked.

"There's more going on there," he said as answer.

"I know, but she's still a woman, even if she has a kid," I said.

Axl had no reply.

Thus, I kept talking.

"I mean, yes, if something happened with them, he'd be getting both of them in his life. And I see that'd be daunting, because he doesn't just have to win Pepper, he has to win Juno. But those are two different things. Because they're two different people. And a man should approach them as two different things. But he can't get either if he doesn't start with one."

There was a long pause before Axl inquired, "What's her gig?"

"Trust," I told him. "Her ex cheated on her and I don't mean he strayed. I mean he was sleeping with another woman their entire relationship."

"Jesus," he muttered.

"Unh-hunh," I agreed. "And that doesn't get into her family, who are very, *very* Christian. Like, her mom and sister don't wear pants, they wear skirts and dresses, because women should not only not wear men's clothes, they shouldn't highlight certain parts of their bodies. They go to revivals. And she told us that her father contends God spoke through him once. He was talking in tongues. She was there to see, said it was lunacy and scared the crap out of her. It happened when she was twelve or thirteen. That's pretty crazy, but I still could go on."

"So her family's not in her life," he deduced.

"She'd like that, them not being in her life. But every so often, they show up, intent to get her back into the fold. Once, she said she wouldn't put it past them to kidnap her or Juno and try to brainwash them into compliance."

Axl's tone was different, brisk and commanding, when he asked, "Does she feel they pose a serious threat?"

God.

My guy.

Such a good guy and *so* protective.

"No, honey," I assured. "She was joking. Or not joking, making a joke while complaining."

"Right."

"So…" I said, hoping he'd fill in the blanks.

"So?" he asked, not filling in the blanks.

Which meant I had to.

"Um, obviously, with all of this, Auggie needs to get a move on."

"Babe."

That word was dripping discouragement.

"She's got no one in her corner, Axl."

I heard a sigh and then, "I get that you'd want your friend to be happy, but maybe they weren't meant to be."

"Mag and Evie found a house, one they both love and even Gert likes. Evie showed us the pictures at the shower."

Gert was Evie's friend, a highly opinionated, very hilarious elderly lady, who for some reason, Mag and Evie took house hunting with them.

Maybe it was because Mag got a huge kick out of her, Evie

adored her, and none of her kids lived close, so they looked out for her and did that by getting her out of her house and listening to her tell them where they should live.

"Hattie—"

"Boone and Ryn also found a house, the next one they're going to flip," I went on.

"Baby."

That was soft and sweet.

But he didn't then say, "I see your point. I'll get on Auggie straightaway."

So it was time to pull out the big guns.

"And I want us to declare Sundays our days where we eat in bed and have lots of sex and maybe expend the effort to go out and sit in the Jacuzzi, but that's all the effort we expend. Of course, that is, when we're not having sex."

"Baby."

And *that* was his purr.

I so totally knew he'd be into that idea.

"Not to mention, it's no coincidence that Smithie's shutdown coincides with Lottie and Mo's two-week honeymoon."

"Ha—"

"So maybe it won't work out," I kept at him. "Maybe they'll be the unfortunate ones in all of us that don't click. But Pepper deserves to have a guy put it on the line for her. Make her feel like more than a mom. Even if for a little while, make her life about more than looking out for, taking care of and protecting her daughter."

"I know she deserves that, honey, and I want that for her too. But you're asking me to push my boy into being that guy who puts it on the line. And I sense, from how pissed he got at me for getting in his face about it, that maybe he's already tried that. It didn't work. And he isn't fired up to go there again. It feels good you think we all got it so goin' on that getting shot down will just deflect off us and we move on. But you gotta know, it sucks for us just like it would for anyone to make a move only to crash and burn."

Interesting.

"Have you ever been shot down?"

"Uh...yeah."

Wow.

"Really?" I asked.

"Babe, it was *you* who shot me down."

Oh.

Right.

"Repeatedly," he went on.

Eek!

"So you can see my hesitation in pushing Aug into going for Pepper," he finished.

I was hearing him, but I wasn't hearing him.

Because I'd turned into the LoHi space that used to be long lines of storage units, but had been repurposed into studios, with a couple of small galleries, shops, a little café, a littler coffee bar and the morning load-up and evening stowage of a few food trucks.

Including, coincidentally, the line of Joy of Food trucks that could be seen around Denver.

And outside my unit, which was tucked into a corner of one of the L-shaped buildings, was Brett's shiny black town car.

Next to it was a sporty Mercedes.

And outside my studio door stood Joe, Brett's driver.

And I was not freaking because Brett was there or upset because they were taking up my two parking spots.

I was freaking *and* upset because Brett was there, obviously with someone, and they were nowhere to be seen outside.

Which meant they were inside.

With my *work*.

"Hattie," Axl called.

"I've gotta go," I told him. "I'm at the studio and Brett's also here."

"Sorry?"

"Brett's here, as in, *here*, as in, I think he's *inside my studio*."

"I'm on my way," he stated.

"You don't have—"

I didn't finish that because he was gone.

I also didn't redial him to tell him he didn't have to intervene with me and whatever Brett was up to, I could handle it, and I didn't because it would do no good.

I also didn't because I had to park in a spot that wasn't mine, two units down and hoof it back to mine...and fast.

"Is he in there?" I asked Joe before I even made it to him.

"Heya, Hattie," Joe said as answer.

"Hey," I returned shortly. "Is he in there?"

"Yep."

Grr!

Brett.

I walked by Joe, pulled open my door, and stopped when I got inside, confused.

Because, yes, Brett was in there.

But he was with Sadie Chavez, Jet's sister-in-law and fellow Rock Chick.

Jet was married to Eddie. Sadie was married to Eddie's brother, Hector.

I saw Sadie had on a beautiful pink blouse, a slim, bone-colored skirt, a fabulous pair of deep rose Malone Souliers mules with their signature thin bands, these in cream across the toe and the top of the foot.

I knew Sadie, of a sort, mostly in an acquaintance-type, friend-of-a-friend deal.

She'd been to Smithie's repeatedly.

She'd also been to the shower last weekend.

So what I didn't know was why she was there.

With Brett.

Though, I could hazard a guess.

When I came in, she turned, smiled and called, "Hey, Hattie."

"Hi, Sadie," I greeted her then looked right to Brett. "I need to talk to you."

"I don't get a 'hey'?" he asked on a smile.

"Hey," I said. "Now can I talk to you a sec?" I returned my attention to Sadie. "Not to be rude. I just have to have a word with Brett real fast."

"Of course," she said.

Brett moved to me.

When he got to me, I reached for his wrist, grabbed hold, turned, and as I was right inside the door, I opened it and called, "We'll be right back," to Sadie.

"Take your time, I'm enjoying myself."

I couldn't imagine how, what with her now going to be alone in a room with a bunch of amateur sculpture, a bunch of detritus from sculpting and a bunch of stacked and boxed materials that would maybe one day be sculpture.

I dragged Brett outside and noticed Joe's eyebrows go right up when I did.

I ignored Joe, turned on Brett, but waited until the door closed.

I let Brett go.

Then I launched in.

"Let me guess, she works at a gallery."

"No," he replied.

Oh.

Well then...

What was Sadie doing there?

"She owns one," he finished.

Ugh.

I dropped my head back and studied the blue Colorado sky.

"Hattie, sweetheart," he called.

I righted my head and looked him straight in the eye.

"You don't get to do that," I said quietly.

"Honey," he said quietly back.

"I share my stuff when I'm ready to share my stuff." And that was never, since he, Sly and Axl were the only ones who'd ever seen it, and I hadn't invited any of them to have a look. "You don't do it for me, and it doesn't get done until I'm ready."

"You have eleven finished pieces in there," he told me.

"How do you know if they're finished?" I asked.

That shut him up.

But not for long.

"If they're not, when they are, I suspect you'll get right on finding somewhere to show, or someone to consign them with."

Hmm.

Sarcasm.

Not a big fan.

"Brett—"

"She flipped for them."

That shut *my* mouth.

"She wants to show you. A clear-out of her gallery, total focus on you."

My skin started to feel tingly.

Brett kept speaking.

"She says, as you've never sold, she has no idea where to price you. But she thinks the girl folded into herself she'd tag for fifteen K, that huge man head would be twenty."

Oh.

My.

Freaking.

God!

"Twenty thousand dollars?" I whispered.

"Yes. And she says she thinks she can get a feature on you in

5280 magazine. She also wants to take some pictures. Because she knows a couple of galleries in LA, one in San Fran, one in Vail and two in Aspen who she thinks will be interested in your work. This, after you debut at her gallery. And they'll have the clientele that'll buy it."

I didn't know what to say, and considering the tingles had taken over to the point my fingers felt numb, I decided to concentrate on that rather than try to find something to say.

"Are those pieces done, Hattie?" he asked.

"Yes," I pushed out.

"Sweetheart, Sadie Chavez has run a successful art gallery in Denver for a long time, through good times, and a seriously bad recession. She's done this because she knows good shit. And she wants to debut you and make a big deal of it. Because your shit is *good shit.*" He got closer. "You're a fantastic dancer, Hattie. But you're a knock-your-socks-off artist."

He lifted an arm straight, finger pointed at the door to my studio.

He then finished softly, "That's your future, baby. You just gotta have the balls to grab hold."

"What if people don't buy it?" I asked.

"They will."

"What if they don't get it?" I asked.

"Art is pain. That studio is filled with your pain. And now it's time to let it go."

He was talking about more than what was in that studio.

I stared up at Brett.

Brett stared down at me.

When he was done staring, he took my hand and squeezed it.

"Are you ready?" he asked.

I couldn't say the words.

So I nodded.

I'd dragged him out by his wrist.

He walked me back in holding my hand.

* * *

Axl showed twenty minutes later.

Brett and Sadie (and Joe) were gone.

I was sitting on my ass in front of "After," knees to my chest, arms wrapped around my calves, toe-to-toe with my sculpture in the same pose, except with my head up, when he pulled open the door.

I looked his way.

He saw where I was, his expression morphed right to worried, and he hustled to me.

He got in a squat beside me and asked, "Baby, are you okay?"

"Yeah. Sadie had another appointment, so she had to go. Brett left with her."

"Sadie? Sadie Chavez?"

"She owns an art gallery by Larimer Square."

"I know."

"She's going to show me. Debut me. Get me in *5280* magazine. Send pictures of my stuff to other galleries. In LA. Aspen. Vail. San Francisco."

"Are you down with that?"

That was the first question he asked, right off the bat, after I said what I just said.

Brett didn't ask.

Axl asked.

That was why Axl was there.

And as much as I owed Brett for kicking me in the ass to do this, it was also why he wasn't.

"I'm scared. She's going to price the pieces really high and that freaks me out. It freaks me out just people seeing them. But I got really tingly when Brett told me she liked my stuff."

"Of course she did. It's fantastic."

And he thought that, I could see it in his face.

That praise was genuine.

I looked across the studio at the head of a man made out of concrete and rebar.

The expression facing us was a man filled with peace and joy. Even rapture.

On the other side, it was the same man, filled with rage, his mouth open in a way you knew he was shouting.

It was my dad when I was doing right.

And when he thought I was doing wrong.

"Hattie," Axl called me gently.

I looked to him. "Do you want her?"

"Sorry?"

I tipped my head to "After."

He looked to me and his face had changed.

He was stunned.

"Are you offering her to me?"

"She should be with you. You understand that art is pain that should never be forgotten."

After I said that, his hand came out. He grazed the backs of his curled fingers along my cheek before he opened them, gliding them into my hair.

Then he repeated, "Are you offering her to me?"

That was a whisper with a vibration reminiscent of his purr, but deeper.

More meaningful.

Incredibly beautiful.

"Yes," I said.

"I absolutely want her."

I felt my eyes start to sting.

"Brett's going to be disappointed," I told him. "Sadie said she'd price her at fifteen thousand dollars. He told me he'd give me seventeen right on the spot and I wouldn't have to pay Sadie's commission. I thought she'd be mad, but she was really pleased for me and told me if I sold her privately, it would be of record and she could more easily price the other pieces."

"I'll give you eighteen for her."

God, he was so sweet.

"Axl, honey, I'm giving her to you for free."

He ignored that. "We'll put her in the corner of the living room. After your show. She needs to be in your show."

How cool were the words *your show*?

Don't answer that.

They were seriously, super, freaking *cool*.

"Yes," I agreed. "But we'll move her there without money exchanging hands. She's yours now."

"She was mine before."

Oh man.

That did it.

The tears spilled over.

"I like you very, very much," I whispered.

"And I like you very, very much, baby," he whispered back.

I stared into his amazing eyes and sniffled.

"Dad'll come to the show, and it'll hurt him," I said so low, it was hard even for me to hear.

"He needs to see it, for more than one reason, baby."

He was right.

Another tear spilled over.

Axl moved his hand out of my hair and engaged the other one so he could catch them with his thumbs.

"It's you," I said.

"What's me?" he asked.

"It's you that came into my life and good things started happening."

"Coincidence."

"I don't think so."

"Hattie, even if that was the case, which it isn't, you laid the groundwork."

Okay.

I couldn't argue that.

"In other words, it was always going to happen. It's just that, now it is," he concluded.

I love you, I thought.

But I did not say.

I reached out with my hands too.

Took hold as I shifted to my hip, then my knees.

I pressed between his splayed thighs and wrapped my arms around his body.

And I took in his beautiful face.

Then I kissed him.

He slid his arms around me and kissed me back.

When I pulled away, I whispered, "I'm going to have a show."

And at that, Axl Pantera smiled at me.

Big and white.

And dazzling.

CHAPTER TWENTY-FOUR

Fly Forever

AXL

The next day at lunchtime, while Axl moved through the restaurant toward his mother's table, his phone chimed.

He dug it out of his side leg pocket, looked down at it, and saw he had a text from Hattie.

The phone recognized his face and the text came up.

> Hope everything goes okay with
> your mom.
> Tell her I said hey.
> xx♥♥oo♥♥

She was thinking of him. Worried about him. Worried how he'd handle whatever was coming.

And she wanted him to know he was on her mind.

Christ, he was in love with this woman.

He stopped on his way long enough to reply,

Will do, babe.
At the restaurant. I'll pick you up
at your place later to go get
your dad. ♥

He then pocketed his phone, resumed walking, aiming his eyes at his mother to see she was watching him.

He smiled at her.

She smiled back and started to push out of her chair.

He moved forward faster, and when he got close, ordered, "Don't get up."

"Rubbish," she said, clearing her chair, turning to him, putting her hands on his shoulders then positioning her face for him to kiss her cheek.

This he did.

Then he held her chair as she sat down, helped her scoot it in, all before he sat down.

He started it.

"Hattie says hey."

"Tell her I said hello back."

He saw she already had a drink. San Pellegrino with lemon and lime.

"Have you been here?" she asked.

"No," he replied, glancing at the menu sitting on his place setting and seeing the prices.

Hawk paid well, but Axl would rather go to Mustard's for a hot dog or Brother's for a hamburger than go to a snobby joint with white tablecloths and pay through the nose for lunch.

Though, he'd consider taking Hattie here for dinner so he could see her in another of her dresses.

Just not on a Sunday.

His lips quirked at that thought.

"I don't even know if you've been here."

At her tone, as well as her words, Axl's attention cut back to her.

And the waiter was at the table.

"Drink for you, sir?" he asked.

"Same as my mom," Axl ordered.

"Anything to start?" the guy pressed on.

"We'll have the large bowl of mussels to share," his mother said.

"Right away," the waiter murmured and took off.

Axl's attention went right back to his mom.

"You okay?" he asked.

"Right now, Lisa is coordinating the movers who are moving me to my new condo. It's close to the Federal Reserve building. Lovely. About twenty-five-hundred square feet. They have a fitness center, a rooftop pool and hot tub and a dog run. I'm thinking of getting a dog."

Jesus Christ.

His mother wasn't going to move out.

Right then, she was *moving out*.

"You're thinking of getting a dog," he repeated.

"Yes. I had a designer furnish the space. Did some small renos. The guest bath was dire. But they're done so it's all set. I'm just taking some pieces that I cherish and my personal belongings. Everything else I'm leaving behind. I haven't had a dog since I was in high school. Your father doesn't like fur on furniture."

Axl sat back in his chair and held her gaze.

She was jumping all over the place so he thought it best to let her get it out.

"I'm thinking Pekingese. Or a bichon frise. Both are so cute. A small dog. You can use the fitness center if you like. Though, you probably have a membership to a gym. But I don't know that either."

"There's a gym in my office building," he told her.

"Ah," she said, reaching to her water.

She took a sip.

Put the glass down.

Gave him her gaze.

And gutted him.

"I didn't know you had a gym at your work. I didn't know if you'd been to this restaurant. You are my heart. You are my soul. I was so humiliated at the woman I allowed myself to become, I avoided any meaningful conversation with you, which would be meaningful time with you, because it might lead you to realize how meaningless your mother had become."

Good fucking Christ.

Immediately, Axl bent forward so deep, the table was cutting into his abs, and reached his hand to her across it.

"Mom, you are not meaningless."

She didn't take his hand.

"You aren't either, Axl. You are so very extraordinary. I was so incredibly proud when you enlisted. I worried for you, so many sleepless nights when you were deployed. But I was proud of you. And so proud you went your own way, and even after you got out, were the man you wanted to be, not the man he wanted to make you be."

"Ma, take my hand."

She still didn't take his hand.

"I didn't stand between him and you. I didn't stop him from all the atrocious things he said to you."

"Mom—"

"I was so very lost, you see. I spent decades reeling, wondering where that girl I used to be had gotten to."

"Please, Ma, take my hand," he begged.

She drew a breath into her nose then reached out and put her hand in his.

He closed his fingers around tight.

"He was a steamroller," he said.

"I am your mother, Axl, and it is my job to look out for you. There's no excuse."

"Do you think he would have let you stop him?" he asked.

"I think I should have tried. In the beginning, I would say things. Though I'd wait until we were alone at night in our room. When I could get my words in, he told me not to coddle you. He said it was no way to make a man, his mother coddling him. I tried to explain it wasn't coddling, it was nurturing. He paid me no mind. Though, I'd eventually become accustomed to that. It was often in our marriage he paid me no mind. But he was so rarely with me. He was always working. Until the wee hours. There was always so much work to do. You know, I cannot even tell you how many times I wished he had a mistress. That would make sense. That would make him at least seem human."

She shook her head forcefully, closing her eyes tight.

She opened them and carried on.

"I shouldn't be saying these things to you."

"Yes, you should. You can lay on me whatever you want."

She looked to her lap.

"Mom," he called.

She lifted her head.

"I hated watching what he did to you, but you were my touchstone in that house. I knew you loved me. I *know* you love me. We never talked about it, but it was there. I had you, and you had me. And that was how we got through. And since I left, I had sleepless nights, worried, because I was out. But you were still in."

"Oh, Axl, darling," she whispered.

"You taught me how to cook. You didn't send your assistant to come pick me up from school or practices, you were always there. And those were our times, just us, driving home, being normal. And every meet, when I'd finish my event, win or lose, I looked for you in the stands. Not him. Because I knew, win but also lose, I'd see pride coming from you, and I only got that from him if I won."

"Sweetheart," she said softly.

"And now you're out. And you're not drinking San Pellegrino. I can't drink. I gotta get back to work. But you're drinking champagne. And tonight, you're going out to dinner with Hattie and me and Hattie's dad. Then you're going to the club with us and watching her dance."

"Axl, really—"

He squeezed her hand tight. "That's what's happening, Mom. Unless you have something special planned."

"I was thinking of trying one of those restaurant delivery services. Your father thinks they're *millennial*. That's his new word for anything that annoys him. Which I've realized are things he doesn't quite understand. Progress, which is something he despises. He wants it to be 1992. When greed was still good and *Basic Instinct* was a hit film and it was okay to villainize femininity. Where he was very approving of Jazzercise, because women should spend a good deal of their time engaging in whatever they could to make themselves attractive to a man. But disapproving of Anita Hill, because what was her issue? Men need to be free to be men and women should just put up with it."

He grinned at her and encouraged, "That's it, Ma. Get it all out. Though, if DoorDash is your big plan for tonight, you're going out with us so we can celebrate. You can DoorDash tomorrow."

Her jaw ticked to the side, she squeezed his hand, and he took her cue, let her go and sat back.

And this was because the waiter was there with his San Pellegrino.

"We also want a bottle of Dom," he told the guy.

The waiter blinked.

Then he smiled. "Of course, right away."

And he was off again.

"I can't drink a bottle by myself, Axl," his mother protested.

"Is Dad paying your cards?"

"I have my own cards now."

"You still have the joint ones?"

"Yes."

"Then he's paying for lunch today and who cares if you leave a half a bottle of Dom?"

That was when she grinned.

She got serious again fast.

"I don't want you to worry, darling. I took some classes. Then I opened a web design business about a year and a half ago. I do it from home."

Holy fuck.

"Seriously?" he asked.

She nodded.

"Does Dad know that?"

She shook her head. "It was easy to do it under his radar. He hasn't asked how my day was or how I spent it for at least ten years."

Fuck, his father was a dick.

"I now have a goodly number of clients," she shared. "Enough I'm nearly full time. I have money coming in, my own accounts, my own cards. Of course, I bought that condo using your father's and my accounts to get financing, but I'll be able to afford it as I do not intend to serve thirty-six years of duty at your father's side and let him cheat me out of my due. He can have the house. I hate that house. It's boring. He can have the cars. I don't want to drive a Jaguar. I want a Mazda. One of their smaller-size SUVs. I test-drove one. They're zippy. I just want the money. And I've engaged an attorney. Colorado is a marital property state. Your father can make it ugly, and he can make it drag on, but he can't circumvent that. And we already have a strategy. Demand every-thing at first, but since I don't want anything but half of our liquid assets, the investment portfolio and his retirement, he'll feel like he's won when that was all I wanted in the first place. And we both know, it's very important for your father to feel he's won, even if he hasn't."

Seemed she now had her ducks in a row.

"Sounds like a good strategy," he noted.

"I hope so," she murmured, reaching again for her water.

After she took a sip and set it back, he called, "Ma."

She looked at him.

"I'm proud of you. I'm happy for you. And if he fucks with you, he'll never see me again."

She didn't look happy about that.

"Axl."

"I'm being very serious."

"It has pained me for years, how he treated you. More, how I didn't intervene. And I offer no defense for either. But, darling, he does love you and that would destroy him."

"Then he better not fuck with you."

"You really shouldn't say the F-word, sweetheart," she murmured. "It's vulgar."

He grinned. "I'll refrain when I'm around you."

She looked horrified. "I hope you don't use it around Hattie."

"Hattie's a millennial, Mom. We've embraced the F-word. We don't think of it as a curse word at all."

She burst out laughing.

Christ, she looked pretty laughing.

He tried to think of the last time he saw his mom laugh.

He couldn't remember.

Jesus.

He also hadn't been a very good son.

"I didn't look out for you either," he admitted.

"That's not your job."

"Yes, it is."

She shook her head, not in a negative, in a "What am I gonna do with my boy?"

"We need to do this more often," he told her.

"I'd like that," she replied, a light beginning to shine in her eyes that wasn't pretty.

It was gorgeous.

"Then we will."

Hard part done.

Good things ahead.

Now it was time to enfold his mother into his life.

"Now, I gotta give you the heads-up about Don, Hattie's dad. It looks like things are on a good path, and he knows not to be a dick to her around me..."

Her eyes got big and her face paled.

But Axl kept going.

"But you never know. So before you meet him and spend time with him, if there's a weird vibe, it'd be good for you to know why it's there."

The mussels came before the Dom.

And mother and son had lunch.

In the end, he had half a glass of champagne.

Because seriously.

It was a celebration.

* * *

Axl was on his way back to the office from lunch when he made his decision.

Hattie said that Don could be a charmer.

And his mom seemed like she had it going on.

But today was a big day and a big change.

And she needed everyone she could get in her corner.

Bottom line...

They were all going to be a family.

So he called Don.

Hattie's dad answered quickly.

"Hey, son. All good?"

It was weird, though not in an entirely bad way, that it kinda felt good when Don called him "son."

"All good, Don. Listen, just so you know, my mom left my father today. She's coming out with us tonight."

"Well, shit, Axl, I'm sorry."

"I'm not. My dad's a dick."

"Right," he muttered.

"She seems like she's doing good, I just wanna make sure that keeps going. They were together for thirty-six years. We gotta look after her."

When he replied, there was a lowering of Don's voice. It was significant.

It said he was taking this seriously.

It also said it meant something to him that he'd been asked.

"We'll see to her, Axl," he promised.

"Great, Don. Thanks."

"Are you picking up your mother?"

"Her name's Rachel and yeah."

"How about I meet you at the restaurant so you and Hattie don't have to be driving all around Denver picking up your parents."

"That'd work, thanks."

"Not a problem. See you then."

And yeah.

There it was.

They were going to be a family.

"Yeah, Don," he replied. "Later."

* * *

As usual, she was the first headliner to come out.

Before she did, they brought the lights down.

And during the opening of the song there was nothing, just a muted shine coming from the black surface of the stage.

So it nearly blinded you when the spotlight came on Hattie, flying through the air on the first drum crash of U2's "Where the Streets Have No Name."

He felt Don shoot straight in his seat, heard his mother's quickly drawn breath.

But Axl didn't take his eyes off her.

She was in a black leotard that had swathes of material crossed over her breasts, a mock turtleneck, exposed shoulders but gathered material tight down her upper arms to her wrists. The back was exposed except for a narrow band along the middle. Some parts of the bodysuit were sheer, and there was a filmy skirt that went to her knees and floated around her.

Her pointe shoes were red.

The beat of the song was fast, Axl had no idea how she kept up, arms out, heels down and crossed, up on pointe, down, up, down, and again, again, again.

But before Bono shared he wants to run, she swept her leg around and up nearly to her nose before it came down.

She turned and took only two steps before she was soaring again.

Back arched at an impossible angle, arms up and graceful, front leg straight, back leg in a curve cutting through the air like it had weight, holding her up.

And she could fly forever.

Christ.

It slowed down a bit then, and she used the entire stage, interpreting the song with every inch of her body, the room dark, the only light following her.

Turns and leaps and all sorts of shit he had no idea what it was called.

And it didn't matter.

There was only one word for it, really.

Beauty.

She started looking at him at "poison rain."

And like it was when she danced for him before, he got her message immediately.

This was their song.

He was her shelter.

His throat closed.

At the end of the song, after another leap, she did pirouette after pirouette after pirouette as the light faded.

And then there was black.

The packed room was utterly silent.

And then it exploded.

The light came on again for Hattie to take her bow.

And she was looking at him.

Axl smiled at his woman.

And she smiled back.

CHAPTER TWENTY-FIVE

Deviled Eggs

AXL

They came in the back door and Cleo was right there to share how she felt about whatever she was feeling.

Cleo didn't get the chance.

Hattie launched in.

"Get this, Sleekmeister General. My mother is dating a dude named Shiloh. He carves logs for a living and reeks of pot."

Cleo assumed her disapproving face, though, it had to be said, that was her normal resting expression. It had just been temporarily replaced by her "What the Fuck Are You Two Doing Interrupting My Naptime" face.

"I know," Hattie agreed.

"Honey," Axl said, his voice shaking.

She whirled on him.

"You think this is funny?" she demanded.

"A little," he lied.

It wasn't a little funny.

It was hilarious.

Her head cocked dangerously and Axl tried to focus on that rather than her gorgeous curls moving with it.

"It's funny my mother ambushes our meet-the-boyfriend brunch by making me *meet her boyfriend*? One she hasn't mentioned word one about? One she's been seeing now *for three months*, again, without mentioning *word one*. One who *carves logs for a living* and *reeks of pot*?"

"I'm seeing you don't see why she did that, considering she was nervous as fuck, Shiloh was nervous as fuck, and you aren't taking this too well."

"He carves logs for a living!" she shrieked.

And Cleo took off.

Apparently, she wasn't a fan of ranting women.

Axl hooked Hattie by the waist and pulled her to him before he wrapped his other arm around her.

Because, even if he also wasn't a fan of ranting women, he was a fan of Hattie.

"Babe, chill out," he urged.

"I cannot believe this," she said.

"Yeah, I got that message all the way home from Mercury Café."

"This is unbelievable," she mostly repeated.

This time he didn't respond.

"I mean, if this goes somewhere, and they're clearly into each other, so it's going somewhere, what kind of provider is he going to be?" she asked preposterously. "I think he was actually high at brunch. I'm not sure it's a good mix, carving wood, which would, I assume, require sharp instruments, and being stoned."

"Wait. Did we get thrown back to 1952 and we gotta worry what kind of provider your mom's boyfriend is gonna be when she's got a successful cake decorating business that she's kept successful for nearly twenty years?" he asked.

She looked chastised at that.

"If that's the case, don't worry," he went on to tease. "I got you covered. And I'm all in for you to wear a short, little apron over your tight skirt and twinset when you make me dinner and greet me at the door with a martini. Though I think we need to interrupt our plans of doing nothing but fucking the rest of the day to go out and buy you a string of pearls."

She slapped his arm halfheartedly then asked, "You know what a twinset is?"

"My mother, until very recently, was the dutiful wife of a prominent attorney. Once a month, she had what she called her Twinset Lunch. Which was supposed to be about being on a guild to raise money for some charity, but from what Mom said, it was a chance for all the women to try to beat each other out on who had the best set of pearls. I think Mom has seven sets. And those were something Dad never bitched about buying her."

She made a face.

Adorable.

"Yeah," he agreed. "Think that's the same thing Mom thought of it."

Her expression changed again, as did her tone.

"You hear from her today?" she asked.

And Axl's mood changed to match her tone.

"Yes, she's going out to buy some workout clothes. There's a gym in her building. She wants to take advantage of it."

"Good," she murmured, what she didn't ask hanging in the air, which was the reason for Axl's mood change.

He answered it anyway. "He's texted seven times so far today."

"Honey," she whispered.

He told her something she knew. "He's pissed, behaving like a dick and acting like this is all about him. Not a surprise."

It could safely be said Sylas Pantera was blindsided in coming home on Friday evening, thinking he'd have dinner with his docile, soul-sucked-out-of-her wife and then do whatever it was his father did when he was winding down from a week.

Only for him to find her closet empty, her vanity vacant, picture frames and pieces around the house missing.

And then, after searching, finding a note on his desk in his home office that shared his wife had left him. She gave him her lawyer's details, asking that, for the time being, they speak only through their attorneys.

So far, the only good news was, Sylas had adhered to this request.

The rest...

Axl predicted thirty seconds after he found that note, Sylas called his son, but Axl wasn't answering. He was with Hattie, Don and his mom.

But after eleven calls, on Saturday morning, Axl picked up.

Once Sylas finished sharing how he discovered his wife was gone, he then ranted for a full ten minutes about respect and commitment before Axl could get a word in to ask if his father really found any of this a surprise.

His dad's response was, "Are you *insane*? My partner for thirty-six years leaves with no discussion, no warning, and I'm not supposed to find it a surprise?"

It was at that, Axl lost it.

"She's not your partner, Dad. She doesn't occupy an office across the fucking hall. She's your wife. The woman you married. The woman you had a child with. The woman you're supposed to love. And that's why she's no longer there. Because you're pissed you lost your partner. You're not destroyed that you lost your wife."

He hung up after that, and since, had not been taking his father's calls or returning his texts.

Both of which there had been many.

After sharing that his dad had been in touch, and he was unsurprisingly not handling things well, he didn't tell his mother more.

She was buying workout clothes and trying to find Pekingese breeders.

She'd had enough of his shit.

And so had Axl.

But Hattie had been around, and she knew Sylas was badgering the witness.

"Maybe you should block him," she suggested. "Just for a few days. Or, um...weeks."

"I'll talk to him eventually. Share I'm not going to listen to his shit. But not on our Sunday. Brunch is done. Sharon and Shiloh are now at home, smoking copious weed and fretting about your reaction to them being together. And it's just you and me."

But he'd lost her in the middle of that.

He knew it when she began to look horrified.

"Oh my God, did I not hide I was freaked about my mom's hippie, stoner boyfriend?"

Christ, she was cute.

"Uh...not so much," he informed her.

She tore from his arms and pulled her bag off her shoulder.

"I need to call her," she mumbled.

She so did.

Axl left her to it, going to the bedroom and dumping his keys and his phone by his nightstand after he set some light rock playing low on the Sonos system that ran in speakers throughout the house.

Perfect afternoon of fucking music.

He grinned.

When he went back into the kitchen to get them drinks, she gave him big eyes, and said into her phone, "I'm happy for you, of course I'm happy. If you're happy, that's all I need. I've wanted that for you for a long time. And he seems like a nice guy. Totally into you. I'm sorry I didn't handle it well. It came as a surprise. Though, Mom, I hope you know, in my eyes, no one is ever going to be good enough for you. But please, apologize to Shiloh for me. I acted—"

She stopped talking when a pounding came at the front door.

Axl was at the fridge.

Hattie was still eyes to him.

And he knew who that was.

She did too at the freaked look now on her face.

Therefore, without hesitation, he turned on his foot and started to prowl out of the kitchen, hearing Hattie say, "I gotta go Mom. I think Axl's father is here."

Yeah, that had come out at brunch, Axl's family drama.

Then again, after Shiloh exhausted sharing his file of pictures of his carved logs that was on his phone, they were so nervous, and Hattie so thrown off guard, conversation had dried up.

Axl made it to the door quickly, saw his father through the three windows at the top, unlocked it and pulled it open.

"This isn't happening right now," he declared.

He should have known better.

This was Sylas Pantera.

What he wanted, he got, took, or if necessary, he hassled, coaxed or charmed until it was his.

So his father pushed in.

Hattie was coming into the living room and Sylas's eyes locked on her.

"Of course you're here," he declared contemptuously.

Uh…

Hell no.

"Dad—" Axl started.

"If I could have some privacy with my son," Sylas spat at Hattie.

Hattie looked to Axl.

"She's not going anywhere. You are," Axl said to his dad. "We're not doing this now. I'll let you know when I'm down to talk."

His father turned to him.

"With no warning, out of the complete blue, your father loses *his wife*, he's grappling with that, and *his son* doesn't have time for him?"

"Hattie and I have plans—"

And that was when it happened.

Sylas leaned toward Axl and roared, "*I don't give a fuck what you've got happening with your slut! Your father needs you!*"

Oh no.

Hell no.

"Axl," Hattie said urgently, wisely racing to him and hitting him full on, standing in front of him, her foot back and bracing her weight, her hands to his chest.

Axl felt that chest rise and fall, straining against her hands, as he stared at his father and tried to keep his shit.

"Honey," she whispered.

"I'm good," he bit out.

He was not.

But he wasn't going to fuck up his father.

At least not now, after he had a moment to get a lock on his shit.

She didn't move.

He darted a glance down to her. "I'm good, Hattie."

She again didn't move for several beats, but when she did, it was only to plaster herself to his side and wrap her arms around his middle.

He slid his arm around her shoulders, and for the first time, did not take a second to enjoy her curls brushing his skin.

"We're done," he announced to his dad.

"We—" Sylas began.

Axl cut him off.

"And I mean that in a very final way. We're done. I don't want to see you again. Not ever."

Hattie's arms got tight.

"You can't be serious," Sylas returned, disbelief in every syllable, not to mention written in the way he held his body.

"We're done, and that's the end," Axl confirmed. "You're out of my life. No going back. But if you fuck over Mom, if you don't make this divorce easy for her, don't give her everything she asks for, you don't know exactly what I do for a living, but if you do that, you'll find out."

Sylas's eyes narrowed. "Are you threatening me?"

"Yes."

"I cannot believe what I'm hearing," Sylas clipped.

"Believe it and I hope you're listening closely. There's no going back, Dad. For me, this isn't any change. Like Mom is coping fine with her new circumstances, there's no change for her either. We had nothing from you. So you not actually being in our lives doesn't make them any different. Except neither of us has to put up with you anymore."

His dad puffed out his chest.

What a fucking peacock.

"Axl Pantera, you're speaking to your father."

Yeah.

A fucking peacock.

"A father loves his son, and he shows it. He's proud of him, and he shows that too."

"I'm proud of you, look at you." Sylas swept an arm up indicating Axl. "You're a man any father would be proud of."

"I'm thirty-four years old and that's the first time in my life you've ever said that to me."

"Nonsense," Sylas bit.

"Trust me," Axl said quietly. "I know. It is not nonsense. Now, just to be clear and very thorough, a father also does not make his son watch him dismantle piece by piece over the years the beautiful, vital woman who is his mother. A father does not make a family all about him. And a father does not come to his son's home and call his woman a name when he knows not one fucking thing about her. Not one fucking thing, Dad. If you said that to me just you and me, I'd lose my goddamn mind. But you said it in front of Hattie, and that's unforgivable."

"You can't be missing this is an emotional time for me," Sylas retorted.

Axl shook his head.

"Your excuses have no meaning. You don't get it. You've never formed the foundation for forgiveness. Shit happens. People fuck up. Situations and emotions get the better of them. That's understandable, as long as you have the foundation of love and respect and trust you can call on to find forgiveness. You don't have that. Not from me. Not from Mom. You were so busy building," he shook his head again, "whatever it is that was so important for you to build, you didn't bother building that."

Sylas jerked his head to Hattie.

"You've been seeing this woman, what? Weeks? And she's so important to you that you're willing to annihilate your relationship with your father in favor of her?"

"This isn't about Hattie, though that was the final straw. I'd already told Mom, you fucked her over, you'd lose me. But you precipitated that. So we're done."

"Axl—" Sylas started.

But there was no more to say.

Carefully, he set Hattie behind him and turned to the door he hadn't closed.

He put a hand on it and used his other to indicate his invitation to his father to leave.

"You can't possibly—" Sylas started.

"I can."

"You aren't—"

"I am."

"Axl, you only have one father," Sylas warned.

"Actually, you're wrong about that. I've never had a father. So again, no change."

Sylas looked like Axl sucker punched him.

It came as no surprise, seeing that, Axl felt nothing.

It took him awhile to recover, and when he did, Sylas moved to the door, but of course, he didn't move through it.

He stopped and looked his son in the eye.

And when he spoke, his tone was conciliatory.

"I see now that this is emotional for all of us. We'll give it some time. Time for both of us to cool down. And then we'll talk it through."

"No, we won't."

"Axl—"

"Good-bye, Dad."

At that juncture, the man had the absolute fucking *balls* to look at Hattie and request quietly, "You'll talk to him?"

"Get your eyes off her," he growled.

Hattie came forward and stood between him and his dad.

"I'll talk to him, Sylas. But I think you should leave now," she said. "Okay? I'm sorry, but it's for the best right now."

Sylas studied her.

Nodded.

Looked to Axl.

Axl saw written stark in his father's face that the man was wrecked.

He still felt nothing.

Because Sylas wasn't wrecked that he lost his wife. He wasn't wrecked at the things his son said to him, the way he fathered making his son feel those things. He wasn't wrecked because their family was wrecked.

He was wrecked because he wasn't getting what he wanted.

He was wrecked because he was walking away a loser.

Those were the only reasons he was wrecked.

Sylas left.

Axl set Hattie aside, closed and locked the door.

He turned to her and she was again plastered to him, this time front to front.

"Okay, take a breath, okay?" she urged.

"Babe—"

"I don't care he said that about me. I honestly don't."

"Well, I do."

"Okay," she said quickly.

He put his hands to her waist. "It's been coming, and I think you know that."

"My dad seems to be turning around," she reminded him. "That's like, a miracle. Your dad could too."

"Your dad loves you," he returned. "He's always loved you. He wanted the best for you. He thought you were special, and he was right. He just got it wrong what was supposed to make you special. And he got fixed on that. He's like one of those soccer dads who stands on the sidelines screaming at the refs and the coaches. I gotta believe, somewhere deep down inside them, they know they've got it wrong. They just got obsessed with this thing with their kid. Because they love them. That is not my dad. I have never been anything to my father but a reflection of him. That's why I had to be the best. That's why I had to win. That's why I had to toe the line. The same with my mom. She wasn't a wife. She was an accessory. I can't even imagine how it would feel to know some asshole conned me into thinking there was love there, and then I lost all sense of self trying to twist myself into being what he wanted me to be to earn the love that should already be mine."

He thought about that.

And then he said, "No, I actually can imagine it. It's just that I gave up on it way before she did."

Her body melting into him, Hattie lifted her hand, started

stroking his jaw, and was silent a beat before she said, "That's so incredibly sad, I hate that so much for you, I have utterly no idea what to say."

"You don't because there's nothing to say. That wasn't fun, but now it's done. Mom has moved on, and not that I needed it, still. He just gave me permission to move on too. So I am."

She let him have that a second.

And then she advised, "Just...don't completely close the door. People can surprise you."

His father wouldn't surprise him.

Sylas Pantera had a ridiculous number of flaws.

His fatal one would be that he was predictable.

Hands still at her waist, he started walking her backward, their destination clear.

"I won't close that door," he assured, even knowing Sylas would never walk through it.

It'd make Hattie happy to think that possibility existed.

So he'd let her do it.

"Good," she murmured, but stopped their progress by again throwing back a foot.

"Babe, it's Sunday," he reminded her.

But she knew.

She only stopped them so she could hop up and wrap her arms around his shoulders, her legs around his hips.

Okay.

Now that shit was done.

Over.

Behind him.

Them.

And moving on.

He put his hands to her ass to assist in holding her there.

But he didn't kiss her until they cleared the door to the bedroom.

Because he didn't want to run into anything.

He wanted to focus on nothing.

But kissing his Hattie.

*   *   *

Hattie plopped the bowl on his stomach before she plopped her body in bed beside him.

"Nachos à la Hattie," she declared.

He looked down at the bowl piled high.

He looked back at her while grabbing it and shoving up to sitting on his ass under the sheets in his bed.

"Babe, this is just tortilla chips you melted grated cheese on in the microwave."

"With artfully dispersed dollops of salsa," she added.

He started laughing.

When he was done, she was grinning and pulling a wedge of "nachos" with the long string of cheese it created from the bowl.

It couldn't be said his girl skimped on cheese.

Another reason to love her.

He waited until she had hers, before he went in for his and shared, "Auggie makes pork rind nachos. After having those, we declared him winner since they're better than Mag's pancakes, Boone's mac and cheese, and my deviled eggs."

She was blinking at him.

Rapidly.

"Deviled eggs?" she asked, still blinking. "What deviled eggs?"

He went for more chips and cheese, saying, "Got a variety of options, but the front-runners are Mexican street corn, Cajun crab and pimento cheese and bacon."

"Are you serious?" she asked.

"You've had my cooking."

"So tell me, Axl Pantera, why we're eating nuked cheese on

tortilla chips when you can make *Mexican street corn deviled eggs*?"

He grinned at her.

"I've gotta spread out the goodness to keep you hooked. I don't want to burn through it too soon, so you take off and find a guy who has new tricks up his sleeve."

When he said that, it was Hattie who was laughing.

He didn't want to, but seeing all that pretty in his bed, his eyes strayed to the flag on his dresser.

Jordan was a connoisseur of a nice ass, and he always could appreciate a great set of tits.

But he'd be all about Axl finding a woman who wanted to spend their Sundays in bed, eating, fucking and laughing.

More.

A woman who didn't want him to give up hope about his irredeemable dad, wishing for Axl that his father would find his way to be redeemed so one day Axl'd have a dad.

When his attention went back to her, she was studiously chewing on a triangle of cheese-coated chip.

She'd seen where his eyes had gone.

"You can ask about him, you know," he said.

"I know," she replied.

And then she didn't ask about him.

"Hattie, I fucked up being a dick about him to you. And the first person who would tell me I did is Jordan. You can ask about him," he reiterated.

She gave him her gaze. "You need to be in that space, and you've had a bad couple of days."

"I need to get to a place where he can be with me in memory and it not hurt."

She gave him a look that he read.

It said that was impossible and he shouldn't expect that.

So he added, "As much. So I need to quit burying him under

the pain of losing him and talk about how good it was to have him while I had him."

That got him another look.

Agreement.

"Do you have pictures of him?" she asked.

"Yeah," he answered.

"Someday, I'd like to see."

"Someday...soon...I'll find 'em and pull 'em out."

"Cool," she said, carefully nonchalant, going for another chip.

After she was done, he did too, telling her, "Something you said in your studio made me think."

She munched and tipped her head to the side. "About what?"

"About art being pain. I got that piece in the living room, and from the minute I bought it, I wondered what I was thinking. Since it's been sitting there, every time I see it, I wonder if having it isn't a little off. Even disrespectful, that a depiction of what took Jordan out was what I have sitting in my living room."

"And?" she prompted quietly when he stopped talking.

"And then you offered me 'After,' and I already knew I was gonna buy it in your show. I didn't care how much it cost. I wanted it from the minute I saw it. Because it was you. And I wanted you. I didn't have any of you back then, so even little pieces would work, I wanted you that bad. But in the end, I knew, I wanted all of you."

She had nothing to say to that.

But now he was getting another look.

Lots of warmth.

Axl kept talking.

"Then, after I was a dick to you about Jordan, I talked with Mo. He has issues. We all do. We look out for each other, but we can't be there twenty-four seven. So, he told me, when he has his moments, Lottie looks after him and I knew that gutted him, because you don't want to lay that kind of heavy on someone you love. Which was what I was trying to protect you from. I didn't want you to shoulder that heavy. But then Mo told me Lottie doesn't mind. She's all over it. Because she loves him and that's a part of him and she wants it all."

Now Hattie was looking at him with an expression he couldn't quite read.

But it looked like surprise.

So he kept explaining.

"Now I get that's why I have that piece in the living room. To remind me of the pain of losing Jordan. Which is something I didn't want, but it's the last thing I got from him. Even as much as that sucks, it's still precious because it means I had him in the first place. I loved the guy, and I was at his back when he died. And when that happened to him, there was no other place I'd want to be. And 'After' is the girl you were, folded in on herself. But you had the nerve and mental toughness to unfold and fly high. That was my girl then, and that's my girl now. But I didn't have you then. Though, when 'After' is here, I'll have you. Then and now. I'll have all of you, even your pain, which is what I need."

This time, when he stopped talking, she started.

"Someone you love?" she whispered.

"Sorry?" he asked.

"You said you don't want to lay the heavy on someone you love."

Well, fuck.

He had said that.

He stared in her eyes.

She stared in his.

They did this a long time.

He broke it.

"I would have wanted to do that with more fanfare, maybe some roses, definitely Mexican street corn deviled eggs."

She didn't laugh.

Didn't even smile.

Tears started shimmering in her eyes.

He thought it was a little freaky, but he couldn't deny it. He loved to see his girl cry, though only when it was tears like that.

She was pretty all the time.

Even a pretty crier.

But at its core, it was the emotion behind it that he loved.

"You're pretty when you cry," he said quietly.

"Dad hated it when I cried."

"Of course he did, he loves you. No parent wants to see their kid cry. I don't mind because you're crying *because* I love you. And, bears repeating, it's pretty."

"I didn't get it," she said.

Okay, not only didn't he understand that, it wasn't what he expected after he told her he loved her.

Her jumping him, yes.

Her getting tears in her eyes, yes.

Her telling him she felt the same, he fucking hoped so.

That, no.

"Didn't get what?"

"I knew I was happy, and I'd never really felt that before you."

There it was, and now the warmth he was getting from her he felt burn in his gut.

She kept going.

"I was happy because I had you, and Dad was turning around, and I love my job. But I was really relieved to get back into the studio. And I was surprised how relieved I was. I thought my art was just an outlet. Something I was messing around with. I'd always been creative. I didn't realize, until recently, that I just did what I did. But one of the things I *didn't* do was allow myself to dream. I was just going through the motions of life. I never let anyone know I did that. My work in the studio. I never gave it any importance. Not because I feared no one would think it was good. Because I was so stuck in a life that was going nowhere, I didn't think there was anywhere to go. I just never thought to dream."

Axl said nothing.

Hattie did.

"And you came into my life. And suddenly, I'm not at Dad's every night. And clearing a drawer for you is the highlight of my day. And every little thing I learn about you is like discovered treasure. Cleo. And the Jacuzzi. And how much you like creamer. The sound of your purr. That you can cook. That I can make you laugh. You made me happy. And being happy, I began to see my life clearer. Or, more to the point, take time to look at it at all. And I began to understand who I was when I wasn't just existing. I love to dance. And I love my art. And I'm going to have a show. And now, I can dare to dream. Because I have what I need. I know who I am. And the thing that makes it safe is that I'm in love with a really great guy who also loves me."

When she quit talking then, the nacho plate hit his nightstand half a second before he hit Hattie.

After a lot of kissing and the same amount of groping, he was tugging at her panties when she said breathily, "You need to save some stamina. I want to try the you-do-yours, I-do-mine porn thing tonight."

Fuck, just that and he felt himself beading.

Christ, his girl.

"Quiet."

He got her panties down over her feet, surged up, Hattie opening her legs as he did.

Yeah.

His girl.

"And maybe explore that light bondage thing you were mentioning," she went on.

Fortunately, it was only Hattie who got dressed in her panties and his tee when she got up to nuke cheese on chips.

So once he positioned, he was all set to slide in.

Which he did.

And fuck.

Connecting with her, he realized he *did* purr.

She huffed out a breath, her pussy closing tight around him, and caught his ass in one hand, claiming the back of his neck with the other.

Gazing down at her, her hair all over his pillow, those gorgeous brown eyes hot and bothered, he started moving.

"Love you, baby," he whispered.

She cocked a leg high, pressed it to his side, planted her other foot in the bed and reared up to meet his strokes.

"Love you too, Axl," she whispered back.

He kissed her.

He fucked her.

They both came.

And after cleanup, he saw the chips and cheese no longer looked so hot.

So Axl put on some sweats and went to the kitchen to assess things.

He didn't have fresh cilantro, but he had everything else.

He went back to her while the eggs were boiling, but he left her again.

And didn't go back until he brought her his Mexican street corn deviled eggs.

They devoured them.

He left the bed again a couple of hours later.

To get their laptops.

CHAPTER TWENTY-SIX

The Women

AXL

"I can't believe this is finally happening," Boone said.

"It hasn't happened yet," Hawk warned.

Axl sat in the backseat of the Hummer, Hawk driving, Boone in the passenger seat, and he watched the Colorado terrain slide by.

Cisco had a place in the foothills.

And this was where, in a team effort, Cisco, Mamá Nana and Ally Zano had convinced Lynn Crowley and Heidi Mueller that it would be safe to meet to discuss what they knew about what was happening in the Denver Police Department.

He took his eyes from the landscape to catch Hawk glancing at him in the mirror.

It was not a secret from the crew that his mother and father had split.

It also wasn't a secret that Sylas's first response had been tactical.

Instead of proceeding with a divorce, he demanded a six-month separation that included intensive marriage counseling.

Axl worried his mother would cave on that.

She did not.

Onward from that, in the three weeks since his mother moved out, unsurprisingly, his father had dicked with her at every turn. He'd canceled the joint cards, blocked access to the joint accounts, and attempted every legal maneuver in the book to drive up her attorney's billable hours in order to break her, at least financially.

Again, Axl worried she'd suffer, and as such, last Friday, he took her to lunch to share he'd cover her if she got buried.

"Oh, Axl, darling. Thank you so much. But I prepared for this," was her response. "I didn't touch any of my earnings from my business since I started. Not to mention, I deposited half of the household and discretionary stipend your father gave me for the last year in my sole account. I have money coming in and a good nest egg. I can outlast him." She'd patted his hand. "But it's good to know I can turn to you for a loan if that occasion arises."

Axl had to get over the fact his father gave his mother a "stipend," something, until then, he did not know, rather than her being free to do whatever she wished with their money.

But he didn't mention that.

Instead, on his way back to work from their lunch, he called his father.

Sylas picked up immediately.

"This is your final warning," was all he said before he hung up.

To his surprise, that worked. His mom had shared with him that morning that her attorney had told her that Sylas had been in touch and he was ready to proceed.

Axl had no idea if it worked because his father was rethinking things now that his family had imploded and it was coming clear he'd irrevocably lost his wife, and he had to make maneuvers to save his relationship with his son. Or if his father had indeed investigated Hawk's operations, and since he had a sense of what Axl did for a living, it was an attempt at self-preservation.

He figured it was the latter.

But in the end, it didn't matter.

The divorce was proceeding, and until it was final, his father had also agreed to a monthly allowance that covered his mother's mortgage and HOA fees with some beyond that besides, so she could breathe easy financially.

But Hawk and his own father were tight. Axl had met Hawk's dad and the man was hilarious. He also thought the world of his son. So Hawk didn't understand that Axl might worry about his mother, but the loss of his father didn't factor.

So Hawk had been keeping a close eye on his man.

Axl didn't tell him there was no cause for concern.

He just went to work and did his job.

Eventually, Hawk would get it.

"Proof," Boone said. "Crime does pay."

When Boone said that, Axl focused on the property they were approaching.

L-shaped. Made mostly of stone, some wood. A nod to rustic and its surroundings.

But the wide, curving drive made of attractive pavers, the stone balustrades along the way topped with lanterns that would light the way in the dark, the two double-doored garages as well as the double-door front entry, and the fact that the compact front exterior didn't quite hide that what was beyond was downright rambling stated this wasn't a rustic mountain cabin at all.

Not to mention Sly, in his suit, with his earpiece, standing outside the front door.

Ally's Mustang was parked outside. As was Mamá Nana's GMC Denali.

Cisco's town car was likely tucked in a garage.

Hawk parked, they got out, and Axl did this with eyes on Sly.

He was talking into his hand.

Their arrival was being announced.

They moved inside and Cisco met them at the front door.

"Nervous," he informed them unnecessarily.

Nearly two month's delay in this meet, they already knew the women would be nervous.

None of them replied, there were varying chin movements, juts or dips, and Cisco led them into his great room.

He'd gone with the nod to rustic here too. Wood, stone, hefty ceiling beams, plaid upholstery on the furniture, leather as well, wool throws.

But the view from three tiers of windows put the price tag on that room.

And it was substantial.

Axl took it in as a matter of course, what he'd do in any situation.

He also noted Mamá had two people with her, likely not simply for her protection, but she'd assured the women they were there for theirs as well.

Ally, as usual, was alone.

Cisco, wisely, had none of his men taking up space which, considering the look of his men, might give bad vibes.

And then there was Lynn Crowley and Heidi Mueller.

In her early thirties, Lynn had straight brown hair, an angular face, a messy outfit with not-very-well-cleaned-off baby spit-up on her shoulder. Even sitting, you could tell she was tall. She was also too thin. In photos he'd seen of her, she'd not been this before her husband died and not simply because she was pregnant.

A mix of fear, worry and grief was wasting her away.

And she exuded all of that.

If what Heidi was giving off didn't edge it out, the room would be filled with Lynn's panic, dread and sadness.

Heidi, on the other hand, was the exact opposite.

In her late forties, blonde, fit, well-dressed, very attractive.

And pissed.

There was grief there. It pinched the sides of her eyes and permeated the look in them.

But the prevailing emotion coming from her was rage.

Interesting, though not surprising.

She hadn't only lost her husband, she'd, personally, been dragged through the media like it was she who committed multiple felonies.

But one of the felonies her husband was allegedly in some way involved with was the murder of Lynn's husband.

A curious duo.

And that was an understatement.

"I believe we all wish this to be done so we can move on," Cisco started it, indicating the room with a movement of his head to share Hawk, Boone and Axl should find their places. Cisco himself sat in a leather armchair, his attention on the women. "So, quickly, I'd like to introduce you to Hawk Delgado and his men, Boone Sadler and Axl Pantera. As has been explained, they've a number of reasons to be involved in this, not the least of which, Boone and Axl's women were targeted by whoever is behind it."

Lynn barely looked at them.

Heidi glared between them like they personally shot her husband.

Hawk took a seat in the only vacant armchair left of the four. Ally was in one, Mamá in the other, Cisco in the third. Lynn and Heidi were sitting on the couch that faced the massive fireplace.

Boone and Axl assumed positions on the periphery, standing.

"And I'm afraid you'll have to begin," Cisco went on, his attention on Heidi. "As we sadly have not much of note to say."

"You know my husband didn't fuck those sex workers like that fake suicide note said he did," Heidi spat at Hawk.

Interesting opener.

"We know," Hawk confirmed.

Regardless that he did, she pressed on that same theme.

"I didn't know what he was up to with the rest of it, but I know he didn't do that."

"Yes, we know that too," Hawk repeated.

She pushed out breath from her nostrils like an angry bull.

She then declared, "They've been messing with Lynn since they took Tony out."

Everyone in the room looked to Lynn.

She was staring at her lap.

Heidi kept on.

"I mean, seriously dicking with her. Calling her. Leaving notes on her doorstep. Passing her in the grocery store and saying shit to her. Sitting outside her fucking day care and watching her go in and come out with her freaking *kids*. It's lunacy."

"As we've mentioned to you, we can discuss protection," Ally stated.

"And as we've mentioned to you, let them know we talked to you?" Heidi snapped. "No way."

Ally looked to Mamá.

So Axl looked to Mamá.

Mamá sat in her armchair, her eyes not leaving Heidi.

"Lance was *messed up* before they killed him," Heidi stated. "I had no idea what he was talking about. I mean, I'm a cop's wife. I know shit can get real. I had twenty years of living with that. But he was a detective. He wasn't on the beat anymore. But he kept talking about, 'If something happens to me.' But he never would answer when I asked why he kept on about it. It was flipping me out. He updated our will to make sure all was in order. He increased his life insurance policy, which by the way, was fucking *voided* because he supposedly killed himself, so that was money well spent."

She tossed a hand Lynn's way.

And kept going.

"Tony didn't know these assholes would kill him. He didn't take out a life insurance policy. Three kids, she's part time, she's fucked. Funeral expenses will eat you alive, trust me. And his pension doesn't cover three kids. I'll tell you that."

Single-handedly, with no backup, no one knowing he was doing it, investigating a syndicate of dirty cops and he didn't get life insurance.

Hell, just being a cop and he didn't have it.

It wasn't smart.

Everyone in that room knew that.

No one said anything.

"So…yeah," Heidi carried on. "When my husband *was murdered*, it didn't come as a big surprise. I knew something was up. Though, Lance killing Kevin and then turning the gun on himself, that is utter *bullshit*. Kevin was an asshole, but he always had Lance's back. I didn't get it. Lance said it was a guy thing. But if things went south with those two, Lance would just walk away. Or ask to be assigned a new partner. Or whatever. He wouldn't shoot him. And he would never, *not ever*, kill himself. Me?" She shook her head. "Our kids? Leave us like that? He'd never do that."

No one said anything.

Though even if there was something to be said, they couldn't.

Heidi wasn't done.

"And Lynn's got all this shit happening, and *she* comes to *me* and says my husband didn't fuck those women. She wants me to know that. My husband…My Lance…He did things…" Suddenly, the rage just spluttered out, and in a whisper, hanging her head, "Goddamn."

Giving Heidi a minute, and for other reasons, everyone now was looking at Lynn.

"Lynn, if you have anything on Tony's investigation, it would help," Hawk carefully urged.

Lynn's gaze grazed through him before it returned to her lap.

"Lynn, we can protect you and your kids without them knowing you have protection," Hawk stated. "And we can end this if we've got even something small to go on. We keep running up against dead ends. We need something to go on."

This was true.

Sylvie and Tucker Creed had tracked down the ME on Lake Powell.

He was unsurprisingly closed-lipped, even after they put the lean on him.

His response to this was not doing the right thing.

Instead, this resulted in him cutting his vacation short, coming home, resigning and looking into relocating.

So they were forced to put pressure on and drop in the right ears his recent, large cash purchases.

Now he was under official investigation.

The bad guys also hadn't taken the bait when the Resurrection MC entered the game. Various brothers in that club were sniffing around what really went down with those transports they got jacked for protecting in their earlier incarnation as the Bounty MC. And they weren't being entirely legal about it.

But...

Nothing.

So now, with the ME under investigation for taking bribes, all their asses were swinging out there.

And they continued to have dick because no one had high hopes that investigation would turn up anything.

The ME contended he and his wife had been saving for years to realize their dream of eventually retiring to their houseboat on Lake Powell. They just didn't keep this savings in a bank.

Regardless how ludicrously lame this excuse was, a man's reputation was on the line, and after years in his position, the medical examiner had never given cause to investigate his findings or his earnings. And as such, it was taking a forensic accountant going through years of the ME and his wife's personal accounts to prove this claim wrong.

And even when that happened, the guy would have to give it up who gave him the money.

But so far, the ME was not giving anything up.

Which could only mean one thing, and that thing was understandable considering four people were dead in this mess.

The medical examiner who falsified his reports on Lance Mueller and Kevin Bogart was more afraid of who paid him off than he was of being found guilty of taking bribes.

In other words, unless something broke, they had and would continue to have dick.

"You don't get it. It's never the same guy," Heidi said.

"Please explain," Hawk requested.

"When they're messing with her. It's never the same guy," Heidi told him.

Fucking hell.

"We know this is big," Hawk shared.

"So you know you can't protect her from half the Denver Police Department," Heidi returned.

"Half?" Ally asked, her voice curt, edgy.

Then again, her dad and brother were cops, and dirty ones didn't sit well normally.

Half the force was fucked right the hell up.

Lynn spoke.

"It isn't half."

Again, she had the room's attention.

"I'm sorry, Lynn, can you—?" Hawk started.

"They'd roll them in. Divert," she said.

"Right," Hawk replied. "And by that you mean?"

She fully lifted her head, straightened her shoulders.

And stated, "People didn't like Tony. By people, I mean his colleagues. Fellow cops. He knew that but he didn't care. They didn't like him because he was by the book. He was a good man. *A good man.* To his core. He said he was by the book because there was a book for a reason. And it wasn't to protect the police. It was to protect the people. And he didn't get it. He honestly did not get it. Because, he said, you become police to protect the people. So the book should be your bible."

Tony Crowley was known as straitlaced and exactly as she described her husband. He was also known to take that to extremes. This made him unpopular with his coworkers.

But you couldn't argue what she was saying.

"They were racially motivated and racially profiling," she declared. "And he saw that they were also targeting women. Mostly fellow officers."

No one said anything.

So Lynn continued.

"That was what he thought it was. In the beginning, he didn't know it was bigger. He didn't know there were dirty cops. He just thought they were bad cops who had no business being on the force. So, whoever these guys are, they convinced others that *Tony* was the problem. And now, because they think Tony talked to me, they think *I'd* be the problem if this became a media nightmare because women are coming forward about stuff and Black people are having *a moment*."

Mamá's eyes moved to Hawk.

"A moment?" Hawk asked Lynn.

"Yeah, he said he heard Kevin call it that. Like four hundred years of slavery and lynchings then decades more of every Black parent having to have 'the talk' with their kids about what to do if a cop pulled them over isn't worthy of *a moment.* When Tony was on the beat, he saw it happening. He could rant about it for hours. 'That's not protecting the people,' he'd say. People of color would look at him in uniform with distrust and it broke his soul. He did what he did to keep them safe, not scare the crap out of them. He worked hard to become a detective and get out of uniform. And he wanted that element out. It isn't all of them. It isn't even half. But when the bad ones convince the other ones that you're not one of them, you don't stand a chance."

She shook her head and her voice got small.

"Tony didn't stand a chance."

Fuck, Axl felt for her.

It had never been remotely okay, a good cop went down in all of this.

But seeing the aftermath in her, hearing the pride she had in her husband, pride that was deserved.

It was killer.

Hawk gave her a second.

Then he broke it down.

"So he was building a case of cops racially profiling, and he stumbled onto something bigger."

"And the women," she stressed, and the way she did made Axl's neck itch.

"And the women," Hawk confirmed he heard her, and the way he did that, Axl knew Hawk hadn't missed her tone.

"Yes, and they killed him for it," she returned.

"Did he mention any names?" Hawk asked.

"Lance Mueller and Kevin Bogart," she stated.

Goddamn it.

Two dead men.

Nothing new.

"That's how I knew about Heidi," she went on. "Because, a couple of days before he died, he got fidgety. He said something wasn't adding up. He said there were sex workers involved. He said it might be about skimming or kickbacks. Maybe blackmail. He said he found something out about Lance Mueller, and he thought that was why he moved from the DPD to Englewood PD. But everyone was talking about how Lance and Kevin moved departments because Kevin had so many sexual harassment strikes. But Lance moved first, and Tony said that didn't jibe, which was part of what he was digging into. And he was finding something. So he told me he thought this was bigger than what he could do on his own and he might have to take it to his higher-ups."

"Did he take it to his higher-ups?" Ally asked.

Lynn shook her head. "I don't know. He was dead in a couple of days. And a day after that, I came home, my house was a mess, and there was a message written on my bathroom mirror in soap that told me to keep my mouth shut. My husband's dead. My kids are asking for Daddy. I notice guys sitting in their cars outside my house. And then the rest begins. I kept my mouth shut."

"Your house was a mess?" Cisco asked.

"They were searching for something," Lynn answered.

"Do you know if they found it?" Cisco pressed.

She shook her head.

"He didn't leave you anything?" Ally pushed it, and she did because it was important. "Notes? Files? Tell you he'd hidden something somewhere?"

"If he did, he didn't tell me. So if he did, they probably got it," Lynn replied. "And no, he would talk about it, but only minimally. Mostly, he kept me out of it."

"The sex workers," Cisco butted in. "Did he mention any names of sex workers? Or, perhaps, names of the men who ran them?"

She shook her head but then it ticked, and she said, "Maybe someone named Dynamite?"

"Why do you say that?" Hawk quickly pressed.

Lynn turned to Hawk. "Because he was on the phone, and when he got off, I noticed he'd doodled while he was talking. And in the scratching on the notepad, there was one word. 'Dynamite' with a bunch of question marks. Outside it being weird, and maybe about some case he was working on, I didn't think anything of it. And in the end, it might not mean anything."

From the looks on faces, everyone had the same response to that.

No one knew anyone called Dynamite on the street.

So maybe it was an individual working woman.

No one in that room knew the names of all the ladies of the evening.

Which meant a chat with Knight, another visit with Brandi and everyone hitting up all their informants to find out.

"So how did you know Lance Mueller didn't do what the bogus suicide note said he was doing with sex workers?" Ally asked. "Did Tony go into specifics about this skimming or blackmail?"

Lynn gave another shake of her head.

"No, he just said Lance Mueller was a lot of things, but he loved his wife and he'd never 'do that.' And there was a rumor about *that* which freaked Tony. Because he said it didn't jibe. He didn't get into it, but it was when he was talking about there being sex workers involved. When I heard about the murder-suicide, and what was in the note, that was when I knew what *that* was. The implication that Lance was taking freebies from working women."

Now Heidi was looking at her lap.

"And maybe something else," Lynn continued. "Something about some motorcycle gang or something."

And...yeah.

Tony had made the connection.

And then he'd been whacked.

But it seemed only Tony knew who he told about this, if he told anyone at all.

Say, if he took it to his superiors, and they were involved, so they made moves to take him out, because the cops on their crew had looked into it, and they knew Tony hadn't made anything he was doing official.

Or if whoever "they" were caught Tony nosing around, and that was enough to make moves to keep him quiet.

"Do you know who he was talking to on the phone?" Cisco asked.

More head shaking from Lynn.

"He was on the phone a lot. He had a network he was building. He said the evidence has to be there and he can't be everywhere the evidence was. So he had to rely on people to keep tabs. That's all he said about it. But I assumed he was talking about people in certain communities, Black and Latino, who could record incidences and report them to him."

Everyone looked to Mamá.

She also shook her head, which meant it wasn't her, and she didn't know who it was.

But the way she looked at Hawk, she was going to find out.

"Most frustrating, though, was trying to get the women in the department to talk to him. He said they thought he'd make things hard for them. They didn't want to be seen as complaining. Like they couldn't take it. Tough it out," Lynn continued.

"But Bogart had sexual harassment complaints lodged against him," Ally pointed out.

Lynn shook her head. "From women in admin, dispatch. Not officers. Tony saw it happening with the female officers. But none of them would come forward. He thought they'd feel there was safety in numbers. But they just refused to make a big deal out of it."

"Was it a big deal?" Cisco asked.

Lynn looked to him. "Tony knew what razzing was. He got razzed every day for being the kind of cop he was. And then some. He wouldn't push it if it was just razzing. In the end, cops are cops. It's a brotherhood, not a sisterhood. They give each other guff, and sometimes, it can seem mean. It's a way to blow off steam. Build camaraderie. This was not that."

For covert purposes, none of the cops on their crew had done any thorough questioning of officers.

Axl had a sense that was probably going to change.

"Lynn," Hawk said gently, "something like this doodle of Dynamite might mean something. I know this is difficult, and it might not come to you right now. But if you remember anything like that, we're in this until the end. We'll follow it to see where it leads."

"After this, I can't..." she looked to Heidi, "*we* can't—"

"With your permission, we're going to have eyes on your houses," Hawk announced. "All entries, including windows. They will be monitored, and recorded, twenty-four seven. We'll also give you panic buttons to carry with you. And we'll install panic buttons in your homes so you can push them and have protection rolling out before you can dial nine-one-one. We'll do the same with cameras on the day-care center. You won't have a protective detail. They won't know any of this is happening. But you will have eyes on you and there will be someone to intervene within minutes if you face a threat."

Both women looked uncertain.

So Hawk kept going.

"It isn't just the people in this room who have your back. This team is larger. We're motivated to see an end to this not only to put a stop to what's happening in the DPD, but to make certain you two and your families are out from under this threat."

When they both continued to appear unsure, Hawk gave them more.

"We don't know who they are, but we know what they want. Now what we need to do is stop them before they get it and disappear. I know I don't have to tell you that Tony needs justice. And Heidi, whatever your husband did, he didn't kill his partner. What he did cannot be undone. But that's what should be known about him. And what should be known about the ones behind this is that they're dirty, they're murderers, and it might not be innocent men who took their raps, but they were innocent of those raps. I understand your fear and that it might be difficult to trust people you don't know. All I can do is assure you that we have significant resources, and they're at your disposal to keep you safe if you choose to accept them."

Heidi and Lynn looked at each other.

Then they looked at Hawk.

"Okay," Lynn said.

"You'll clear my husband's name?" Heidi asked.

Hawk nodded, but replied, "Of what he didn't do. Absolutely."

Heidi took a beat.

Then she said, "Okay."

That ended the meeting.

Ally, Mamá and Cisco were about taking care of the women.

Hawk, Boone and Axl moved back out to the Hummer.

Hawk had turned around in the huge drive and had just started them down it when he said, "I wanna know who Dynamite is before we're down the mountain. And I want to know where to find whoever that is."

Boone got out his phone.

Axl did too.

EPILOGUE
Soar

AXL

That evening, Axl walked into his house with his phone at his ear and his eyes scanning the refrigerator door.

"Ghost," Jorge stated. "And I'm sure it won't surprise you to know she's been outta sight for months. People saying she just vanished. Word she's a sex worker. Also word she's a junkie. Can't get a lock on it. Now, she's just nowhere. She could be dead. She could have relocated. Vance is on it."

They were talking about Dynamite, who he now knew was a ghost, something that didn't help them. Also something they unfortunately hadn't been able to ascertain before Hawk drove them down the mountain.

Now he knew why.

Because she was a ghost.

And Vance, Lee Nightingale's man, was on it because he was not only Lee's best tracker, he was the best tracker any of them had.

Which meant he was the best tracker not only in the state of Colorado, but the entire Rocky Mountain region.

As in, unless Dynamite was encased in lime, which she hopefully was not, and maybe even if she was, Vance would eventually find her.

"Brandi?" he asked Jorge.

Having gotten a greeting-non-greeting from Cleo, who saw him, took him in, established he was still capable of feeding her, then walked away, he continued looking for a note from his woman.

This because her car wasn't in the garage and she hadn't sent him a text to say she wasn't going to be home when he got there.

"Still elusive. No one knows where she is. Cisco and Ally are still on that," Jorge told him.

He was in his bedroom, seeing no note on his nightstand, so he stopped and looked around.

"I'm not having good thoughts about Brandi not being locatable. She's not the sharpest tack and she's been untraceable for weeks," Axl remarked.

"I think we need to brace for the fact that we are far from the only ones who know that Brandi blabs for dollars. And it wasn't long after you and Aug talked to her that you connected the dots on the setup and handed that shit to the police in an official capacity, which meant Hattie's stalking stopped," Jorge replied. "They took out two of their own. If Brandi becomes a liability, they wouldn't blink in erasing her. And she might not be a bright bulb, but she knows this is ugly. So it might be her that decided on a new location that doesn't include the Denver Metro Area or anywhere near it."

If he was her, he'd be gone about ten minutes after he and Aug left her apartment.

He was not her, which was why he wasn't stupid enough to be on her side of the game.

"So right now, dead in the water . . . again," he finished.

"Yeah. For now," Jorge confirmed.

Axl heard him, but he was focused on something else.

He'd found Hattie's note.

As well as other.

"Lee's got guys on the camera work," Jorge said in his ear as Axl moved to his dresser. "Lynn's feeds will come into our monitors. Heidi's will go to Nightingale."

"Right," Axl murmured, staring at the top of his dresser.

"That's it for tonight. Meet tomorrow with all the players to brief and reassess," Jorge said. "Nine, at our offices."

"See you there," Axl said distractedly.

"Right, brother, uh . . . you good?"

Axl stared at the picture frame by Jordan's flag, more precisely what was in it, and said, "Yeah, I'm great. Hattie left me a present and I just found it."

"Cool." Jorge sounded amused. "Later."

"Later, man," Axl said and disconnected, eyes still to the picture.

They'd been on leave.

They'd taken it in the Keys.

Beach bar.

A babe in a bikini top and short sarong who had a thing for Jordan took that shot of them.

Three inches taller than him, Jordan had been fucking around, got Axl in a headlock.

They were both pretty significantly drunk and laughing.

During that vacation, they'd sprung for separate rooms.

It had been a good call.

That night, Jordan had tagged the girl in the sarong.

Axl had spent the night, and the rest of his leave, hooking up with a tall blonde who gave shit head and he'd discovered had fake tits. But it wasn't a bust because she was seriously funny and she was a local, so she knew all the best restaurants.

Call him crazy, but he'd take laughs, good food and good company during a vacation fling over good head and real tits any day.

Every once in a while, she still texted him. Mostly hilarious memes and gifs and pictures of the funny faces made by the baby she had with her now husband.

So yeah.

Definitely worth sloppy blowjobs.

Sarong girl had only lasted the night.

Jordan had fucked his way through the Keys, stating, "One day, I'll find the right one. And then playtime will be done. Since I want a lot of kids, I'm gonna have to get on that. So I don't got a lot of time to have this kind of fun. Which means I gotta get what I can while I can get it."

Jordan had been wrong, he didn't find the right one.

But he was also right, he didn't have a lot of time.

So it was good he took what he could get.

And had fun while it lasted.

Axl had pulled out the photos yesterday, their Sunday, and shown them to Hattie.

And he'd laughed when he'd told her about their time in the Keys.

Today, she'd found a frame and put Jordan—the real Jordan, the one he needed to remember, the one he got drunk with and laughed with and caroused with, the one who knew he'd be faithful to his wife and make a lot of kids—*that* Jordan was now in his house.

There was also Hattie's note on the dresser, and when Axl could tear his eyes from the picture, and his mind from the memories, he picked it up.

Honey,
  I'm at the studio.
    Can you meet me there?

xx-Hattie

He felt a frisson trace up the back of his neck.

Because she didn't text that or give him a call.

She put that note by that picture on her dresser.

And wanted him at her studio.

He dropped the note on the dresser, took another look at the picture in the frame, and calling good-bye to Cleo, who had no reply, he went back out to his Jeep and drove to her studio.

Her Rogue was parked outside of it.

She was starting week two of her time off from Smithie's. There had been a lot going on before, with life, his mom and dad, another meet with her mom and boyfriend (that went a lot better, thankfully), Lottie's bachelorette party, Mo's bachelor party, and the wedding a week ago where Axl got to spend all day with her wearing that amazing bridesmaid dress celebrating their two friends getting hitched.

But when she could get there, she was in her studio a lot.

Including the last week, when she was up with him at six or earlier, and they kissed in the garage before getting in their respective cars and taking off for their days.

His meaning he'd go to work, and hers meaning she'd go to her art (his house, by the way, had become their default, and her two drawers were filled, his extra closet half filled—he dug her space, especially her bedroom, but his place had Pac-Man).

Sundays were the only days she took off.

Sadie had transferred several pieces to her back room in prep for the show that was happening in a few weeks, so Hattie had more room to create.

Axl hadn't been there since the day she got her show.

He knocked twice before he went in.

The first thing he saw was scuttling across the floor.

Two balls of fluff with black faces, curled tails, one with black-tipped brown fur on her body, the other had a creamier coat, both had white chests.

His mom's Pekingese.

Making up for lost time, and lost opportunities to spoil pets, Mom didn't get one puppy, she got two. A sister and brother.

His mom had named them Molly and Wellington, or Welly.

Hattie called them Floof One (Molly) and Floof Two (Welly).

They jumped around his boots, so obviously he had no choice but to pick them both up and give them a squeeze.

He got puppy breath in his face and puppy saliva on his jaw as he walked in, wondering why his mother's dogs were in Hattie's studio and wondering where Hattie was in her studio.

But moving in, he circumvented a big crate, which probably meant Sadie was taking more pieces away.

And that was when he saw it.

He stopped dead with two puppies squirming in his hands.

And he took it in.

Life-size, a man made of steel. Some small sheets and triangles, but mostly ribbons and straws of it forming a body, head, face and hair.

The eyes, though, looked to be smooth aquamarines.

The figure was in a deep squat, one knee bent, his other almost, but not quite, on the ground.

His arms, though, were straight up.

And suspended precariously on rebar you could see running through the ribbons of steel that made up his body, his fingers were wrapped around the waist of a woman made of concrete.

And she was soaring.

Over his right shoulder, one leg front, one leg behind, her back, neck and head arched, arms out to her sides.

Him.

And Hattie.

"Your mom had a client meeting tonight," her voice came from behind him.

He turned.

She stood there leaning against the crate in her work clothes, cutoff jean shorts and a tank, ratty old red Keds that were serious cool, her hair in a big bunch on the top of her head, curls dropping down the sides and around her neck.

No makeup.

Total pretty.

Her gaze went to the puppies in his hands, then to his eyes.

And she kept talking.

"She didn't trust these little guys alone in her new condo with her new furniture as Welly is being stubborn about house training and she's a pushover about not putting them in their crates because Molly hates the crate. So I told her they could come to the studio. I need to drop them off on the way home."

His voice was gruff when he stated, "I told her the breed was stubborn."

"No, you told her they were stubborn and *sloth-like*," she corrected.

"Because that's what the website said," he reminded her. "She's committing to hopefully a couple decades with these things." He jostled the fur balls that were wriggling in his hands. "She needed to know what she was in for."

Her face changed.

Fuck.

So goddamn pretty.

"Sometimes," she said softly, "it doesn't matter. If a being is precious, even the bad parts are parts you need."

He swallowed.

And his voice was downright rough when he asked, "What's that?"

She knew what he was asking when her eyes went beyond him to the sculpture.

But they came right back to him.

"You. And me."

Good Christ.

Good Christ.

Fuck.

The puppies kept squirming.

Axl kept hold on them.

"I don't hold you up, baby," he said softly.

She tipped her head to the side. "You don't?"

"No."

She looked beyond him.

"Well," she said to her sculpture, studying it as if attempting to decipher it. "I suppose one take is that he's holding her up. Another is he helps her soar."

Good Christ.

Good Christ.

He bent and put the dogs down.

They scampered.

Welly right to Hattie.

Molly disappeared behind some chunks of stone.

Hattie kept talking.

"Sadie saw it today when she brought her guys to do some crating. They helped me mount her. She weighs a ton. Not literally. But close. She looks strong, but she's hollow. Though, only in the literal sense, not figuratively. Figuratively, she's just delicate."

Jesus.

She was killing him.

"Please come here," he said.

She didn't come there.

She went on, "She wants it for the show. Sadie does. I said I have to ask you." She looked at him again. "Is it okay it's in the show?"

"That's your call," he told her. "Now, please come here."

She looked back to the piece. "I think, if Sadie has the space for it, it should be in the show. Kind of before, with all the other stuff, and after. You know, a then and now. That's its title, by the way. 'After 2.' There's after Dad. And now after you. The title isn't original. But it is apropos."

After you.

"Baby, *please come here*," he begged.

She came there.

He pulled her in his arms and shoved his face in her neck.

"It's not for sale," he declared to her skin.

"No. I called Dad. He told me he'd keep it in his backyard until…"

She didn't finish that.

He did. "We get our place and it has its place."

"Yes," she said softly.

He lifted his head. "Until then, as you know, I don't have a backyard. My place butts the fence and the fence butts the alley."

"I know, but as much as I love your pad, Axl, you can't raise kids in it. They need their own space. And we'll need our own space. And your place will really only be just our space until we find a different space when the concept of 'our' expands."

Their kids'll need space.

And they'll need space.

His throat felt tight.

"Right," he pushed through it.

"My mom's backyard isn't big enough for it either. Your mom has no backyard. So it's Dad's. For now. He sounded kinda excited about it. Even though I made sure he knew eventually, it'd be moved."

"Right."

"I'm supposed to get you a plaque," she said confusingly.

"What?" he asked, not following.

"Evie and Ryn told me when I showed them this today," she tipped her head to the sculpture. "Now that it's official, you know, you and me, you need a plaque for your workstation."

He felt his lips curve up because this had become a thing.

Evie started it with Mag. Got him a #1 BOYFRIEND plaque to sit at his workstation. It changed when they got engaged. It'd no doubt change again when they got married.

Ryn did the same, and the plaque Boone had declared him her hero.

"They suggested, 'Axl Pantera, The Wind Beneath My Wings,'" she told him.

"Please, fuck, do not give me a plaque that says that."

She grinned up at him.

Her grin faded and she traced his cheekbone with her thumb, murmuring, "I'll figure out something."

"Baby," he called, and her gaze went from her thumb, which was now at the corner of his mouth, to his eyes. "I love it."

"Good," she whispered.

"And I love you."

"Good," she repeated, still whispering.

"Thanks for adding Jordan to my house."

Her warm brown eyes melted.

"You're welcome."

"Wanna move in?" he asked.

She did a slow blink.

When she was done doing that, there was no describing what was in her eyes.

It was just a feeling.

And that feeling had a focal point in the left side of his chest.

And then she said, "Absolutely."

And when she was done doing *that*…

Well, that was when he kissed her.

While he was doing it, Molly started yapping.

And Welly used the distraction to pee in the corner.

* * *

HAWK

Hawk folded into the backseat of the town car next to Cisco.

"Joe," Cisco said the minute he closed his door.

The car started moving.

Hawk had taken in that Cisco had come prepared for this late-night meeting.

Gone was the man's usual suit, he was in jeans, boots and a sweater.

They were nice jeans, boots and sweater. Hawk knew they cost more than he would ever pay for clothes (not more than his wife would pay for his clothes, which was why he had jeans, boots and sweaters in his closet much like that).

But Cisco wasn't going casual because the workday was done.

He wasn't feeling anything hindering his movements tonight.

"Don't got a good feeling?" he asked.

"I never enjoy a chat with Brandi," Cisco replied.

They agreed on something.

"You get why she wanted this talk, just you and me?" Hawk went on.

For the first time since he entered the car, Cisco turned his head to look at Hawk, "I have no idea."

"Credit where it's due, you've been solid through this, man," Hawk said to him.

Cisco turned again to face forward. "I had motivation."

"The women."

Cisco didn't reply.

Hawk faced forward as well and murmured, "Heard rumors."

"Never believe rumors."

These ones, considering Cisco's recent behavior, Hawk was prone to believe.

"It's happened in Denver before," Hawk stated.

And it had.

Twice.

When Darius Tucker and Shirleen Jackson exited the game and went legit.

And when Marcus Sloan and Ren Zano did the same and became partners in a legal operation.

"Yes, and when that happened, we got Benito Valenzuela," Cisco reminded him.

Not much surprised Hawk Delgado.

That surprised him.

He turned to the man again. "You're saying—"

Cisco also turned to him. "I'm not saying anything."

"No," Hawk stated firmly. "You're saying you're making moves to get out, doing it protecting Denver from a psychopath like Valenzuela."

What Cisco said next didn't confirm.

And it absolutely did.

"Hypothetically, if one were to endeavor not to make the mistakes made before him, actually learn from history for once, in reviewing how those before had taken their bows, one would note that the mistake they all made was that they didn't select then train their successor in the proper way to go about things."

Hawk felt one side of his mouth tick up.

Cisco ignored it and faced forward.

They were silent the rest of the way.

Not that B had ever been mighty, but even if there wasn't far to fall, where she was now, she'd fallen to it.

It aspired to be a flophouse.

Christ.

"Charming," Cisco murmured as he opened his door and got out.

Hawk did the same.

And with Joe at their back, they moved to the front door of the complex that might actually have no management. It looked abandoned.

So it was a squat.

Hawk didn't miss Cisco had sent men ahead and they were positioned.

He also hadn't missed the piece on Cisco's hip.

He was also strapped.

Once inside, there wasn't a lot of light, and what there was, was coming from candles since the electricity had been turned off. There was almost zero furniture except mattresses that had probably been hauled from a dump. Last, there were a number of smells, none of them pleasant.

And when they made it to the room where B had taken up residence, they saw the only real piece of furniture in the place.

The chair from where she was currently reigning.

She had a standing lamp next to her throwing light. That lamp had an extension cord that ran out the window, so she was stealing the juice from somewhere else.

And her phone in her hand was raised.

Her taloned thumb was moving over it when they came in.

She put her phone down.

And when they stopped in front of her, she declared, "This is the last time you see me."

Christ, he hoped so.

Hawk nor Cisco spoke.

"You hear me? I'm out after this. And by out, I mean *gone*. No one gonna yank B's chain no more," she kept at them.

"We hear you, B, now why are we here?" Cisco said on an annoyed breath.

"They have a message for you."

Shit.

He kept his eyes on Brandi and so did Cisco.

"And that message is?" Cisco prompted when she said nothing.

"We fold," she said.

Hawk stood still and silent.

Cisco did the same.

Brandi said no more.

They didn't ask for it because they both knew no more was to be said.

In unison, they both turned around and walked out.

Joe had them on the road, taking them back to where Hawk had left his Camaro when Cisco spoke.

"You believe that?" Cisco asked.

"Absolutely not," Hawk answered.

Cisco sighed.

Hawk crossed his arms on his chest.

They were feeling the pressure.

Which was good.

But that was horseshit.

No one was laying down their cards.

The game was still on.

* * *

PEPPER

"You've gotta go."

His breaths were still labored.

So were mine.

But his face was in my neck so I could feel his.

They felt beautiful.

He was also still inside me, mostly because he just came.

And so had I.

That felt even more beautiful.

"Sweetheart," he whispered.

This shouldn't have happened.

This never should have happened.

I pushed against his chest.

"Auggie, you have to go."

He lifted his head and looked down at me through the dark.

"Pepper, that was good."

No.

It was *so* good.

Frantic, I-can't-wait-to-be-inside-you, I-can't-wait-to-get-you-inside-me, wall sex right inside my front door?

That was not about ending a dry spell.

That was about Auggie.

Auggie and me.

Auggie and me and how *unbelievably fucking good* we were together.

On this thought, with a fair sight more desperation, I pushed again at his chest, trying to squirm away from him.

He kept hold.

And put his mouth to my ear.

"Baby, that was hot, but it was fast, and it was done before things were said. Now we gotta talk."

"No." I shook my head. "No talking. No nothing. That was a mistake."

"It wasn't a mistake."

"It was totally a mistake. *You* are a mistake. *This* is a mistake. It's all a huge *mistake*."

He lifted his head. "I'm a mistake?"

I hated the tone of his voice.

Disbelieving.

Kinda pissed.

A thread of hurt.

God.

But I couldn't go back on it.

I couldn't.

This shit was not going to happen to me again.

And I wasn't going to put Juno through it.

"Yes, Auggie." I squirmed again and this time I got away.

My panties were somewhere on the floor. Fortunately, the skirt of my tank t-shirt dress was easy to shimmy back down.

I went to my front door that Aug slammed behind him after he stalked me into my house and before he'd pinned me to the wall.

And the reminder of all of that sent quivers down my inner thighs.

I opened the door and stood abreast of it, eyes to my feet.

"Pepper, sweetheart, you don't want me walking out that door," Auggie warned.

No, I don't, I thought. *I really, really don't.*

But I couldn't have what I wanted.

I never could.

I'd learned that repeatedly.

Don't reach, you might get it and find out (A) you didn't want it in the first place, or (B) it didn't want you.

So I said nothing.

He stopped in front of me. I could see the toes of his boots close to mine that were exposed by my flat sandals.

There was something very...*wonderful* about that.

His boots.

My sandals.

His masculine.

My toenails painted pale pink.

Him right there.

With me.

"Pepper, look at me."

"You've gotta go," I repeated.

"Juno's with him."

That made the back of my neck itch.

Then again, whenever my girl was gone, doing her time with her dad, I had that feeling.

"Yes, she is."

"So we can talk."

"We're not talking."

"Pepper—"

My head shot up and I snapped, "God! I shouldn't have to say it again! Get out, Auggie! That was stupid and it was weak and it's not happening again. I'm already mortified enough I let you fuck me. You're just making it worse."

He got in my face and growled, "I'm not gonna play this game."

"I'm not playing a game."

"I know women like you. And yes, you are."

He knew women like me?

I didn't ask, mostly because he didn't give me the opportunity.

"Thanks for the hot fuck, babe," he said. "At least that made it worth putting up with this bullshit play."

And then he was gone.

I closed the door behind him.

Put my forehead to it.

"Huge mistake," I whispered.

But I knew.

I could tell myself that again and again and again.

But I'd seen the girls with their guys.

So I could repeat it for eternity, and I'd never believe.

No, Augustus Hero was not a mistake.

The mistake would be if he took a chance on me.

Now *that* would be a mistake.

Huge.

* * *

LEE

His phone went, waking him up.

His wife, Indy, was buried under him.

It was their thing.

It was also a necessity.

His woman was a mover when she slept. If he didn't pin her to the bed, his shins would be covered in bruises by morning and she'd possibly smack him in the face waking him up in the middle of the night.

Repeatedly.

He rolled off her, reached out, nabbed his phone, looked at his screen and any vestiges of sleep fled.

He took the call.

"Willie," he greeted.

"Need your time," Willie answered.

Willie Moses.

A good friend for years, since high school.

A cop, on the beat. A sergeant, never had a dream of detective, he was good with people and the street was in his blood.

"Now?" Lee asked.

"Now," Willie answered.

"Text me, brother," Lee told him.

"Got it," Willie said and then disconnected.

Lee rolled back to Indy.

Before he could give her a kiss, she muttered drowsily as well as irritably, "Remind me again why I married you?"

"Multiple orgasms and we made two super fuckin' cute kids," he replied.

"Oh yeah, that's why," she said.

He grinned, aimed, touched his mouth to hers, then made certain the covers were still on top of her as he got out of bed.

By the time he returned, she'd be totally tangled up in them.

Which was good, he'd have to wake her to get her untangled, and him, Indy, two sleeping kids, two awake adults and a bed meant he'd get a fantastic welcome back.

He dressed, took keys, phone and a weapon with him to his car, got in and drove to where the text instructed: a dark corner of a parking lot at Mile High Stadium.

Eddie was already there.

Figured.

Lee parked next to Eddie's truck, got out and moved to Eddie, who was leaning against his front bumper.

"Hank coming?" he asked.

"Since I didn't know you were coming, no clue," Eddie answered.

"Got a clue about this middle-of-the-night mystery?" Lee went on.

Eddie shook his head. "Nope."

They heard it before they saw it.

A car approaching, headlights out.

Both put hands to their guns at hips and repositioned so Lee's vehicle was between them and it.

It stopped and Willie could be seen in the driver's seat.

It appeared there was a Black woman with short cropped hair in the seat beside him.

They both got out.

Lee didn't take his eyes off the woman.

She was tall. Slender shoulders, round hips, dark skin, strong features.

She had confidence in her movements, so much, it was better described as power.

She stopped at the hood of the car and leaned against it, crossing her feet at the ankles, her arms on her chest.

Willie approached Lee and Eddie and got a lot closer.

He, too, stopped.

"Thought you boys might wanna meet Dynamite," he said.

And then one side of his lips curled up in a smile.

* * *

AXL

It was only two days after he saw Hattie's sculpture of them before it was delivered.

And this time, Elvira didn't give any shit about it like she did when Boone got his.

Neither did any of the guys.

Now, when it happened, it was what it was.

He'd just returned to the office from being out in the field and it was sitting at the head of his workstation.

Light blue plastic, white words, slid into an aluminum stand.

Cheap.

Simple.

Everything.

The plaque said,

AXL PANTERA

"THEN AND NOW"

He got out his phone immediately and texted Hattie.

I love it.

Hattie texted back in less than a minute.

Good.

Don't miss the romance the Dream Team has been waiting for—Pepper and Auggie's love story is coming in *Dream Keeper*!

AVAILABLE LATE 2021

Please turn the page for a preview.

CHAPTER ONE

A Perfect World

PEPPER

My phone chimed with the eleventh text I'd gotten in an hour and I *just* managed not to pull it out of my purse and throw it in the nearest garbage can.

Okay.

All right.

Deep breath and...

Center.

Bottom line: I needed to get over it because I didn't want to be a hater. Hating was such an ugly thing. I didn't like how it made me feel and I didn't want it around my daughter. And when the world at large was so full of negativity and hate that it was pushing in sometimes on an hourly basis, the best way to keep that kind of thing from burying my little girl was, when I had her, do my all not to be a hater.

So I had to guard against the hate.

Even if the holidays were coming up and it always got bad during the holidays.

Bad in the sense of these texts I was currently getting from my sister, because she (and Mom and Dad) always thought holidays were the perfect time to win me around to their way of thinking.

Or, to be blunt (and honest), indoctrinate me and Juno into their way of life.

A way of life I'd turned my back on years ago.

You had to hand it to them, they never gave up.

But that was a stretch for a silver lining because it was also a not-great thing that *they never gave up*.

And it couldn't be denied, I hated it (rephrase: disliked it intensely) when they put my sister forward to appeal to me in a sisterly/generation-sharing way.

Making this worse, I had to divide my time with my daughter, giving some of it up to her father which was never fun, but especially unfun during the holidays.

In a perfect world, my baby would be with me all the time.

In a *perfectly* perfect world, my baby's daddy would not be a liar and a cheater, and we'd all be together all the time.

It was not a perfect world.

This year, I sensed it was going to be even worse because her dad had a(nother) new woman in his life, and from what I was getting, she was all in to win Corbin by showing she could be the best stepmom in Denver.

That happened a lot (the new woman and her wanting to win Corbin by using Juno) and it always involved messing with Juno's heart. And then, when Corbin dumped her (and he would eventually dump her), part of Juno's heart would go with her.

It hurt my baby girl.

It hurt to watch.

It also hurt because I was powerless to do anything about it.

In the beginning, I'd tried to talk to Corbin and warn him about introducing his girlfriends to his daughter too soon.

He not only didn't want to hear me give him advice on how to father, he didn't want to hear from me at all.

Though, even if he didn't want to hear from me, he spent a lot of time making sure I heard from him on a variety of subjects that had to do with co-parenting (and other topics).

This regardless that Juno was eight and for the most part, we had it down (and topping that, he never listened to me and did his own thing anyway—it was like he was going for maximum frustration, and as usual with Corbin, exceeding all expectations).

And I didn't need any of this right now.

It was career day for Juno's class and Juno loved me. She thought I could do anything. As such, she did not get that her mom—who had been a stripper, but was now a featured dancer at a former strip club (even so, you could absolutely still describe what we did as exotic dancing, we just no longer bared all)—was not the person teachers wanted talking to their kids about their future career prospects.

But Juno thought I was cool.

Juno thought I hung the moon and that my besties, Lottie, Ryn, Hattie and Evie were the stars (all of them also dancers, except Evie, who used to be one, but now she was a student).

So Juno didn't hesitate to ask me to come and chat with her class.

I had a little presentation to give. It was a lot about the choreography, costumes, lighting, music choices and working with the stage technicians, and less about how I found new and interesting ways to take off most of my clothes (obviously).

But I was nervous.

I could dance while disrobing with a crowd watching, but standing in front of them and talking to them?

Nope.

Making matters worse, they were having career days all semester, one each Tuesday. The kids invited parents or other folks in their lives to come in and chat with the class. Thus, I knew she'd asked her dad to come that day too, and as referenced earlier, he and I did not get along.

Juno was probably trying to see to my feelings and instead of telling me her father was going to be there, she'd warned me "someone else is coming."

It was a little weird she didn't just say, "Dad's coming to bore everyone with anecdotes about being a baller real estate agent."

But sometimes she got a little weird when her dad had a new woman in his life.

Therefore, during these times, I had to let her be how she needed to be, even if that was weird.

Then be prepared to pick up the pieces after.

This was what was on my mind after I got past checking in at the front office and was walking down the hall toward Juno's classroom.

But even if my headspace was taken up with all of that, when I turned the corner to the hallway where Juno's classroom was, nothing would have made me miss the astonishing and totally unforeseen fact that Augustus "Auggie" Hero—hot guy, ex-military, current-commando, member of my immediate posse, man I was supposed to be dating since Lottie tried to fix us up months ago, man I'd broken down and had wall sex with not long ago and then ended that episode *very badly*—*that* Auggie Hero was holding up the wall beside the door to Juno's classroom with his broad shoulders.

But his head was turned, and his black eyes were on me.

Now there…

Embodied in that man…

Was a true perfect world.

But I felt my heart start racing and that had nothing to do with the fact he was gorgeous.

What was he doing here?

God, God, God.

It was important to repeat that he was a current commando.

A commando who, for unknown reasons, was loitering in the hallway of an elementary school.

Was…?

God!

Was there some threat to Juno?

I rushed to him, my high heels echoing against the tile in the quiet hall, and I didn't hesitate to grab onto his forearm that was crossed on his chest and lean in close so I could say low, "Is everything okay?"

He stared down at me.

Then he tipped his chin and looked at my fingers curled around his forearm.

He looked back at me when I squeezed his sinewy flesh and snapped, "Auggie! Is something wrong? Is Juno unsafe?"

At my question, his face changed.

In my panic, I hadn't really registered his expression before, but now it couldn't be missed that it was hyper alert.

I was already hyper alert but I did not take it as a good sign he'd gone hyper alert even if it wasn't a surprise, considering all that had been swirling around the Dream Team for nearly a year.

That Dream Team being Evie, Ryn, Hattie, Lottie…and me.

The Dream Team's men being (in order to the women) Mag, Boone, Axl, Mo…and as mentioned, Auggie was supposed to be (however was not) mine.

Like she'd tried to do for Auggie and me, Lottie had fixed up all the others. Since, there had been weddings, engagements, moving in and buying houses together in that mix.

My fixup just didn't work.

And yeah, that was on me, because, again, my daughter had to deal with my family and the revolving door of women that Corbin introduced into her life.

She was not going to put up with that from me.

And it was important at that juncture to mention that all the drama that had been swirling around the Dream Team included death and dirty cops and kidnappings and stalking and shootouts, and it bore repeating...*death*.

As in *murders*.

So...yeah, Auggie Hero, Badass Extraordinaire standing outside my daughter's classroom freaked me.

Big time.

His voice—something I particularly liked about him, it was deep but smooth (not silky and elegant, instead soft and calming)—came at me.

"Is there a reason Juno wouldn't be safe?"

My voice was rising. "I don't know! You tell me."

"Pepper, I didn't come up to me and ask if Juno was safe."

Okay...

Wait.

What?

"Then why are you standing outside Juno's classroom?"

His strong, heavily stubbled chin jutted slightly to the side.

"I'm here for career day," he declared. "Juno called. She wants me to talk to her class about going into the military."

I blinked up at him.

"You didn't know?" he asked.

No.

I.

Did.

Not.

Know.

That.

My.

Daughter.

Asked.

Augustus Hero.

To talk to her class on the same day I was going to talk to her class!

How did Juno...?

Why did Juno...?

What the hell?

"Her father isn't coming?" I asked Auggie.

He shook his head once. "No clue. I just know I'm here and now you're here. That's all I know."

I stood there, staring at him, at a loss for words because my daughter had somehow found a way to call Auggie and ask him to come and talk to her class during career day.

She did not have a cell phone.

As far as I knew, she didn't use my mobile.

Though, we were one of the last of a dying breed that had a landline, also as far as I knew, Auggie's phone number was not a part of the collective conscious.

How did she call him?

Further, I didn't know if she had a quota on how many people she could ask to come speak to the class, but if she did, and considering the fact that her father was not there, that meant possibly she'd picked Auggie over Corbin.

Even if Corbin was a cheat and an asshole and I had many (what I thought were) serious questions about his concept of parenting, Corbin was good-looking. He was confident. He dressed well. He had encyclopedic knowledge of Bruce Willis films, *Seinfeld* and *The Office.* And he was indeed baller at real estate. So he was interesting, could hold a conversation and probably had motivating tidbits to share with a third-grade class.

Auggie, on the other hand, was the most beautiful man I'd ever laid eyes on and every time I saw him I was reminded of this fact.

That thick black-black hair that curled at the ends. His hooded brow, deep-set onyx eyes and dense eyebrows that had a wicked-gorgeous arch. The slight flair to the nostrils of his strong, attractive nose. His excruciatingly perfect lips. His tall, lean, muscled body that was not too tall or too lean or too muscled, it was all *just right*.

Not to mention, I had noted in all of these months since Lottie had begun her fixups and we'd all intermingled copiously, that Auggie was funny.

Auggie was playful.

Auggie liked to tease.

There was some boy to this man that would never go away.

And there was something so insanely compelling about a man who was downright beautiful in a classical sense (he looked like a Greek god, for goodness sakes) being the kind of guy you knew would make you laugh in bed. Who would get into the spirit of Halloween and Christmas in a way the joy would never go out of it. Who wouldn't sweat the small stuff and would guide you to that same.

I dealt with a lot of small stuff in my life every single day.

It'd be good not to sweat it.

And he wasn't only a veteran, he was currently a commando.

He'd been on the team that had rescued Evie from a kidnapping, and that effort had reportedly included smoke bombs and confusion tactics, so I had secondhand knowledge that he was the real deal.

He was probably the single coolest person you could ask to speak at a third-grade career day.

The only cooler person I could think of would be Hawk Delgado, Auggie's boss, because I had suspicions that the cover story was false to protect his identity and Hawk had singlehandedly found and eliminated Osama bin Laden.

But as such, and for other reasons, he probably couldn't talk to eight-year-olds about that.

"Pepper, you're touching me," Auggie stated unhappily.

At these words, I shot back a step, letting him go, but I did this still staring at him.

Now in horror.

Oh God, how had I forgotten?

The last time I'd spent any real time with him was when we'd had sex in my foyer.

And although it had been *amazing*, after it was over, I'd freaked way the heck out and then kicked him out.

He did not want to be kicked out.

He wanted to explore what we both had been sensing, but what had become clear against the wall of my entryway was happening for us.

But I wouldn't hear of it.

Juno had to survive her father's revolving door of babes. She wasn't going to have to do that with her mother.

I'd made a pact with myself.

No men in Juno's life until she was mature enough to sort through that emotionally.

I had decided this would be when she was around fourteen or fifteen, though I'd consider it at thirteen, but also possibly push it back to sixteen if she was having a difficult adolescence.

I knew this was going to be a *very long* row to hoe for me (case in point, standing right there with all the perfection that was Auggie Hero and not being able to make him mine).

But there were sacrifices you made as a mother that were necessary to make.

This was one of them.

I had told not one single soul about this pact I'd made with myself.

None of my friends were moms, they wouldn't get it.

Added to that, none of my friends had started a family with the love of their lives, or even had just settled in with the love of their life, sleeping beside him for years, only to learn he'd been cheating on them *the whole time they were together*.

Yep.

The *whole* time.

They didn't get what it felt like to have your heart broken, your trust decimated, all your dreams for your future shattered *and* have to watch your daughter experience the same thing.

They didn't get that.

I went through that.

But more importantly, Juno went through it.

Top all of it with the shit my dad, mom and sister pulled on a regular basis and okay, sure. Maybe I was overprotective. Maybe this pact was over the top.

Maybe.

But as a single mother, I didn't have the luxury of dealing in maybes.

I needed to do what I needed to do to keep my baby safe and healthy, physically and emotionally.

And I was going to do it.

"I'm taking it Juno didn't tell you she asked me to be here," he remarked, breaking into my explanatory (justifying?) thoughts.

"No," I mumbled.

"You got a problem with me being here?" he asked.

ABOUT THE AUTHOR

Kristen Ashley is the award-winning and *New York Times* best-selling author of over seventy romance novels, including the Rock Chick, Colorado Mountain, Dream Man, Chaos, and Fantasyland series. Her books have been translated into fourteen languages, with over three million copies sold.

Born in Gary and raised in Brownsburg, Indiana, Kristen was a fourth-generation graduate of Purdue University. Since, she has lived in Denver, the West Country of England, and she now resides in Phoenix. She worked as a charity executive for eighteen years prior to beginning her independent publishing career. She now writes full time.

Because friendship, family, and a strong sisterhood are prevailing themes through all of Kristen's novels, Kristen has created the Rock Chick Nation, a series of programs designed to give back to her readers and promote a strong female community. Its programs include Rock Chick Rewards, which raises funds for reader-nominated nonprofit women's organizations and has donated over $146,000.

You can learn more at:
    KristenAshley.net
    Twitter @KristenAshley68
    Facebook.com/KristenAshleyBooks
    Instagram @KristenAshleyBooks